P9-DXR-654

PRAISE FOR
MISSING AND ENDANGERED

"Fans of police procedurals with a Southwestern flair
will love Joanna's determination to manage
marriage, motherhood, and policing in this 19th
Joanna Brady book."
—*Library Journal*

"The two parallel cases provide plenty of action,
while keeping a premium on character studies
and violence to a minimum.
Once again, the compassionate, intelligent Joanna
balances a busy home life
and a complex job with aplomb.
This long-running series consistently entertains."
—*Publishers Weekly*

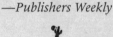

"What is refreshing is the way [Jance] shows
how law enforcement are not just numbers
and robots but people with families
and a personal home-life.
As with all her novels,
readers will not be disappointed."
—MilitaryPress.com

PRAISE FOR JOANNA BRADY AND
NEW YORK TIMES
BESTSELLING AUTHOR
J. A. Jance

"The Arizona desert comes to life
in the mysteries of J. A. Jance."
—*Arizona Republic* on *Judgment Call*

"Jance starts her books fast . . .
and keeps things moving with cinematic panache. . . .
You want an accessible thriller?
Jance is your gal."
—*Los Angeles Times*

"Addictive. . . .
Jance will charm you into reading
everything by her you can find."
—*Statesman Journal* (Oregon)

"An excellent writer."
—*Chattanooga Times*

"Compelling . . . Satisfying."
—*USA Today*

"Entertaining . . .
Jance makes it interesting;
she never forgets the human side."
—*Mercury News* (San Jose)

"Jance skillfully avoids the predictable."
—*South Florida Sun Sentinel*

"Characters so real
you want to reach out and hug—
or strangle—them.
Her dialogue always rings true."
—*Cleveland Plain-Dealer*

"Jance delivers a devilish page-turner."
—*People*

"Joanna Brady's a delightful character—
close in toughness to Warshawski
but willing to work within the confines
on mainstream law enforcement."
—*Chicago Tribune*

By J. A. Jance

Joanna Brady Mysteries

J. P. Beaumont Mysteries

Walker Family Novels

Ali Reynolds Novels

Poetry

ATTENTION: ORGANIZATIONS AND CORPORATIONS
HarperCollins books may be purchased for educational, business,
or sales promotional use. For information, please e-mail the Special
Markets Department at SPsales@harpercollins.com.

J. A. JANCE

MISSING AND ENDANGERED

A BRADY NOVEL OF SUSPENSE

WILLIAM MORROW

An Imprint of HarperCollins*Publishers*

This is a work of fiction. Names, characters, places, and incidents are products of the author's imagination or are used fictitiously and are not to be construed as real. Any resemblance to actual events, locales, organizations, or persons, living or dead, is entirely coincidental.

Excerpt from *Nothing to Lose* copyright © 2022 by J. A. Jance.

MISSING AND ENDANGERED. Copyright © 2021 by J. A. Jance. All rights reserved. Printed in the United States of America. No part of this book may be used or reproduced in any manner whatsoever without written permission except in the case of brief quotations embodied in critical articles and reviews. For information, address HarperCollins Publishers, 195 Broadway, New York, NY 10007.

First William Morrow mass market printing: October 2021
First William Morrow international paperback printing: February 2021
First William Morrow hardcover printing: February 2021

Print Edition ISBN: 978-0-06-285347-9
Digital Edition ISBN: 978-0-06-285348-6

Designed by Kyle O'Brien
Cover design by Richard L. Aquan
Cover photographs © Chris Cornish (shrine); © Shutterstock

William Morrow and HarperCollins are registered trademarks of HarperCollins Publishers in the United States of America and other countries.

21 22 23 24 25   CWM   10 9 8 7 6 5 4 3 2 1

If you purchased this book without a cover, you should be aware that this book is stolen property. It was reported as "unsold and destroyed" to the publisher, and neither the author nor the publisher has received any payment for this "stripped book."

For Terry, and for Kathy and Rusty

MISSING AND ENDANGERED

🌵 PROLOGUE

LATE ON Wednesday afternoon, the first week in December, Sheriff Joanna Brady sat at her desk, mired in paperwork. She was laying out the details of her request for a budget increase for the next fiscal year, something that had to be in the hands of the county supervisors well before their next scheduled Friday morning meeting. At this point Joanna's department was grossly understaffed, and only an increase in the bottom line would allow her to hire more sworn officers. Unfortunately, right this minute Joanna's heart wasn't in it.

When her cell phone rang with her daughter's photo showing on the screen, Joanna welcomed the interruption. "Hey," she said, more cheerily than she would have thought possible. "How's it going?"

"It's snowing," Jenny said, not sounding the least bit happy about it. She was in her second year at Northern Arizona University in Flagstaff, where she had quickly run out of patience with Flag's winter weather. That had happened during the second blizzard of her freshman year, and now, to her utter dismay, this year's *Farmers' Almanac* was predicting yet another season of record-breaking snowfall. "We'll probably have another foot by morning," she added gloomily.

Joanna had to bite her tongue to keep from men-

1

tioning that Jenny could have chosen to go to school in Tucson, where it was much warmer and seldom if ever snowed, but the offer of a scholarship and a spot on NAU's rodeo team had carried the day.

"How are things with you?" Jenny asked.

"Fine," Joanna replied, but that was an outright lie, because things definitely weren't fine, not even close. As Jenny rattled on about her day and about the latest rivalries on the rodeo team, her mother's mind wandered back to a conversation with Detective Ernie Carpenter earlier that afternoon.

Ernie, who had been Joanna's lead investigator for as long as she'd been sheriff, had let himself into her office unannounced and then closed the door behind him before dropping into one of her visitor's chairs.

"It's back," he said.

Joanna struggled for several long moments, trying to come to terms with exactly what "it" was, but then, observing his somber demeanor, she got his drift.

"The cancer?" she asked.

He nodded.

Years before, Ernie had been treated for prostate cancer, choosing to go the radiation-seeds route. Since then he'd been in remission, and Joanna had almost forgotten about that original diagnosis. Now she realized she'd been noticing that he seemed to have lost some weight recently and was looking a little more worn than usual.

"It's metastasized," he added. "It's in my lymph nodes and my liver."

"I'm so sorry," Joanna murmured, "so very sorry. Does anyone else know?"

"Only Rose," he said. "I'm not ready for the guys

around here to start treating me like the cancer guy with one foot in the grave, even if it's true."

Joanna couldn't help half smiling at that. When it came to gallows humor, Ernie Carpenter had always been at the top of the class.

"So here's the deal," Ernie continued. "I'm letting you know that I'm pulling the plug as of January first. Rosie and I have talked it over. The seeds gave me a pretty good run, but it looks like that's coming to an end. I'm not going to put myself through some kind of godawful round of treatment that would maybe give me a few more months at best but zero quality of life. That's not fair to me, and it's sure as hell not fair to Rose. I'm going to take my retirement, and the two of us will hit the road. We'll travel while I can travel, and when I can't do that anymore, we'll come home."

He left off there. The recurrence was bad enough news, but the idea that Ernie planned to forgo any additional treatment was stunning. Joanna's first instinct was to ask, *Are you sure?* But the set of Ernie's jaw caused her to stifle. Yes, he was sure. He and Rose were sure. They had obviously reached this conclusion together. This was their business and nobody else's.

"How can I help?" Joanna asked quickly. "What can I do?"

"Keep this under your hat, for one thing," he replied. "You find sympathy in the dictionary between shit and syphilis, and I'm not interested in sympathy. I wanted to give you a heads-up in advance so you can start getting your ducks in a row as far as detectives are concerned, but I don't want a lot of hoopla about this. I'll tell Jaime, of course. He's my partner, and I owe it to him, but that's it. I'm not telling anyone else."

Joanna thought about that before speaking up. "I'll give you a week," she said.

Ernie seemed taken aback. Clearly that kind of terse response was not what he'd expected. "I beg your pardon?"

"You have until a week from today to tell Jaime whatever you decide to tell him about why you're retiring. You can let him know about the cancer or not—that's entirely up to you—but after that, all bets are off. If you don't want to be labeled 'cancer guy' on your way out the door, you'd better put on your big-boy underwear and announce your upcoming retirement, because there's no way in hell I'm letting you leave this department without a retirement party, and that will need to be scheduled ASAP. Got it?"

Sitting there at her desk, she met Ernie's gaze and held it. He was the first one who blinked.

"Yes, ma'am," he said finally. "I hear you loud and clear." He had stood up to leave just then but paused at the door and added, "By the way, I'll be using up some of my vacation time and taking tomorrow and the next day off. Rose and I are going to Phoenix to pick up an RV, and we'll be spending the night."

"Good-o," Joanna said with a wave. "Travel safe."

When the door closed behind him, Joanna was left alone with the term "RV" echoing in her heart. When her mother and stepfather—Eleanor and George Winfield—had hit retirement age, they, too, had dived into the RV life, expecting to spend many "golden years" cruising the USofA. Unfortunately, that plan had been cut short. A hail of bullets fired by a troubled teenager from a highway overpass had forever ended George and Eleanor's travels together. Joanna dreaded the idea that Rosie and Ernie's traveling days, too, would soon end in a somewhat different but equally tragic way. So it was hardly any wonder that when she'd turned back to writing her report, she hadn't been up to the task.

"Well, Mom?" Jenny's exasperated voice broke into Joanna's reverie. "Have you heard a word I said?"

"Sorry," Joanna replied. "Something was going on, and I was distracted. What were you saying?"

"I was asking if you and Dad would mind if I brought someone home for Christmas vacation."

The fact that Jenny routinely referred to her stepfather as "Dad" was something that never failed to gladden Joanna's heart. But Jenny was planning on bringing someone home for Christmas? Who? A boyfriend, maybe? Jenny had friends who were boys—most notably Nick Saunders, the kid from St. George, Utah, who was also on the NAU rodeo team. He and Jenny boarded their horses at the same place in Flag and sometimes looked after each other's mount when one or the other was out of town. Joanna knew the two were good friends, but if there were any romantic links between them, the subject had never come up. And if this was someone else, who was he and what were his intentions?

"Who is he?" Joanna asked.

Jenny laughed aloud. "It's not a he, Mom," she said. "It's a she—Beth, my roommate. That's her name, remember? Beth Rankin."

Jenny's reply sent Joanna spinning down yet another mental rabbit hole. Halfway through her sophomore year, this was the first time Jenny had suggested bringing one of her college friends home for a visit. But having someone stay over for several days might be a problem. Family members were well accustomed to the many inconveniences of having one-year-old Sage and seven-year-old Denny in the house. A college student might not be up for that. And then there was the challenge of sleeping arrangements.

"With the guest room changed into a nursery . . ." Joanna began.

"Don't worry, Mom," Jenny put in quickly. "I'll bunk on the sofa in the living room, and Beth can stay in my room. She had a huge blowup with her folks over Thanksgiving, and she isn't planning on going home. The idea of having her stuck on campus all alone during winter break is just . . ."

"Of course she can come," Joanna said quickly. "Didn't you tell me she's an only child?"

"Definitely," Jenny returned, "with an over-the-top helicopter mom."

"You might want to warn her in advance that a household with a one-year-old and a seven-year-old may be a little more than she bargained for."

"I'll pass that along," Jenny said. "But maybe being around Sage will do the same thing for Beth that it did for me."

"What's that?"

"Being around a baby made it blazingly clear that I'm nowhere near ready to have one," Jenny answered. "Sort of like making the case for birth control without anyone having to say a word."

It was Joanna's turn to laugh. "In other words, delivering the 'birds and bees' talk by remote control."

"You've got it—indirect but very effective."

They both laughed at that.

"All right," Joanna said. "Tell Beth she's more than welcome. As for you? Thank you."

"Thank me for what?"

"For being the kind of daughter you are," Joanna said. "For making me laugh and for reminding me what the season for giving is all about."

"You're welcome," Jenny said, "but now that I've called you, I'm going to call Dad, too, and make sure my bringing home company is okay with him as well."

"Good idea," Joanna said. "No, make that an excellent idea, but I can't imagine he'll say no."

"I know, but I'll call him anyway. I don't want him to think we're ganging up on him."

"Okay," Joanna said. "Bye, then."

When the call ended, Joanna felt as though she'd just been run through an emotional spin cycle. Glancing at her watch, she was surprised to see that it was after five. That meant that her secretary, Kristin Gregovich, had most likely already bailed. Just to be sure, Joanna walked over to the door Ernie had left closed on his way out and opened it. Sure enough, the chair behind Kristin's desk was empty, as was the dog bed next to it where Spike, the department's recently medically retired K-9, spent his days.

Kristin's husband, Terry, happened to be Joanna's K-9 officer. During a shoot-out nearly a year earlier, Spike had taken a bullet that had been intended for Joanna and very nearly died as a result. Spike's extensive injuries had made his returning to active duty impossible. When his replacement, a newly trained pit bull named Mojo, appeared on the scene, Spike had been disconsolate each morning to see Mojo ride off in Terry's patrol vehicle. Taking pity on the grieving dog, Kristin had asked Joanna if she could bring Spike along with her. These days Spike spent his workdays dozing on a dog bed beside Kristin's desk while Mojo went out on patrol.

With the outer office completely deserted, Joanna didn't linger. "Okay," she said to the empty room. "Since everyone else has called it quits for the day, I guess I'll do the same."

She went back into the office long enough to gather up her laptop and stuff it into her briefcase. Then she headed home, leaving through the private door at the back of her office, an exit that led directly to her reserved parking place just outside.

Joanna had a short commute—eight minutes door-to-door—from the Cochise County Justice Center to her home at High Lonesome Ranch. She sometimes wished it were longer, to give her a larger buffer between her life as an Arizona sheriff and her life as a wife and mother, between dealing with bad guys and dealing with kids, between fighting bureaucracy and handling dirty diapers. The bureaucracy battle would be never-ending, but Joanna's daughter Sage was now more than a year old, and with any kind of luck the diaper era would be coming to an end in a matter of months.

At the moment Joanna's husband, Butch Dixon, was off on the second leg of a book tour for his latest novel, book number five, *A Step Too Far*. His lighthearted, genre-jumping stories might have been cozies but for the fact that his main protagonist, Kimberly Charles, was a law-enforcement officer. The books were set in a small and entirely fictional town in southern Arizona, but the strong resemblance between Sheriff Brady and Butch's fictional Sheriff Charles was hardly coincidental.

Butch's editor often referred to him as a solid "midlist" author, and for authors in that category going on tour was mandatory. In this instance conflicting scheduling issues had required breaking the tour into two separate parts. The half before Thanksgiving had focused on out-of-state appearances. The second half featured drivable events located in and around Arizona and New Mexico. For the earlier part of the tour—the national one—Butch had used media escorts. For more local venues, he was driving himself.

With Butch out of town, Joanna checked his schedule daily. Today she knew he had a three-hour dinner break between the end of his afternoon event in Mesa and the start of an evening one at White Tank Library in Waddell, Arizona. Joanna had never heard of Waddell until she Googled it and learned it was a Phoenix suburb located at the base of a mountain range on the far western side of the Valley of the Sun. In terms of the Phoenix metropolitan area, Waddell was about as far from Mesa as humanly possible.

Once in the car, Joanna plugged in her phone and dialed Butch's number. "How's your day going?" she asked when he picked up.

"Pretty well," he said. "I'm grabbing a burger at a Denny's in Avondale right now, so I don't have to fight rush-hour traffic all the way from central Phoenix to White Tank. Since I'm on my own, I can't use express lanes, and that's a pain."

"How was attendance this afternoon?" Joanna asked.

"Red Mountain in Mesa was a full house," he replied, "but people are still surprised when Gayle Dixon turns out to be male instead of female. I get the feeling that the bookstores aren't exactly thrilled to have an author out on the road this late in the season. With Christmas on the way, it's as though I'm more of an annoyance to them than I am a help."

"Speaking of Christmas," Joanna said, "I just had a call from Jenny. She was asking if it was okay for her to bring someone along home for Christmas vacation."

"I know," Butch said. "She called me about that, too. I was afraid it was going to turn out to be a boy, and they were coming home to announce an engagement. I told her sure, the more the merrier. I met Beth last fall when I drove up to Flag to help Jenny and Maggie get settled in before school started."

Maggie was Jenny's quarter horse—the equine half of a prizewinning barrel-racing team.

"Beth struck me as being very quiet," Butch added. "She's evidently smart enough but very shy. Jenny's so outgoing, I wondered how they'd get along."

"Based on that Christmas invite, I'd say they're doing fine," Joanna assured him. "By the way, Jenny's last final is on Friday, the fifteenth. I'm guessing they'll show up sometime late on Friday evening or else sometime during the day on Saturday."

"That's what she told me, too," Butch said. "When I come home this weekend, I'll have to get my rear in gear if I want to have Christmas decorating done and holiday baking in hand before they show up."

Butch was due home on Saturday. Joanna had been looking forward to the two of them enjoying a relaxing weekend together. Her vision for the upcoming weekend didn't include the hustle and bustle of getting ready for Christmas.

"Why not leave most of that for the girls to do after they get here?" Joanna suggested. "Jenny's always loved decorating, and since Dennis is seven now, he's big enough to be a help this year, too. Ditto for making Christmas goodies. Put all three of them to work in the kitchen. It'll give them something to do."

"Besides staring at their cell-phone screens you mean?"

"Exactly," Joanna agreed with a laugh.

"Based on what Jenny had to say about the weather up in Flag, I'm really glad New York left the northern end of the state off the tour schedule this time around. Phoenix traffic is a pain, but it's better than driving in snow and ice." Then, after a brief pause, he added, "So what are your plans for tonight?"

"The Christmas cards didn't go out last week, which means they have to go out by Friday at the latest," Joanna told him with a sigh. "In other words, tonight I'll be up to my eyeballs in doing those. Eva Lou said she would stop by this afternoon to help address envelopes. I left her copies of the lists, but I'm the one who has to do all the signing and stuffing."

Eva Lou Brady had been Joanna's first mother-in-law. After Andy Brady's untimely death, Eva Lou and her husband, Jim Bob, had stayed close to their daughter-in-law and granddaughter, a relationship that hadn't diminished once Butch appeared on the scene. They had welcomed him with open arms, treating him as though he were their own son-in-law rather than a widowed daughter-in-law's second husband, and once Dennis and Sage had turned up, they had welcomed them with the same kind of loving enthusiasm. Jenny was their first grandchild. Dennis and Sage counted as numbers two and three.

Joanna's folks—her father and mother as well as a beloved stepfather—were all gone now. Butch's parents—

his father, Don, and his incredibly toxic mother, Margaret—were full-time RVers who, to Butch's immense relief, preferred to spend most of their time east of the Mississippi. That meant that in the grandparent department Jim Bob and Eva Lou Brady were the only ones left standing.

"Eva Lou's a doll," Butch said, "and I'm so glad she's helping out, but I should have worked on the Christmas-card issue before I left on tour."

"You did," Joanna reminded him. "For one thing, you wrote, laid out, and printed the Christmas newsletter, but if I remember correctly, at about the same time you had a horrendous batch of copyediting to do."

"Right," Butch muttered, "with a brand-new copyeditor who was more than a little challenging."

"So get off your cross about the Christmas cards," she told him, as she pressed the remote and opened the garage door. "You're good."

"Sounds like you're home."

"I am," she said. "I'll let you go. Give me a call once the event is over and you get back to the hotel."

"Will," he said. "Love you."

"I love you, too," Joanna murmured. "I love you a lot."

CHAPTER 1

WHEN JOANNA opened the car door, the irresistible aroma of cooking food—most likely a beef stew—filled the garage, and she uttered a small prayer of thanks for the presence of Carol Sunderson in their lives.

Carol was Joanna and Butch's not-quite-live-in nanny/ housekeeper. Years earlier Carol and her physically disabled husband, Leonard, had been living in a rented and extremely decrepit mobile home while caring for two preteen boys, grandchildren who'd been abandoned by their drug-addicted daughter. Leonard had perished in a house fire caused by a faulty electrical circuit that their landlord could and should have corrected.

The fire had left Carol and the two boys, Danny and Rick, homeless. All this had come about several months after Joanna and Butch had moved from High Lonesome's original ranch house into the new one they'd had built a little farther up the road. For a time they'd had renters in the old house, but when the renters decamped within days of the Sunderson mobile-home fire, Joanna had suggested letting Carol and her grandsons live there for free.

Carol Sunderson might have been poor, but she was also proud. Unable to afford rent of any kind but disinclined to accept charity, she had offered to help out in the Brady/Dixon household in lieu of paying rent.

Joanna had encouraged Carol to take her former landlord to court, where years later he'd been held liable
for damages in Leonard Sunderson's death. A court-
awarded settlement had improved Carol's financial
situation immeasurably, but her living arrangement
with Joanna and Butch remained in place. She and the
boys continued to live rent-free in Joanna's old house
while Carol helped out as needed in the new one.

The grandsons, Rick and Danny, were almost grown.
Rick was a senior in high school. He had a driver's
license, an old clunker of a car, and a part-time job
in town delivering pizza. Danny, a sophomore, was
currently making a name for himself on Bisbee High
School's varsity basketball team. With her boys able to
come and go relatively independently, Carol was a daily
calming presence in Butch and Joanna's busy home. Joanna's position as sheriff called for long hours at times,
and without Carol's logistical assistance in terms of
household management Butch wouldn't have been able
to write books much less go on tour.

Joanna entered the house via the laundry room,
pausing there long enough to stow her weapons in the
gun safe. Once that was done, she closed the metal
shutters that covered the exterior windows and doors.
High Lonesome ranch was located at the base of the
Mule Mountains on the far western edge of the Sulphur
Springs Valley. As the crow flies, the two houses were
less than ten miles from the border with Mexico. In
recent years, because of the drastic increase in cartel-
related smuggling, living there had become riskier.
That was the reason Butch and Joanna had installed
rolling shutter systems and security window screens
on both houses. Joanna had always loved sleeping with

the windows open, so sleeping in what amounted to a locked vault wasn't her first choice, but better to be safe than sorry.

Entering the warm kitchen, Joanna found herself in a kind of controlled bedlam. Sage, squealing with delight, rocketed around the room in her walker, leaving behind a trail of Cheerios. Lucky, the deaf black Lab Jenny had rescued years earlier, followed dutifully in Sage's tracks, sniffing out and scarfing up abandoned Cheerios as he went. Carol stood at the counter, dishing stew out of their relatively new programmable pressure cooker into a serving bowl while a frowning Denny concentrated on setting the table. He stood at Joanna's end of the kitchen nook with a table knife in his right hand and with that hand placed over the left side of his heart. That way he could be sure the knife would be placed on the correct side of his mother's plate.

"Soup's almost on," Carol announced. "You might want to get Sage out of the cart, change her, and strap her into the high chair."

"Will do," Joanna said, giving the housekeeper a mock salute before capturing the child, lifting her out of the walker, and heading for the nursery. A few minutes later, as Joanna strapped Sage into her high chair, she noticed that the table was set for only four. On nights like this, Carol usually cooked enough for everybody and her crew ate here in the kitchen right along with everyone else.

"The boys aren't coming?" Joanna asked.

"Rick's working, and Danny has a basketball game in Douglas. I'll take some stew home for them to eat later on."

"Are you going to the game?" Joanna asked.

"I don't know," Carol said. "The varsity game starts at seven. Danny wanted me to come, but I wasn't sure if you'd be home in time."

Joanna's not showing up at home on time was often a sore subject with Butch—and occasionally with Carol, too.

"Well," Joanna said, "I'm home now, so you should be able to go. I'm perfectly capable of cleaning up the kitchen and putting the kids to bed."

While Joanna supervised Denny and Sage, Carol bolted down some dinner of her own. Then, after loading stew into plastic containers for each of her boys, she headed out. Left to handle the evening tasks on her own, Joanna discovered that they took longer than she'd expected. It was after eight thirty before she had the kids bathed and in bed and the kitchen cleaned up as well. Only then did she sit down at the dining-room table—the space deemed Christmas Card Central—to deal with the task at hand.

When Joanna had first decided to run for the office of sheriff, it hadn't occurred to her that she would end up having to become a politician as well. Her first husband, Andy, had been a deputy sheriff running for office against his boss, then the current sheriff, when he'd been gunned down by a drug-cartel hit man on his way home from work. During the reception after Andy's funeral, one of the guests had broached the idea that maybe Joanna should run for office in Andy's stead. When she finally agreed to do so, it had been more to get people to shut up about it than with any expectation of winning. And once the election was over and she'd won, she took office without realizing that she was on a path that would bring her to her life's work, that of being a professional law-enforcement officer—a LEO. For most LEOs being a cop is just that, but being sheriff is different. Sheriffs have to do the job, yes, but in order to keep it they have to run for office. That reality had forced Joanna to become a politician, and that was what had brought her up against the Christmas-card problem.

In ordinary times—meaning prior to Joanna's becoming sheriff of Cochise County—a single box of twenty-five cards would have been enough to do the trick. In terms of her personal list, that was still true—holding steady at twenty-five or so. Those were long-time friends and relations—the ones who got the family holiday newsletter with a collection of chatty year-in-review updates written and arranged by Butch and illustrated with selected photos: Denny with his two front teeth missing, Jenny in a cowboy hat sitting astride Maggie as both horse and rider celebrated their latest barrel-racing win, Sage and Denny posing with a professional mall Santa in a photo that Butch had managed to have taken the day after Thanksgiving. For that one Denny had been grinning from ear to ear while Sage screamed her head off. Santa photos were like that, Joanna supposed—you win some, you lose some.

Once she went to work on the cards, Joanna discovered that Eva Lou had approached the problem in an efficient and typically logical fashion. All the envelopes had been addressed in Eva Lou's flawless, old-school penmanship. Once addressed, the envelopes had been divided into two distinct groupings. Eva Lou had slipped cards and neatly folded copies of the newsletter under the flap of each envelope in the personal stack. In the other stack, plain envelopes awaited cards only. The personal stack was much smaller, so Joanna tackled it first—signing both the cards and newsletters and adding personal notes as needed.

She was done with that one and starting on the larger stack when her phone rang with Butch on the line. "You must be done," she said. "How'd it go?"

"Well enough, I guess," he answered with a singular lack of enthusiasm. "I'm getting pretty tired of giving the same old talk and answering the same old questions, but I love telling stories, so I should shut up and enjoy it, right?"

"Right," she replied.

"What are you doing?" he asked.

"Christmas cards," she answered bleakly. "Eva Lou got all the envelopes addressed. I did the personal list first before starting on the others."

"As in saving the best for last?" he quipped.

"Not exactly," she answered.

"What's going on at work?"

And that's when Joanna realized she hadn't told Butch about Ernie Carpenter's bad news. Ernie might have sworn Joanna to secrecy inside the department, but that didn't mean she couldn't share the news with Butch. More accustomed to using a keyboard than writing by hand, Joanna leaned back in her chair to rest her aching shoulder as she told Butch what had happened.

"This is awful news for Ernie and Rose, but it's also going to leave your detective division pretty shorthanded, won't it?" Butch observed when she finished.

"Very," Joanna agreed with a sigh. "I'll be down to only two detectives, Jaime and Deb."

Jaime was Jaime Carbajal, Ernie's longtime partner

and the other half of what had always been known as "the Double C's." Deb was Deb Howell, who had been promoted from deputy to detective due primarily to Ernie's careful mentoring.

Joanna had expected Deputy Jeremy Stock to be next up in the detective ranks. He had passed the exam, and she'd been waiting to bring him on board when his hidden life as a fatally abusive husband and father had come to light. Not only had he murdered his remaining family members before taking his own life, he'd come dangerously close to taking Joanna's as well. And Joanna's next candidate for promotion, Deputy Daniel Hernandez, had recently left her department in order to take a job with Tucson PD at substantially higher wages.

"Didn't you tell me Garth Raymond passed the test?" Butch asked.

Joanna nodded. "Yes, with flying colors," she replied. "The problem is, he's my youngest deputy. He took the test on a dare because some of the other guys were hassling him about his being a 'college boy.' He outscored all of them, so yes, Garth is a 'college boy' and smart as a whip, but he's also been with the department less than two years. If I end up fast-tracking him to detective, I'm worried there'll be some blowback."

"Young and smart sounds like a good combination," Butch observed. "After what Garth did to save that girl out in Skeleton Canyon last year, it seems to me as though he's also an altogether good human being. In other words, if I were you, I'd discount young and go for smart."

"I'll bear that in mind," Joanna said.

"And you should probably give Myron a call," Butch

added. "If you're going to give Ernie an appropriate send-off, the clubhouse at Rob Roy Links is the place to do it right, but with the holidays in full swing his banquet facilities may already be totally booked."

Myron Thomas had managed to establish and maintain one of the best golf courses in southeastern Arizona, creating a resortworthy facility out of what had once been farmland along the San Pedro River.

"A big party there will cost money," Joanna said. "The board of supervisors will never approve of having the department pay for it."

"Then we'll pay for it," Butch declared, "as in you and me, babe. Fortunately, I just turned in a manuscript, and that delivery-and-acceptance check is burning a hole in my pocket."

Butch's career as a mystery writer had grown into something neither of them had ever anticipated, and having chunks of discretionary cash show up occasionally for them to use as needed was a real blessing.

"Thank you," Joanna said. "I'll give him a call first thing tomorrow."

"Okay," Butch said, "I'm doing an early-morning TV interview, so I'd best hit the sack. What about you?"

"I'm going to keep plugging away on the cards a while longer," she told him. "Have a good night. I miss you."

She did keep plugging. On the nonpersonal side, there were no newsletters to sign and stuff, but the process still took time. Here she could easily have opted for using cards with her signature supplied by the printer, but these messages were going out to many of her supporters and loyal volunteers. Joanna felt that, at the very least, each of these folks deserved the courtesy of a personal signature on their holiday greeting. And that was why the cards had to be done entirely at home. Marliss Shackleford, a local newspaper reporter and Joanna's personal nemesis, was always on the lookout for the slightest misstep on Joanna's part, and if there'd been any hint that Joanna was doing politicking while on the job, Marliss would have made sure it was headline news in the *Bisbee Bee*.

At eleven, and not quite halfway through the second batch, she gave up and put down her pen. There was no sense in staying up any later in an attempt to finish them.

"Come on, dogs," she said aloud. "It's time to go get busy."

Lady, Joanna's Australian shepherd, got to her feet and headed for the laundry-room door. Lucky, deaf as a post and sound asleep, didn't move a muscle. Joanna reached down, touched him awake, and then delivered the same command in sign language.

Joanna opened the garage door to let the dogs out and then stood in the open doorway, waiting for them to finish. The night was clear and bitingly cold. The dark sky overhead was alive with glimmering stars. In the shadow of the Mule Mountains, the lights from Bisbee didn't detract from the nighttime sky, nor did the lights from Douglas and Agua Prieta, twenty-five miles away.

Standing there, enjoying both the chill and the stars, Joanna focused on one star that clearly outshone all the rest. She wasn't sure what star it was—Venus, most likely—but it reminded her of the star, the one that had shone over Bethlehem. After all, wasn't this a time for peace on earth and goodwill to men? As a sense of peace really did settle over her, Joanna called to the dogs.

"Come on, guys," she said. "Let's go to bed."

Lucky and Lady came at once, and they all went inside, but as far as peace on earth was concerned? Joanna Brady couldn't have been more wrong.

CHAPTER 2

IT WAS almost midnight, and Beth Rankin sat on the cold tile of the bathroom floor, leaning against the chill of the porcelain tub and waiting for her phone call. She had silenced the ringer so as not to awaken her room-mate, Jennifer Brady, sound asleep in the room they shared in Conover Hall at Northern Arizona University. The last thing Beth wanted was for Jenny to wake up and start asking questions about who would be calling so late at night.

Beth supposed she ought to be using the time for studying rather than just sitting here staring at her silent cell phone. After all, finals were coming up. She needed to do well. Her late grandmother, Granny Lockhart, had bequeathed her a generous trust for the sole purpose of enabling Beth to attend college, but that bequest came with strings attached, including keeping up with her classes and getting good grades. If Beth were to blow it and end up dropping out of school, that money would be forfeited, with no way of ever getting it back.

Shivering and in a futile effort to keep warm, Beth drew her Lumberjack sweatshirt more tightly around her body and pulled the hood up over her ears. Her mother wouldn't have approved. Madeline Rankin thought sweatshirts, especially hoodies, were vulgar and common. She claimed they made ordinary people look like gangbangers, not that her mother had ever met one of those. Beth had purchased the forbidden sweat- shirt in the bookstore that first week of school in the vain hope of fitting in. The strategy hadn't worked. The other kids, with the possible exception of Jenny, looked on Beth as though she came from another planet. And maybe she did. Maybe Hastings, Nebraska, *was* another planet, even though she didn't live there anymore. That was where she had grown up, but none of her family still lived in Hastings. This past October her parents had sold out and had moved—lock, stock, and barrel— into Beth's deceased grandmother's old place in Saddle- Brooke, a fifty-five-plus community near Tucson.

Beth had visited her grandmother there once, and she hadn't minded it then—mostly, she supposed, because she hadn't minded her grandmother. Granny Lockhart was one of the nicest people Beth had ever met. Too bad Granny's niceness hadn't been passed along to her daughter, Madeline. Granny had been easygoing and fun. Beth's mother was neither.

Beth's first visit to SaddleBrooke once her mother was in charge—the one over Thanksgiving weekend— had been a total disaster. At home Beth had lived under Madeline's many strictly enforced guidelines, including a lights-out deadline of 10:00 P.M., no exceptions. The night before Thanksgiving, Madeline had noticed a light under the guest-room door at midnight. She had stormed inside and caught her daughter red-handed, talking on the phone with Ronald. Madeline had pitched a connip- tion fit, not only because of the lateness of the hour but also because of the presence of the phone.

For religious reasons, Madeline didn't approve of de- vices of any kind. Typewriters were okay, up to a point, she supposed, but as for computers, cell phones, and iPads? No way! Those were not allowed in her house under any circumstances!

Naturally, that was the other piece of forbidden fruit, in addition to the sweatshirt, that Beth had purchased that first week of being away at school—her very first and very own cell phone. She'd wanted to purchase her own laptop as well, but with all the other expenses of starting school, her monthly stipend hadn't been able to stretch that far. Fortunately, her new roommate, Jennifer, had allowed Beth to use her laptop until a month later, when Beth's next stipend came in and she was able to purchase one of her own. For that first month or so, the phone was all Beth had needed.

When her mother had barged in on her that night, naturally Beth had ended Ron's call. What followed had been a blazing shouting match between mother and daughter in which Madeline had demanded Beth hand over the phone, something Beth refused to do. It was her private property, and she was keeping it. The exchange became so heated that eventually Beth's dad, Kenneth, had bestirred himself long enough to insert himself into the fray, not that he'd had a word to say in Beth's defense. He never did. In any disagreement between mother and daughter, Beth's dad always took Madeline's side. Only now was Beth beginning to realize that maybe it was easier for him to do that and take the path of least resistance. There was little doubt that if he'd come down in Beth's favor, Madeline would have made his life a living hell.

In any event, the fight between Beth and her mother, staged in the early-morning hours of Thanksgiving Day, had been epic. Finally, with her mother still standing there screeching at her, calling her daughter an ungrateful wretch among other choice names, Beth had calmly climbed out of bed, gotten dressed, packed her things, and left the house in the middle of the night, curfew be damned!

It was a three-mile hike from her folks' place out to the highway—a difficult three-mile hike at that, especially since Beth was dragging a Rollaboard behind her and wearing a heavily loaded backpack. It had been cold, too, but not that cold. After all, she was accustomed to winters in Nebraska, and those were cold down to the bone.

Since Beth was without a vehicle, her father had driven up to Flagstaff to bring her to SaddleBrooke. Now she had to get back on her own. During the trip down, she hadn't paid that much attention to the landscape around her or to the roads they were traveling. Once she finally reached SaddleBrooke's main entrance, she was dismayed to see that the highway outside the development was virtually deserted at this time of night. Beth had thought maybe she'd be able to flag down a bus and purchase a ticket, but she soon discovered that no buses were available, leaving her with only one option—hitchhiking.

She knew that sticking out her thumb in the middle of the night was a dangerous proposition, especially for girls her size—a petite five foot three. But she had already figured out that there were lots of dangerous places these days, including college campuses. With that in mind, she'd started carrying a switchblade in her pocket and a can of wasp spray in her purse, just in case she needed them.

A seemingly unnecessary stoplight at SaddleBrooke's

brightly illuminated entrance blinked endlessly through its cycle of green, orange, and red, while Beth stood there for what felt like forever. Twice, approaching vehicles raised her hopes by slowing, but each time they ended up turning into SaddleBrooke rather than stopping. At last a pickup truck came speeding through the green light, only to slow to a crawl on the far side of the intersection. To Beth's surprise, the backup lights came on as the driver put the vehicle in reverse. When the truck finally stopped in front of her, the driver buzzed down the passenger window. "Need a ride?" he asked.

Feeling wary, Beth loaded her luggage into the bed of the truck and then climbed into the passenger seat. Fortunately, her Good Samaritan, as nice as could be, turned out to be a guard at the prison in Florence. He was on his way to fill in for someone else who'd gone home sick. Once at the prison, he parked Beth in a lobby and found a buddy of his who was willing to give her a ride to Apache Junction once his shift ended at 6:00 A.M.

From Apache Junction on, there'd been lots more traffic, and none of the people who'd offered her rides had been the least bit out of line either. Her experiences along the road led Beth to conclude that maybe hitchhiking wasn't nearly as dangerous as everyone, and most especially her mother, claimed it was. Even so, it was still late afternoon on Thanksgiving Day before Beth finally made it back to Conover Hall on the NAU campus. For dinner she'd made do with cheese, crackers, and a soda from a 7-Eleven just off campus. Beth hadn't spoken to either one of her parents since then, and she had no intention of doing so. She was done with them, and, she supposed, they were done with her as well.

Yawning, Beth checked the time—ten past twelve. Ron's late-night phone calls—make that his *midnight* phone calls—were a challenge. Initially they had e-mailed back and forth using Jenny's computer until Beth purchased her own. Now, however, even though Beth had a laptop of her own, they communicated almost entirely by one-way video chats. Due to Ron's job requirements, midnight was the only time of day when he could speak to her, and even then he had to initiate the calls. Ron had Beth's number; his number was always blocked and his image blurred for security reasons. Beth didn't regard that as an entirely satisfactory arrangement, but she went along with it. And once he finally did get around to calling, they usually talked for an hour or more.

Going to bed late and getting up early left Beth perpetually sleep-deprived. No wonder she fell asleep in her classes. No wonder she couldn't hold her head up when it came time to do homework. It was lucky Beth was smart enough to get by anyway. Independent study through library excursions intended to augment her mother's bare-bones homeschooling meant that Beth was already familiar with a good deal of the material being presented in her freshman-level classes. She suspected she'd be able to pass most of her courses without cracking a book, but she needed to maintain the 3.0 GPA that Granny Lockhart's trust required.

With a sigh Beth looked at her phone once more. Ron was later than usual, and she needed to get to bed soon. She had an early class on Thursday mornings, but she didn't want to go to bed without talking to him.

This was the best part of her day. She needed to hear his voice, needed to listen to the sweet things he said to and about her. His loving words each night were all that made her life worthwhile.

But now, sitting there alone, Beth thought about her parents. She had long rebelled against the teachings of the beloved pastor at her parents' church. After Madeline and Kenneth Rankin married, they had fallen in with a small but strict religious sect. Pastor Ike, the sect's original founder, was the one who had decreed that electronic devices were the source of all evil, a belief Madeline Rankin had accepted with a willing heart.

Pastor Ike also insisted that children educated at public schools were doomed to become pawns of the devil, which led to Madeline's decision to homeschool her daughter. Granny Lockhart, a librarian and a lifelong reader, had sent her own daughter to public schools. Naturally, Madeline's path to rebellion had led her in the opposite direction, becoming an indifferent student who hated reading and despised books, choices that made her embrace Pastor Ike's teachings without any reservation.

Madeline's contempt for learning should have precluded her from homeschooling her daughter, especially a child who happened to be exceptionally bright. By the time Beth was twelve, she had easily outstripped her mother's limited grasp of both math and science. When it became apparent to all concerned, even Madeline, that Beth wouldn't be able to progress further without outside help, rather than enrolling her in the local public school system Madeline had sought help from their neighborhood library. Madeline might not have liked books, but she was willing to tolerate her daughter's love for reading, and that one chink in her Pastor Ike armor was all it had taken to set Beth on a brand-new path.

Once set loose among shelves loaded with books, Beth had become a voracious reader, devouring everything in sight. She read biographies and autobiographies of world leaders, scientists, and philosophers. For math and science, she turned to things that were essentially college-level textbooks, most of which were well beyond Madeline's limited capabilities to understand. But among the books Beth dragged home, the ones Madeline deemed to be approved reading material, Beth had managed to smuggle in some unapproved items as well—mysteries and romances, mostly. They were the kinds of stories where dashing young men arrived on the scene in the nick of time and carried vulnerable women off to live far better lives than they would have had otherwise.

But there was more to be found in libraries than just illicit books. Beth found computers there that had to be used in order to access materials. With Madeline nearby and sniffing her disapproval, Beth, under the guidance of a helpful library aide, laid hands on a computer keyboard for the very first time. Once that happened, Madeline's previously unchallenged influence over her daughter's life officially ended.

Beth soon discovered that library-based computers had far more to offer than just access to the computerized card catalog. With her face hidden behind a screen, she had cracked open the door to the outside world, including the miracle of Internet dating.

Eve, upon encountering that long-ago apple in the Garden of Eden, could not have been more thrilled than

Beth was once she learned that by posting her profile on a Web site, she might end up meeting someone who was similarly minded, someone for whom she might be the perfect match. She had made a tentative start there, but it wasn't until after she arrived at NAU that she connected with Ron.

It had happened right at the end of orientation week. Jenny had known all about setting up electronic devices, and her help had been invaluable in making Beth's phone operational, creating accounts and passwords, and getting her logged on to the Internet.

And then, on Saturday night at the end of that week, with her roommate out for the evening, Beth had used Jenny's laptop to post her profile on a different dating site from the one she'd tried before. Minutes later Ron had responded. Several others did, too, but those didn't count and she didn't bother replying. No, she saw finding Ron as a combination of beginner's luck and divine intervention.

Ronald Cameron was twenty-four and very good-looking. He was a recent college graduate, with an entry-level job working cybersecurity for the U.S. government. He lived in Washington, D.C. He loved to read. His parents were divorced. Like Beth, he had grown up with a domineering mother. He had just bought his first-ever new car. In other words, he checked every one of Beth Rankin's boxes.

With all that in mind, Beth's freshman-orientation week at NAU had been far more than a mere introduction to college life. It was also her introduction to the world at large, all of it made possible by the generosity and wisdom of her grandmother, Elizabeth Lockhart.

Granny Lockhart had never approved of the way

Madeline raised Beth, insisting that homeschooling was destined to stunt Beth's intellectual and social development, but it was only in death that the old woman had been able to deal out her ultimately winning hand. After Elizabeth's passing, Madeline had been annoyed and Beth puzzled when Hugo Marsh, her grandparents' longtime attorney, had insisted that seventeen-year-old Beth join her parents for the reading of her grandmother's will.

By the time the process was over, a furious Madeline had been totally outmaneuvered. Elizabeth Lockhart had left her fully mortgage-free home in SaddleBrooke to her daughter and son-in-law, but she'd gone through all the legal and financial hoops necessary to create what was essentially a generation-skipping trust. Everything else went into that, enough to provide for her namesake's undergraduate education and then some.

Both the will and the trust came with several ironclad stipulations. One said that anyone going against the will would automatically be precluded from benefiting from it. That specification alone had left Madeline in a state of seething fury.

But there were rules attached to Beth's part of the bargain, too. In order to be eligible to benefit from the trust, Beth was required to attend Elizabeth Lockhart's alma mater, Northern Arizona University, in Flagstaff, Arizona. While an undergraduate, she was required to maintain at least a 3.0 average. Upon graduation any funds remaining in the trust were to be released to Beth and to no one else for her to use however she saw fit. Any noncompliance meant that all remaining funds would automatically revert to a secondary beneficiary, Granny Lockhart's preferred charity—a national women's organization devoted to handing out scholarships. If Beth chose not to go on to college at all or if she attended some other school or dropped out prior to graduation, she was out of luck.

Madeline had fully expected for Beth to remain at home while attending school, preferably at a local community college. She most especially didn't want her sheltered daughter going off to some faraway school where she would be exposed to all the wicked goings-on that seemed to be so much a part of college life these days. But according to Granny Lockhart's wishes, it was NAU or nothing. Madeline's parents had always been well-off, and she'd assumed that, as their daughter, she would be their primary heir. The idea that any of what she regarded as "her money" would end up in the hands of some kind of women's scholarship fund drove Madeline nuts, but there wasn't a thing she could do about it.

Left with no alternative and unwilling to pay for Beth's schooling on her own, Madeline had grudgingly taken possession of the house in SaddleBrooke, allowed her daughter to enroll as a freshman at NAU, and kept her mouth shut—right up until Thanksgiving weekend, when Beth had gone so far off the rails as to bring one of those forbidden, filth-filled cell-phone things into Madeline's home. For Madeline that was the last straw, and for Beth it was the next rung on her ladder to independence.

The phone buzzed in Beth's hand. Ron at last. "Hey, babe," he said, "how's my sweet Betsy from Pike?"

Beth didn't like it when he called her that. The term came from a corny old folk song about Betsy crossing the prairie with her husband, Ike. The reason Beth hated the song so much was the Ike part. The name reminded her too much of home and church and Pastor Ike—of everything Beth Rankin was trying to escape. She wanted to tell Ron that she would rather be called Beth or even Elizabeth, but she wasn't brave enough. She let the words pass without making an objection.

"Oh, Ron," she breathed. Just the sound of his voice sent her heart fluttering wildly in her chest. "I'm so glad you called. I was afraid we wouldn't have a chance to talk tonight. I love you so much, and I didn't want to miss it."

CHAPTER 3

WITH BUTCH off on tour, the early-morning scramble was the bane of Joanna's existence. Getting everyone up, dressed, fed, and ready for school and work was complicated to say the least, and doing so in a timely manner was almost impossible. That Thursday morning Denny might have missed his bus and Joanna most certainly would have been late to work if Carol hadn't shown up around seven thirty to finish pulling all the critical pieces together.

On Joanna's drive between home and office, she took a piece of Butch's advice to heart and placed a call to the main number at Rob Roy Links. Myron Thomas usually stayed on each night to oversee the closing of the restaurant and bar, so she didn't expect him to answer, but she left a message asking if his party room would be available for a retirement gathering sometime during December. By the time she pulled in to her parking place at the Justice Center, she had switched gears from mommy duty to cop duty and was ready to go back to work on that budget request.

She was deep into that when Chief Deputy Tom Hadlock stormed into her office a little before ten. "We've got a problem," he said.

"What's wrong?"

"An OIS."

OIS was copspeak for officer-involved shooting, and having one of those in her department was unwelcome news indeed. Joanna was on her feet and reaching for her Kevlar vest, hanging on a nearby coatrack, before Tom finished speaking.

"Who?" she demanded, as she slipped on the vest. "Anybody hurt?"

She didn't usually wear one when she was in her office, but she always did when she was out on calls, and she insisted that her people do the same. Hopefully that would be the case here.

"Deputy Ruiz," Tom answered. "And it sounds like he's hurt real bad."

A sudden chill seemed to fill the room. *Not another deputy!* Joanna thought despairingly. "Where did this happen?" she demanded.

"Armando went out to Whetstone first thing this morning to deliver a no-contact order. He was at an address on Sheila Street right at the edge of town when it all went south. He sent out a shots-fired/officer-down call, requesting backup and medical assistance. Officers and EMTs from Huachuca City are on their way."

"What about the shooter?" Joanna asked.

"Down and unresponsive at this point," Tom replied. "He may be deceased."

Joanna let out her breath. *Not only an officer-involved shooting but a fatal one at that!* "Do we have any idea how this happened?"

"Details are sketchy right now. The only witness is the shooter's estranged wife. She's the one who dialed 911, screaming that a cop had just shot her husband."

"That would be the woman who swore out the no-contact order?" Joanna asked.

"Evidently."

Joanna's temper soared. "If she didn't want any contact with the man, what the hell was she doing there?" she demanded. "Why not just stay away and leave him alone?"

"Who knows?" Tom asked. "Who the hell knows?"

Joanna grabbed her purse and started for the door. "Okay," she said, "are any of our patrol units nearby?"

"The closest one right now is Garth Raymond. He was investigating an abandoned vehicle on Davis Road east of Tombstone. He's been notified and is headed to the scene."

"I'm headed there, too," Joanna said grimly, "and I'm keeping my fingers crossed. I've already lost one deputy. I don't want to lose another." It was years now since Deputy Dan Sloan had been fatally shot, and his loss remained an open wound not only in the department but also in Joanna's heart.

Joanna made it to the door before turning back to her chief deputy. "Okay, Tom, please keep me posted. I'll need the names of everyone involved as well as the exact location—a physical address—of the crime scene. You'll need to alert both the Department of Public Safety and the county attorney's office. DPS will be handling the actual investigation, but if Arlee Jones isn't in on the ground floor on something like this, he'll make our lives hell on earth."

Arlee Jones had served as the county attorney for as long as Joanna could remember. Well into his seventies, he should have been past his pull-by date, but he was also a political animal through and through. He was the proverbial "good old boy," someone who won reelection time after time, seemingly without having to lift a finger.

He and Joanna had crossed swords on more than one occasion. It was his job to determine whether an officer-involved shooting was justifiable, and she didn't want Arlee Jones looking into the Whetstone situation with a chip on his shoulder.

As for Joanna? In the car with her seat belt fastened and the transmission in reverse, she was confident about how this situation would sort itself out. Armando Ruiz was an experienced officer, one who didn't take shortcuts. She felt sure he must have had good reason to utilize deadly force. She also had a complete understanding of the bare seconds cops have to make those life-or-death, shoot/don't-shoot decisions. Other people—especially folks in the media—would no doubt buzz around, second-guessing the man's choice to their hearts' content, but it was a decision Deputy Ruiz himself would have to live with for the rest of his life.

Soon Joanna was speeding westbound on Highway 80, her flashing lights ablaze and siren screeching. With a dead civilian and a gravely wounded officer, what had started out as a normal morning was now infinitely more complicated. Driving through Bisbee's Lowell neighborhood and past Lavender Pit, she listened in on the urgent radio chatter going back and forth between Dispatch and personnel in the field. That was how she heard, for the first time, that EMTs at the scene were calling for an air ambulance to transport Armando to the trauma unit at Banner–University Medical Center in Tucson. Gravely wounded indeed!

When Andy had been shot and left to die, no one had knocked on Joanna's door to deliver the devastating news because she was the one who'd found him. That wasn't the case with Armando. Officers from other jurisdictions were currently on the scene, but it was Joanna's sacred duty to be the one to let Amy Ruiz know what had happened. So although Joanna originally set out to go directly to the crime scene, she soon changed her mind.

Mentally, she ticked off everything she knew about Armando Ruiz. He was in his thirties and had been a deputy for the past seven years. He and his wife, Amy, lived in Sierra Vista along with their three school-age kids—all of them boys. Joanna was relatively certain Amy Ruiz was a schoolteacher, but she didn't know which school or what grade level. After a moment's thought, however, she realized that there was someone at her disposal who might be able to fill in a few of those blanks.

"Siri," she ordered, "call Frank Montoya at work."

During Joanna's first run for office, she had faced two formidable opponents, both of them Cochise County deputies—Dick Voland and Frank Montoya. Her victory had been met with a good deal of bad-mouthing, to the effect that her running for office had been little more than a bid for sympathy. In addition, there was concern about having an amateur—someone whose knowledge of law enforcement was secondhand at best—heading up the department.

In order to defuse the situation and stifle the criticism, Joanna had baffled supporters and critics alike by naming her two former opponents to serve jointly as co–chief deputies.

It had been an instinctive but inspired choice. While Joanna went to work learning the ins and outs of law enforcement, Montoya and Voland had been on hand to supply the necessary professional expertise. Dick

Voland had left a couple years later to start his own private-investigation firm. At about the same time, he'd hooked up with Joanna's least favorite reporter, Marliss Shackleford, a match-not-made-in-heaven that had eventually come to grief. Frank had stayed on with Joanna's department until fairly recently, when the lucrative offer of becoming chief of police in Sierra Vista had lured him away.

At the time Armando Ruiz was hired, Frank had been in charge of doing the initial interviews, and Joanna seemed to remember that Frank and Armando had some shared Sierra Vista connections.

"Hey," Frank said when he came on the line. "I hear you've got some excitement out Whetstone way. How bad is it?"

"Pretty bad," Joanna replied. "Deputy Ruiz was serving a no-contact order and ended up in a shoot-out with the recipient. The protection-order guy is dead at the scene. Armando is being airlifted to a trauma unit in Tucson."

"Whoa," Frank murmured.

"You can say that again, but Armando is the reason I'm calling. I'm on my way to Sierra Vista right now, and I need to let Amy know what's going on. We have emergency numbers for her, but this isn't the kind of news that should be delivered by telephone. The thing is, I have no idea where she works. . . ."

"She teaches second grade at Carmichael Elementary," Frank supplied. "Do you want me to go talk to her?"

A call was coming in from Tom Hadlock.

"Thanks, Frank," Joanna said, "but this is my responsibility. I should be the one to do that, but right now I need to take another call."

"If there's anything else I can do, let me know," he said.

"Will do," she responded before switching over. "Okay, Tom," she told him, "brief me. What have we got?"

"The address for the crime scene is 2101 North Sheila Street, Whetstone. I know you're driving, so I just texted it to you. The no-contact order was sworn out yesterday by Madison Hogan, the estranged wife of one Leon Hogan. At this point I don't know if Deputy Ruiz even got a chance to deliver it, because it's still not clear why or how the situation devolved into a shoot-out. According to the EMTs, they found Armando lying on the ground next to the driver's door of his vehicle, and there was no visible sign of any court order at the scene. What we do know for sure is that several shots were fired."

"Any witnesses?" Joanna asked.

"Other than the wife, probably not," Tom replied. "A woman who lives up the street heard the shots and called 911, but she didn't actually see anything. When officers from Huachuca City arrived, they found Madison Hogan kneeling over her husband's body. She was covered with blood, screaming like a banshee and naked as a jaybird."

"Naked?" Joanna asked.

"Stark naked," Tom returned. "She kept trying to run into the house, saying she needed to go get her kids, but Officer Larry Dunn from Huachuca City PD wouldn't let her. He gave her a blanket and put her in the back of his patrol car. Sometime later a neighbor—the same one who called 911—showed up and brought Ms. Hogan a robe to wear. By the way, the neighbor's name is Alice Kidder."

"No, wait," Joanna interrupted. "Go back. Did you say kids?"

"Yes, the Hogans' two kids were there. A girl named Kendall, age seven, and a boy named Peter, age five."

Joanna caught her breath. Kendall Hogan and Denny Dixon were exactly the same age. This was a weekday. If Kendall was in second grade, why wasn't she in school?

"Did they see what happened?"

"Can't tell," Tom said. "Officer Dunn, one of the first responders from Huachuca City, found them locked in the trailer's back bedroom."

"Locked inside?" Joanna echoed.

"Yup," Tom said. "Dunn told me that the property's previous renter was a known drug dealer. There was a padlock-and-hasp arrangement on the doorframe outside the second bedroom. Maybe that's where he kept his excess inventory. Dunn said that today the padlock was nowhere to be found, but someone had stuck a table knife through the hasp in order to keep the kids contained."

"Where are they now?"

"The kids? Officer Dunn took them out through the trailer's back door and handed them over to the neighbor. With their father's body still out front. . . ."

"Understood," Joanna replied. "I'm glad they weren't subjected to seeing him like that, and keeping the kids separated from their mother at the moment is the right thing to do."

"Speaking of the mother, I just listened to the 911 tape," Tom continued. "That part about her being a screaming banshee was on the money. That's all you can hear—her carrying on something fierce, but it's possible to make out a few of her words here and there. 'You killed him! You didn't have to do that. How could you?'"

"So the husband came out of the house with guns blazing, and the wife, who's supposedly divorcing the guy, now decides this is all Deputy Ruiz's fault?"

"Exactly," Tom muttered grimly. "That's just the way DV calls go."

Joanna knew her chief deputy was right about that. All too often in domestic-violence situations, the people involved stop fighting each other long enough to turn on anyone who tries to intervene—law-enforcement officers included. Unfortunately, Joanna herself had recently had an up-close-and-personal experience with a domestic-violence perpetrator.

"So about this Hogan character," Tom resumed. "He evidently moved into the trailer just a couple of months ago. His driver's license still lists a Sierra Vista address. I did a quick check with Records at Sierra Vista PD. They report there've been several contacts at the Hogan residence over the past year or so."

"All domestic-violence calls?" Joanna asked.

"You got it."

"It sounds as though the late Mr. Hogan was your basic wife-beater," Joanna concluded.

"Not so fast," Tom replied. "According to reports on each of those incidents, Madison Hogan appeared to be the aggressor while Leon was the one with visible injuries—cuts, bruises, and scratches mostly, and on one occasion a very black eye after she lit into him with the business end of a hairbrush."

"The wife was the one taken into custody?"

"That's about the size of it," Tom agreed, "but guess

what else? Each and every time, Leon refused to press charges."

"No surprises there either," Joanna muttered.

That was another hard-earned law-enforcement lesson—domestic-violence victims are often reluctant to press charges against their abusers, either out of fear of retaliation or else out of misplaced love. All too often, the bad guy comes to the victim after the incident swearing his or her eternal love and vowing that it will never, ever happen again, and the victim always falls for it. That was just the way things were. As for male victims? They almost never came forward.

"Hang on a minute," Tom said. "I've got another call." Joanna waited on hold for the better part of five minutes, thinking about how easy it had been to jump to the conclusion that the husband had perpetrated those earlier incidents, including the one with the hairbrush. Unfortunately, today he'd been armed with a handgun.

Finally Tom Hadlock came back on the line. "Okay," he said, "here's an update. Deputy Raymond just arrived on the scene. With Garth on the other side of the county, I've asked Deputy Creighton to take up a position near Willcox so he'll be able to cover all of the Sulphur Springs Valley as well as the I-10 corridor."

Cochise County, Joanna's jurisdiction, was eighty miles wide and eighty miles tall. With only a bare minimum of sworn officers on duty at any given time, an emergency like this required moving assets around like pieces on a gigantic desertscape chessboard.

"Good decision," Joanna told him. "Now, what about DPS? When are they due?"

"The Tucson sector has advised us that one of their investigators is having to come from Casa Grande. The

other is from Tucson. They're expected to show up together eventually, but we don't have an ETA. At this
time I'd say they're still an hour or more out. In addition, DPS is shorthanded on CSIs at the moment, so
they're requesting that our CSIs respond to the scene."

Joanna knew that the DPS investigators involved
wouldn't be happy at this turn of events, but it wasn't
her problem. Since their own department had made the
call, they could either like it or lump it.

"Are Dave and Casey on their way then?" she asked.

"They are," Tom answered, "and so is Doc Baldwin."

Joanna's trusted two-person CSI team was made
up of Dave Hollicker and Casey Ledford. Dr. Kendra
Baldwin was the Cochise County medical examiner.

"What about Detectives Carbajal and Howell?" Tom
asked. "Should I send them along as well?"

Joanna thought about that for a moment. If the DPS
resented having to use another department's CSIs, having
her detectives show up at the crime scene would make
things that much worse.

"Nope," she said. "The DPS guys will most likely
already have their noses out of joint at having to work
with our CSIs, so let's leave Deb and Jaime out of the
mix. In the meantime I'm coming up on Sierra Vista
and need to get off the phone. I've got a lead on a current location for Deputy Ruiz's wife. I'm planning on
stopping by to tell her what's happened before heading
over to Whetstone. I'll call you back when I'm done
with the notification. And be sure to tell Deputy Raymond to keep those two kids separate from their mother
until someone has a chance to interview them. If it turns
out they did witness the shooting, we'll need statements
from both of them."

"Roger that," Tom said.

Joanna ended the call and then summoned Siri. "Please give me driving directions to Carmichael Elementary School in Sierra Vista, Arizona."

Eight minutes later Joanna pulled in to a visitor space in the school's parking lot. When she walked into the office, a sour-faced woman glared at her from the far side of a chest-high counter.

"We don't allow guns in here," she snarled. "Didn't you see the sign?" she added, pointing to the no-guns-allowed notice stenciled on the office door.

When Joanna was first elected, she had worn civilian clothing. Too many wrecked sets of pantyhose and damaged pantsuits and skirts had sent her in search of more durable choices in attire. These days she usually wore the same uniform her officers did, with both her name and her badge displayed front and center and with a holstered weapon on her hip. The total illogic of forbidding an armed and fully trained police officer to set foot on the school grounds carrying his or her weapons was enough to set Joanna's teeth on edge.

"I'm Sheriff Joanna Brady," she announced. "I have zero intention of relinquishing my weapon. If you'd like to take it away from me, you're welcome to try. In the meantime I need to speak to the principal about an urgent matter."

The woman hesitated, looking as though she were prepared to argue the point. The slight delay sent Joanna's quick temper up another notch. "Now!" she added forcefully.

Shaking her head, the woman shuffled over to an open door and spoke into it. "Ms. Hayes, there's someone here to see you—the sheriff. She says it's urgent, but you need to know she's got a gun."

"Did you tell her this is a gun-free zone?"

"Why don't you try telling her that yourself? Or maybe we should call the school resource officer."

"I'll handle it," another female voice said in the background.

The woman who emerged from the office was probably ten years Joanna's senior. Surprisingly enough, she approached with a tight-lipped smile on her face.

"Welcome to Carmichael Elementary, Sheriff Brady. I'm Wanda Hayes, the principal. What can we do for you today?" she asked, staring pointedly at Joanna's holstered weapon.

"I need to speak to Amy Ruiz."

"Ms. Ruiz is in class right now, and I can't allow you to go wandering the halls. Lunchtime will start in about twenty minutes and—"

Joanna stopped her short. "Amy's husband, Deputy Armando Ruiz, has been seriously wounded and is currently being airlifted to a trauma unit in Tucson. I'm here to deliver that news in person. And you might want to think about arranging for a substitute teacher. I have a feeling Amy's going to be off work for the next several days."

As Joanna spoke, the supercilious smile faded from the principal's face. "Call Ms. Ruiz and ask her to come to the office," she said over her shoulder to the woman still lingering in the background. "When you do, tell her I'm coming down to cover her class." Then, to Joanna, she added, "When she gets here, you'll need privacy. You're welcome to use my office."

"Thank you," Joanna said.

The intercom setup was at the far end of the counter. As Wanda Hayes hurried off down the corridor, the other woman did as she was told. "Ms. Ruiz," she said into the microphone. "Please report to the office."

Inside the office designated as Wanda Hayes's private domain, Joanna had a choice to make. She could either sit in the chair behind the desk and take command of the situation or she could be a caring human being and use one of the two visitor chairs. She chose the latter. When an anxious and breathless Amy Ruiz hurried through the doorway a few minutes later, she came to a sudden halt the moment she spotted Joanna's uniform.

"Oh, no," she whispered, "not Armando!"

For a moment Joanna Brady was unable to utter a word. All she could do was nod.

Her face white with shock, Amy staggered to the other chair and dropped heavily into it. "Is he . . . ?"

"No," Joanna managed at last. "He's not dead, but he's been grievously wounded—shot while attempting to deliver a no-contact order. He's being airlifted to Banner in Tucson, where he'll probably need to undergo surgery. If you're not comfortable driving there on your own, I'll be glad to take you myself, or else I can have one of my deputies drive you there."

Unfortunately, Joanna knew exactly how this felt—the disorienting shock of having your life turned upside down, of losing that which you held most dear. From the stricken look on Amy's face to the lack of comprehension in her eyes, Joanna wasn't sure how many of her words had actually penetrated.

"No," Amy said at last, as if shaking herself awake. "I should probably drive myself. That way I'll have a vehicle to use."

"What about your kids?" Joanna asked. "It's probably for the best if they don't go with you at this point. Do you have someone who can pick them up from school and look after them?"

Amy stared at Joanna numbly for several long seconds before she finally nodded. "My folks," she said. "I'll call Mom. She'll pick them up and take them home to their place. But what happened, Sheriff Brady? Tell me."

"As I said, Armando was sent out early this morning to deliver a no-contact order to a man living in Whetstone. We still don't have all the details. Officers and EMTs from Huachuca City were the first to arrive on the scene, and they're the ones who requested an air ambulance. One of my own deputies is still on his way, although he may have arrived by now. From what I've been told, the man named in the protection order emerged from the residence with a weapon in hand and began shooting. Armando was hit but still managed to return fire."

"What about the other man?" Amy asked. "What happened to him?"

There was no way to sugarcoat this. "He's deceased," Joanna replied simply. "He was declared dead at the scene."

"You mean Armando killed him?" Amy demanded in disbelief. "Armando shot someone, and he's dead?"

Joanna nodded.

"Oh, my God!" Amy wailed. "My Armando a killer! He could never do such a thing! He'll never be able to live with somebody's death on his conscience!"

The only problem with that statement had to do with the fact that in order for Armando to have his conscience bother him, he would need to survive. That was

Joanna's immediate thought, but she said nothing to that effect.

"We understand that at the time the shooter presented a clear and present danger to any number of people. Had Armando not returned fire, other innocent people might well have perished. Your husband is an excellent officer," Joanna added. "There'll need to be a thorough investigation, of course, but I have no doubt it will end with his being exonerated. In the meantime, though, you shouldn't worry about any of that. You need to get to the hospital. He's probably already there, and you should be, too."

"What if he dies?" Amy barely whispered her darkest fear. "How will I be able to go on if he's not here?"

"You'll go on because you have to," Joanna said softly. "You'll do it because you have kids, and that means you don't have a choice."

"How can you even say such a thing?" Amy demanded. "You have no right."

"I do have a right," Joanna countered softly, "because I've been there, too. My husband, Andy, was also once a deputy. He was gunned down on his way home from work."

Amy's eyes widened in surprise. "Oh, no," she said. "I had no idea. I'm so sorry. Did he make it?"

Joanna reached out, took one of Amy's trembling hands, and held it close. "No, he didn't," she answered finally, "but I did, and so will you."

CHAPTER 4

WHEN JOANNA returned to the school's parking lot, she found two Interceptors parked side by side. One was a year older than hers and came with Sierra Vista markings. Frank Montoya, in full uniform, stood leaning against the front bumper of that one.

"Are you driving Amy to the hospital or am I?" he wanted to know.

"She said she wanted to drive herself."

Frank shook his head. "That is so not happening," he declared. "Amy's bound to be upset, which means she's in no condition to drive. Besides, she'll probably need to make dozens of phone calls along the way. As for you? You need to be at the crime scene. I'll take her, and if anyone has nerve enough to ask how come," he added with a grin, "we'll call it mutual aid."

Unable to help herself, Joanna hugged the man. "Thank you," she said. "Amy had to go back to her classroom to get her things. She turned me down flat when I offered to drive her, but maybe she'll listen to reason if it comes from you."

"Maybe," he said. "Now, you get going and leave Amy Ruiz to me. By the way, who'll be looking after her kids?"

"Her parents."

"Good," he said, "I know the Harpers. They're excellent people. They'll take good care of their grandkids, and I'll take good care of their daughter."

Grateful beyond words for Frank's help and not quite trusting her ability to speak, Joanna simply nodded and climbed into her own vehicle. After dictating Leon Hogan's address into her GPS, she drove away without bothering with either lights or sirens. And she didn't speed either. The emergency aspect of the case was over. Amy had been notified in a timely fashion. The injured had been transported, and the dead would be carted off soon enough. For right now Sheriff Joanna Brady needed some space and some quiet.

In terms of emotions, Joanna's conversation with Amy Ruiz had cost her dearly. For one thing, Armando was Joanna's deputy, meaning that in a very real way he was her responsibility. Whether Armando lived or died—whether he recovered or didn't—his wife and children were also Joanna's responsibility. And the fact that Joanna had indeed walked in Amy's shoes all those years earlier gave her a firsthand understanding of all the emotional pitfalls that lay in store for the entire Ruiz family.

She was headed for the highway, praying for all of them, when Butch called. "I heard about what's going on," he said. "Your shooting's all over the news up here in Phoenix. Which deputy?"

"Armando Ruiz," Joanna replied.

"What about you?" Butch asked. "Are you okay?"

"Medium," Joanna said, "or maybe not that good. I just finished notifying his wife about the shooting. Amy was at school and had no idea anything was amiss."

"How's she doing?"

"She's holding herself together at the moment, but I

don't know how long that will last. I doubt it's all sunk in yet. Frank Montoya just showed up at the school to drive her to the hospital."

"The news report said that the injured deputy had been airlifted to Tucson," Butch said. "Is Armando going to make it?"

"Jury's out on that," Joanna said. "Somehow the bullet bypassed his vest. He was hit in the gut. According to Tom Hadlock, Armando's currently undergoing emergency surgery at Banner Medical in Tucson."

"How did it happen?"

"Armando was delivering a no-contact order. The guy went berserk and came out shooting. He's dead, and there's a good chance Armando won't make it either."

"This isn't your fault, Joey," Butch said after a pause. "You can't hold yourself responsible."

Joanna couldn't help but smile when Butch called her by his pet name for her. "You know me too well," she said, because that's exactly what she was doing— blaming herself.

"The news said it happened out in Whetstone. Have you been to the crime scene?"

"I'm on my way now, but there probably won't be much for me to do. My people will be sidelined, because the Department of Public Safety will be in charge of the actual investigation."

"In my experience," Butch observed, "you don't do well on the sidelines. And if you don't believe me, check out your two failed attempts at maternity leave. It might be a good idea for you to take yourself elsewhere."

The gibe about her inability to stay off work when she was supposedly on maternity leave was well deserved.

"Thanks," she said. "I'll bear that in mind."

"All right, then," Butch said. "I'm on my way out to do both an interview and a signing. Call if you need to. If I'm busy, I'll have my phone on airplane mode and call you back when I can."

"Thank you," she said. "I really did need to hear your voice."

"You're welcome," he said. "You know I've got your back."

"Yes," she agreed. "I know you do."

"Stay safe," he reminded her.

"Will," she returned. "Bye-bye."

As Joanna turned onto Sheila Street in Whetstone twenty minutes later, she saw the cluster of official vehicles parked haphazardly along the dirt shoulder half a mile away. A few of them probably belonged to some of her people. And it made sense for them to have parked on the street rather than entering the property and disturbing the crime scene. But Joanna was equally sure that if news of the shooting was already being reported on Phoenix television stations two hundred miles away, there was most likely an active media presence here at the scene.

The moment that idea crossed her mind, she saw confirmation that she wasn't wrong. One of the first vehicles she passed was the very recognizable white RAV4 belonging to none other than a local pain-in-the-ass columnist named Marliss Shackleford.

A Huachuca City officer, attempting to prevent unauthorized vehicles from accessing the scene, flagged Joanna down. She was stopping to display her ID when Marliss, frizzy hair and all, stepped up to the window, pushed her way past the cop, and leaned inside.

Joanna tried to give the woman the brush-off. "Excuse me, Marliss, but I'm in a hurry. Would you mind?"

Marliss, with the camera side of her iPhone pointed in Joanna's direction, didn't take the hint. "Is Leon Hogan the victim who's deceased?" she asked.

Joanna knew from past experience that this annoying woman spent the better part of her day with one ear glued to her home-based police scanner. That meant that day or night she always knew exactly what was going on with Joanna's department.

Joanna didn't waste any time crafting a diplomatic response. "Next-of-kin notifications have not been done. That means we're not releasing any names to the public."

Marliss wasn't the least bit deterred by Joanna's terse reply. "I understand Deputy Ruiz is seriously wounded and has been airlifted to the trauma unit at Banner Medical in Tucson. Any word on his condition?"

"No comment," Joanna said through gritted teeth. "Now, move out of the way, Marliss. I need to get going."

Reluctantly, Marliss retracted her head, allowing Joanna to pull forward enough to be parallel with the next shoulder-parked vehicle—the M.E.'s minivan, sometimes referred to as the "body wagon."

Looking around, Joanna saw that her stop in Sierra Vista had made for a seriously late arrival at the crime scene. Doc Baldwin and her people were huddled on the front porch of the single-wide mobile home, most likely already at work with their preliminary examination of the body, while Casey Ledford and Dave Hollicker were combing the weedy yard for shell casings, with Casey laying down evidence markers while Dave followed along, camera in hand. Dogging the CSIs' heels was none other than County Attorney Arlee Jones.

Joanna stood still long enough to examine her surroundings. Whoever had assigned the arbitrary name of Sheila Street to that washboarded stretch of dirt road had vastly overstated the case. It wasn't a street at all, but it was the last bit of roadway inside Whetstone proper. The collection of houses strung loosely along its eastern flank were backed by nothing but open range. No grazing cattle were visible at the moment, but barbed-wire fencing surrounded each residence and every driveway included a livestock-deterring cattle guard.

Garth Raymond's patrol vehicle, parked just beyond the cattle guard and directly behind Armando's, barred anyone else from entering the property. The driver's-side door on Armando's vehicle still hung open. Joanna, on the far side of the cattle guard, was several car lengths away. Even so, she could see the horrifying bloodstains marring the inside of the door panel, showing exactly where Deputy Ruiz had been standing at the time he was hit. All around the car, Joanna saw the telltale scatter of medical debris left behind by EMTs fighting to save Armando's life.

Beyond Deputy Ruiz's patrol car, Joanna spotted the body of Leon Hogan. It lay fully exposed on a small wooden porch outside the front door of the single-wide trailer. Dr. Baldwin and her henchmen were clustered nearby, doing whatever was necessary prior to transporting the body.

In search of a better vantage point, Joanna made her way across the cattle guard. One thing in particular stood out. There was not a hint of cover on that porch. In other words, the dead man must have been standing in full sight, facing Armando and firing away. From Joanna's point of view, that added up to only one thing—suicide by cop. Leon Hogan might have been fine when it came to pulling the trigger on someone else, but he hadn't had guts enough to take his own life.

She stood for a moment longer, surveying the sad scene. An aging GMC pickup was tucked in under a sagging carport at the near end of the mobile home, a fourteen-by-seventy. The yard around it was nothing but hard-packed dirt, littered with dead weeds and trash. Clearly no one involved was overly concerned about performing any kind of routine maintenance.

Joanna was still lost in thought when Deputy Garth Raymond hurried up to greet her.

"What's the story?" she asked.

"As near as I can tell, most but not all of the confrontation took place right here in the front yard. Armando must have been in the process of leaving when the woman came racing out of the house with the man taking potshots at her as she ran. He missed her and hit Deputy Ruiz instead, even though Ruiz tried to take cover behind his patrol car. Chances are Hogan wasn't even aiming at Armando."

"Any sign of that no-contact order?" Joanna asked.

Garth nodded. "Casey Ledford told me she found it on the living-room floor, soaked in spilled coffee and next to a tipped-over end table. My guess is the coffee got spilled at the same time the table got knocked over."

"What about the kids?" Joanna asked. "How are they?"

"Okay," Garth said. "Evidently they heard what was going on but didn't actually see it. They were in a bedroom where the windows are too high for them to look out. After I got here, I walked over to the neighbor's house to check on the kids. The little girl, Kendall, told me that while she and her brother were playing in the bedroom, her parents were in the living room. She said she heard the doorbell ring. Right after that, someone closed the bedroom door. That was followed by some loud noises inside the house, but it wasn't until after the shooting that the kids found out they were locked inside the bedroom and couldn't get out."

"But before that?" Joanna asked.

"Kendall told me that after the doorbell rang, at some point, she heard her parents arguing—yelling at each other in the living room along with a 'sort of wrestling sound.' That's what she called it—a wrestling sound."

"Which would suggest some kind of physical altercation," Joanna concluded.

"Yes," Garth agreed, "an altercation followed by gunfire. Kendall said that when she started hearing gunshots, she made Peter hide under a bed to keep him safe."

Hearing that made Joanna's heart hurt. Seven-year-olds should never have to protect their younger siblings from gunfire. And considering the relative strength of the thin metal siding on the exteriors of mobile homes, hiding under the bed wouldn't have done much good.

"Go on," she said.

"Once the gunfire ended, the kids reported hearing someone screaming. After that they heard some sirens. Kendall said they tried to get out of the room then, but the door was locked from the outside. At that point she climbed up on a dresser and started pounding on the window until . . ." Garth paused and consulted a pocket-size notebook. ". . . until Officer Larry Dunn from Huachuca City unlocked the door and delivered them to the neighbor."

"If she was able to pound on the window, are you sure the kids didn't see what happened?"

"I asked Kendall about that flat out, and she said no. I'm guessing that even when she was up on the dresser, her father's body was out of sight."

"That's a relief," Joanna breathed.

It would be awful if the two kids turned out to be the only eyewitnesses. Being forced to go to court and talk about seeing their father gunned down and their naked, blood-spattered mother outside howling at the sky were the kinds of things that could fuel a lifetime's worth of nightmares.

"Did you tell them their father was dead?" Joanna asked.

Looking at his feet, Garth shook his head. "No, ma'am," he said somberly. "I didn't think it was my place."

Joanna gave her young deputy an encouraging pat on his upper arm. "You're right about that, Deputy Raymond," she told him. "But sounds like it took Officer Dunn a while before he could get to the kids."

Garth nodded. "That's right. He had to contain the woman first. He heard Kendall pounding on the window. The mother was determined to race back into the house. He finally had to lock her up in the backseat of his patrol car."

In the background Joanna heard the distant wail of a siren. No doubt guys from DPS were about to stage a dramatic arrival. Shutting the sound out, Joanna turned back to Garth.

"I wonder if being locked inside the bedroom was a usual occurrence or an unusual one," she mused.

Garth shrugged. "No idea," he said. "I didn't ask."

"If you have a chance to talk to Casey, ask her to be

sure to dust both that table knife and the padlock hasp
for prints," Joanna told him. "I'd like to know exactly
who locked those kids inside the bedroom and why."

Garth looked puzzled. "You want *me* to ask her?" he
asked. "Why don't *you*?"

Joanna gazed down the road, studying the progress
of an approaching vehicle leaving behind a rooster tail
of dust.

"Because I'm not supposed to be here, and I won't
be," she answered. "For that matter, neither are you.
This is an officer-involved shooting, and the DPS cav-
alry is about to arrive on the scene to take charge of
the investigation. Once they're here, I'm pretty sure I'll
be given my walking papers. In the meantime what's
become of Madison Hogan? Is she still here?"

Garth shook his head. "No, Ms. Hogan was hysterical and hyperventilating. Once the EMTs got Armando
loaded onto the helicopter, they determined that she
should be transported as well, by ambulance rather than
by helicopter. They took her to the ER at Sierra Vista
Memorial for observation."

"Thanks for the briefing, Garth. I appreciate it."

Joanna turned back to the road just in time to see
an unmarked SUV roll to a stop and park next to her
Interceptor, effectively blocking her in. Knowing that
her presence at the scene would be a bone of contention,
Joanna had been careful not to venture any farther into
the yard than the far edge of the cattle guard.

Doors on the SUV were flung open, and two suit-
clad men, an older one and a younger, stepped out onto
the dirt road. They stood there for a moment, glancing
around the scene as if getting their bearings. Joanna
happened to be close enough to the new arrivals to be

able to make out their features. The younger one was a complete stranger to her. Unfortunately, the older one was not. Dave Newton was someone with whom she had crossed paths and swords on a previous occasion. Joanna didn't like him one bit. From the look of displeasure on his face when he caught sight of her, the feeling was mutual.

"Sheriff Brady," he said dismissively, sauntering up to her. "What are you doing here? I understand a member of your trigger-happy department has been up to your old tricks."

Joanna did a slow burn at the words "trigger-happy." That suggested from the outset that Newton had arrived on the scene already predisposed to find some kind of wrongdoing on Deputy Ruiz's part. Not only that, but for him to speak to her in such a derogatory fashion in front of one of her own officers was utterly beyond the pale. With some effort she managed to keep a tight rein on her temper and reply in a reasonably civil tone.

"Good afternoon to you, too, Detective Newton," she said, addressing him with icy politeness. Turning to Newton's partner, she extended her hand in greeting—a courtesy she hadn't bestowed on Newton. "And you are?" she asked.

Newton was a grizzled fiftysomething. His partner wasn't a day over thirty. The younger man responded with a winning smile.

"Name's Liam Jackson, ma'am," he replied, "Detective Liam Jackson. Glad to meet you."

"You haven't answered my question," Newton insisted, prying Joanna's attention away from the younger man. "What are you doing here, Sheriff Brady? My instructions were clear. We may be having to use your

CSIs, but this is a DPS investigation from beginning to end. We're in charge."

"Understood," she agreed, "and this is as close as I've been to the crime scene, but I wanted to be here in person to hand things over to you. This is Deputy Garth Raymond. He was the first member of my department to respond to Deputy Ruiz's officer-down call, although officers from Huachuca City PD arrived before he did. Garth will be able to supply you with the names of everyone who's been here, including the EMTs."

Looking around the scene, Newton frowned. "You don't have any investigators here, do you?"

"As requested, Casey Ledford and Dave Hollicker, my CSIs, are here, as is County Attorney Arlee Jones," Joanna replied. "No one else from my department is on the scene. I'xve told everyone that we're handling this by the book. And now that you're here to take charge, I'll be on my way."

"Where to?" Newton asked suspiciously.

Joanna bristled. Where she was going was none of Newton's business, but she answered the question anyway. "I'm on my way to Tucson," she replied. "Deputy Ruiz is currently undergoing emergency surgery at Banner Medical. He's one of my people, Detective Newton, and my place is with his wife in the waiting room outside the OR."

"Just remember," Newton cautioned, "under no circumstances are you to speak to him about this case. Do I make myself clear?"

"Perfectly," Joanna said. "By the way," she added, "you'll need to move your vehicle. It looks like yours has me blocked in."

"Sure thing," Detective Jackson said cheerfully. "Right away."

Pulling car keys from his pocket, the younger man headed over to the SUV with Joanna following on his heels. She didn't need to look back at Newton to confirm that he was sending a superior sneer in her direction. By publicly dissing her and banning her from the scene, he probably thought he'd won, but to Joanna's way of thinking, this dustup was only the first round. Maybe she couldn't talk to Armando Ruiz, but that didn't mean she couldn't listen in when other people did.

She'd taken Butch's advice and had seemingly accepted her sidelining with good grace, but if Newton tried pushing Arlee Jones around in the same manner in which he'd treated her, the man was in for a big surprise. The Cochise County attorney happened to be the guy who would have the final say about whether or not Armando Ruiz would be facing charges. Jones was also a stubborn old coot and not the least bit pushable. He could be gotten around, however, and Sheriff Joanna Brady had more than eight years' worth of practice in doing just that.

CHAPTER 5

JOANNA MIGHT have looked calm, cool, and collected as she departed the crime scene, but when she called Butch a few minutes later, she was in full rant mode.

"You'll never believe who DPS sent out—that asshole Dave Newton!" she fumed. "And like the jerk he is, he lit into me right there in public, dressing me down in front of one of my deputies and sending me packing from the crime scene."

"Wait," Butch said. "Who's Dave Newton?" Then, after a pause he added, "Now I remember—Mr. Soccer Ball Guy, right?"

Years earlier a fleeing homicide suspect had carjacked a minivan containing two young children from the Texas Canyon Rest Area on I-10 before heading west. Joanna and a very inexperienced deputy had been several exits ahead of the speeding minivan and had given chase. Since there were only two westbound lanes, Joanna's department had coordinated with a number of eighteen-wheelers to create a moving roadblock that had forced the suspect onto a secondary road that, unknown to the carjacker, came to a dead end several miles away. Finally, with no choice but to stop, the armed bad guy had attempted to use one of the kids as a human shield, an action that had left Joanna with very few options.

Taking cover behind the van, Joanna had hit the ground. Despite the fact that she was exceedingly pregnant with Denny at the time, she'd lain on her protruding belly and had shot under the body of the minivan, nailing the jerk in the foot and smashing his ankle to bits.

Joanna's father, D. H. Lathrop, had loved those old black-and-white cowboy movies where the good guy shoots the gun out of the bad guy's hand. This wasn't exactly the same thing, but it had done the trick. The kids had been rescued and the handcuffed suspect packed off to a hospital. The injury was serious enough that not only was the killer now spending life in prison without parole, he was doing so with an amputated foot—an outcome Joanna didn't regret in the least.

But because the incident was an officer-involved shooting, DPS had been called in to investigate, with none other than Detective Newton running the show. During an interview with Joanna, an arrogant Newton had taken issue with her version of events, suggesting that it would have been impossible for "someone in her condition" to lie on her belly and shoot well enough to hit the suspect in the ankle and do so on purpose. That's when Joanna had issued her soccer-ball challenge.

"Okay," she'd told him. "You lie on a soccer ball. I'll lie on my belly, and we'll see which one is the better shot!"

Not surprisingly, Newton had declined to participate, and eventually he'd been forced to exonerate Joanna as well, but that's how she continued to think of him and refer to him—Soccer Ball Newton.

"Exactly," Joanna replied finally. "That's the one."

"I'm guessing with that kind of history there's a lot of bad blood on both sides."

"You could say that," Joanna agreed, "and I'm afraid some of it is going to get splashed onto Deputy Ruiz. If Newton can come up with a way to claim that Armando is at fault, he will."

"But you didn't call him on that, did you?"

"No," Joanna said. "You'd be proud of me. I managed to keep my mouth shut for a change."

"So where are you headed now?" Butch asked. "Back to the office?"

"No, I'm on my way to the hospital in Tucson. Frank Montoya is driving Amy Ruiz to the hospital, but someone should be there with her when Armando comes out of the OR, and I'm nominating myself for that duty. Why not? If I can't be working the homicide, I could just as well make myself useful."

"How did you rope Frank Montoya into taxi duty?" Butch asked.

"I didn't," she said. "He flat-out volunteered. When I left the school after notifying Amy, he was there waiting and offering to give her a ride."

"He's a good guy," Butch said. "I'm sorry your department lost him."

"Boy howdy," Joanna returned. "That makes two of us."

"My last Phoenix appearance is tonight," Butch said. "The ones in Tucson start tomorrow. With all this going on, do you want me to cancel and come home?"

Butch's question made Joanna realize that with everything that had been going on, she hadn't told Carol Sunderson about any of it.

"I don't know," she said. "Let me talk it over with Carol and give you a call back."

Just then call waiting sounded. "It's Tom Hadlock," she told Butch. "I'd better go."

"Updates?" she asked once she'd switched over to the other call.

"Deputy Ruiz is in surgery as of twenty minutes ago," the chief deputy told her. "It's expected to take several hours."

A surgery lasting several hours was not good news, but at least Armando was still alive.

"All right," she said. "I'm on my way to the hospital and don't know how long I'll stay. Frank Montoya is bringing Amy there while her folks look after their kids. And speaking of kids. What's going on with Kendall and Peter Hogan? If their father is dead and their mother is hospitalized, are there any nearby relatives who can look after them?"

"None that I can find," Tom answered. "Leon Hogan was in the army and stationed at Fort Huachuca. He's originally from Cody, Wyoming, and his parents still live there. I've organized a next-of-kin notification with Cody PD, but that hasn't happened yet. I'll let you know when it's done. In the meantime I've contacted Child Protective Services. They'll be sending someone to Alice Kidder's house to take charge of the children until such time as their mother is released from the hospital."

"From what Garth told me, those kids might have plenty to say. Do we know if DPS is interviewing them?"

"No idea," Tom answered, "but the word I'm getting from Casey Ledford and Dave Hollicker is that this Newton character is a complete jackass, so we'd best not ask."

"You're right there," Joanna agreed. "He is an ass with a capital *A*."

Tom let that pass without comment. "If you're on your way to Tucson, how long do you plan to stay?"

"Beats me. Probably several hours, but I'll need to check with my sitter. In the meantime DPS is on the scene and already sent me packing. By now they've probably done the same with Deputy Raymond."

"Okay," Tom said. "I'll keep the lights on here."

Good to her word, Joanna called Carol Sunderson the moment the previous call ended. "It's handled," Carol said. "I'll have the boys come here for dinner, and then they can go home while I stay here with Denny and Sage. It's not a problem. You do what you need to do and don't worry about a thing."

"Butch said that if need be, he can cancel his Tucson appearances and come home."

"He doesn't need to do that either," Carol insisted. "We'll be just fine on our own."

As Joanna drove on, for the thousandth time she thanked her lucky stars that Carol Sunderson was in their lives. How many working parents *weren't* blessed with that kind of stable child-care arrangement?

Gradually the radio chatter dissolved into road noise, and Joanna found herself thinking about the costs and consequences of domestic violence, not just in terms of loss of life but also in terms of shattered hopes and dreams. According to Records at Sierra Vista PD, Madison Hogan might have been the primary aggressor in those earlier domestic-violence callouts to the Hogan residence, but now Leon, the DV victim, was the one who was dead. How often did that happen?

Starting out in law enforcement—after Joanna's election but before she'd put herself through the rigors of police-academy training—she'd already known that domestic-violence calls were inherently hazardous for first responders—cops and EMTs alike. For years, though, her knowledge of domestic violence had been more of the textbook variety. She'd had no personal experience with that kind of behavior—not with her first husband, Andrew Brady, nor with her father, and certainly not with Butch. But her hand-to-hand battle with Jeremy Stock had taught her that people who commit domestic violence can often look like the guy next door. In fact, they might just *be* the guy next door.

Joanna couldn't help but wonder if having that kind of traumatic experience in her own background made her a more effective leader or a less effective one? If today's events were any indication, the jury on that was still up for grabs.

These days whenever Joanna's officers were being summoned to domestic-violence calls, she had to fight to remain calm and in command when what she really wanted to do was give way to panic, get far from the conflict, and bury her head under the covers.

That morning she'd been unaware Deputy Ruiz had been dispatched to deliver Madison Hogan's protection order. That had somehow slipped under her radar, but even if it hadn't, would she have insisted on sending a backup officer along with him? The truth is, probably not, because she didn't have the manpower.

And then there was the situation with body cameras. A year earlier Joanna's request for funds to purchase bodycams had been x-ed out of her budget. According to Tom Hadlock, once the shooting ended, Madison Hogan had promptly started pointing the finger at Deputy Ruiz. Had he been wearing a body camera, most likely the video footage would have exonerated him completely, but now should the incident in Whetstone devolve into a he said/she said situation, Soccer Ball Guy would probably take Madison's word as the gospel.

But it was the word "gospel" in her mental meanderings that brought Joanna up short. She immediately redialed Tom's number.

"Does Reverend Maculyea know about any of this?" Joanna asked.

Marianne Maculyea and Joanna Brady had been best friends from junior high on. Not only was Reverend Maculyea Joanna's pastor at Tombstone Canyon United Methodist Church, she was also chaplain to local law-enforcement agencies as well as to the Bisbee Fire Department.

"She does," Tom answered. "I called her first thing. She has a pre-wedding counseling session scheduled this afternoon at four. Since the wedding's this weekend, she can't postpone, but she'll be heading to Tucson as soon as the appointment is over."

When Joanna had plucked Tom Hadlock out of his jail-commander slot and installed him as her chief deputy, she'd despaired of his ever making the grade, but now, nearly two years in, he appeared to be firing on all cylinders. The idea that he'd thought to notify Marianne Maculyea without having to be specifically asked to do so was a big checkmark in his favor. If Marianne was coming to the hospital, Joanna would be there to serve as backup for Amy Ruiz and Marianne would be backup for Joanna. That made for a win-win.

As Joanna approached the hospital grounds on Campbell, she barely recognized the place. It seemed to have doubled in size from when she'd been here with Andy all those years ago. The main entrance was different. The parking structure was different. Even so, as soon as she stepped inside the building itself, it seemed all too oppressively familiar. Andy had been shot elsewhere, but it was here in this hospital where she'd finally lost him. And she knew that in coming here Marianne would suffer a similar flashback.

Years earlier, after being childless for years, Marianne and her husband, Jeff, had brought twin baby girls—Ruth and Esther—home from an orphanage in China. Esther's health had been precarious from the start, and when surgeons at the then University Medical Center had attempted a heart transplant, Esther hadn't survived. Ruth, healthy and sassy, now happily spent her spare time out in the garage with her dad, learning to be a wrench-wielding gearhead. Jeffy, the surprise bundle of joy who had arrived long after Jeff and Marianne had given up hope of ever having biological children, was a quiet kid who loved books and drawing.

Even though Jeff's and Marianne's lives appeared to be complete now, Joanna knew that her friend carried an unhealed wound in her heart. Coming here automatically forced Joanna to revisit Andy's death, and Marianne would be dealing with Esther's. For both of them, their good deeds in caring for Amy Ruiz would not go unpunished.

Joanna made her way to the OR waiting room, expecting at any moment to be accosted by someone objecting to the presence of her firearm, but no one said a word. Before exiting the elevator on the OR floor, she said a silent prayer asking for guidance, and then, squaring her shoulders, she entered the waiting room. She expected to find Amy Ruiz already there, but she wasn't. The room was full of people, all of them strangers.

Joanna tucked herself away in a corner seat and waited. She sat there for a while, but then, remembering she'd been putting the final touches on her budget request that morning, she pulled out her iPad. Butch had fixed her laptop so she could access files remotely from the tablet. She wasn't nearly as fast typing on the iPad's flat keyboard as on a real one, but she could do editing just fine. And that's what she did. While she was at it, she put in an additional request. She still had access to the line item that had included the amount necessary for body cameras. She added that one in, right along with her request for extra personnel.

If Dave Newton's investigation failed to exonerate Armando and some kind of multimillion-dollar lawsuit resulted, Joanna would be able to show in dollars and cents how spending a small amount of money on body-cams might have made all the difference.

She had just finished putting the final touches on that and sending it when Frank Montoya came in with Amy leaning on his arm. They stopped at the nurses' station long enough, Joanna suspected, for Amy to be given a beeper that would let her know when Armando had been moved from the OR to a recovery room.

When Frank and Amy turned to search the room, Joanna waved them into the two unoccupied chairs she'd been saving for them. Amy looked like hell. When Joanna saw her earlier, before delivering the news, she'd seemed completely put together. Now her makeup was gone, her hair was a mess, and the despair on her face was apparent for all to see.

"He's still in surgery," Amy announced, "and I need to use the restroom."

As she walked away, Joanna turned to Frank. "I thought you'd be here first."

"So did I," he said, "but Amy insisted on getting her kids organized and packing a bag to bring along. I think she knows she'll be here for several days."

"She's not wrong about that," Joanna said grimly. "I'm pretty sure she will be."

"She cried most of the way here, so she's probably cried out at this point," Frank continued. "The problem is, much as I hate to do it, I have to drop her and run. I have a meeting coming up later this afternoon that I must attend."

"You've done way more than your share," Joanna told him gratefully. "I'll be here, and so will Marianne Maculyea."

CHAPTER 6

JOANNA AND Amy Ruiz sat together for the next two hours, but they mostly didn't talk. Amy was busy fielding phone calls from relatives and well-wishers, and although Joanna knew that the calls were all well intentioned, she could see that every time Amy had to repeat the story of what had happened and tell people Armando was still in surgery, it depleted her that much more.

Finally, when Amy was briefly between phone calls, Joanna reached over and touched the woman's knee.

"The people who are calling you all mean well, but they don't have any idea that they're draining away your strength. Turn off the phone. People can leave messages, and you can return them at your leisure. Have you had anything to eat?"

Amy shook her head. "Not since breakfast," she said. "But I'm not hungry."

"You still need to eat," Joanna said firmly, sounding just like her mother. It was the same thing Eleanor Lathrop Winfield would have said, with the exact same inflection. "If nothing else, you can pick at a bowl of chicken noodle soup, but it's going to be a very long night, and if you don't get some nourishment, you'll crash and burn."

"This sounds like the voice of experience speaking," Amy said, giving Joanna a wan smile.

Joanna nodded. "After Andy was shot, this is where they brought him. And then, when I lost him . . ." She paused, remembering, and then swallowed hard before she continued. "After a while things got so bad that I had to get away, so I took off on foot. I had no idea of where I was going or what I was going to do. I ended up at a hotel a few blocks from here—a place called the Arizona Inn. Have you ever heard of it?"

Amy shook her head.

"I went inside and tried to eat some lunch," Joanna continued. "I ordered food, but I couldn't eat it. I left most of my sandwich on the plate, and then I went outside. It's a resort, you see—an oasis, really—with beautiful plush lawns and gardens. There was this little palm-frond-covered patio with a Ping-Pong table and four big blue wooden chairs, one in each corner.

"I was sitting in one of them, crying my eyes out, when this old lady came walking up to me. She looked ancient, probably somewhere in her nineties at least. One leg was in a brace of some kind, so she walked with a funny gait, but she stomped up to me like she owned the place and asked me if I was a guest. I wasn't, of course, and I was sure she was about to throw me out, but then something strange happened. She asked me what was wrong and what she could do to help. All of a sudden, I spilled out the whole story—to a complete stranger. Then she took my arm and walked me to the lobby entrance, as though we'd been friends forever. I'll never forget the words she said as she sent me on my way. 'It will take time, my dear, but someday things will be better for you. Just you wait and see.'"

"And she was right?" Amy asked.

"Yes," Joanna replied after a moment, "she was right, but it took a long time. That's why I think things will be better for you, too, eventually, but right now it's time for baby steps. We're going to go down to the cafeteria. You may not swallow a bite of food, but I hope you'll at least try."

Chicken soup was one of the items on the cafeteria menu, and that seemed like a good choice. Since break-fast had been a very long time ago, Joanna ordered two bowls instead of one. Joanna ate hers. Amy did not. She stirred at it absently but swallowed only a taste or two. They spoke very little, and Joanna didn't push it. There wasn't that much to say. The road ahead for the Ruiz family held two stark and very different choices—either Armando would recover from his injuries or he would not.

Amy's beeper buzzed just after four. She leaped up like a frightened rabbit and started to clear the table. "You go," Joanna said. "I'll take care of this."

Joanna was heading for the hospital elevator when a call came through from Arlee Jones. "Who the hell does Dave Newton think he is, coming into my county and telling me what I can and can't do?" Cochise County's chief prosecutor demanded.

Joanna's first encounter with Newton had been in Pima County as opposed to Cochise, so it hadn't fallen under Arlee Jones's aegis.

"He is a bit of a jerk," Joanna replied. She could have said a whole lot more, but she didn't.

"He's way more than 'a bit,'" Arlee countered. "And he was walking around dissing Dave and Casey, acting as though our people don't have any idea what they're doing."

He was dissing their boss, too. That's what Joanna thought, but she didn't say it aloud.

"What's the deal with the fingerprints on the table knife?" Arlee asked. "Casey said you wanted them."

Joanna took a breath and launched into an explanation. "Garth Raymond said that according to at least one of the Hogan kids they were playing in the bedroom when Armando showed up with the protection order. After the doorbell rang, someone—they didn't see who—locked them inside the bedroom. After that they heard sounds of a struggle, followed by gunshots. At least I believe that's the correct chronology. And so I'm curious. Who locked them in the bedroom, their father or their mother? Since Madison Hogan swore out the protection order just yesterday, how come she was stark naked at her husband's residence early this morning?"

"She was naked because they had just gotten out of bed," Arlee replied.

"How do you know that?"

"Because I asked her," Arlee replied. "When I got tired of watching Detective Newton strutting around the crime scene like some puffed-up peacock, I took myself to the hospital and talked to the wife. Madison told me she called Mr. Hogan to ask for Christmas money for the kids. He said he'd give her some, but only if she and the kids came out to his place in Whetstone to spend the night. She decided that since the protection order hadn't been delivered, her going there wouldn't be a problem. I can't help but feel sorry for the poor guy. He probably thought he'd get a piece of tail for his trouble. Instead he ended up with a bullet in his chest."

Arlee Jones wasn't exactly a font of political correctness.

"Frank Montoya told me that while the Hogans were still together and living in Sierra Vista, his department had responded to several domestic-violence incidents at their residence. In all those cases, Madison was deemed to be the aggressor. So where did the gun come from? Whose was it? What kind?"

"A Glock 17," Arlee answered. "Dave Hollicker found a bunch of spent casings around the front door of the mobile home near where we found Leon Hogan's body. They also found a single casing in the living room of the trailer, along with a bullet hole and a bullet in the living-room ceiling."

"That coincides with what the little girl told Deputy Raymond—that the fight started inside the house and then moved outside, where, presumably, Leon Hogan was firing his weapon as he approached Deputy Ruiz."

"That's how it looks to me," Arlee agreed. "Leon Hogan came out firing, and both Deputy Ruiz and Madison Hogan took cover behind the door of his vehicle. Hogan fired several shots. There was plenty of brass on the pouch and several slugs hit Armando's vehicle, but only one bullet actually hit the door."

"The one that hit him?"

"That's right. It shattered the driver's-side window and then ricocheted off the frame before striking Armando in the gut. I don't think Hogan could shoot for beans, and the fact that Armando got hit was more of a fluke than anything else. How is he, by the way?"

"Just out of surgery," Joanna said. "He's in Recovery right now, so there's no word on his condition. Amy, his wife, is with him."

"Good to hear he made it through surgery," Arlee said. "Now I just wish someone could take Newton down a peg or two. From what I saw, Armando Ruiz acted in self-defense, but that doesn't mean those guys from DPS can't drag out the investigation, making Armando's life as miserable as possible for as long as possible—make yours miserable, too, for that matter."

"It wouldn't be the first time," Joanna said, "but think about those poor Hogan kids. Their lives are pretty miserable at the moment, too. There's a good chance one of them saw their naked mother screaming over the body of their dead father."

"Unfortunately, that's something they'll never be able to unsee," Arlee Jones observed sadly.

For the first time ever, Joanna felt a real human connection to the crusty old prosecutor.

"Where are they right now?" she asked.

"The Hogan kids?" Arlee asked.

"Yes."

"Back with their mother, I suppose," Arlee replied. "Madison was hysterical when the EMTs brought her to the hospital in Sierra Vista. The doctors there gave her something to calm her down and take the edge off, but they were getting ready to release her about the time I was leaving. CPS was right to remove the kids from the crime scene, but I can't see any reason for them not to be returned to their mother's custody."

"Were they interviewed before they went back to her?" Joanna asked.

"I thought they should have been," Arlee replied, "but Newton said otherwise. Those state-run three-letter folks stick together. When DPS says jump, CPS says how far."

Joanna thought about that for a moment. "Even so," she said finally, "something about all this just doesn't feel right."

"Not to me either," Arlee agreed, "but I think I should get off the phone. I'm sure I've bothered you long enough. I had to rant and rave about Newton to someone, and you were the only one I could think of."

"Feel free," Joanna said. "Anytime."

He ended the call. Reluctant to carry on her conversation with Arlee in a crowded elevator, Joanna had stayed in the downstairs corridor while they talked. Off the phone with him, she stayed where she was and dialed Casey Ledford's number.

"Dave Newton is a complete asshole," Casey said when she answered.

Joanna laughed in spite of herself. "It doesn't sound like he's busy winning friends and influencing people today," she said. "I was just on the phone with Arlee Jones. He was singing the same song, different verse."

"How's Armando?" Casey wanted to know.

"Out of surgery," Joanna replied. "His wife is with him. I'm about to go upstairs to check on his condition, but let me ask you a question. How are *you* doing?"

"We've gathered what we can from the crime scene, and that includes the table knife you asked for, the one from the hallway just outside the kids' bedroom."

"And the fight started inside the house, in the living room?"

"That's how it looks. We're packing up right now so we can go back to the lab and start processing."

"Okay," Joanna said. "Let me know what you find."

"Off the record, right?" Casey asked.

"Yes," Joanna said. "Definitely off the record."

Her next call was to Detective Deb Howell.

"How's Armando?" the detective wanted to know. Joanna gave her the same answer she'd given to Casey.

"I guess you got pushed off the case the same way we did," Deb grumbled. "What's there to investigate? It sounds to me as though the guy had a gun in his hand and was shooting to kill. Why wouldn't Armando use deadly force?"

"I agree," Joanna said. "But that's not why I'm calling."

"Why, then?" Deb asked. "What do you need?"

"I'd like you to look into Madison Hogan."

"The dead guy's wife? Why? What's this all about?"

"Leon and Madison Hogan had a contentious marriage," Joanna replied. "According to Frank there were several incidents of domestic violence at their residence prior to Leon's moving out. In each case the husband was the one with visible injuries and Madison was the one who was taken into custody."

"My understanding is we're not to have anything to do with Armando's case."

"This has nothing to do with the shooting itself. This is about the Hogans' two kids, Kendall and Peter."

"What about them?"

"When officers arrived on the scene, the kids were locked in a bedroom. The little girl told Deputy Raymond that just before a fight broke out in the living room, someone shut the door and locked them inside by shoving a table knife through a hasp on the outside of the door."

"Who locks kids inside bedrooms?" Deb demanded.

"Good question," Joanna returned. "And why? The whole thing seems off to me somehow. Armando was there to deliver a protection order that Madison Hogan swore out yesterday, yet she evidently took the kids to Leon's place to spend the night. She told Arlee Jones that she went there in hopes of getting money from Leon to buy Christmas presents for the kids, but I wonder if that's true. It was a school night. What were the kids doing at their father's mobile home in Whetstone this morning when they should have been at school in Sierra Vista?"

"I don't understand," Deb said. "What are you saying?"

"I'm just wondering if Madison Hogan had some other underlying reason for going to Whetstone, something that has nothing to do with Christmas presents. But that's Dave Newton's problem, not ours. For right now I'm worried about the kids."

"What about them?"

"Maybe I'm nuts, but what if Leon Hogan wasn't the only victim of domestic violence living in that household? Maybe he's not the one who locked the kids in that bedroom. What if their mother did?"

A brief but telling silence followed. "Considering what we all know about Jeremy Stock, I don't think you're nuts," Deb replied. "And believe me, Sheriff Brady, I'm all over it. Do you have any idea which school the two kids attend?"

"Not a clue," Joanna answered, "but check with Frank Montoya. He knows where the family lives, so he'll know which school."

CHAPTER 7

IT WAS dark outside and well past dinnertime, but Kendall could tell that no dinner would be forthcoming. Fortunately, that nice Mrs. Kidder, Daddy's neighbor, had made toast and scrambled eggs for them for breakfast, and Mrs. Ambrose, that lady from Child Something or Other, had bought them a burger from McDonald's before she brought them back home. She said their mother had been ill and had been in the emergency room, but now that she was home, they could go home, too. And then she had sat there in the living room with them while their mother told them that Daddy was gone.

Kendall had known that from the beginning, but Peter hadn't known until later, after their mother told them to go to their room and stay there.

"What does gone mean?" Peter had asked. "Will we still be able to see Daddy on weekends?"

Kendall had explained. "It means he's dead."

"Like Coon you mean?"

Coon had been the family dog, a bluetick hound, one with long floppy ears and a very cold nose. Daddy had brought Coon home as a puppy the year Kendall was five. Coon was supposed to be Kendall's dog, but he had really belonged to Peter more than he did to her. He slept at the foot of Peter's bed, and when they were home, he was always nearby. When Daddy left, he was going to take Coon with him, but Peter had cried and begged for the dog to stay with them, and he had. Then, a few weeks later, Kendall had come home from school and found Peter on the bed with his head buried in the pillow, crying like crazy.

"What's wrong?" Kendall had asked.

When Peter had come home from school that day, Mommy had told him that Coon had somehow gotten out of the yard, been hit by a car, and died. She said the vet tried, but he couldn't save him.

Kendall had never believed that story. If Coon was dead, it had more to do with the fact that Mom's new boyfriend, Randy, hated him than it did with Coon getting out of the yard. But she didn't mention that to Peter any more than she had told him earlier that their father was dead, even though she'd known that long before their mother got around to telling them.

As soon as she'd heard that first gunshot, she'd made Peter hide under the bed. After that the shots had come thick and fast. When they ended and the screaming started, Kendall had tried the door only to discover that it was locked from the outside. Wanting to know what had happened, she'd climbed up on top of the dresser and peeked out the window. The moment she saw Daddy lying on the porch with a big patch of blood spreading on his shirt and with his eyes open and staring at the sky, she knew he was dead. She'd seen dead people before, but only on TV, not in real life. This was definitely real. Daddy had told her that he was going to fix it so she and Peter could come live with him, but now she knew that was never going to happen.

After Mrs. Ambrose left, Mommy had told Kendall

and Peter that people were coming over that night and they needed to stay in their room. Randy was there, and some other people were there, too. Kendall could hear them laughing, talking, smoking, and probably drinking, too. Mommy did that a lot. It sounded like it was a party, which didn't seem right, not with Daddy dead.

In the meantime Kendall and Peter lay on the floor in their bedroom with Peter's Spider-Man coloring book between them. Peter was weird and liked to color upside down, so he was on one side of the book and she was on the other, listening while he jabbered away about which color he was going to use next. She was glad that her brother was busy and talking. Then he said something that caught her attention.

"I'm hungry," he said. "Let's go get something to eat."

Kendall had hoped that that late-afternoon hamburger had been enough. Now she knew that it wasn't. She also knew that leaving their bedroom wasn't an option. She'd done that once when Mommy had friends over. She tiptoed out of the room and had been creeping down the hallway toward the bathroom when she saw some man she didn't know going into Mommy's bedroom. She must have made a noise. Just then Randy turned up behind Kendall, grabbed her by the shoulder, and spun her around. She'd never liked him. Randy had mean eyes and a nasty way about him, but that night was the first time he'd really scared her.

"Don't make a sound," he told her, giving her a stiff shake. "You go back to your bedroom right now," he'd ordered, hissing the words and shaking his finger in her face. "And don't you come out again either. Or else."

Kendall didn't know what "or else" meant, and she

didn't want to find out. She didn't want Peter to find out either. So when there were evening visitors at the house, the kids usually stayed in their room no matter what—hunger included.

Even before Randy and his pals started hanging around, there'd been times when Mommy sent them to bed without remembering they hadn't had any dinner. As a result Kendall had taken to sneaking food—cookies, crackers, and sometimes even dry cereal—into their room and hiding the items away in the closet in case they were ever needed. Tonight they were.

"How would you like a marshmallow sandwich right here in the room?" Kendall asked.

Peter shook his head. "There's no such thing as a marshmallow sandwich," he said.

"Yes there is."

"Is not. Show me."

And so Kendall did. After making Peter close his eyes, she got up from her place on the floor and went over to the chair by the door where she had dropped her backpack. Daddy had always loved cooking outside on his Weber grill, and once he moved out and went to live in Whetstone, the grill had gone with him. When Kendall and Peter would go to stay with him on weekends, that's what he would make for them to eat—burgers, hot dogs, or sometimes even steaks—all of them cooked on the grill. And after dinner he always made s'mores for dessert.

Last night when Mommy told them to go to bed, she and Daddy had still been in the living room. On their way through the kitchen, Kendall had spotted a partially used bag of marshmallows and several unopened packets of graham crackers sitting on the counter. She'd gathered them up and carried them into their bedroom. She'd used one of her scrunchies to close the marsh-mallow bag before stuffing it and the packets of graham crackers into her backpack. She produced them now, pulling them out of the backpack one by one with the same kind of flourish a magician might use when pulling rabbits out of a hat.

Daddy always bought the huge marshmallows, not the medium ones or the tiny ones. These were big enough that when you stuck them between two crackers, it looked like a real sandwich. Kendall had to admit that she missed the crunchy burned crust that Daddy always left on the outside of the marshmallows, but she didn't complain, and neither did Peter. It was something for them to eat, and by then they were both hungry.

"Put on your jammies," Kendall ordered when they finished eating and as she stowed the remaining food in the corner of the closet. "It's time for bed."

"I need to go to the bathroom first," Peter said. "I need to pee."

"You can't," she said. "The door's locked."

That wasn't true. Kendall was only pretending the door was locked, and she did that so Peter wouldn't step out into the hallway and run into Randy the same way she had. As for the peeing problem? She'd created a solution for that.

"You'll have to use the jar," she told him.

After her encounter with Randy, Kendall had cleaned out an empty peanut-butter jar, one with a lid on it, that she kept in the closet for times when the kids needed to go to bed and there was partying going on outside their door. Unfortunately, there was no work-around for brushing their teeth.

Peter scowled. "Do I have to?"

"Yes, you have to."

"But why? Peeing in the jar is gross."

"Peeing in your pants is worse," she said.

Faced with that inarguable truth, Peter heaved a heartfelt sigh and did as he was told. Had he tried the door, he would have discovered that it wasn't locked at all, but fortunately Kendall was very good at pretending, just like earlier today when she'd had to pretend that Daddy wasn't dead. After seeing the scene outside their bedroom window, she'd climbed down from the dresser without letting Peter look outside and without telling him the truth, either. Sometime after that—a seemingly long time—a police officer had opened the door and let them out. The whole time he was walking them over to Mrs. Kidder's house, he hadn't said anything about what had happened to Daddy, and neither had the other cop, the one who'd talked to them later. Since the officers hadn't mentioned a word about Daddy being dead, neither did Kendall. She just pretended it hadn't happened, even though it had.

Kendall also pretended that she hadn't seen the gun. It had been lying on the front porch right next to Daddy's hand, but she knew it wasn't Daddy's. He didn't have a gun. The one on the porch was probably the one her mother usually carried around in her purse. They'd had a lesson on guns at school one day, and Kendall had come away knowing that guns shouldn't be left lying around out in the open like that. At least that's what her second-grade teacher, Mrs. Baird, had told them. "Guns are dangerous," she'd said. "They need to be handled properly and shouldn't be left in places where children have access to them."

Kendall didn't bother trying to repeat those words to Peter. She just did her best to make sure he never got anywhere near Mommy's purse.

"Can we go to school tomorrow?" Peter asked once they were both in bed, lying in the dark with Kendall in the top bunk and Peter in the lower one.

Peter liked school because of the free breakfasts and free lunches. Kendall liked school because she loved her teacher. Mrs. Baird didn't yell at people the way Mommy did. Mrs. Baird was always smiling. She said please and thank you. Mommy didn't do any of those things.

"We can't," she said. "You heard what Mommy said. We have to stay home until after the funeral."

"What's a funeral?" Peter asked.

Kendall wasn't exactly sure what a funeral was— something to do with dead people—something to do with Daddy. She had asked Mom when that would be— the funeral, that is—and Mom said she didn't know, that someone else would have to tell them.

"I think it's like a party for dead people," Kendall answered. "Grandma Puckett is coming."

"Will Daddy's mommy and daddy come, too?" Peter asked.

Kendall had met Daddy's parents only once when they came to Mommy and Daddy's wedding. She knew that they lived far away, so they didn't visit often.

"I don't know," she answered with a shrug.

But Kendall was glad they'd be having company, even if it was only Grandma Puckett. When she came to visit, there was usually a lot of yelling. Mommy didn't seem to like her mother very much, but when she was there, the food was always better. It turns out Grandma

Puckett didn't approve of people having cold cereal for dinner. The other good thing about having Grandma visit was that Randy generally stayed away.

Peter was quiet for a long time after that. Kendall thought he had fallen asleep, but then he spoke again. "I wish Coon were here," he said. "He always kept my feet warm."

"I wish he was here, too," Kendall replied.

Only when she heard Peter's breathing steady did Kendall Hogan finally give herself permission to stop pretending and to stop being brave. Only then did she give way to the tears she'd been holding back all day because she hadn't wanted Peter to see her crying. She wept as though her heart was broken, because it was.

Daddy and Coon were both gone, and neither of them would be coming back. Ever.

CHAPTER 8

IT TURNED out to be a very long evening. When Joanna went back upstairs, she found Marianne Maculyea sitting with Amy in the OR waiting room. The three of them were there together when the surgeon arrived to deliver his difficult news. Armando had survived the surgery and was now in recovery. He told Amy that they'd managed to successfully resection her husband's bowel. Once released from the hospital, Armando would be wearing a colostomy bag, something that might or might not be reversible at some point in the future. For now the biggest danger was the possibility of infection. Once out of recovery, he would be moved to the ICU, where, heavily sedated, he could be monitored for any sign of infection. In other words, there was nothing for Amy or anyone else to do but watch and wait.

Shortly after eight that evening, Armando was transferred to the ICU, and the others moved to a different waiting room. About that time Amy's father, Glenn Harper, showed up, arriving with a buddy in tow and with Amy's car keys in hand. He listened in silence while his daughter laid out the situation, including the fact that in the morning Armando's sister would be driving their mother over to Tucson from Las Cruces and dropping Amy's mother-in-law off to stay as long as her help was needed. Glenn Harper, a retired U.S.

Army colonel, was used to taking charge, and he did so as soon as Amy finished.

"Okay," he said. "Sounds like you're in for a long haul, and I'm glad to hear Consuelo is coming. The kids can stay with Mom and me for as long as necessary. While Armando's in the ICU, you'll only be able to see him for a few minutes every hour, so you'll be better off trying to get some rest, rather than sitting here in the waiting room all night long. I've reserved a room for you at a hotel over on Speedway called the Aloft. It's just down the street on the corner of Speedway and Campbell—within walking distance if need be. Once Consuelo shows up, the two of you can spell each other, with one of you here at the hospital while the other grabs some sleep in the room."

"Dad," Amy said, fighting back tears. "You shouldn't have."

"Yes I should. You're my girl, and looking after you is my job. Have you eaten anything?"

Amy glanced in Joanna's direction and shook her head. "Not really," she answered.

"All right, then," he concluded. "In order to take care of Armando, the best thing we can do right now is take care of you. To that end I'm going to make sure you have some dinner and get you checked into the hotel. The hospital will call if you're needed."

Joanna knew that Glenn Harper was right. There was nothing to be gained by Amy's toughing the night out on a hard chair in an ICU waiting room. She was surprised, however, when Amy knuckled under almost immediately and obediently did as she was told. She slipped into Armando's room long enough to kiss him good night before allowing her father to escort her from the waiting room. With Amy gone and with nothing more for Joanna and Marianne to do, they headed out as well.

As they rode down in the elevator, Marianne murmured sadly, "Aloft used to be the Four Points, you know."

Joanna nodded, because she knew what Marianne meant. The Four Points was the hotel where she and Jeff had been staying when they'd lost Esther. Reaching out, Joanna took her friend's hand and squeezed it. "I know," she said. "This place holds far too many bad memories for both of us."

Minutes later, after Joanna had turned off Kino Parkway onto I-10, Butch called. "What's going on?" he wanted to know.

Joanna brought him up to date. He sighed when she finished. "So even after Armando recovers from surgery, he still won't be able to return to active duty?"

"Definitely not with a stoma," Joanna replied. "A desk job will be the best he can do for the time being and maybe for good."

"Which means you're going to be even more short-handed in terms of sworn officers than you already are."

"Looks like it," she agreed. "I'll have to cross that bridge when I come to it. For right now all we can do is hope and pray Armando doesn't come down with some kind of infection. That bullet didn't kill him, but sepsis could."

Joanna made the hundred-mile drive from Tucson in good time and was home in bed by eleven. Even so, it was almost three before she finally fell asleep. It was fine to tell Butch that she'd deal with the personnel crisis later, but that didn't mean she herself believed it. Finding, hiring, and training qualified people was a difficult, time-consuming process, and keeping them on board after they were hired and trained was even more challenging.

In the end all the tossing and turning did for Joanna was cause her to oversleep. The next morning, by the time she woke up and staggered out of the bedroom in search of coffee, Carol was on duty and she and Sage were already back from taking Denny to catch the bus. Carol, with her own cup of coffee poured and on the table next to her, sat beside Sage's high chair supervising her breakfast.

"You had a late night," Carol observed, "and don't bother telling me about it. I already know why. It made the front page. I picked up your copy of the *Bee* on our way back from the bus stop."

The *Bisbee Bee* was delivered on a daily basis by an auto-route driver who shoved each day's copy into the metal newspaper cone attached to their mailbox post. This morning's edition sat on the table next to Carol's silverware. She pushed the paper across the table until it was close enough for Joanna to read the headline:

Father of Two
Shot by Deputy
by
Marliss Shackleford

"Father of Two Shot by Deputy," Joanna thought. *Why not "Armed Gunman"?* But the answer to that was clear enough, and most likely the article would be more of the same. Armed or not, the father was the victim here, which meant that the deputy was in the wrong.

"I don't have time to read this right now," she said, tossing the offending paper in the general neighborhood of her purse. "I need to shower, dress, and get to work."

By the time she reached the Justice Center, roll call was over. After touching base with Tom Hadlock and bringing him up to date on Armando's condition, Joanna retreated to her own office, where her first call was to Amy Ruiz. Armando's condition had been upgraded to serious but stable, with no signs of a developing infection. In addition, Amy's mother-in-law and sister-in-law had gotten an early start leaving Las Cruces and were due at the hospital any minute. All of that was good news, and Joanna was able to turn to her pile of neglected correspondence and daily routine matters with a happier heart.

Much later, with her desk finally cleared, she closed the door to her office and read the *Bisbee Bee* article all the way through:

Leon Hogan, age 29 and a father of two, was gunned down yesterday at his residence in Whetstone by Cochise County Deputy Sheriff Armando Ruiz. Deputy Ruiz had been sent to the home to deliver a no-contact order obtained by Hogan's estranged wife a day earlier.

Shortly after the document was delivered, a confrontation occurred between the two men which ended in gunfire. Mr. Hogan was declared dead at the scene. Deputy Ruiz, age 31 and the father of three, was airlifted to the trauma unit at Banner–University Medical Center in Tucson, where he underwent emergency surgery. His condition is currently listed as serious.

The officer-involved shooting is currently under investigation by officers from the Arizona Department of Public Safety.

"I never meant for any of this to happen," said Madison Hogan. "I was just trying to prevent trouble, not cause it. And my poor kids. They were inside the house when all this happened, and the cops wouldn't even let me go inside to take care of them."

Ms. Hogan admitted that the couple was having marital difficulties and living separately. "But we were working on our issues and trying to make things better. Now my poor kids are fatherless."

Armando Ruiz, originally from Las Cruces, New Mexico, has been a deputy with the Cochise County Sheriff's Department for the past seven years, where, according to Chief Deputy Thomas Hadlock, he has served with distinction.

So far the Cochise County Sheriff's Department has refrained from making any statements regarding the officer-involved shooting, and Sheriff Joanna Brady herself has been unavailable for comment.

Joanna was livid. *I wasn't unavailable for comment when you stuck your head in my window!* she thought savagely. *I said "No comment" right out loud, remember?* Unsurprisingly, Marliss Shackleford didn't respond to that query.

Deputy Ruiz and his wife, Amy, a teacher at Carmichael Elementary, along with their three children reside in Sierra Vista.

Mr. Hogan, born in Cody, Wyoming, served

in the U.S. Army and did two tours of duty in the Middle East. He was honorably discharged in 2012 while stationed at Fort Huachuca.

The couple had resided in Sierra Vista until Mr. Hogan moved to a separate residence in Whetstone three months ago. For the past three years, he's been the manager and head mechanic at the local Lube&Oil Tek franchise on Fry Boulevard.

Funeral services for Mr. Hogan are pending. Ms. Hogan has created a GoFundMe account to help pay for her husband's final expenses.

At that point Joanna wadded up the paper and heaved it across the room in exasperation. Count on Marliss to do a hit job. Yes, Leon Hogan was dead, but Armando Ruiz was in the hospital fighting for his life. Who was going to set up a GoFundMe account for him? And if someone did, would Marliss Shackleford be willing to give that effort a little free publicity as well?

There was a knock on the door. "Come in," Joanna called.

Detective Deb Howell entered, pausing long enough to pick up the discarded newspaper on the way. "I read this, too," she said. "I'm assuming it belongs in the trash?"

Joanna nodded, and Deb dropped the offending item into a wastebasket situated next to Joanna's desk.

"Thank you," she said.

"Leon Hogan was definitely the focus of the piece," Deb said. "Armando? Not so much."

Joanna was glad to hear she wasn't the only one who'd reacted to the article in that fashion. "What's up?" she asked.

"Jaime just got called to investigate a fatality traffic accident north of Elfrida. Since there are only two of us on duty, we drew straws, and he got the short one. He and Dave Hollicker are working that. In the meantime I've been in touch with Casey."

Joanna held up a cautioning hand. "Is that a good idea?" she asked.

"I'm not here to discuss any details of the Whetstone shooting," Deb assured. "I've been given to understand by any number of people that discussing that case is completely verboten. This is about the kids."

"And?" Joanna prodded.

"Casey has identified two separate sets of finger-prints on the table knife."

"Whose are they?"

"One set belongs to Officer Larry Dunn of Huachuca City PD. The other belongs to Madison Hogan. Sierra Vista had her prints on file because of those previous domestic-violence arrests."

"According to what Kendall Hogan told Garth, the bedroom door got shut and locked between the time the doorbell rang and the moment the shots rang out," Joanna asserted quietly. "That would suggest that Madison might have expected some kind of trouble once the protection order was delivered and she wanted to keep the kids out of it."

Deb nodded. "That's my take on it, too."

"What about the handgun?" Joanna asked. "Any prints on that?"

Deb nodded. "Two sets of prints there, too, only this time they belong to Leon and Madison Hogan, with his prints overlaying hers. But what's really interesting about the Glock is the guy who owns it."

"Who?"

"Casey checked the registration and traced it back to a guy named Randall J. Williams."

"Never heard of him," Joanna said. "Who's he?"

"Mr. Williams is a relative newcomer to the area who bills himself as some kind of cowboy artist. He lives in a trailer out near Miracle Valley."

"What's his connection to all this?"

"Once you brought up the domestic-violence issue yesterday afternoon, I got my rear in gear. I went straight out to Sierra Vista and started chatting up folks who live in the Hogans' neighborhood. Everyone figured I was there because of the shooting, and I didn't exactly disabuse them of that notion. The Hogans' up-the-street neighbor, Lois Watson, was especially helpful, and let's just say I'm glad Madison is Lois's neighbor and not mine."

"Why?"

"According to Lois, once Leon moved out, Madison started partying almost every night, with people drinking and carousing until all hours. They parked their cars up and down the street, blocking driveways right and left, including Lois's. She tried talking to Madison about it, but nothing happened. Lois has a security camera, but she also started keeping track of the plate numbers in a little notebook. She was able to give me a complete, day-by-day list."

"You ran them?"

"I certainly did. A 4Runner that shows up almost every night belongs to none other than our Mr. Williams of Miracle Valley fame."

"That's a very interesting connection," Joanna said.

"I think so, too," Deb agreed. "And it leads me to believe that maybe he's Madison's boyfriend."

"Which tells us that Madison is probably the one

who brought the murder weapon to the crime scene, because it seems unlikely Williams would have willingly handed a weapon over to his girlfriend's estranged husband."

"Yup," Deb replied. "Not unless he had a death wish."

A long pause followed. From her first view of the crime scene, Joanna had assumed that she was looking at a case of suicide by cop. Now something else occurred to her.

"Maybe Madison came to see Leon intending to take him out. Maybe that's why, despite the protection order, she brought the kids and went on that overnight with her ex in the first place, but when it came time to do the job, he wrested the weapon from her. She ran out of the house, trying to get away . . ."

". . . and Armando was collateral damage," Deb concluded.

Joanna nodded. "At first I thought this was suicide by cop. Now maybe it's more like homicide by cop. So it seems to me we need to know more about Randall Williams and a hell of a lot more about Madison Hogan."

"I have one more item of interest about her," Deb volunteered. "After hearing back from Records at Sierra Vista PD, just for the hell of it, I ran both Leon's and Madison's names through *our* Records department."

"And?"

"I came up with one hit—with Animal Control."

Deb's answer left Joanna totally mystified. "Animal Control?" she echoed.

"Three months ago, which is probably only days after Leon moved to Whetstone, Madison turned up at Animal Control prepared to relinquish ownership of a two-year-old bluetick hound named Coon. When someone is giving up an animal like that, the paperwork asks for a reason. Madison claimed that she and her husband were getting a divorce. She said her husband had left the dog with her, and she couldn't afford to care for it. Which reminds me, so far I've been unable to find any trace of ongoing divorce proceedings between Leon and Madison Hogan."

"So she lied about that, too," Joanna concluded. "There's a difference between being separated and being divorced. What happened to the dog?"

"Jeannine placed it with an old codger down near Double Adobe who has a real soft spot in his heart for rescuing hounds of all kinds. He had two blueticks and three redticks. Now it's three and three."

Jeannine Phillips was Joanna's Animal Control officer. Since taking over that position, she'd transformed what had once been a "mostly kill" shelter into a "mostly adopt" one.

"Okay," Joanna said. "I'll give Madison Hogan a few points on that score. She might have had a gun, but at least she didn't shoot the damned dog. Keep digging into Madison Hogan, though, and see what else you can find."

"Trust me," Detective Howell said, rising to her feet. "I'm on it. I'll keep you posted."

As soon as Deb left the office, Joanna picked up her phone and dialed Casey Ledford.

"Deb was just here," Joanna said. "Thanks for running the prints on that knife."

"You're welcome," Casey said.

"Did you mention the knife to Dave Newton?"

"I had to," Casey answered. "With clear signs that a confrontation of some kind had occurred in the living room, it seemed likely that the whole residence would be regarded as a crime scene. I have to say, however, that when I told him about the knife situation, he didn't seem especially interested."

"I'm not surprised," Joanna said. "The man has twenty-twenty tunnel vision. He's only concerned about getting the goods on Armando. Any prints on the shell casings you found?"

"Yes," Casey answered. "I've run them. No hits so far. They don't match Madison Hogan's prints, and they don't match Leon's either."

"Which means that a third party is most likely involved one way or another," Joanna said. "What about gunshot residue? Did you run any GSR tests?"

"For sure on Leon Hogan," Casey replied, "and GSR was definitely present on both his hands and clothing. I contacted the hospital in Tucson, and they collected samples from Deputy Ruiz's hands as well. I also asked them to collect Armando's clothing as evidence so it could be tested later."

"Good," Joanna said. "What about Madison? Did anyone run GSR tests on her?"

"Not so far as I know," Casey answered. "If so, they would have been placed in evidence and I would have been the one doing the analyzing. But I'm not sure why you're looking into Madison."

"I'm not quite sure of that myself," Joanna said. "When I figure it out, I'll let you know. In the meantime thanks for the info. Now I'll let you go. If Newton finds out you've been speaking to me, there'll be hell to pay. I don't want to put you in his crosshairs, too."

Joanna hung up and sat there for a time thinking. From everything she'd been told, Madison Hogan had emerged from the house naked as a jaybird. If she had fired that first gunshot, the one inside the house, there would have been GSR on her hands and body at the time of the shooting, not that that would necessarily have proved anything. Whatever had been there the day before would certainly no longer be present more than twenty-four hours later. Had Dave Newton been half the investigator he thought himself to be, he would have ordered GSRs from everyone on the scene—Madison Hogan included. The problem was, this was Newton's ball game, not Joanna's. When it came to the Whetstone shooting incident itself, Joanna needed to stay out of it.

But Madison was the suspect in multiple domestic-violence incidents. If she'd had access to one deadly weapon, she could probably lay hands on another with the greatest of ease. Did that pose a danger for her children—for Kendall and Peter? In Joanna's mind the answer to that question was an unqualified yes, and she wouldn't be backing off until she was sure those two kids were no longer in jeopardy.

Not ever.

CHAPTER 9

FOR THE first time all semester, Jennifer Ann Brady was pissed at her roommate. She also had a headache and was pretty sure she'd blown her first final, organic chemistry. It was an upper-division course. She might have been a first-semester sophomore on campus, but due to a collection of advanced-placement classes she had enough credits to qualify as a junior.

What she'd learned in biology and chemistry classes at Bisbee High School had been good enough to enable her to pass advanced-placement exams on both those subjects, but passing tests didn't necessarily give you the same kind of foundation as that to be gained by doing actual classwork. At NAU organic chemistry was designed to function as a first sort, separating promising students from unpromising ones and sending the latter into degree programs less demanding than those called for in, say, premed or prevet programs. And that's what Jenny wanted do more than anything else in life—she wanted to become a veterinarian.

So she'd spent the whole semester struggling with the classwork. When finals came around, she'd needed to burn the midnight oil, last night being a case in point. She had long since adjusted to the fact that her room-mate was a night owl who seemed to stay up until all hours every single night. Earplugs and a sleeping mask helped with that most of the time. It was also annoying that Beth was pretty close to brilliant and had spent her whole first semester breezing through classes without so much as cracking a book.

When Jenny had finally called it quits the previous night and was ready to go to bed just before one o'clock in the morning, Beth had been in the bathroom. Jenny hadn't been paying that much attention. She didn't know how long Beth had been there. Wanting to respect her roommate's privacy, she'd waited ten minutes. Finally, desperately needing to get some sleep, she knocked on the door.

"I need to go to bed."

"Just a minute," Beth had said.

The shower hadn't been on before, but it came on then. Five minutes later a wet-haired Beth had finally emerged, tying the belt on her robe.

"Sorry," she added. "I was taking a shower."

Which turned out to be a lie. The vented fan in the bathroom was a joke. When somebody took a hot shower, the place steamed up like crazy. Jenny entered the room to find there wasn't a trace of steam in the air or even on the mirror. If Beth had really been taking a shower, it would have been a cold one, and no one in his or her right mind would take a cold shower in the middle of the night in mid-December.

For some time now, Jenny had wondered about the inordinate amount of time Beth spent in the bathroom. Conover Hall was supposedly a nonsmoking facility, which should have included being a nonvaping building as well. But if that's what Beth was doing, wouldn't there at least have been a hint of smoke or flavor of some kind left behind? As far as Jenny could tell, there was none.

When the two girls met, back at the beginning of the school year, Jenny had taken the younger girl to be astonishingly innocent and naïve, and maybe she was. But in her bed that night, Jenny had wondered about that for the first time. What if Beth Rankin was really a capable liar? What if the stories she'd told about her unreasonable and domineering mother weren't true? What if the difficulties Beth claimed to have with her parents were actually her fault rather than theirs? And what if the person Jenny had just invited to come home with her for Christmas wasn't at all who Jenny thought she was?

She'd lain awake in bed worrying about that. Then she slept through her alarm. She'd come within minutes of being late for her test. She was sure that at least some of the answers she'd given were wrong, but she didn't have the heart to look them up. Thankfully, this was the only final she had today. If she'd had to face another, she might just have given up altogether.

She went back to the dorm. She took an Aleve and lay on her bed, nursing her headache right along with her wounded pride. When the headache finally let up a little, Jenny stacked some pillows behind her, sat up, and reached for her iPad.

She had been nine going on ten when her father died. She didn't remember that much about it, but of course she'd known that he was a deputy sheriff at the time he was murdered. Jenny didn't remember any specific conversations, but she suspected that first her father and later her mother had both understated the life-or-death risks that went along with being in law enforcement.

Yet gradually Jenny had figured it out all the same.

She didn't really remember much about her father's funeral, but when one of her mother's deputies had been gunned down, it was almost as though the whole town had come to a complete stop. And seeing her mother standing next to a black-clad but very pregnant Sunny Sloan at her husband's funeral was an image that was now engraved on Jenny's heart.

And then there was Jeremy Stock, one of her mother's own deputies, who had lost his marbles and very nearly killed his boss. The remembered terror of that night—of not knowing whether her mother would live or die—had made the dangers all too real. Jenny had also come to understand that politics and public relations had a lot to do with what was going on in her mother's life. As a result, even when she was away at school, she tried to keep up with what was going on in her hometown, because more often than not something about her mother's department would be mentioned in the news.

The day before, Jenny had been focused on studying, so it wasn't until Friday afternoon that she found out about what had happened to Deputy Ruiz. She immediately dialed her mother's number.

"I just now saw Marliss Shackleford's article," Jenny said when her mother answered. "Is Deputy Ruiz going to be all right?"

"He seems to be recovering," her mother said after a pause. "That was the word I had earlier this morning, but I haven't been in touch this afternoon. I should probably give Amy a call once we're off the phone. I was going to go up today, but we decided it was Tom Hadlock's turn to represent the department. I need to get home and finish working on the Christmas cards, although I have to say that seems incredibly unimportant right now.

"How are things with you?"

Jenny sighed. "I had my organic chemistry final today, and I may have blown it."

"I doubt that," her mother said. "When it comes to taking tests, you're right up there with the best of them."

Jenny didn't want to go into any detail about how Beth Rankin had upset her test-taking applecart that day. Instead she changed the subject.

"Marliss Shackleford's article said that the incident is being investigated by the Department of Public Safety. How come?"

"Because that's the way officer-involved shootings work," Joanna explained. "The idea is that if we investigated our own people and encountered wrongdoing on their part, we might be tempted to cover it up."

"But it sounded like Deputy Ruiz was firing back at someone who was already shooting at him. How could that be anything other than self-defense?"

Joanna laughed. "Good question," she said. "Maybe you should consider going to law school instead of veterinary school."

"How's Dad doing?"

"He's in Tucson right now with appearances there both tonight and tomorrow. He should be home on Saturday. I can hardly wait. Single motherhood isn't what it's cracked up to be. I know I did it with you for a while, but you were older. With two little kids? Take it from me, two kids need two parents. But enough about us. When's your next final?"

"Tomorrow afternoon at one. It's for a psych class. That one shouldn't be nearly as tough as the one I took this morning. I'll go over my class notes, but I should be fine."

"What about Maggie?" Joanna asked. "Are you going to be bringing her home when you come?"

"No," Jenny said. "Nick is staying here over the holidays. He'll look after her. Even with four-wheel drive, dragging her around in a horse trailer when there's a chance of ice and snow on the road seems like a bad idea."

"Speaking of coming home," Joanna added. "Dad was all hot to trot to get all the Christmas decorating and baking done before you arrive. I told him not to worry. That it would give you and Beth something to do to keep you off the streets."

If I'm even speaking to her by then, Jenny thought.

She and her mother talked for a few minutes longer. An hour later, while Jenny was still poring over her psych-class notes, Beth Rankin showed up bearing gifts in the form of a pepperoni pizza and two iced-down sodas.

In terms of peace offerings, it couldn't have been better. By the time the pizza box was empty, all was forgiven and Jenny and Beth Rankin were friends once more, and Jenny's earlier qualms about taking Beth home were forgotten.

CHAPTER 10

A CALL from Joanna's chief deputy late in the afternoon boosted her spirits.

"Armando's awake and talking," Tom Hadlock reported. "I let Dave Newton know so he could come interview him, but I didn't call the DPS guys with that news until after I heard what Armando had to say to Amy and his mother."

"Mr. DPS is not going to be happy about that."

"Too bad," Tom replied.

"What did Armando have to say?"

"He said that when he went to deliver the protection order, Leon appeared to be under the influence, but he was in his own home at the time. Since it's not against the law to be drunk at home, Armando handed over the paperwork and left. He was on his way back to his vehicle when he heard a gunshot behind him. It sounded like it came from inside the house, so he turned around to look. The next thing he knew, a woman came streaking up to him, and I do mean streaking. She didn't have a stitch of clothing on. At the time Armando had no idea who she was, but we now know that the woman in question was Leon's wife, Madison Hogan. She was screaming something like, 'He's gonna kill me! He's gonna kill me!' She took cover behind Armando's patrol vehicle, and so did he. That's when Leon Hogan

110

came charging out onto the porch, firing like crazy. Armando did the only thing he could do and returned fire. Getting hit was pure bad luck. But the whole thing sounds pretty cut-and-dried to me. It's got suicide by cop written all over it."

Joanna might have changed her mind on that score, but Tom was just ramping up, and she let him continue his rant without interruption.

"If Dave Newton doesn't shape up and call it justifiable homicide," Tom continued, "I'm half tempted to punch his lights out. What the hell was Armando supposed to do? Throw down his weapon and let the guy plug him? We've got a nearly dead deputy and a patrol car full of bullet holes. If Armando hadn't returned fire, he wouldn't be in a hospital right now. He'd be in the morgue."

"Yes, he would," Joanna agreed. "Give Armando my best, and let him know I'm thinking about him."

"Will do," Tom said.

Joanna spent the rest of the day redoing the duty roster, making up for Armando's absence as best she could. If there were callouts when people were off duty, she'd be having to pay overtime, and the budget would take a definite hit. That complex work was interrupted by several calls from reporters. Tom Hadlock was her media-relations guy. With him out of the office, dealing with journalists fell to her. Fortunately for her, Marliss Shackleford wasn't among the callers.

It was close to time for her to go home and time for the Rob Roy restaurant to open when she put in a call to Myron Thomas, reserving the club's banquet room for the evening of December 26 as the site for Ernie's retirement bash.

She was barely off the phone with that when Ernie presented himself in the doorway. "What are you doing here?" Joanna asked. "I distinctly remember your saying you'd be taking two days off."

"I heard about Armando," he said. "I know DPS is in charge of the investigation, but I wanted to come in to see if I could help out. Where is everybody? Both Jaime and Deb are nowhere to be found."

"I believe Jaime is currently conducting a vehicular-homicide investigation between Elfrida and Willcox. As for Deb? I suspect she's out in Sierra Vista following up on a couple of leads concerning the well-being of Leon and Madison Hogan's two children."

Over the next several minutes, Joanna laid out her concerns about Kendall and Peter Hogan.

"Anything I can do tonight to help?" Ernie asked when she finished. "I'm still a member of this team, you know, and if there's work to be done, I'm here to do it."

"Yes," Joanna said, "but not right now. Tomorrow will be fine, but FYI, you should know that I just now reserved the Rob Roy banquet room for your retirement party. It's scheduled for December twenty-sixth."

"All right, then," Ernie said with a somber nod. "I'll start letting people know I'm leaving. Any idea who you might bring on board as your new detective?"

"Not yet," Joanna answered.

"Well," Ernie added, "if I were you, I'd take a close look at Garth Raymond. He's young, but he's got a lot on the ball."

"Thanks," Joanna said. "I'll bear that in mind."

Once Ernie left her office, Joanna did the same, heading home somewhat earlier than usual. She helped with dinner and got the kids down for the night. Then, after changing into her nightgown and robe, she went to work on the remaining Christmas cards, determined to finish those off before bedtime. She was making good progress when, right around ten, both dogs got up and headed for the back door. Assuming they were ready to go out one last time, Joanna followed. She opened the back door and security shutters just as a pair of arriving headlights swung into the yard.

Alarmed, she was about to head for the gun safe when Lady let out a joyous bark and went galloping toward the approaching vehicle. Lucky, deaf since birth, had never quite mastered the art of barking, but he went racing toward the car as well just as Joanna heard the garage door on the far side of the house rolling open.

When Butch had designed their new home, she had looked at the original drawings and shaken her head. "Most people have a two-car garage. This looks like a four-bedroom, two-garage house."

"It is," he had said, "and don't worry. Once Jenny starts to drive, we'll need it."

He'd been right about that. Both Joanna's work vehicle, the Interceptor, and her Buick Enclave occupied her garage, while Butch's latest Subaru stayed in his. With Jenny off at school, the second parking spot in his garage was currently open.

Closing the door, Joanna went back inside. She met up with Butch just as he and the two cavorting dogs entered through the family room. Once he dropped his bags, she gave him a heartfelt hug. "What are you doing here? I thought you were staying in Tucson tonight and tomorrow."

"The Green Valley event started at six and was over before eight. Since it was still early, I canceled my hotel room and came home. I can drive back and forth to Tucson for tomorrow's Oro Valley event. People who live in Tucson and work at Fort Huachuca make that kind of commute every day of the week."

"Have you eaten?"

"No, but after being on the road and eating restaurant food, what I want more than anything is a peanut butter and honey sandwich. The only way to get one of those in a fine dining establishment is to order off the kiddie menu."

"Do you want me to fix it?" Joanna asked.

"No, I will," he told her with a grin. "You never slather on nearly enough peanut butter."

While he headed for the kitchen, Joanna went back to the dining-room table. She didn't have that many cards to go—only fifty or so—and it seemed silly to stop when she was that close to the end. Shortly after she returned to her task, Butch entered the room, bringing along both his sandwich and a glass of milk. He sat down next to her. Once the sandwich was gone, Butch began stuffing signed cards into envelopes and sealing them shut.

As they worked, she brought him up to date on everything she'd learned in the course of the afternoon.

"The murder weapon is registered to one of the wife's pals?" Butch asked when she told him about the Glock.

"Maybe," Joanna hedged. "We think Williams might be Madison's boyfriend, but we don't know that for sure."

"And you think Madison brought it to the crime scene?"

"That's how it seems." Joanna nodded. "She might have fired that first shot—the one Armando heard coming from inside the house as he was on his way to his vehicle."

"You're saying you think it's possible she started the whole thing?"

"Maybe," Joanna said, "but at this point there's no way to prove it, and there probably won't be."

"No GSR?" Butch asked.

Suddenly a light went off in Joanna's head. "I wonder what happened to the robe?"

"What robe?"

"While Madison was sitting in the back of that Huachuca City patrol car, someone—one of the neighbors—brought a robe for her to wear. I wonder what happened to it—if it went to the hospital with Madison or if the EMTs returned it to the neighbor?"

"Why would you need to find the robe?"

"She might not have been wearing it at the time of the shooting, but if she fired that first shot, she would have had GSR on her hands, and there could be cast-off traces of it inside the sleeves." Joanna glanced at her watch. It said 11:23. "Too late to call Ernie," she said.

"Call Ernie?" a puzzled Butch asked. "Why would you need Ernie to go chasing after Madison's GSR? Wouldn't that be up to Detective Soccer Ball?"

"My primary concern right now is the Hogan kids," Joanna said. "We know their mother has had multiple domestic-violence arrests if not convictions. If she was brandishing and firing a weapon at her former husband's home, what does that say about her qualifications for being Mother of the Year? Not only that, as soon as Madison was let loose from the ER, Child Protective Services sent the kids right back home to their mom."

Butch reached across the table, took one of Joanna's

hands in his, and gave his wife a searching look. "I see where you're going with all this, Joey," he said. "For some reason you've decided that Madison Hogan is an unsuitable mother. How come?"

"She locked her kids in the bedroom, for one thing," Joanna said defensively.

"And?"

"She swore out that protection order against her husband and then dragged her kids out to his house to spend the night."

"Maybe she changed her mind," Butch offered. "People going through divorces do all kinds of stupid things—including changing their minds about protection orders."

"So you think I'm wrong?" Joanna asked.

Butch chose his words carefully. "I think there's a possibility that you might be jumping to conclusions," he said.

Joanna thought about that for a moment. "Maybe I am," she said. "I almost hope you're right, because suitable or not, she's the mother they're stuck with."

"But you're not going to back off?"

"Nope," said Joanna, signing the very last card and passing it over to Butch. "First of all, I want to know about the GSR on that robe. Depending on what we find out, I'll go from there."

"To bed, then?" Butch asked.

Joanna nodded. They were headed for their bedroom when Joanna stuck her hand in the pocket of her robe and discovered the dollar bill she'd left there.

"Oh, wait," she said. "I almost forgot. It's Tooth Fairy day. This morning Sage showed up with a new tooth, and this afternoon Denny lost one."

"One tooth in and one out," Butch said. "That seems like an even trade to me."

With that, Joanna hurried off to Denny's bedroom and exchanged a dollar bill for the tooth in the specially designed Tooth Fairy pillow that Grandma Eva Lou had given him. Back in their bedroom, Joanna opened the top drawer of her dresser. Inside, there were two small white boxes, one with Denny's name on it and the other with Jenny's. One day there would be a box with Sage's name on it as well.

Joanna dropped the baby tooth into Denny's box and then returned it to her drawer. She wasn't sure why she carefully saved all those teeth, except for the one of Jenny's that had disappeared when she bit into a bean burrito. Someday she'd give them to the kids. Then it would be up to them to decide if they wanted to keep them or throw them away.

For right now, though, they belonged to Joanna, and she planned on keeping them until she was ready to let them go. As she headed for bed, however, her thoughts returned to Kendall and Peter Hogan. Was anyone hanging on to their lost baby teeth?

Joanna hoped so, but it didn't seem likely.

CHAPTER 11

BETH RANKIN, who had never before had any friends to speak of, now had two. Sure, she'd known a few kids her age, from church mostly. In a brief bow to Beth's physical fitness and assuming that all activities would be conducted under parental scrutiny, her mother had tried enrolling Beth first in swimming lessons and later in gymnastics. Both pursuits had turned out to be dismal failures. Swimming had come to grief because Beth was terrified of water, and the swim instructor was totally unable to effect any changes in that. Gymnastics had ended abruptly when her mother had declared team uniforms to be immodest.

Beth had been thrilled to leave swimming behind, and she hadn't minded quitting gymnastics either. She'd had nothing in common with the other girls. Their lives centered on electronic devices and connections—on things like e-mail and video games and Instagram and chat rooms. As for the kids she met at church, the ones her mother would have preferred she socialize with? Out of spite Beth had refused to pal around with any of them. If they were good enough for her mother, they weren't good enough for her.

Now Beth had two friends in her life—Jenny and Ron—and last night she'd been caught in a crossfire between them. One of the things she loved most about

Ron was that he was interested in her. He wanted to know everything about her. He wanted to know her favorite color? Green. The name of her favorite pet? Blue Boy, a now-deceased parakeet, was the only one she'd ever had. Her favorite TV show? That was easy. She didn't have one. Her favorite author? She had two possibles, J. K. Rowling and Arthur Conan Doyle. Her favorite food? Pizza, now that she'd finally had a chance to actually try it.

Ron talked to her about the classes she was taking, the books she'd read, the movies she'd seen—there weren't many of those. And every time they spoke, he never failed to tell her how special she was and how smart. He had never met anyone like her before, and he could hardly wait until he got done with the special project he was working on so he could fly out to meet her.

He also said he thought she was beautiful. That was something that most definitely had never happened to Beth before. So when he started asking her to send him selfies, she didn't see any harm in it. In fact, the first selfie she sent to him was the first one she ever took. As soon as he got it, he wrote back telling her no wonder green was her favorite color, adding that the only way most people had eyes that green was if they wore contact lenses.

Of course he sent one of himself. It turned out the guy was a hunk and everything those romance writers were always talking about—tall, dark, and handsome. Just thinking about him took Beth's breath away. How could she possibly be so incredibly lucky as to have someone like Ron in her life?

So when he asked her to send a photo of herself in her bra, it had creeped her out in a way but excited her, too.

He didn't see her as a kid. Ron saw her as a woman—a real woman—and someone he wanted to spend his life with. Besides, when he asked and she said no, he didn't hassle her about it. A couple of weeks later, on his birthday, she sent a bra picture to him as a surprise. Of course he'd loved it, and naturally, too, he'd wanted more—a photo of her completely nude.

When it came to discussing the birds and the bees, there was only one piece of advice Madeline Rankin had ever bestowed on her daughter. "Mark my words," she'd said, "if you give a boy one thing, he's going to want more."

Madeline had probably expected her comment to function as a deterrent, but it had the opposite effect. If her mother was against it, Beth was for it. Two nights ago, when it had been time to say good night, Beth had promised Ron that the following night they would do their chat with her completely in the nude.

Their video chats were one-way only. Ron said that security restrictions at his job made it necessary for him to keep his current image blurred on-screen, but that didn't matter to Beth. In fact, that somehow made the whole idea seem even more mysterious and exciting. Once they started, he'd been thrilled beyond measure. He wanted to see all of her, exploring her body one piece at a time, as though he were taking a guided tour. For Beth the experience had been both terrifying and exhilarating—right up until Jenny knocked on the door.

In the course of all their many midnight calls, that had never happened before. Usually Jenny was asleep long before Beth and Ron got on the phone. Thank God Jenny hadn't come barging in. Beth had been standing up at the time. The phone had fallen all the way to the floor. It was a miracle it hadn't broken. She'd turned on the shower and wet her hair, hoping the noise from that would be enough to keep Jenny from hearing her tell Ron about what had happened and saying good-bye.

Jenny had made it clear that she'd been pissed when Beth came out of the bathroom. And things this morning hadn't been any better between them. Beth had worried about it all day long and wondered how she could go about making things right. Thankfully, bringing home pizza had done the trick.

Beth and Jenny were good again, and Beth was relieved beyond words. She wanted to have Ron in her life, but she needed Jenny, too. The last thing she wanted was for Jenny to rescind the invitation for Beth to come to Bisbee over Christmas vacation.

She sure as hell didn't want to go to SaddleBrooke! And by eleven thirty that night, Beth was camped out in the bathroom awaiting Ron's call.

CHAPTER 12

WITH BUTCH at home, Joanna slept better than she had for days. When she woke up on Saturday morning to the aroma of baking waffles, her life was complete. Waffles were Denny's personal favorite—and Joanna's, too, for that matter. Traditionally that's what they had for breakfast the morning after Butch came home from a book tour.

When she walked into the kitchen in her robe to collect her coffee, Denny was downing his second waffle while Sage, in her high chair, worked her way through a serving of bite-size waffle pieces with Lucky waiting nearby in hopes of capturing anything that missed her mouth and landed on the floor.

"Thanks for letting me sleep in," she said.

"After the week you've had, you deserve it," Butch said with a grin. "Your waffle is coming right up."

Joanna took her coffee and took her customary place in the breakfast nook.

"You're off today, aren't you?"

Joanna nodded. "Today and tomorrow both," she replied.

Settled into her third term in office, Joanna was attempting to do a better job of splitting her time between home and work. She and Tom Hadlock now routinely spelled each other on weekends. They were both on

122

call, of course, especially if something serious went down, but every other weekend they took turns being first up, and this was Joanna's scheduled weekend off.

"So here's an idea," Butch said, handing her a plate loaded with a steaming waffle. "As I understand it, today Denny has an overnight playdate at Jeff and Marianne's, with us due to pick him up after church tomorrow, right?"

Joanna nodded.

"How about this?" Butch continued. "The book signing at Sun City Oro Valley starts at one P.M. Why don't you and Sage come along? After the signing we can do some Christmas shopping. If Sage happens to see what we're buying, I'm pretty sure she won't tell. And when we're done shopping, we can stop off for a nice dinner on the way home. Come to think of it, if you want to, we could maybe even swing by the hospital to check on Deputy Ruiz while we're at it."

Joanna reached for the butter. "Sounds like you had this all plotted out well before I ever set foot in the kitchen."

"You know me," he returned with a grin. "When it comes to writing books or living life, I'm all about outlining."

"And I'm all about spur-of-the-moment," Joanna countered. "But what if Sage raises a fuss during your talk?"

"So what?" Butch returned. "Loyal fans will love it. After all, how many times does an author's baby show up at a signing? As for the people who still can't wrap their heads around the idea that Gayle Dixon is actually a guy? Having Sage there will make them that much more confused."

"I'm not sure," Joanna said, feigning a frown.

"How come?"

"The three of us going on a family outing on a week-end? Doesn't it sound a little too normal?"

"We feel pretty normal to me," he said.

"All right, then," she said. "Count me in."

After breakfast, while Joanna was in the bedroom getting dressed, she took her phone off the charger and called Ernie. "You asked if there was something you could do to help out," she said when he answered, "and there is."

"What?"

"I need you to track down the robe that Madison Hogan was wearing in that Huachuca City squad car. It's possible it went to the hospital with her, the EMTs might still have it, or it might have gone back to the woman who lent it to her originally—Alice Kidder, one of Leon Hogan's neighbors over in Whetstone."

"If I happen to find this robe," Ernie asked, "what do you want me to do with it?"

"If somebody's already run it through the laundry, you don't need to do anything. If they haven't, take it into evidence and bring it back to Casey. Tell her I want her to look for cast-off GSR on the insides of both sleeves."

"Will do," Ernie replied. "And I'll let you know how it's going."

"Good," Joanna said. When she emerged from the bedroom, she didn't exactly mention her conversation with Ernie to Butch. Maybe Butch was right and Joanna *was* jumping to conclusions, but that didn't mean she was ready to call it quits. It also didn't mean she was prepared to discuss it.

As Joanna loaded up a pair of traveling thermal coffee cups, Butch loaded the kids and their gear into the car. With him going on tour, they had transferred Sage's car seat from his Subaru to Joanna's more spacious Enclave, and that's what they drove that day. They left the house at ten, dropped Denny off at Jeff and Marianne's, and were having lunch at a Burger King in Tucson on the far north end of Oracle Road by a quarter to twelve.

At the signing Sage behaved perfectly. She snoozed through her father's literary presentation without making so much as a peep. When Butch introduced his wife and daughter to the audience, the crowd responded with enthusiastic applause. Later, during the signing itself, Joanna discovered that Butch had been on the money about the way his many retiree fans would feel about Sage's presence—they absolutely loved it! When it came time for selfies, there were lots of people who wanted Sage and Butch in the photo with them, but there were more than a few who had zero interest in having Butch's face included. Their selfies featured Sage as the star attraction. Fortunately, she responded way better to the attention from all those cell-phone-wielding, silver-haired grandma types than she had to being photographed with Santa a few weeks earlier.

Their next stop was at the hospital. They had already discussed that Butch and Sage would hang out in the lobby while Joanna went up to Armando's room. What they didn't expect was to run into the two DPS detectives who were on their way out the front entrance as they were entering.

"What are you doing here?" Newton asked, while looking disapprovingly at each of them in turn.

"I'm here to visit my deputy," Joanna replied. "This

is my husband, Butch Dixon, and my daughter, Sage. Butch, these are Detectives Dave Newton and Liam Jackson of the Department of Public Safety."

Butch obligingly offered his hand. While both detectives accepted the greeting, Newton's gaze returned almost immediately to Sage.

"I would have thought your baby would be much older by now," he said with a frown.

"The baby you're thinking of *is* older," Joanna replied. "His name is Dennis, and he's seven. Sage is baby number two."

Detective Newton appeared to be nonplussed at that, as though he couldn't quite deal with the idea that Sheriff Joanna Brady had not one but two young children. Overcoming his momentary confusion, the DPS officer quickly reverted to form.

"Well," he growled, "what I said yesterday still goes. We've interviewed Deputy Ruiz, but if you speak to him today, you are to make no references to the shooting investigation. Is that clear, Sheriff Brady?"

"Oh, it's clear all right, Detective Newton," she told him. "I wouldn't think of it."

"Soccer Ball Guy must not have kids of his own," Butch muttered once the others were out of earshot. "He doesn't seem to be up to speed when it comes to child development."

"You're probably right about that," Joanna said. "And any kids he didn't have should count themselves lucky."

At the desk in the lobby, Butch and Joanna learned that Armando had been moved from the ICU to a regular room. While Butch and Sage hung out in the hospital lobby, Joanna went upstairs to a room that was awash in flowers and overflowing with people. Amy and her three boys were front and center, as were her parents, Glenn and Suzanne Harper, while a soft-spoken Hispanic woman hovered in the background. When it was time for introductions, the latter turned out to be Consuelo Ruiz, Armando's mother, who seemed beyond pleased to learn that the sheriff herself had come to visit.

It was easy to see that the crush of visitors was more than Armando could handle. As the Harpers gathered up the three boys to head back to Sierra Vista, Joanna turned to Amy. Her coloring was bad. There were dark circles under her eyes, and she looked as though she was weary beyond bearing.

"How are you doing?" Joanna asked kindly.

"All right, I guess," Amy answered faintly, although she sounded anything but all right.

"How's he doing?" Joanna asked.

"Better," Amy said, "and far better than his doctors expected. There's no sign of an infection, but he's tired right now, especially after those other investigators were here. Talking to them really wore him out."

"Yes," Joanna said. "I ran into the DPS guys on my way in."

Amy frowned. "The older one isn't very nice, is he?"

"Not very," Joanna agreed, "but he has a job to do."

"He acted as though he thinks Armando somehow provoked Leon Hogan into shooting at him—as though all of this is Armando's fault."

"Don't worry, Amy," Joanna said reassuringly. "From what I've been told, the physical evidence isn't going to support that kind of assumption. Armando might have shot Leon Hogan, but he didn't do anything wrong. It was clearly in self-defense. That makes it justifiable homicide."

"You're sure?" Amy asked nervously. Clearly Dave Newton's presence and attitude had troubled her.

"I'm sure," Joanna replied.

Just then a nurse came in to check Armando's vitals.

"It's very kind of you to come all this way to visit," Amy said. "You and Chief Deputy Hadlock, too."

"Armando is my deputy," Joanna said simply, as if that were explanation enough. "When we leave here, we'll be squeezing in some shopping. It turns out Christmas is coming at warp speed."

"I know," Amy said faintly. "I'm not ready for that either, and I don't think I'm going to be."

Once the nurse left, Joanna spent a few minutes visiting with Armando. She could see he was done, so she didn't stay long. Out in the hallway, however, she paused long enough to send Tom Hadlock a text:

At the hospital. Armando seems to be doing better. Amy? Not so much. She's in way over her head. The department has to make sure Christmas comes to their house. If we don't do something, Santa's going to miss them this year. Talk to me about this on Monday.

Down in the lobby, she found Butch seated on a sofa with his face in his phone while Sage lay sacked out on a blanket next to him.

"That was quick," he said, looking up at her.

Joanna nodded. "It was a full house up there. The last thing they needed was another visitor."

"How's he doing?"

"Better than expected," Joanna replied, "but Amy's running on empty. She's worried sick about Armando, of course, but she's also got three little kids and has no clue about how she'll manage to make Christmas happen for them. I just sent Tom a text. Armando is one of ours. We have to make sure we handle his family's Christmas."

"Sounds doable," Butch said. "As of now, I'm apparently unemployed for the time being. No wait, maybe not. My agent says I have another book to write, but I already told her I'm not starting on it until after Christmas."

They gathered Sage, carried her back to the car, and loaded her inside without waking her.

"Why can't grown-ups sleep like that?" Joanna wondered as she fastened her own seat belt.

"Grown-ups know too much," Butch told her. "Babies don't. So where are we going to shop?"

They hit Tucson Mall, Costco, Target, and the Apple Store in short order. Butch needed a new computer in the worst way. Even though it wouldn't be wrapped up and under a tree, it was exactly what he wanted. They worked their way through the list—Lego sets for Denny, Jeffy, and Ruth, an Amazon gift card for Jeff and Marianne, an immense teddy bear for Sage, a new purse for Carol, and clothes for her boys (Carol had provided the required sizes!). Jenny had put in a request for a particular pair of Tony Lama boots.

"What do we do about Beth Rankin?" Butch asked as they walked past shelves stocked with purses in Dillard's.

"No idea," Joanna said. "Once we meet her, maybe we'll be able to figure that out."

Three hours later Butch was loading the last of their many purchases into the Enclave's cargo area. "It was a close fit," he said, climbing into the driver's seat once he finished. "If we'd bought anything else, you'd have to hold it on your lap." He fastened his seat belt, started the engine, and put the car in gear. "By the way, you may have noticed you weren't on the list," he added with a sly glance in Joanna's direction.

"As a matter of fact, I did notice that," she admitted. "It made me feel a little left out."

"Don't worry. It turns out your shopping is already done," Butch told her. "Signed, sealed, delivered, and wrapped, even."

"Care to give me a hint?" she asked.

"No way," he said. "Not gonna happen. Now, guess where we're going for dinner?"

"I have no idea."

Butch glanced at his watch. "We've got a dinner reservation at Rob Roy," he said. "It's a little out of our way, but Myron's holding a table for us. He says he's got my name on his best rib eye."

"When did you talk to Myron?" Joanna asked.

"While you were upstairs at the hospital. By the way, he and I are double-teaming you. We'll have a great dinner, yes, but you'll also be able to get a head start on organizing the menu for Ernie's party."

Joanna nodded. "That's probably a good idea," she said. "If it was left up to me, I probably wouldn't get around to party planning until the last minute."

"No," Butch told her, "you wouldn't get around to it until *after* the last minute."

Joanna said nothing more. She knew he was right, and there was no point in belaboring the issue.

During most of the drive from Tucson to Palominas, Sage was wide awake and raising hell in her car seat.

It was nerve-racking, but by the time they got to the restaurant, she had worn herself out enough that she fell asleep again and stayed that way. Butch and Joanna ate their dinner in peace. Afterward Myron stopped by their table and laid out the menu options for Ernie's party. It wouldn't be a sit-down kind of affair. They would be serving what Myron referred to as "heavy hors d'oeuvres—less expensive than a full deal meal," he said, "but I promise, no one will go away hungry."

After dinner they drove back home, unloaded the car, put Sage to bed, and then went to bed themselves. Joanna drifted off with the idea in her head that she would sleep late in the morning and spend the rest of the day doing absolutely nothing. That all changed the next morning when she set foot in the living room and found it full of assorted boxes. A prelit but as-yet-undecorated Christmas tree had been moved into its traditional place of honor in front of the living-room window. Butch was on his knees, busily installing the tree skirt.

"It's about time you dragged yourself out of bed," he said over his shoulder. "You're late for the party."

"It doesn't look like a party to me," Joanna grumbled. "This looks like work."

"But not *work* work," Butch corrected. "I'm willing to leave the cookie baking and candy making until after the girls get here, but I want the house dressed for Christmas sooner than that, and today's the day."

"Aye-aye, sir," Joanna said wearily. "What do you want me to do?"

"Tree to start with," he said. "Ribbons first and then balls."

"And what are we going to do with Sage?"

"Don't worry about her. Carol said if she had to

choose between taking care of Sage or decorating a tree, she'd rather take Sage—and she did. That gave me a chance to start bringing in boxes."

"Why didn't *I* get to choose?" Joanna asked.

"Because you got drafted," he told her. "Now, get to work."

And she did. Other than going to church and bringing Denny home, they worked on decorating all day long. Late in the afternoon, a text came in from Ernie Carpenter:

> Finally caught up with Alice Kidder. Casey's not in today, but the robe is secured in an evidence locker in the lab. Going to dinner with Jaime and Delcia. I'll tell them tonight.

Joanna read the text with some satisfaction, but it was satisfaction tinged with sadness. She had succeeded in getting Ernie off the dime in terms of letting people know he was leaving the department. Unfortunately for Joanna, that made his imminent departure all the more real, and she for one knew she was going to miss him terribly.

CHAPTER 13

BETH HAD thought Saturday was bad, but as she awakened late on Sunday morning, things were infinitely worse. Yes, the Thursday-night/Friday-morning phone call with Ron had ended badly when Jenny so rudely interrupted things. Beth had worried about that all day long, but it was worry mixed with anticipation. It had been her hope and expectation that no real damage had been done and that the next night she and Ron would be able to pick up where they'd left off. She hoped that now that Ron had had a chance to see her . . . well, video tour . . . maybe he would return the favor by showing her his.

Beth had fixed things with Jenny by bringing home pizza, but remedying the situation with Ron wasn't nearly as simple as bringing home pizza. For one thing, on Friday night he didn't call—not at all! She'd been in the bathroom at the appointed hour as usual, but nothing happened. No call came in. And it wasn't as though she could call him. His number was always blocked.

She sat there waiting for so long that she finally lay down on the floor and fell asleep. When she woke up, stiff, sore, and freezing cold at five o'clock in the morning, there were no missed calls on her phone, and that made for a Saturday of absolute agony. What if Ron had

133

broken up with her? What if he never called her again? What if she'd lost him for good? What if it was over?

She did her best to conceal how upset she was, but Jenny had noticed anyway.

"Is something wrong?" she'd asked.

"I'm just worried about the test I took yesterday," Beth had replied quickly. That wasn't true, of course. She'd done fine on the test—aced it, most likely—but the excuse had sounded real enough. Besides, it was the only thing she could think of.

The rodeo team was due to have their annual Christmas party that night. Sororities and fraternities on campus were busy holding winter formals. The rodeo team's version was a combination barn dance/steak fry with an ax-throwing contest tossed in for good measure. Each team member was welcome to invite a guest, and Jenny had asked if Beth wanted to go. Naturally, Beth had begged off.

"Sorry," she said. "It just doesn't sound like my thing."

"Too bad," Jenny replied. "It might have cheered you up."

So Beth had spent most of the evening alone and literally pacing the floor in their very small room. It wasn't fair that she couldn't call Ron, not even to apologize despite the fact that she'd done nothing wrong. It wasn't fair that he held all the power in the relationship and she had none. It wasn't fair that he could drop her just like that—for no reason, really—and leave her twisting in the wind. Didn't he know how much she loved him? Didn't he know how much she cared? Didn't he understand how much she needed him in her life?

Jenny came in around eleven thirty. She changed into

her jammies, stuck earplugs in her ears, put on her eye mask, and got into bed while a heartsick Beth went into the bathroom and resumed what she now regarded as a futile vigil.

To Beth's immense relief, her phone rang at ten past twelve. Her heart rejoiced until she heard Ron's voice.

"You cut me off!" he snarled accusingly.

She recoiled from the menacing tone. He had never spoken to her that way, and it shocked her into momentary silence. "I didn't mean to," she stammered finally. "My roommate was right outside the door. She needed to use the bathroom so she could go to sleep. She had an exam in the morning and—"

"Jennifer Brady is a bitch," Ron growled. "You shouldn't let her boss you around that way. You shouldn't let her boss *us* around."

Beth was surprised. She didn't remember even mentioning Jenny's last name to Ron. She must have done so somewhere in the course of their many conversations, but since Beth was in full apology mode, she didn't give the matter much thought.

"I'm so sorry," she said, "really I am. I didn't mean to hurt your feelings."

"Well, you did," he said. "That's one of the reasons I call you in the middle of the night—so we won't be disturbing anyone else and so we won't be interrupted. To have someone horning in like that . . ."

"Please," Beth pleaded, "can't we just let this go? Can't we just forget about it?"

But Ron wasn't about to let anything go. "You need a new roommate," he said. "Either she should move out or you should. It's the end of the semester. That shouldn't be too hard to arrange."

The problem was, Beth didn't want to lose Jenny as a roommate. She was the only person on the whole NAU campus who'd been nice to Beth from the start—the only one.

"I'll try," she murmured quietly.

"You'd better do more than try," he responded.

Ron didn't come right out and add *or else* to that sentence. He didn't have to. It was understood.

"And if I were you, I'd think twice about spending Christmas down in Bisbee with your roommate and her family. If you really want me in your life, you'll get Jennifer Brady out of it."

Beth tried desperately to think of something to say in response, but Ron didn't give her a chance.

"I have to go now," he said abruptly. "Something's come up."

And just like that, the phone went dead and he was gone. There was no way to call him back—no way to change things around so their conversation ended in a less contentious fashion. Ron had made it abundantly clear: Beth had to choose. She could have Ron in her life or she could have Jenny—one or the other, but not both.

For a time Beth stared at the screen of her phone, willing it to ring again, but of course it didn't. She managed to keep her tears at bay for a time, but when the realization that he wouldn't call back finally hit home, Beth Rankin dissolved into racking sobs, slipping helplessly to the floor and using a bath towel to muffle the sound of her weeping.

Her new life—the one that had opened up for her when she first set foot on the NAU campus last fall—lay in ruins. It had lasted all of three short, glorious months, but now it was over. Finished. With Ron out of her life, most likely for good, Beth Rankin had nothing left to live for, nothing at all.

She cried herself to sleep, and for the second night in a row she slept on the bathroom floor.

"What are you doing in here?" Jenny demanded the next morning when she pushed the bathroom door open and found Beth lying next to the tub. "Did you fall? Are you all right?"

Beth struggled to emerge from the fog. "I wasn't feeling well," she said, getting to her feet. "I started feeling nauseated during the night. I came in here and sat down on the floor next to the toilet because I was afraid I was going to throw up. I must have fallen asleep."

"Sorry to wake you, then," Jenny said, "but I've got to get ready to go. Maggie and I have a coaching session scheduled for this morning."

Moving like she was half drunk, Beth staggered out of the bathroom and stumbled over to her bed. She fell into it and pulled the covers up over her head, pretending to be asleep. She wasn't asleep. She was just waiting for Jenny to leave. As soon as Beth was alone, she once again dissolved into a storm of tears. She cried until she couldn't cry anymore, and then, finally, she fell into a dreamless sleep.

CHAPTER 14

WITH BUTCH at home and fully in charge, Joanna's Monday morning was a breeze. When she came out to the kitchen to collect her first cup of coffee, Denny was dressed for school and both kids were almost done with breakfast.

"I can't tell you how glad I am the book tour is over," she told Butch after giving him a good-morning smooch.

"That makes two of us," he said, "although I have to say that waking up to the occasional room-service breakfast isn't really a terrible hardship."

Joanna went back to the bedroom, where she showered and dressed. When she emerged for a second time, Denny had been dropped off at the bus stop and her own breakfast was on the table. All of that added up to her being at her office ten minutes early. She was there in plenty of time for roll call. After that, she and Tom Hadlock had a powwow in her office.

"I got your text about taking care of Christmas for Armando's family," he said. "I'll handle it. Karen Griffith out in the front office is friends with Amy's mother, Suzanne. Karen says she'll get in touch with Suzanne and find out what the Ruiz boys are hoping Santa will bring them so we can make a list. And you can be sure Amy isn't forgotten, either."

"Thanks, Tom," Joanna said. "Now, what's going on? Any word on the DPS investigation?"

The chief deputy shook his head. "Not a whisper," he said, "and I take that as good news. If Dave Newton had something to brag about, you can bet your bippy he'd be doing just that—shouting it to the high heavens. The evidence all seems to line up with what Armando's told us. The CSIs found a total of nine shell casings at the scene that were fired from the Glock—one inside the mobile home and eight outside it. There was an additional casing located next to Armando's patrol car. That one was apparently fired by his service weapon, and it says a lot about hitting the practice range. Leon fired nine times and nailed Armando once. Armando was a one-and-done."

Joanna was grateful there were no civilians within earshot of Tom's politically incorrect but valid evaluation of the shooting scores.

"Tell me again about the shot fired inside the mobile home."

"Dave Hollicker dug the bullet out of a ceiling tile. It looks to him like that shot was aimed straight up into the air rather than at any kind of angle."

"Suggesting that the shot could have occurred in the course of some kind of struggle?"

Tom nodded. "Possibly."

"What else went on?" she asked.

"Not a whole lot," Tom responded. "Jaime finished up his preliminary investigation on that wreck over by Willcox. We were going on the assumption that it was a DUI-related fatality. The driver had imbibed in a cocktail or two, but according to Doc Baldwin he had a heart attack. That's what caused the wreck in the first place. It's also what killed him.

"Other than that we handed out a few DUIs here and there, including a guy who hit a steer in that patch of open range on Highway 181 just north of Five Mile Creek. Killed the steer and totaled the car, but the driver's lucky. Between his seat belt and air bags, he walked away with only minor injuries. Nonetheless, he's currently cooling his heels in our jail for the time being—driving drunk with no insurance and driving on a suspended license.

"The only other thing of note, also alcohol-related, was a little donnybrook out on Robbs Road just north of the LeRoy Airport. Several members of a visiting motorcycle gang were partying at one of the mobile homes parked out there. Two of the guys at the party, who happen to be a pair of brothers, got into a knock-down, drag-out fight. They were busy tearing up the place when the lady of the house—using the term loosely—clocked one of them over the head with a frying pan."

"A frying pan?" Joanna asked. "A real frying pan?"

"Yup," Tom replied, "one of those no-kidding, heavy-as-hell, cast-iron skillets. The guy was still out cold when Deputy Raymond showed up. EMTs hauled him off to the hospital in Willcox with a possible concussion. His sparring partner was arrested at the scene, charged with disturbing the peace and resisting, and is currently being held in our lockup. Once the guy in the hospital is released, he'll end up in jail as well."

"What about the lady wielding the frying pan?"

"Deputies Creighton and Raymond were at the scene. They were considering arresting her on a domestic-violence charge, since concussion guy happens to be her husband. The other partygoers raised hell about that—said the two drunks probably would have killed each other had she not intervened—so they let it go."

"Probably a good decision on their part," Joanna offered.

"Outnumbered by a motorcycle gang?" Tom said. "You'd better believe it was a good decision. I'da done the same thing in a heartbeat."

Once Tom left her office, Joanna turned to her Monday-morning paperwork. She did so with a happy heart, because she was reasonably sure that Tom's assessment of the Dave Newton situation was correct. If he and Jackson had come up with any discrepancies in Armando Ruiz's story, Newton would be broadcasting them far and wide.

She spent the better part of two hours refining and polishing her budget request before loading it into e-mails and sending it off to members of the board of supervisors and copying Tom Hadlock in the process.

It was getting on toward lunch when Casey Ledford came into her office. "Did you hear?" she asked.

"Hear what?" Joanna asked.

"Ernie's pulling the plug," Casey replied. "He just drove into the parking lot in an enormous RV. It has signs on both sides that say 'Gone Fishing.'"

"Sounds like he's made up his mind, then," Joanna observed, but the RV ploy told her how the game would be played. Ernie would retire, making no mention that his cancer was back. That was his call and fair enough, but at least he'd done what Joanna had asked. He was notifying people in the department that he was out of there. There was no need for him to say how come.

"Did you know?" Casey asked.

"I might've had a clue," Joanna admitted.

"He's a good guy," Casey said, "and I'm sorry to see him go, but that's not why I'm here."

"Is this about the GSR?"

Casey nodded. "I found traces on the robe inside the sleeves down by the wrists, most prominently on the right-hand side and to a lesser degree on the left. I also found traces higher up in the sleeves, again with measurably more residue present on the right-hand side than on the left. We know from the crime scene that Leon was left-handed. What about Madison?"

"No idea."

"At any rate, there isn't enough residue inside either sleeve to reach the threshold of proving that she actually fired a weapon, although she was most likely in close contact with one when it went off."

"Can you draw any conclusions?"

"Based on the location of the bullet hole we found inside the house, I'd say this suggests there was an altercation of some kind during which both Leon and Madison Hogan were both trying to gain possession of the weapon."

"What I think," Joanna said, "is that she brought the weapon to Leon's house with every intention of using it on him and then trying to stage the scene so it looked like suicide. Instead Leon ended up turning the tables on her long enough to chase her out of the house."

"Makes sense," Casey said, "but what about those two poor kids? What's going to happen to them?"

Joanna shook her head. "I'd say that with their father dead and their mother most likely a gun-wielding maniac, they're pretty much up shit creek."

"At least she locked them in the bedroom before everything went down."

"For whatever that's worth," Joanna grumbled.

Casey stood up. "All right, then," she said. "If there's anything more you need, let me know."

"Thanks," Joanna replied. "I will."

As soon as Casey left her office, Joanna picked up her phone and dialed Deb Howell's number.

"Where are you?" Joanna asked.

"I'm on my way to have a chat with Arlene Ambrose, the CPS social worker who took charge of Kendall and Peter after the shooting. I don't know what if anything she'll tell me. At the very least, I'm going to try to get her to think about launching an investigation into the kids' welfare on her end."

"Here's something that might help light a fire under her," Joanna said. "Casey found traces of GSR on the borrowed robe Madison Hogan wore yesterday. A possible conclusion is that Madison was in possession of the Glock at the time she drove the kids to Leon's house in Whetstone."

"A woman with a history of domestic-violence arrests and a Glock in hand doesn't make for motherhood and apple pie," Deb said. "I'm not sure that'll be enough to get Mrs. Ambrose off the dime, but I'll do my best. On another topic, though, I just found out about Ernie. Did you know he's leaving?"

Obviously, word about Ernie's looming departure was spreading fast.

"I'm pretty sure he mentioned it," Joanna said. What she failed to say was exactly when the issue of Ernie's retirement had been broached for the first time.

"He told Jaime and Delcia last night and let me know this morning," Deb continued. "He's always been here, and I'm going to miss him terribly. If it hadn't been for Ernie, I wouldn't be a detective right now."

"Don't be so sure about that," Joanna counseled. "You're right about his helping you along. Ernie saw your potential early on and was instrumental in getting you to focus it, but I'm pretty sure that even if it took a little longer, you would have made the grade on your own. Now, though, it'll be up to you and Jaime to return the favor. Whoever I promote is probably going to need a leg up."

"Like Garth Raymond, maybe?" Deb asked.

Deb's question gave Joanna a subtle hint as to which candidate her current crop of detectives favored. "Too soon to say," she replied.

"Will there be a retirement party?"

"You'd better believe it," Joanna said. "It'll be at the Rob Roy the evening of the twenty-sixth, and I expect you and Jaime to roast Ernie within an inch of his life."

"Roger that," Deb said. "I'll be there with bells on."

As Joanna ended the call with Deb, the landline phone on her desk rang.

"Good morning," Dr. Kendra Baldwin said when Joanna picked up. "I'm sure Dave Newton would go apoplectic at my calling you, but I just sent my finalized copy of Leon Hogan's autopsy report to him and thought I owed you a courtesy call as well."

"Let me guess," Joanna said. "Our shooting victim died of a single gunshot wound to the chest."

"Well, yes," Kendra agreed, "there's that. But there are a few additional details as well. For one thing, there were very recent scratches all over his face. Like he'd been in a serious hand-to-hand altercation shortly before he was shot and his opponent was trying to fend him off."

Joanna thought back to what Casey had told her a

few minutes earlier about the bullet hole in the living-room ceiling and the suggestion that the shot had been fired in the course of a struggle to gain control of the weapon.

"Could the scratches have come from someone attacking him?" Joanna suggested.

"Possibly," Dr. Baldwin allowed.

"Was he drunk?" Joanna asked.

"Drunk?" Kendra sounded a bit puzzled. "I found no blood-alcohol content at all."

"Armando told his wife that when Leon Hogan came to the door that morning he appeared to be under the influence."

"He may have been," Kendra conceded. "If so, it wasn't due to booze. If there was something else in his system, it'll show up in the tox screen. No telling how long that will take. By the way, I mentioned all of this to Dave Newton. He had glommed onto what Armando said about Leon Hogan being under the influence. He was not at all happy when I told him no alcohol was involved."

Joanna was busy putting puzzle pieces together, and she hit on the other thing Casey had mentioned—that there'd been signs of struggle in Leon Hogan's living room, with dregs of coffee spilled on the protective order itself. Was it possible that Madison Hogan had slipped something into Leon's coffee in an effort to incapacitate him? And if so, was there a chance that evidence of her doing so might linger on some of that coffee-stained paperwork?

Kendra was still speaking. ". . . to the Taylor/Finch Funeral Home in Sierra Vista. They'll be the ones handling the services."

"Anything else of interest?" Joanna asked.

"I spoke to Armando's surgeon early on, requesting a forensic examination of the slug removed during the surgery. A microscopic examination shows the presence of powdered glass on the bullet."

"Because it hit him after going through the safety glass in his car window?" Joanna asked.

"Yes," the M.E. replied. "But that safety glass might also have helped save his life. Leon fired from up on a porch. The angle was such that the bullet in question came through the car window on a slightly downward trajectory, striking the window frame along the way. That combination—the window frame and the window itself—might have slowed the velocity of the bullet enough that Armando's internal damage is less severe than it would have been otherwise."

"What you're saying," Joanna murmured, "is thank God for safety glass."

As soon as the call with the M.E. ended, Joanna dialed the lab and passed along everything Doc Baldwin had told her.

"All right," Casey said. "Once Dave Hollicker gets back from Elfrida, I'll have him take a close look at that window frame. Anything else?"

"One thing more," Joanna said. "Would it be possible to examine the coffee stains left on that protection order? There's a chance Madison Hogan might have slipped Leon something, and using his morning coffee to deliver it would be a good bet."

"A mass spectrometer could tell us that in a blink," Casey said.

"But since we don't have one of those," Joanna muttered, "that's probably a no go."

"Not exactly," Casey said, "because you know who does have one? The Department of Public Safety. And you just happen to be talking to someone—that would be me, the CSI assigned to the case—who can request they use it."

"How does it work, and how soon can it happen?"

"They'll need a sample of the document itself, but I can put a rush on it and ask for the test to be done as soon as I can get the evidence to their lab in Phoenix."

"Get it ready, then," Joanna ordered. "As soon as it is, I'll have Tom Hadlock assign a deputy to make the delivery. Tox screens take forever. We want this done sooner rather than later."

CHAPTER 15

THAT MORNING when Joanna left home, Butch had sent along a tuna sandwich for her lunch. She ate it while seated at her desk doing the boring but necessary administrative work her position as sheriff demanded. Movies and television shows made it sound as though people in her line of work bounced from one piece of high drama to the next, without anything in between.

Unfortunately, what went on in all that "in between" space was both complicated and excruciatingly dull. How many vehicles did her department have? How many of them needed new tires at any given moment? How many computers out in the front office would need to be replaced? Was someone keeping up with the department's cybersecurity needs? How many prisoners passed through the jail? How much was the county paying to feed them on any given day? And if you happened to have a jail guard who was doing things he shouldn't with a female prisoner? Firing his ass was also Joanna's responsibility—and she had done so, by the way—immediately.

Late in the afternoon, Kristin tapped on the door. "Someone to see you, Sheriff Brady."

The seriousness in Kristin's tone caught Joanna's attention. "Who?" she asked, looking up from her paperwork.

"A Mr. Lyndell Hogan," Kristin replied.

"Leon's father?"

Kristin nodded.

"By all means send him in," Joanna said.

Joanna stepped out from behind her desk to welcome her visitor. The man who entered the room was an older gentleman, probably somewhere in his sixties. He was dressed in cowboy attire—jeans, boots, and a western shirt—and carried a worn Stetson in both hands. His long, silvery hair was pulled back into a ponytail, and an equally silver handlebar mustache graced his upper lip.

"Howdy, Sheriff Brady," he said, extending a hand as Joanna came forward to meet him. "Hope you don't mind my dropping in on you like this," he said in a soft drawl that reminded Joanna of her late father, D. H. Lathrop. "I was told if I needed any information, I should contact a guy named Dave Newton, but he doesn't seem interested in getting back to me. Since you're the local sheriff, I thought I'd come straight to the horse's mouth."

"I'm so sorry for your loss, Mr. Hogan," Joanna said.

"Thank you, ma'am. Appreciate it. My names Lyndell, but please call me Lyn."

Joanna glanced behind him. "Is your wife here, too?"

"No, ma'am, Izzy's a bit tuckered out. It's a long drive from Cody to here. I parked her at the hotel so she could take a nap."

"You drove here from Wyoming?"

"Yes, ma'am," he said, having a seat and placing the hat in his lap. "Took some time to find people to look after our livestock, so we didn't leave until Friday morning. We had twenty-four hours and forty-six minutes of pure driving time, divided up over four days. Driving straight through wasn't an option. We ran into some real bad weather in Colorado—a blizzard that pretty much stopped us in our tracks for the better part of a day and a half."

Joanna sat down to face him, and Lyndell continued. "Most people might've flown at a time like this, but Izzy's folks died in a plane crash when she was just a little girl. She hasn't set foot in a plane all her life, and she's not about to start now."

"How can I help?" Joanna asked.

"Well, ma'am, " Lyn said, "seeing as how my son has turned up dead, I'd like to know the reason why."

"You do realize this isn't my department's investigation," Joanna began. "Since one of my officers was involved—"

"Yes, yes, yes, I know," Lyndell Hogan said impatiently, waving aside her objection. "Officer-involved shooting and all that. And if I could get that Dave Newton fella to call me back, I'd be talking to him. But he hasn't, so I'm talking to you, and I'm asking you straight out. Just how much did Madison Gale have to do with it?"

Joanna blinked at that. "Madison Gale?" she repeated.

"Leastways that's the name she was going by at the time Leon married her. So answer my question."

Joanna knew her reply needed to be circumspect. "We know that Madison was at the scene when all this happened," she said, "but so far we have no hard evidence to suggest that she was directly involved."

"I'd bet money she was," Lyn said. "Was she screwing around with that officer who shot Leon by any chance?"

"Absolutely not!" Joanna declared. "Deputy Ruiz

went to your son's residence to deliver a protection order. Armando Ruiz is a good guy, a married man with a wife and three kids. To my knowledge, prior to this week he'd had no previous interactions either with your son or with Madison."

"Wait," Hogan said. "You're saying my son finally wised up and asked for a protection order against that witch? We've been telling him to do that for months."

"I'm afraid it was the other way around," Joanna replied. "Madison swore out a protection order on him."

"That's ridiculous, when all this time she's the one who's been beating the crap out of him."

"You knew she could be violent, then?"

"Absolutely," Lyn asserted.

"If she lied to get the protection order, maybe we should start by having you tell me what you know," Joanna said quietly. "But would you mind if I invited one of my detectives to join us?"

"Not at all," Hogan said. "The more people who know the truth about that little hussy, the better off we'll be."

When Joanna called over to the bullpen, Ernie Carpenter was the only guy available. He lumbered into her office, where after a brief introduction he took a seat next to her visitor.

"Mr. Hogan here seems to be under the impression that Madison might have had something to do with his son's death. I'm hoping he can provide us with some background information."

Ernie nodded sagely. "Seems like a good idea," he said. "So how about if you start at the beginning, Mr. Hogan?"

Lyn heaved a deep sigh and ran his hands around the

brim of his hat as if searching for a place to start. "You need to understand that me and my boy didn't always see eye to eye," he said finally. "Fact is, once Leon hit high school, the two of us butted heads most all the time. We've got this cattle ranch, you see. I wanted him to go off to college, be an aggie, and then come home and take over running the place, but he didn't want nothin' to do with it—not with running the ranch and not with going to college neither. Soon as he was old enough to do so on his own, he enlisted in the army. Told his mom he wanted to be a mechanic and the army would train him for that for free. And he was right about that. They evidently turned him into a first-rate mechanic.

"I was mad as hell when he left, but you know how mothers are. Izzy stayed in touch with him the whole time. I kept thinking he'd wise up and come home. He did three two-year hitches, spent some time in the Middle East, and then ended up being stationed at Fort Huachuca, working in the motor pool. That's when he hooked up with Madison."

"How long ago was that?" Joanna asked.

Lyn shrugged. "I don't know exactly. Four years ago, maybe?"

"Wait," Joanna said. "The two kids are seven and five. Are you saying your son wasn't Kendall and Peter's biological father?"

"Nope," Hogan replied. "Madison and the two kids came as a package deal, but I can tell you, once things started going downhill, those kids were the only reason Leon stuck around. He had adopted them, you know. Kendall had some other last name to begin with. I forget what it was, and Peter's last name was Gale. When

Leon adopted them, they all ended up with the same name—his. And that was the one thing that kept him from filing for a divorce, you see. He was their adoptive father, and their stepfather, too. He didn't think there was any way in hell that the courts would grant him a shared-custody arrangement, much less full custody. Especially when Madison told him that if he ever tried to divorce her, she'd say he'd been molesting the little girl—which he hadn't, by the way. My son loved that little girl beyond bearing."

Joanna was astonished. It had never occurred to her that Leon was anything other than Kendall and Peter's biological father. And what Lyndell Hogan was saying was inarguably true. In a custody hearing, a stepfather wouldn't stand a fighting chance, especially one who'd had a child-molestation charge lobbed against him. Proven or not, that was something that would have stuck to Leon Hogan like glue. After all, when Joanna had first heard there were domestic-violence issues in the household, hadn't she assumed that Leon had been the one at fault? It wasn't just divorce courts that were biased in that direction.

Suddenly Joanna had a much clearer idea of why Leon would have been reluctant to press charges during those previous domestic-violence incidents. He'd been doing his best to hold the marriage together, maybe for no other reason than to create a line of defense between two young kids and a potentially violent mother.

"You told us earlier that you and your son were estranged," Ernie offered. "So how come you know so much about all of this?"

"I think I told you I come from a long line of ranchers. Our place has been in our family for three generations now. Years back a lot of our ranch hands came through that old bracero program. One of the best of those guys was named Eduardo Moreno. He had worked for my dad for years before he married a local girl and was able to become a U.S. citizen. Their youngest son, Jorge, and I grew up as best friends. We played football, baseball, and basketball together all through high school, but Jorge was always the smart one. After graduating we both went to the University of Wyoming. I was an aggie, Jorge was prelaw. I went back home and became a rancher. Jorge went to law school, became an attorney, and eventually settled in Tucson—Jorge Moreno. Ever heard of him?"

Joanna and Ernie shook their heads in unison.

"We lost track of each other over time, but then, a couple years back there was a big piece about Jorge in our alumni magazine, because he'd been given some prestigious award. And that's when I found out that he's built a national name for himself in representing husbands who are being booted around during the course of family divorce proceedings, and most especially ones who are fighting to be granted custody of their kids.

"As I said, Leon and I had been estranged, but once Izzy told me what was going on, I called Leon up, put him in touch with Jorge, and told him that whatever the bill was, I'd pay it. And that's what broke the ice between us. Leon was incredibly grateful for the help. When it came time for him to move out, I helped him with that, too—paid his first and last months' rent and security deposit. It was a small price to pay—pocket change, really—to get my son back."

Lyndell Hogan paused for a moment, fighting back tears and searching for words. "Except I didn't get him back," he said at last. "Now he's dead."

Hogan pulled a hankie out of his pocket and dabbed at his eyes. Then he turned his gaze on Joanna. "That's my story," he said. "What can you tell me?"

Before Joanna could say anything, Ernie asked another question. "When your son was telling you about all his difficulties, how did the two of you communicate—by phone, e-mails, texts?"

Lyn frowned. "Mostly by text," he said, "although there were some e-mails, too. Why?"

"And do you routinely erase text messages?" Ernie asked.

"Hell no, why would I? As much as I use that phone, it's not like it's going to get so full of stuff that it blows up. But you haven't told me why you're asking."

"Because it sounds to me as though your son really cared about those kids—as though he thought of them as his kids rather than hers."

Hogan nodded and said nothing.

"With Leon gone, Madison is all those kids have left."

Lyn Hogan nodded again. "Yes," he said. "Their mother and us—Izzy and me. Madison may not think much of us as grandparents, but that's how we think of ourselves. Leon went to court to make those kids his. In my book that means they're ours, too."

"So if something were to happen to Madison, would you and your wife be willing to take the kids?" Ernie asked.

"In a heartbeat," Lyndell Hogan declared, "and without a moment's hesitation. And if it comes to taking her to court to ask for custody of the kids, we're up for that, too. As far as I'm concerned, if there were ever an unfit mother, Madison Hogan is it!"

"In that case," Ernie said, "having access to those

contemporaneous texts and e-mails would go a long way to telling the real story about what was going on behind closed doors while Leon was still here. It would also give Leon a chance to speak out on his kids' behalf from beyond the grave. It might be possible for the court to consider it as deathbed testimony. Mind if I take a look?"

There was a long silence after that. It wasn't easy, but Joanna somehow managed to stifle the impulse to get up and hug Ernie Carpenter around the neck. Finally Lyndell Hogan reached into his shirt pocket and pulled out his phone. He logged in with several swipes and taps before passing it over to Ernie.

"Here you go," Lyn said. "Be my guest. I turned it on. All you have to do is go to my text and e-mail folders. Everything is in there—all of it. What he sent to me, what I sent to him, and a lot of what he sent back and forth to Jorge. Since I was paying the bill, Leon copied me on most of their correspondence."

For the better part of a minute, Ernie studied the screen in stony silence. Finally he looked back at Lyndell. "We'll be able to get all this material from Leon's phone, too, but doing that will take warrants, time, and all kinds of technical effort that we don't necessarily have available. It'll go a hell of a lot faster if we simply copy what's already here."

"Suit yourself," Lyn said. "Copy away."

Ernie glanced at his watch. "Maybe I can catch Kristin before she takes off." Without another word Ernie took the phone and left the room.

When Frank Montoya accepted the job in Sierra Vista, his departure had left Joanna in a world of hurt when it came to having someone who was up to speed on all things cyber. Fortunately, her secretary, Kristin Gregovich, had stepped into that void and was the department's current IT guru.

While Ernie was gone, Joanna did her best to bring Lyndell Hogan up to speed, sharing what information she could about the ongoing investigation. In actual fact she probably told him more than she should have, but that was too bad. If Dave Newton found out about it and raised hell? That was a risk Joanna was willing to take.

In her telling, however, she left out some of the story—their suspicion that Madison was the one who'd brought the murder weapon to the crime scene, the fact that rather than being drunk during the confrontation there was a chance that Leon had been drugged, and the very real probability that Madison had locked the children in the second bedroom before launching what, by way of Armando Ruiz, would turn out to be a fatal attack.

Yes, Joanna told the story, but she did leave a few things out. *Not lies,* she told herself, *more like sins of omission.*

When Ernie returned at last, phone in hand, he passed the device over to Lyndell. "Got it," he said, "all of it. I'd like to drive up to Tucson tomorrow and have a one-on-one with Mr. Moreno. Under most circumstances an attorney wouldn't be able to speak to us. But your son is dead, and with you paying Mr. Moreno's retainer, I think it's safe to say that if you gave him permission to break attorney-client privilege, I think he would."

"I think so, too," said Lyndell Hogan, slipping the phone into his pocket and rising to his feet. "I'll give him a call as soon as I get back to the hotel to let him know you're coming. What's your name again?"

"Detective Ernie Carpenter," came the reply, "with the Cochise County Sheriff's Department."

Joanna waited until Lyndell Hogan left the room, and then she darted around her desk and gave Ernie a hug. "File sexual-harassment charges if you like, but that was damned fine work."

"You're going to miss me when I'm gone," he said with a grin.

"You're wrong about that," she told him. "I already do."

CHAPTER 16

JOANNA WAS about to head for the parking lot when her phone rang, and she sank back down in her chair to answer.

"I've got several pieces of news for you," Detective Howell said.

"Did you talk to Mrs. Ambrose?" Joanna asked.

"Yes," Deb said, "and that was a lot like talking to a wall. She didn't tell me much, although she did allow as how the kids, and most especially the little girl, didn't seem exactly overjoyed to be dropped off at home. According to Mrs. Ambrose, under the circumstances that kind of behavior wasn't at all unusual."

"It sounds as though the CPS lead goes nowhere."

"Yes," Deb said, "but I had better luck with Kendall's second-grade teacher, Mrs. Baird. Believe it or not, Kendall is in second grade at the same school where Amy Ruiz teaches. There are three second-grade classes at Carmichael. Amy may not have tumbled to the connection, but Frank did as soon as I asked him which school the Hogan kids would attend.

"So I talked to Mrs. Baird, and she expressed some real concerns. For one thing, she's caught Kendall rescuing food out of the trash cans in the cafeteria to take home to eat. She says that the other kids tend to tease

Kendall because she doesn't always have clean clothes or clean hair."

"So there's bullying," Joanna concluded.

"Mrs. Baird has gone so far as to suggest as much to the principal, but she told Mrs. Baird it was just kids being kids and she shouldn't worry about it."

"Which is to say she's sweeping it under the rug."

"But here's something that isn't kids being kids," Deb said. "Mrs. Baird gave me a piece of notebook paper that she said Kendall gave her sometime last week. Kendall showed Mrs. Baird a word she'd printed on the paper and asked what it meant."

"What word?"

"H-O-R."

"What *does* that mean?" Joanna asked.

"That's what Mrs. Baird asked Kendall, and she sounded it out. 'H-O-R' equals 'WHORE'! She said that one of the girls who lives up the street was saying that's what her mommy calls Kendall's mommy—a whore."

Joanna's heart gave a squeeze.

"Mrs. Baird said she was going to bring this to the principal's attention," Deb continued, "but she was out of town at a conference. She was waiting for her to come back, but then after all the uproar with the shooting and with Kendall absent from school this week, she decided not to."

"Did she tell you which class mommy was spreading that ugly rumor?" Joanna asked.

"I don't think she knows, but if we ever get a chance to speak to Kendall, I'll ask her. I'll bet *she* knows."

"I'll bet she does, too," Joanna agreed.

She glanced at her watch. It was approaching dinnertime, and she didn't want to be late getting home.

"But that's not all," Deb continued excitedly before Joanna could cut her off. "I just left Lube&Oil Tek, where Leon was the manager. I spent the better part of an hour with one of his mechanics, a guy named Ricky Amado. You'll never guess what Ricky said the moment I showed him my ID."

"What?"

"'That bitch killed him, didn't she!'"

"That bitch in question being Madison Hogan?"

"Right. Ricky asked me if I'd ever seen the woman in the flesh. I told him no, that I wasn't directly connected to the officer-involved shooting so I hadn't met her. He said, 'She's a dish, at least she used to be, but she's also a real piece of work.' For instance, did you know Kendall and Peter Hogan aren't even Leon's?"

"I know that now," Joanna said. "Leon Hogan's dad and mom drove in from Wyoming. He dropped by the office this afternoon. He's the one who told me."

"Ricky told me she used to be a real looker with a *Playboy*-centerfold body and the personality of the Wicked Witch of the West. Back when Leon first met her, she was working as a bartender out at the Nite Owl and was barely making ends meet. Ricky said he thought Leon fell for the kids before he even fell for her. He seemed to think he was going to ride to the rescue and save all of them."

"Except Madison wasn't much interested in being rescued."

"According to what Leon told Ricky, she's more of a good-time girl, with the kids little more than inconvenient afterthoughts. Once Leon and Madison tied the knot, he went to court and officially adopted them. Since their biological fathers had long since disappeared, Madison made no objection to changing their last names to Hogan."

"Calling Madison Hogan a piece of work doesn't quite cover it," Joanna observed.

"Just wait," Deb said. "Once Madison started showing her true colors, Leon didn't know what to do. He stuck it out for as long as he could for the sake of the kids, because he knew that if he tried to divorce her, once the case came before a judge, he wouldn't have a chance of keeping the kids, but all that changed—"

"When Leon's father stepped in and offered to pay for a high-end attorney who was willing to duke it out in court," Joanna supplied.

"You got it." Deb said. "In the meantime, while they were getting their ducks in a row, the attorney advised Leon that even if he moved out, he should still go on paying Madison's expenses so she couldn't claim he'd deserted them, and in order to keep Leon's money rolling in, she let the kids stay with him on weekends."

"I'm assuming Madison had better things to do on the weekends than look after her kids."

"That's what Ricky said, too—that leaving the kids with Leon on weekends left her free to do whatever she wanted with her latest boyfriend, Randy Williams."

"So Ricky knew about Randy?" Joanna asked.

"And so did Leon," Deb said. "It was common knowledge, but Leon ignored it for the same reason he ignored everything else."

"To protect Kendall and Peter?"

"Exactly," Deb said. "But just because he hadn't filed for a divorce, Leon hadn't stopped moving forward. He told Ricky that his attorney had already rewritten his will, leaving everything he owned to be held in trust for Kendall and Peter until they come of age."

"Which makes sense," Joanna said. "I'm sure he didn't want Madison to be able to lay hands on any of his estate. But since he was living in a rented trailer on the outskirts of Whetstone, that probably won't amount to much."

"You'd be surprised," Deb replied. "As the franchise manager, he had a hundred-thousand-dollar group life-insurance policy. He also had the beginnings of a 401(k). A month or so ago, he changed beneficiaries on both of those, cutting Madison out completely and leaving the proceeds in equal shares to Kendall and Peter."

In her previous life, Joanna had spent time working in the insurance industry. "Filing for a divorce happens in public, but rewriting your will and changing beneficiaries on insurance policies or 401(k)s are private transactions that could have been accomplished without Madison's having a clue," Joanna surmised aloud. "With Leon dead she's probably under the impression that she's looking at a big payday."

"Not anymore," Deb said. "Once I talked to Ricky, I called Lube&Oil's corporate headquarters in L.A. The head of HR told me Madison Hogan had called her office earlier today, asking how she should go about filing a death-benefit claim."

"Not exactly letting any grass grow under her feet," Joanna observed.

"And only to be told she was out of luck," Deb replied, "although she's probably looking for a work-around on those revised beneficiary arrangements."

"There won't be," Joanna said. "Beneficiary arrangements are ironclad and can't be changed after the fact. This all sounds like huge progress, Deb. Anything else?"

"One thing more. Ricky said that Madison was planning to drop by to see Leon when he got home from work on Wednesday—that she was coming for dinner and bringing the kids. Ricky thought she maybe wanted to get back together, but Leon said he was pretty sure she'd be hitting him up for money to buy Christmas presents for the kids. Leon, being a good guy, was fine with that."

"I don't think Madison was dropping by to collect money for Christmas presents from Leon," Joanna said. "I think she was coming to kill him."

And that was when she finally had a chance to tell Deb about the fact that despite Armando Ruiz's claim that Leon had seemed to be impaired at the time of the shooting, alcohol content was entirely missing from his system.

"You think she slipped him something?" Deb asked.

"I do."

"We have got to get those poor kids away from that horrid woman." Deb breathed. "She's a menace."

"I couldn't agree more," Joanna said, "but I've got to hang up now. I'm already late for dinner. If I don't show up pretty soon, you'll have another homicide to solve, because Butch Dixon will kill me."

CHAPTER 17

IT HAD been the worst weekend of Beth Rankin's life. All day on Saturday, she'd agonized over the likelihood that Ron might never call her back. Then, after the ugly way that call had ended, she'd spent all day Sunday worrying that he would.

It wasn't fair for him to demand that she stop being friends with Jenny. It wasn't fair that he dictate she should stay on campus during Christmas vacation rather than go to Bisbee to have fun. What gave him the right to boss her around?

And besides, what did he have against Jenny in the first place? How did he know that Jenny's mother was in law enforcement? But even if Joanna Brady was a cop, what did it matter? What business of it was Ron's? What did he care?

As Sunday afternoon waned into evening, Beth finally started getting mad. Not as mad as she'd been the night she stomped out of her mother's house in Saddle-Brooke, but close enough.

She and Ron were boyfriend and girlfriend, maybe, but they weren't married. They weren't even engaged. And if this was the kind of bossy, overbearing person Ronald Cameron was, they probably never would be either. Beth had spent her whole life up till now being bossed around by other people—first by her mother and by Pastor Ike, too. She wasn't going to allow her new wings to be clipped by someone else—not even Ron. If he called tonight, she decided, she would tell him so—in no uncertain terms.

Sunday night, when she crept into the bathroom just before midnight, her whole body was quaking, but she was determined. Beth wasn't going to give Jenny up, not as a friend and not as a roommate either. And she was going to go wherever she pleased for Christmas vacation. It was Beth's life after all, and she got to decide.

So when the phone rang at two minutes past twelve, her fingers trembled as she accepted the call. "Hello."

"Hey, Sweet Betsy from Pike," Ron said. "I hope you had a nice day!"

Beth had never quite believed it when people claimed they'd been "triggered" by something they heard or saw. She hadn't believed it possible, but suddenly that was exactly what happened to her. In an instant she went from being cautiously tentative to being furious, because here he was calling her up as though nothing at all had happened. As though she hadn't spent the whole weekend mired in a pit of despair—as though the suffering he'd put her through the last several days was meaningless.

"Don't call me that," she snapped. "I'm not Betsy. My name is Elizabeth. You can call me Elizabeth or you can call me Beth, but do not call me Betsy."

"Hold on," Ron objected. "Get off your high horse. I just called to say hi and to ask how you're doing."

But Beth had her back up now. She was more angry than hurt. "You're the one on a high horse," she retorted. "You're the one who thinks you can boss everybody around. Well, you can't. You can't tell me what to do. You can't tell me who I can be friends with and who I can't. And if I want to go to Bisbee for Christmas, I will. Don't call me again. We're done."

Then she hung up. She had turned off her phone, left the bathroom, crawled into bed, and fallen asleep, because it really was over. Ron hadn't broken up with her; she had broken up with him. For the first time in forever, Beth Rankin felt as though she'd taken control of her own life.

CHAPTER 18

LUCKY AND Lady were waiting in the laundry room when Joanna arrived, and it seemed as though they were the only ones happy to see her. No one else was visible, and no one called a greeting either. She put her weapons away and then ventured farther into the house. The kitchen was deserted. Dinner was clearly over, and she had missed it—again. Her phone call with Deb had lasted far longer than it should have. A covered dish of some kind sitting in isolated splendor in the microwave hinted that the lay of the land on the home front wasn't particularly welcoming.

Walking past that, she paused in the doorway long enough to check out the combination dining room/ living room. When she left for work that morning, the two rooms had been awash in partially filled boxes that had once been chock-full of Christmas decorations. All those decorations were out on display now. Holiday trappings covered every possible flat surface, while the boxes themselves had vanished from view.

"Anybody home?" Joanna called.

"Family room," Butch responded. "We're working on the train, and your dinner's in the microwave." It wasn't exactly an ecstatic welcome-home, and it seemed like a good idea for her to make herself scarce. She went over to the microwave, punched the reheat button, and waited. She was in the doghouse, and deservedly so, and the fact that Butch preferred that she eat her solitary dinner rather than help out in the family room wasn't a good sign.

When Joanna first met Butch, she'd been attending the Arizona Police Academy in Peoria. When it came to meals, Butch's diner, the Roundhouse Bar and Grill just up the street, had been the restaurant of choice. The food was good, but the real attraction had been his model trains.

Butch Dixon was a railroad buff. All the decor on the walls inside the restaurant had a railroad connection, but nothing could top the collection of model trains that constantly circled the perimeter of the dining room. They traveled on several different tracks laid on wooden shelving that had been installed a foot below the room's dropped ceiling. Because there were different tracks, the trains could run in opposite directions without ever crashing into each other. Butch and his model-railroading friends had created a series of miniature dioramas along the tracks that depicted towns, cities, parks, farms, and ranches. There were trees in the forests, saguaros in the deserts, windmills on the ranches, and barns and livestock on the farms.

When Joanna first set foot in the Roundhouse, she loved the food but thought the train-based decor was a bit over the top. She was still a fairly new widow at the time and certainly hadn't been looking for any kind of romantic connection. When she met Butch Dixon, the Roundhouse's owner and head cook, she found him intriguing, but that was it. She wasn't interested in having a boyfriend at all, to say nothing of a long-distance one.

Butch's life was based in Peoria and in his restaurant, while Joanna's was located four hours away in Cochise County. In her book that was that.

Except it wasn't. A few months later, the city of Peoria had come along and offered Butch a buyout that he couldn't refuse. He took the money and ran, intent on two very different pursuits. One was to follow his lifelong dream of becoming a writer. The other was to win over a petite and somewhat contrary red-haired woman who'd walked into the Roundhouse and turned his life on end.

Once they married, and when it came time to build their new house, Butch had insisted that his model trains had to come along for the ride. The arrangement in the family room at High Lonesome Ranch was similar to the one formerly in the restaurant, but on a much smaller scale. Here again the tracks rested on shelving just below ceiling level, but this was a simpler display with fewer tracks and, as a consequence, far fewer trains.

These days Butch, with Denny's increasingly capable assistance, switched out the display from time to time, retiring some trains, bringing out others, and changing the scenery to match the season.

After eating her solitary leftovers and cleaning up the resulting mess in the kitchen, Joanna ventured warily into the room where Butch and Denny were creating a display Butch liked to call "Trains in Winter," complete with tiny lit Christmas trees lining the tracks. A chaos of boxes, some empty and some not, covered the floor. Butch, perched on a ladder, stood above the fray while Denny handed things up to him. Sage, confined to a playpen, seemed happy to remain on the periphery of all the action.

"Hey, Mom," Denny said, catching sight of her. "What do you think?"

The wonderful thing about Denny is that he didn't mind when she missed dinner. Chances are, he hadn't even noticed.

"It's amazing!" Joanna said without exaggeration, because it *was* amazing. No doubt it would be even more so once Butch's trains started buzzing around on their shelf-laid tracks.

"What can I do?" she asked.

"Check out all the Christmas trees," Butch said, "and make sure they light up before Denny hands them to me."

For the next hour and a half, they worked on the train display. By the time trains started moving around the decorated tracks, Butch seemed a little less grumpy. Because it was a school night, they had to pause then and get the kids to bed. Once that happened, they returned to the family room to close up and put away boxes. That was when the phone rang with Jenny's face showing in caller ID.

"Hey," Joanna said when she answered. "I'll put you on speaker. Dad and I are in the family room cleaning up the debris field left behind by this year's Trains in Winter project."

"You're already working on that?" Jenny sounded dismayed. "The trains are usually the last thing we work on."

"And they were this time, too," Joanna agreed. "That's because everything else is done. We put up the tree yesterday. The living room and dining room are both decorated to the hilt, and all boxes from there are put away. Believe me, we're on a roll around here."

"But will there be anything left for me to do when I

get there?" Jenny asked. Clearly she didn't like feeling as though she'd been excluded from the process, and that made sense, since in previous years she'd been in charge of most of the Christmas decorating.

"Don't worry," Butch assured her. "There'll be plenty of wrapping for you to do—wrapping and baking both—so how about if we change topics. How are your finals going?"

"I'm almost to the end of them," Jenny said. "Only two more to go, one tomorrow and one on Friday morning at eight o'clock. That one will be easy peasy. I'll be done, packed, and headed down I-17 by noon, which should put me ahead of most of the traffic."

"When is Beth's last final?" Butch asked.

"That's on Friday, too, but slightly later. Even so, we should still be on the road by noon."

"Her folks live in Tucson, don't they?" Butch asked.

"In SaddleBrooke," Jenny answered.

"Meaning close to Tucson but not exactly inside the city limits," Butch commented. "Are you going to stop by and see them on the way?"

"I doubt that. I don't think Beth wants to."

"So she's still at loggerheads with them?"

"Yup, big time."

"What seems to be the problem?" Butch asked.

Joanna was often mystified at how Butch always seemed to know so much more about Jenny's private life than her mother did.

"I think it's all about Beth's boyfriend," Jenny answered. "Her folks seem to hate the guy."

"Will they come around?" Butch asked.

"Maybe," Jenny replied. "Not necessarily because they'll have a change of heart, but because the boyfriend seems to be turning into a short-timer. Things on that score seem to have gone haywire recently. Beth's been down in the dumps for days now. She's been a mess all weekend."

"You think they're breaking up?" Butch asked.

"That's how I see it," Jenny replied. "Beth hasn't been doing much sleeping or eating. She's so distracted right now that I'm surprised she's able to *take* finals, much less *pass* them."

The exchange gave Joanna a possible answer to her earlier question. Butch knew about Jenny's life because he asked detailed questions and then—surprise, surprise—he actually listened to her answers. As for Joanna? She hadn't the slightest clue about where Beth Rankin's parents lived, and she certainly didn't care whether or not this girl she didn't know was breaking up with her current boyfriend.

"Have you met the guy?" Butch asked.

"Naw," Jenny replied. "Beth met Ronald Cameron online at some kind of dating site. He's into computers in a big way—cybersecurity, I think. He lives in Washington, D.C. I doubt we'd have anything in common. As you already know, geeks have never been my thing. I'm a lot more likely to go for guys who prefer riding horses and herding cattle to tapping keyboards."

"Computer guys probably make more money than cowboys do," Butch suggested, "but that's all right. I don't necessarily trust geeky computer guys either."

They all laughed at that, and then Joanna changed the subject.

"What do the weather reports look like for Friday afternoon?" she asked.

Right that minute she was far less concerned about

the possibility of collegiate love affairs going bad than she was about her daughter having to drive home from Flagstaff in adverse road conditions.

"It's supposed to be clear and dry by then," Jenny said. "Perfect weather for driving."

"Good," Joanna said, "but I'll still be worried until you're here safe and sound."

"Mom," Jenny said, "you worry too much."

In actual fact it wasn't a matter of Joanna Brady's worrying too much. It was a matter of her worrying too much about the wrong things.

"Take care anyway," she advised her daughter. "And good luck with those last two finals."

"She doesn't need luck," Butch declared in the background. "That girl of ours has her finals aced."

Once the phone call was over, Joanna noticed that some of the earlier tension had drained away. As they finished cleaning up in the family room, she began recounting everything that had happened in the course of the day. By the time she finished, they were on their way to bed.

"You might have been stuck at your desk all day, but your people were out working like crazy," Butch said. "No wonder you were late to dinner."

"I'm sorry. . . ."

Butch waved off her apology. "Not to worry," he said. "You're forgiven. It's par for the course, and I'm over it."

"But I shouldn't—"

"Joey, you have a job to do. People are counting on you. And don't pay that much attention if I get my nose out of joint occasionally."

Joanna was lying in bed and not quite asleep when

Butch spoke again. "So you think Madison was behind this whole thing?" he asked.

"I do," Joanna said, "and I believe that insurance money was the motive."

"Will you be able to charge her with anything?"

"I doubt it. I think she fully intended to take him out herself, most likely staging things to make it look like he'd attacked her. Unfortunately for Armando, he showed up at that critical juncture and things went in a very different direction."

Butch was quiet for several moments after that. Joanna decided he'd probably dropped off to sleep, but then he spoke again. "Leon was right, you know."

"About what—changing his beneficiary?"

"That yes, but also about it being unlikely he'd get a fair shake in any kind of custody dispute. Biological fathers get screwed over in divorce proceedings all the time. As an adoptive father who also happened to be a stepfather, I don't think he would have stood a chance in a court of law, no matter what kind of high-powered lawyer Lyndell Hogan was footing the bill for. And now, no matter what kind of mother Madison Hogan is, her kids are stuck with her."

Moments later Butch started snoring while Joanna tossed and turned. Murder was bad enough, but this was an even worse outcome than usual. It seemed likely that Kendall and Peter Hogan would be raised by a woman who might well get away with their father's murder.

CHAPTER 19

WITH PETER asleep below her, Kendall lay on the top bunk and listened to the voices coming from the kitchen, where Grandma Puckett was having what she called her "nightly cocktail" and Mommy was drinking beer. No doubt they were both smoking cigarettes. Mrs. Baird said smoking was bad for people's lungs, but maybe Mommy and Grandma Puckett didn't know that.

Tonight Kendall had left the bedroom door cracked open. That meant cigarette smoke drifted into the room, but it also meant she could hear what was being said.

"How can it be there's no insurance?" Grandma Puckett demanded. "I thought Leon had a big life-insurance policy where he worked."

"He did, but I don't get any of it," Mommy said, "not a dime. He changed the beneficiary arrangement a few weeks ago. He did it behind my back, without saying a word about it. He left all the proceeds to the kids in a way that cuts me out of it completely. It's supposed to be held in trust for them until they're of age."

Kendall didn't know what insurance was, and she didn't understand what that b-word was or what "of age" meant either, but whatever those things added up to, they had made her mother furious. She'd been on the phone earlier in the afternoon, talking to someone else about those very things—especially insurance and the b-word. Once Mommy got off the phone, she started yelling and throwing things every which way. There'd always been a picture of Daddy in his army uniform, hanging on the wall in the living room. Mommy had torn that down and smashed it into a million pieces. Then she turned to Kendall.

"Clean that up," she'd ordered, pointing at the mess she'd just made. "Get rid of that broken glass before one of you kids steps on it and cuts a foot."

Kendall had used a broom and a dustpan and cleaned up the mess as well as she could. There were lots of tiny pieces of glass on the floor. She didn't know if she'd gotten all of them. She hoped so. As for the picture itself? If Daddy was gone, she didn't want to forget how he looked, so she slipped the photo out of its frame and smuggled it into the back of her closet, where she hid it away along with the rest of her treasures.

About that time Grandma Puckett had shown up after driving down from Casa Grande. Randy had been there hanging around during the phone call, but the moment Grandma Puckett arrived, he'd taken off. She didn't like him, and he didn't like her. Kendall thought that was just fine, especially if it meant Randy would make himself scarce.

By then it had been getting on toward dinnertime. Grandma Puckett had taken one look in the fridge, found it to be mostly empty, and announced that she was taking everybody out for dinner. For Kendall that was very good news. At breakfast that morning, she'd emptied the last crumbs of Lucky Charms into two bowls, one for her and one for Peter. Once she took a bite, though, the milk tasted funny, so she'd ended up dumping out both bowls, and they'd eaten toast with peanut butter on it for breakfast.

If they'd gone to school that day, they would have had both breakfast and lunch. But they weren't going to school right now, so for lunch they'd had another marshmallow sandwich on the floor of their bedroom. For dinner at Denny's, though, they had a true feast. Both of them had Grand Slams, and not kiddie Grand Slams either. Peter had the Slugger with pancakes and hash browns, while Kendall ordered her favorite, the one with French toast, both of them accompanied by milk shakes.

"Don't you ever feed these kids?" Grandma Puckett asked. "They act like they're starving."

She smiled when she said that—like she was making a joke or something, but Kendall didn't think it was funny. Sometimes it felt like she and Peter really *were* starving.

On the way home from dinner, they stopped off at Safeway and Grandma Puckett bought more groceries than Kendall had seen since Daddy moved out of the house. There was fresh milk and bread and eggs, boxes of cereal, packages of sliced luncheon meat and cheeses. There was even a bottle of orange juice. It had been a long time since they'd had orange juice at home.

Full for a change and relieved to know that Randy wasn't just down the hall, Kendall was about to doze off when the sound of a ringing doorbell roused her. Grandma Puckett must have gone to the door. A moment later she returned. "It's Lyndell and Isabella Hogan," she said. "They're waiting outside. They're staying at the Copper Queen in Bisbee, but they were hoping to see the kids tonight."

Kendall's heart leaped. Daddy's parents were here?

"Well, they're not seeing the kids!" Mommy said. "Tell them to go away."

"For Pete's sake, Maddie!" Grandma Puckett exclaimed. "They're Leon's parents. They've come all the way from Wyoming."

"They could have come from Australia for all I care," Mommy said, raising her voice. "I don't want to see them, and the kids can't see them either. Leon was trying to kill me! If that cop hadn't been there, he would have succeeded, too, but you still think I should roll out the red carpet for them? Not on your life. I don't mind if they come to the funeral. That's up to them, but if you think I'm going to have those people in my house or chumming around with my kids, think again."

Kendall's heart constricted. Daddy had been trying to kill Mommy? That couldn't be true! No way! He wouldn't have done that, not ever. Mommy had come after Daddy sometimes, but never the other way around.

"This is just so wrong," Grandma Puckett was saying, but it sounded as though she was walking away from the kitchen. Kendall heard the front door open again. A few words were exchanged, and then the door closed again.

From the kitchen Kendall heard the thunk of an empty beer bottle landing in the trash. The refrigerator door squeaked open and shut. Mommy was probably getting another beer. Their fridge sometimes ran out of milk, but it was never in any danger of running out of beer.

"Speaking of the funeral," Grandma said, picking up the conversation. "What are you going to wear? For that matter, what are the kids going to wear?"

"I'll find something," Mommy said. "I've lost weight, so now some of my old clothes fit me again. As for the kids? Whatever they wear to school will be fine."

A couple times a year, Mommy would go to Goodwill and come home with bags of clothing. Some of it fit and some didn't. Kendall knew that a few of the kids made fun of them because their supposedly "new" clothes weren't new at all.

"I'll take them shopping tomorrow," Grandma Puckett announced. "I noticed tonight that Peter's pant legs are at least three inches too short, and Kendall's shoes have seen better days."

"That's totally up to you," Mommy said. "The last thing I want to do is spend the day dragging kids in and out of stores. Besides, I have an appointment with the funeral director in the morning. You can take the kids shopping while I take care of that."

"How much is the funeral going to cost?"

"I have no idea," Mommy said. "Some money has come into that GoFundMe account—about three thousand dollars the last I checked. But I told the guy at the funeral home that we've got to keep the price down to a bare minimum. Cremation and an urn—that's it. I'm not paying for a casket just so they can burn it to cinders. Randy told me that if I come up short, he'll take care of the difference."

"Big of him," Grandma Puckett said, but it didn't sound like she meant it as a compliment.

"Don't you start saying bad things about Randy," Mommy objected, her voice rising in pitch. "He takes good care of me."

So did Daddy, Kendall thought as she finally drifted off to sleep. *But he took care of all of us.*

CHAPTER 20

JOANNA'S PHONE was ringing as she stepped out of the shower the next morning. When she picked it up, Casey Ledford's face was showing in caller ID.

"You're at work early," Joanna observed when she answered.

"I'm not at work yet," Casey replied. "A text from DPS came in while I was eating breakfast. Stains on the protective order test positive for scopolamine. If you happen to be doing CSI work for one of the big shots at DPS, you get first-rate service."

"Are you saying you want to make the switch and go work for them?" Joanna asked.

"Not on your life," Casey said with a laugh. "Chances are the place is teeming with plenty of other people just like Dave Newton."

"So what's the next step?" Joanna asked. "Not that you're allowed to tell me, that is."

"That'll be Dave Newton's call. He was copied on the same text that just showed up here, and it certainly lends credence to Armando's claim that Leon Hogan was impaired at the time of the shooting. Once I get into the office and have a chance to enhance them, I'll be sending him and you some of our crime scene photos."

Joanna was puzzled. "What kind of crime scene photos?" she asked.

"Just wait and see," Casey said. "I think you'll find them interesting."

"Why?"

"Because I don't think Madison Hogan had time to clean up her mess before she went racing out of that living room."

In the kitchen Joanna found that Denny had been delivered to his bus stop and a previously read copy of the *Bisbee Bee* lay on the table next to her place setting. She started to reach for it, but Butch stopped her.

"Don't bother reading it," he said. "Marliss has outdone herself with a puff piece on Dave Newton. It's all about how rogue law-enforcement officers operating out of mismanaged jurisdictions must be held to account when it comes to line-of-duty shootings that put innocent civilians in harm's way. Those aren't the exact words Marliss used, but you get the picture."

"I certainly do."

"Who was that on the phone?" Butch asked. "I heard it ringing while you were in the bathroom."

"It was Casey," Joanna answered. "The protective order tested positive for the presence of scopolamine."

"Which means that Madison had doped Leon Hogan sometime prior to when bullets started flying."

"Yes, it does."

"What's next, then?" Butch asked.

"Who knows?" Joanna replied. "For right now the ball is in Dave Newton's court."

She left the house right at seven thirty, and her phone rang before she made it out to High Lonesome Road. Jenny's face showed in caller ID.

"Hey," Joanna said. "I thought you had a final first thing this morning."

"I do," Jenny said. "I'm on my way there now, but I need some roommate advice."

Instantly Joanna felt out of her league. She'd had two husbands but no roommates—ever. By the time she was Jenny's age, she and Andy were married and already had a baby. When it came to roommate issues, Joanna Brady knew absolutely nothing.

"About what?" she asked.

"About Beth," Jenny answered. "I wanted to talk to you about this last night, but with Dad on the phone I just couldn't."

"Talk about what?" Joanna asked.

"Beth was still asleep when I left the dorm this morning, but she spent most of the weekend crying her eyes out. I'm pretty sure she's never had a boyfriend before, and losing this one is real hard on her. I've tried to get her to talk to me about it, but she won't. She just says that it's hopeless—that her life is over and there's nothing anyone can do about it. I don't know how to help her, Mom. I'm afraid she's going to go off the deep end."

Joanna heard an unfamiliar note of panic in her daughter's voice. "When you say 'off the deep end,' are you saying you're afraid she might harm herself?"

Jenny hesitated for a moment before she replied. "I am, actually," she admitted.

"Doesn't NAU have counselors on staff?"

"They do," Jenny answered. "I already suggested she look into seeing one, but Beth said no way was she going to talk to one of them 'over this.' Those were her exact words. That's what she said: quote/unquote, 'over this.'"

"So does 'over this' mean something other than

boyfriend troubles?" Joanna asked. "If she meant her boyfriend . . . What's his name again?"

"Ron—Ronald Cameron."

"Right, of Washington, D.C. So if it's all about Ron, wouldn't she have said 'over him'?"

"Beats me," Jenny said gloomily. "I have no idea if the breakup is his idea or hers, but what I do know for sure is that Beth's taking it really, really hard."

"How long were they together?" Joanna asked.

"Not that long, since shortly after school started last fall," Jenny said. "They've never actually met in person, but they talk back and forth almost every day. I think Beth truly loves the guy. At least she thinks she does."

That was something Joanna couldn't quite understand. How could you possibly fall in love with somebody you'd never met in person? But then she thought about Sage and Denny and Jenny herself. She had loved them long before meeting them in person as living, breathing human beings. And that set of thoughts kept Joanna from saying the first thing that came to mind. She said the second thing instead.

"Maybe you should call him," she said. "If they've been in constant contact for this long, even if they're splitting up, chances are he still cares enough about her that he wouldn't want something bad to happen to her."

Like suicide. That was Joanna's chilling interior thought, one she didn't mention aloud to her daughter.

"All right, Mom," Jenny said. "Thanks. I'm here now. I've got to go in. Wish me luck."

CHAPTER 21

BY THE time Joanna arrived at the department, Casey Ledford was already sitting in the lobby just outside Joanna's office, chatting with Kristin.

"What's up?" Joanna asked.

Casey passed her an array of colored photos, the previously mentioned crime scene photos. There were five of them in all, arranged in a fan like a hand of cards.

"Take a look," Casey said.

Joanna did as she was told. The first picture was of a coffee table. An indecipherable piece of paper lay in the middle of the table, with a pool of liquid spilling across it. Some of the dark liquid remained on the table itself, but most of it had soaked into the paperwork, creating a large brown stain. To the left of the puddle, a coffee cup lay on its side, with its handle pointing away from the spill. At the far end of the coffee table was another tipped-over cup and another puddle of spilled coffee. Yes, this cup, too, lay on its side, but with the handle right at the edge of the table, so indications were that whoever had been sitting on the sofa and using that cup had most likely been right-handed.

The next enlargement focused on the coffee-stained paper itself, with the camera lens close enough that the words on the document, including those obscured by the coffee, were still legible. Leon and Madison Hogan's names were both front and center.

"The protection order?" Joanna asked, glancing in Casey's direction.

The CSI nodded. "Keep looking," she said.

The next three photos were all of the same thing—the tipped-over coffee cup at the far end of the table—and each was somewhat larger than the previous one. It wasn't until Joanna was studying the final photo that she saw what Casey had wanted her to see in the first place—a dark smudge of lipstick along the rim of the cup.

"So the cup with the lipstick on it must be Madison's."

Casey nodded again.

"Did you happen to collect samples from this one?"

"Unfortunately, no," Casey said regretfully, "but I doubt that it had been tampered with. No one at the scene indicated that Madison was impaired in any way. Hysterical and out of control yes, but not drugged up."

"You passed this information along to Dave Newton?"

"Absolutely," Casey said. "And if he asks me, I'm planning on telling him that I showed it to you, too."

"So she goes there and doses poor Leon with scopolamine in hopes of taking him out. Then, when Leon gets hold of her gun, she runs from the house, and he comes out shooting at her, so confused and doped up that he probably has no idea what he's doing."

Casey nodded. "The fact that he actually hit Armando was nothing but sheer bad luck."

"And utterly senseless," Joanna added, handing the photos back to Casey. "Thanks for letting me see these."

Casey took the photos and left. Forty-five minutes later, while Joanna was working her way through that day's incoming mail, Kristin reached out to her over the intercom.

"Detective Liam Jackson to see you, Sheriff Brady."

Joanna had to smile. Her office door was almost always open, and most people simply walked inside. Kristin was clearly putting on airs for this out-of-town, Department of Public Safety interloper.

"Sure," Joanna said. "Send him right in."

"Good morning, ma'am," Liam said.

Joanna couldn't help but like the guy. She had developed a BS filter that enabled her to separate phony politeness from the real thing. This was definitely the latter.

"What can I do for you?" she asked.

"Dave wanted me to let you know that we're pulling up stakes and heading back to the barn."

"You mean you've finished your investigation?"

Liam nodded. "We just had a meeting with your county attorney and showed him what we had so far. Mr. Jones told us that in light of additional evidence that surfaced overnight, it's reasonable to assume Leon Hogan was under the influence of scopolamine at the time of the shooting. Mr. Jones's determination is that in returning fire, Deputy Ruiz was acting in self-defense and that his use of deadly force was justified."

Saying nothing, Joanna sat very still for a moment, allowing a wave of relief to wash over her. Armando was in the clear as far as charges were concerned. Of course, it was typical of Dave Newton that he wasn't man enough to show up and admit his defeat to Joanna in person.

"Thank you so much, Liam," she murmured at last. "I appreciate your letting me know, although I suspect that your partner was hoping for a somewhat different outcome."

Liam nodded, giving her a noncommittal shrug accompanied by a wry grin. "Sometimes you eat the bear," he said. "Sometimes the bear eats you."

And sometimes when you eat bear meat, you end up with trichinosis, Joanna thought, but she didn't say so aloud.

"Does that mean that when Deputy Ruiz recovers, I won't need to keep him on administrative leave?"

"That's correct."

"Does anyone else know?" she asked.

"Not yet," Liam replied. "Only you."

As soon as Liam departed, Joanna hurried to Tom Hadlock's door and stuck her head in the office. "Arlee Jones has spoken," she said. "He's ruled Leon Hogan's death as justifiable homicide. No charges will be filed. I'd like you to hold a presser and let people know."

"Where are you going?"

"Tucson," she said. "This is news Armando and Amy Ruiz need to hear in person."

"Do you want me to send out a departmentwide announcement?" Tom asked.

Kristin had created and maintained a special-distribution list so that in case of some dire emergency a notification could go out to the cell-phone numbers of every member of Joanna's department at the press of a button. In this case, however, it would be sending out good news rather than bad.

"Yes," Joanna said, "make it short and sweet, something like 'An independent investigation by the Arizona

Department of Public Safety has determined that Cochise County Deputy Armando Ruiz was acting in self-defense in the shooting death of Whetstone resident Leon Hogan.' That'll just about do it."

Hadlock gave his boss a sly grin. "Are you sure you don't want me to add a 'Neener, neener, Detective Newton!' on the bottom of that message?"

The fact that Tom was beginning to develop a sense of humor came as something of a shock to Joanna, and she burst out laughing.

"No, thanks," she said. "Let's go with understated elegance, but remember: Don't send out the text until I give you the go-ahead. I want to let Amy and Armando know before anyone else does."

As Joanna drove out of the parking lot, Marliss Shackleford's RAV4 was driving in. Fortunately for Joanna, Marliss was now Tom Hadlock's problem. Too bad for him.

Motoring up and over the Divide, Joanna was lost in thought. Armando might have been exonerated, but Leon Hogan was still dead and his children were still in the custody of their remaining parent, who had possibly not only drugged their father but also intended to kill him.

What was Joanna's responsibility here? For one thing, Madison had the presumption of innocence. For another, Joanna understood that standard Child Protective Services protocols attempted to keep families together at all costs. But was this a family that should be kept together? Obviously, Leon himself hadn't thought so. That's why he'd been consulting with a divorce attorney—a divorce attorney who lived in Tucson. And not just any attorney—an attorney who happened to be Leon's father's childhood pal. Lyndell Hogan had been paying the attorney's fees on his son's behalf. That being the case, maybe the attorney would be willing to discuss what had really been going on.

Before Lyn Hogan had left Joanna's office the previous day, he'd given her his cell number in case she needed to be in touch. She'd added it to her contacts list as a matter of habit.

"Siri," she said aloud, getting the AI's attention. "Call Lyndell Hogan."

"Lyn Hogan speaking," he answered after picking up.

Joanna took a deep breath. Since the case surrounding the shooting was no longer active, neither was the prohibition against her discussing it. With that in mind, she wasn't going to pull any punches.

"It's Sheriff Brady," she told him. "There have been some new developments overnight. Lab results indicate that someone administered scopolamine to your son shortly before the shooting."

"Sco- what?" he asked, sounding genuinely puzzled.

"Scopolamine," Joanna answered. "On the street it's known as a date-rape drug and is sometimes referred to as 'devil's breath.' It's a tasteless clear liquid. Once dropped into someone's drink—that would be coffee in Leon's case—it's undetectable. Often victims become confused or even pass out cold. When the drug wears off, they usually have little or no memory of what happened either immediately before or after ingesting the drug."

"In other words, when my son came out of the house with that gun in his hand, he wasn't in his right mind and had no idea what he was doing."

"Correct," Joanna replied. "I'm surprised he could stand on his own, much less shoot. He would have been completely out of control. Earlier today the Department of Public Safety submitted their findings about the incident to the county attorney. Arlee Jones has now ruled your son's death to be justifiable homicide."

"But it happened because he was drugged," Lyn said.

"Yes."

"Who gave the stuff to him, Madison?"

"That's how it looks."

"Why?"

"We believe she was after the hundred thousand dollars' worth of group life insurance that Leon had at work. Unfortunately for her, shortly before this happened, Leon changed his beneficiary designation. As things now stand, all proceeds will be held in trust for the kids. She won't be getting a dime."

"Thank God for small blessings," Lyn murmured. "Are you going to arrest her and charge her?"

"Probably not," Joanna replied. "The presence of scopolamine is real enough, but the rest of it—the idea that she went to Whetstone possibly with the intention of killing him—is all speculation on our part. Without a full confession, I don't think there's a chance that we'd be able to get a jury to convict her. It would be so much wasted effort. My main concern right now is with the kids."

"Mine, too," Hogan said. "Izzy and I tried stopping by the house last night. Madison's mom came to the door, but Madison refused to let us in or even see us."

"And didn't let you see the kids either."

"They were probably in bed. We didn't even ask, but the idea of them being left with her . . ."

"That's why I'm calling you, Mr. Hogan," Joanna said. "Some items have come to light that make me wonder if leaving the two children in their mother's care is in their best interests."

"What kinds of things?"

Joanna recounted what Deb had learned in the previous day's interviews—that Kendall had been reluctant to go home, that there seemed to be a steady stream of late-night partying going on at Madison's residence, that Kendall was being bullied at school for being dirty and because her clothing wasn't clean, that she'd been caught rescuing food from the trash cans in the cafeteria. Somehow Joanna left out the part about Kendall and Peter being locked in the bedroom at the time Leon Hogan was gunned down.

"What can I do?" Lyn asked when Joanna finished her recitation.

"I'd like to speak to your son's divorce attorney," Joanna said.

"Jorge," Hogan said. "Jorge Moreno."

"He's a friend of yours, right?"

"Correct."

"And in a way Jorge was representing your interests as well as your son's. I don't know if that connection is enough to release him from his attorney-client privilege, but if he knows that the kids are being mistreated in some fashion and can talk to me about it, there might be a chance for us to help them."

"Where are you right now?" Hogan asked.

"I'm on my way to Tucson. I have an errand to run."

"Is it all right for me to give Jorge your number?"

"Absolutely."

"Okay," Lyn Hogan said. "I'm pretty sure he'll give you a call."

CHAPTER 22

THE NEXT morning, when Grandma Puckett took Peter and Kendall to IHOP for breakfast, they couldn't have been happier. Daddy had taken them there sometimes, but Mommy never did. Kendall had blueberry pancakes, while Peter ordered the ones made with chocolate chips. Grandma Puckett had scrambled eggs and toast.

There was a question Kendall had been wanting to ask. She'd been thinking about it in bed overnight, but it wasn't until breakfast that she managed to work up her nerve.

"Could Peter and me come live with you in Casa Grande?" Kendall asked quietly.

Grandma put down her coffee cup. "'Could Peter and I come,' not 'Peter and me,'" she corrected. "But, Kendall, I'm far too old to be raising kids. Why would you even ask such a thing?"

Because you feed us, Kendall thought, chasing a stray blueberry around on her plate. *Because you're nice to us.*

There were lots of things Kendall could have said, but she chose the one she thought might work. "Because I don't like Randy," she said aloud. "He scares me. He has mean eyes."

Grandma's expression hardened, but when she spoke,

her voice was full of concern. "Scares you how?" she wanted to know. "Has he ever hurt you?"

Kendall nodded.

"How? What did he do?"

"He grabbed me by the shoulder and shook me—real hard. His thumb left a bruise right here." Kendall pointed to a spot just under her collarbone.

"Has he ever hurt Peter?"

Kendall shook her head. "I try to keep Peter out of Randy's way so that won't happen," she whispered.

A waitress stopped by the table and refilled Grandma Puckett's coffee cup.

"I don't like Randy either," Peter muttered when the waitress walked away. "I saw him kick Coon once."

"Your dog?" Grandma asked, frowning. "That's terrible. I noticed the dog wasn't here, but . . ."

"Mommy said he got out of the yard and got hit by a car," Kendall supplied.

"And the vet couldn't fix him," Peter added. "So Coon's dead, too, just like Daddy."

"I'm so sorry to hear that," Grandma said. "You really loved that dog, didn't you?"

Peter nodded. "He always slept at the bottom of my bed and kept my feet warm."

After IHOP they went to Walmart. Kendall was amazed. While she pushed the grocery cart, Grandma Puckett filled it up with all kinds of things—pairs of pants, shirts, socks, and underwear for both of them. They each got two new pairs of shoes, "one for school and one for dress-up," Grandma Puckett said.

Kendall thought that the word "dress-up" really meant that those were the shoes they should wear to Daddy's funeral. The same held true for the dress

shirt and clip-on tie for Peter and the pretty new dark
blue dress for Kendall—the nicest one she ever remembered having. Not only that, they both ended
up with brand-new jackets—warm ones. There were
other things, too, like new toothbrushes and tubes of
toothpaste. Kendall thought this was way better than
Christmas.

When they got to the checkout counter, Grandma
didn't complain about how much everything cost. She
just got out her credit card, put it in the slot, and pretty
soon the receipt came out. Kendall never remembered
seeing one quite that long.

"Are you sure we couldn't come stay with you?"
Kendall asked once they were back in the car.

She kept hoping that between breakfast and now
Grandma might have changed her mind. Instead, she
just shook her head.

"Sorry, Kendall," Grandma said. "The place where I
live is only for old people. You're too young."

On the way home from Walmart, they stopped off at
a place where Peter could get a haircut and Kendall a
trim. Grandma said Peter's hair was so long that he was
starting to look like a girl. When they went back to the
house, Mommy wasn't there. Kendall and Peter helped
unload the car. Grandma had them carry all the bags
into the kids' bedroom so she could help them take off
the sales tags and put everything away. Instead of doing
his share of the work, Peter climbed onto the lower
bunk and fell asleep.

When it came time to hang things in the closet,
Grandma started taking out the existing items she
thought were too small for Kendall to wear. She was
right—some of them had been too small on the day

Mommy brought them home. But the deeper Grandma went into the closet, the more Kendall worried about what she'd find there, and it didn't take long for that worry to become a reality.

Grandma Puckett leaned down. When she straightened back up, she was holding the empty peanut butter jar. "What's this?" she asked with a frown.

"It's for Peter," Kendall said.

"Why would Peter need an empty peanut butter jar?"

"To pee in," Kendall said quietly.

"Why not use the bathroom?"

"It's for when Randy's here," Kendall said. "He gets mad if we come out of our room when he's here."

Grandma set the jar down and turned back to the closet. This time she emerged holding the almost empty package of graham crackers along with the bag containing the remainder of the marshmallows. Kendall said nothing.

"Well?" Grandma pressed.

"It's food, I guess," Kendall mumbled, staring at the floor.

"Food should be kept in a kitchen cabinet, not in a bedroom closet where it might attract mice or bugs or all kinds of other vermin," Grandma said. "What's it doing here?"

"Because . . ." Kendall began. Grandma's voice had sounded angry, and Kendall was sure she was in trouble.

"Well?" Grandma insisted.

"Because sometimes Mommy forgets about dinner," Kendall admitted quietly.

"You mean she forgets to feed you?"

Kendall nodded again.

And then something totally unexpected happened.

Grandma turned around and returned the marshmallows, graham crackers, and even the peanut butter jar to their original hiding places in the closet exactly as she'd found them. The next thing Kendall knew, Grandma Puckett had pulled her into a fierce hug, holding her so tightly that Kendall could barely breathe.

"I'm so, so sorry," Grandma whispered in her ear. It sounded like maybe she was crying, but Kendall couldn't be sure.

"I didn't raise your mother to be like this, you know," Grandma said. "I thought your daddy would be a good influence on her—that maybe he could fix her. But he didn't—couldn't. What are we going to do about this, Kendall? What on earth can we do?"

Kendall didn't answer, because she had no idea.

Mommy came home a little while later. She was acting weird, staggering a bit and not exactly talking straight. Kendall had seen her like this before, but usually not in the middle of the day. It was the kind of thing that happened late at night, when the beer was flowing and people—mostly strangers—were out in the kitchen talking and laughing.

Kendall was on her way to the kitchen, but when Grandma and Mommy started arguing, she froze where she was and went no farther.

"How often do you forget to feed the kids dinner?" Grandma demanded.

"What makes you think I don't feed my kids?" Mommy asked right back. "Who told you a story like that, tattletale Kendall?"

"It doesn't matter who told me. What matters is whether it's true. Do you forget to feed them or not?"

"It's none of your business. You can't show up at my

house and call me a bad mother to my face. You may be my mother, but you've got no right to do that, none at all."

That's when the front door opened. Kendall held her breath. If it had been anyone else, the doorbell would have rung first, but Randy never used the bell or knocked. He always barged right in as though he owned the place.

He must have heard the sound of raised voices. "What's going on?" he wanted to know.

"It's my mother," Mommy said. "She has nerve enough to come into my household and accuse me of being a bad mother—of not taking care of my kids, of not feeding them."

"You said that to her?" Randy demanded. "You said that to your own daughter?"

Kendall recognized the menace in his voice because she'd heard it before. She crept back into the room and cowered against Peter's bunk.

"Yes I did," Grandma said defiantly. "I not only said it, I meant it. Maddie may be my daughter, but she isn't a fit mother."

"Get out of here, you old cow!" Randy bellowed. "You get the hell out of here and don't come back!"

"Believe me," Grandma said. "I'm going."

Huddled next to the bottom bunk, Kendall heard Grandma walk past on her way to the guest room. Minutes later she came back, dragging her Rollaboard. She slammed the door as she left the house, without having exchanged another word with either Mommy or Randy.

A few minutes later, a brokenhearted Kendall climbed onto the bottom bunk next to Peter. With Grandma

Puckett also gone now, everything was lost. It would be just the two of them from here on—Kendall and Peter—against everyone else.

After a time, with Peter's warm body snuggled against hers, Kendall fell asleep, too.

CHAPTER 23

BY THE time Beth awakened the next morning, Jenny was already gone, but for the first time in weeks Beth felt rested and ravenously hungry. She went straight to the food court and treated herself to a huge breakfast. She had two back-to-back finals that day. When the second one was over, she felt as though she'd done well, which—considering how miserable the weekend had been—was pretty much miraculous.

She was trudging back to Conover Hall when a text came in on her phone. The phone had been in her pocket with the ringer turned to silent during the exams. She knew that other kids sometimes used their phones to cheat during tests, but Beth didn't. Feeling the familiar buzz in her pocket, she pulled the phone out—dreading that the incoming text might be from Ron while at the same time hoping that it would be. When she looked at the phone, however, she was surprised to see that the message was from Conrad Milton, a kid in her humanities class. In fact, he had waved at her a few minutes ago as she was leaving the room after finishing the test. She didn't know Conrad all that well. During the course of the semester, they'd shared class notes a couple of times, and that was the only reason he was in her contacts list. But when she read his message, she was beyond stunned.

Hey, there, Sweet Betsy from Pike. Thank you for
the guided tour. I never knew you were such a hot
mama. Care to go out sometime?

Horrified, Beth stood stock-still, as if frozen to the
ground, unable to comprehend the words she'd just read.
How could Conrad possibly know to call her Sweet
Betsy from Pike? And he had seen her "guided tour"?
That could only mean that Ron had sent Conrad the
photos—the ones that showed her naked body. Feeling
as though the phone were suddenly on fire, she pitched
it into the nearest snowbank.

The depths of Ron's betrayal momentarily robbed
Beth of the ability to breathe, leaving her close to faint-
ing dead away. As she stood there swaying, an older
gentleman, probably a professor of some kind, must
have noticed her distress.

"Excuse me, my dear," he said, approaching her with
concern written on his face. "Are you all right? Do you
need help?"

Beth shrank away from him with a look of abject
terror on her face, as if he were reaching out to drag
her into some dark abyss, as though he, too, a complete
stranger, had somehow seen her naked.

She turned and raced up the sidewalk and back to
Conover Hall, with tears streaming down her cheeks
and with her heart hammering in her chest. It was all
she could do to make the key work in order to enter the
room. Thank God, it was empty. Jenny wasn't there.

Beth threw herself facedown on the bed and lay there
sobbing. Gradually the sobs subsided as the terrible
truth dawned. She had defied Ron, and he'd struck back,

humiliating her in public in a way that robbed her of every shred of dignity.

How did Ron know Conrad Milton? Were they friends or acquaintances somehow? And how did Ron know that Beth and Conrad were connected? And then she figured it out. It was because of her phone and the contacts list in her phone. Ron was a cybersecurity expert. Somehow he must have gained access to her phone and to the information inside it. So had he sent copies of the video to everyone in her contacts list? To Jenny, even?

And if that were the case, how would Beth ever be able to look anyone she knew in the face without wondering if they'd seen the pictures, too?

For the first time in her life—for the first time ever—Beth Rankin wanted to die. She lay in bed for a long time after her tears finally abated, but she knew she couldn't stay there. She didn't want to be in the room when Jenny came back. She didn't want to face her. She didn't want to face anyone.

At last Beth stood up. She hadn't bothered removing either her jacket or her boots when she came in. She simply got off the bed and left. She took nothing with her, not even her purse. Like a wounded animal, she simply fled—first out of the room and then out of the dorm. She had no idea where she was going or what she would do when she got there. She simply knew she was leaving and she wasn't coming back.

CHAPTER 24

JORGE MORENO called Joanna before she made it as far as the Tucson city limits. "I've just spoken to Lyn Hogan," he said after introducing himself. "He tells me you'd like to speak to me and that you're coming to Tucson today."

"I am," she answered. "I need to pay a visit to one of my deputies at Banner Medical first, but I could drop by after that if it would be convenient."

"About two?" Jorge asked. "My office is on Broadway, in a low-rise between Alvernon and Swan." He gave her an address.

"Two it is," Joanna said. "See you then."

When Joanna arrived at Armando's room, the place was still awash in flowers, but the mood was decidedly less somber than it had been the last time she was there. Armando was actually eating lunch when she came in, and Amy, looking decidedly less stressed, greeted Joanna with a smile.

"You're looking a lot more chipper than you did on Saturday," Joanna said to Armando.

He nodded. "This is the first time they've given me actual food," he said. "Chicken noodle soup and red Jell-O may not sound especially appetizing to most people, but it feels like a feast to me."

"Still no signs of an infection," Amy put in. "The

203

doctors said that if he stays clear, he may be able to go home early next week."

Joanna understood that taking Armando home with a colostomy bag would be a challenging issue for everyone concerned, but the fact that he would be going home at all helped make the complexities fade into the background.

"I have some more good news for you," Joanna announced. "The DPS investigation has concluded. Based on their recommendations, Arlee Jones has declared that you fired in self-defense. That means the shooting is justifiable and you're in the clear."

"I may be in the clear, but Leon Hogan is still dead," Armando said bleakly. "And he's dead by my hand."

Joanna understood that, too. She also realized that the guilt of having taken another person's life was something that would stay with Armando Ruiz for the remainder of his days on earth. She hoped what she said next might lighten that burden, but it wouldn't erase it— nothing would.

"You may have pulled the trigger, but it's not your fault," Joanna said. She went on to explain the M.E.'s findings and the presumption that at the time of the shooting, Leon had been operating under the influence of scopolamine.

"I thought he was drunk out of his mind," Armando said when she finished.

"He was out of his mind," Joanna said. "He just wasn't drunk."

"So who drugged him, his wife?"

Joanna nodded. "We think she might have come there planning on killing him, but he ended up wresting the gun away from her."

"Can you prove it?"

"Not so far," Joanna said.

"So I end up killing the guy for her and getting shot while she gets away with murder?"

Joanna nodded again. "That's how it looks."

"I just found out from my friend Katie that the Hogan kids go to my school—to Carmichael," Amy interjected from her chair in the corner.

"Katie?" Joanna asked.

"Katie Baird," Amy said. "We both teach second grade. Kendall Hogan is in her class. From what Katie said, it sounds like the situation in the Hogan household is a bit of a mess."

"More than a bit," Joanna allowed, but she didn't say any more than that. She left a few minutes later. Casey Ledford called as Joanna headed back to her car in the parking garage.

"I've got news," Casey said.

Joanna recognized the excitement in her CSI's voice. "What kind?" she asked.

"After we learned about the scopolamine, I took another look at the contents of Madison Hogan's purse. It was collected from the crime scene, and I had previously inventoried what was inside it, but this morning I started to wonder about that scopolamine. If it turned up at Leon Hogan's residence, how did it get there?"

"And?"

"I remembered there was a bottle of over-the-counter eyedrops in the purse. On a hunch I ran an analysis, and guess what? No eyedrops—scopolamine."

"With Madison's fingerprints on the bottle, I hope?" Joanna asked.

"You've got it," Casey answered.

"So we might be able to get her on attempted homicide at least."

"And maybe even more," Casey said. "Deb's been talking to one of her pals over at the DEA. They've been keeping an eye on Madison's boyfriend, Randy Williams. He's suspected of being a small-time drug dealer with delusions of grandeur. He's in the process of attempting to set up a network with a cartel-related smuggler. The cartel guy is the one the DEA really wants to nail, so they've been keeping hands off as far as Randy is concerned. They're hoping we'll do the same."

"They expect us to just leave him alone?" Joanna demanded.

"That's what it sounds like."

"I happen to know Eugene Autry, the local DEA agent in charge," Joanna said. "He's based right here in Tucson. As soon as I finish up with my next appointment, I'll be dropping by Gene's office for a surprise visit."

She hurried into Jorge Moreno's office at the stroke of 2:00 P.M. The man who came out to the desk to greet her wore cowboy boots under a suit with a distinctly western cut. Joanna had known attorneys who assumed western attire in order to make a statement. She suspected that as far as Jorge and Lyn Hogan were concerned, they both dressed as cowboys because that's what they were, born and bred.

"I hope you don't mind," Jorge said as he ushered Joanna into a conference room. "Lyn Hogan asked me if he could be a part of what's being said here, and since he's paying my fees, that seemed only fair. I told him we'd put him on speaker."

Having Leon's father involved meant that Joanna wouldn't be able to discuss any of what she'd just learned from Casey, but that was all right. She was happy to forge ahead with what she had so far.

"I don't mind at all," she said. "I think we're all on the same page here. My primary concern is for the kids."

Jorge nodded seriously. "Mine, too," he said.

Once both Lyn and Izzy Hogan had been added to the mix via speakerphone, Jorge turned to Joanna. "So what do you want to know?" he asked.

"Our understanding is that Leon Hogan retained you to represent him in a custody fight connected to divorcing his wife, Madison."

Jorge nodded. "He came to me when he discovered that his wife was conducting an affair with someone he thought to be an especially unsavory character."

"Randy Williams?"

Jorge nodded again. "You're aware that after Leon married Madison, he went to court and adopted her kids?"

"Yes," Joanna said, "Peter and Kendall."

"Leon adored those kids from the start, but after he and Madison married, he started to see a whole other side to the woman."

"The violence, you mean?"

"He realized early on that she often lashed out at the kids, but he had no idea of the real extent of it. When he tried to tell her he thought she was being too hard on them, she turned on him instead."

"Hence the domestic-violence incidents," Joanna said.

"Those, but there's more to it than just that," Jorge

said. "Madison was working as a bartender at a bar when she and Leon first met."

"The Nite Owl?" Joanna asked.

Jorge opened a file folder that had been lying on the conference table when they entered. He shuffled through several pages. "Yes," he said. "That's it—the Nite Owl. At the time Madison told him that she was an occasional marijuana user, but eventually he figured out that her drug use was more serious than occasional—and not limited to marijuana either. He tried talking her into going into rehab. She refused. When Leon found out Madison was carrying on with a boyfriend behind his back while he was at work, that pretty much did it for Leon, especially after he heard rumors that Madison had lost her job and that Randy was pimping her out. Leon was desperate to get away from her, but he was worried sick about leaving Kendall and Peter stuck in that kind of mess."

Remembering what Deb had learned about Kendall's bullying situation at school, Joanna felt half sick. The neighborhood kid who'd been teasing her hadn't been wrong. Kendall's mother really was a whore—regardless of how you spelled it.

"I advised both Leon and my friend Lyn here that if Leon had any hope of gaining custody of those kids, we couldn't risk filing for a divorce until we had the goods on Madison. To that end I engaged the services of a private investigator—a Mr. Richard Voland. I believe you and he may have crossed paths at some time in the past."

Joanna could barely believe her ears. Her former chief deputy had been Leon Hogan's private eye?

"Yes," she said aloud. "Dick and I worked together for a number of years."

"Mr. Voland had been working behind the scenes to create a dossier on Madison Hogan and on her boyfriend, Randy Williams. By last week we had collected enough information about their activities that I thought we could move forward. I had expected to file within the next week or so, but then . . ." Jorge shrugged.

"But then Leon died."

Jorge nodded.

"So if you were intent on moving forward, you must have thought you had sufficient evidence to prove that Madison was an unfit mother."

"Not quite," Jorge said. "We were waiting on one more interview. Leon told us that the next-best person for us to talk to would be his mother-in-law, Jacqueline Puckett. Mr. Voland told me that she's currently in Sierra Vista and he's hoping to interview her sometime this afternoon. Depending on the results of that interview, it's my understanding that Lyn and Izzy here are prepared to go to court and sue for custody of the children."

Joanna was stunned. Grandparents going to court to declare their former daughter-in-law an unfit mother wasn't unheard of, but it would almost take an act of God for them to be granted full custody.

"Allegations against Madison are that serious?" Joanna asked.

"In my opinion," Jorge Moreno said, "the answer to that question is yes. Leon thought she neglected them— that she often left them unsupervised and didn't attend to their nutritional needs. Leon was the one who saw to it that they were vaccinated so they could enroll in school. Until he came along, neither Peter nor Kendall had ever seen a dentist. Then there was the situation with the dog."

"What dog?" Joanna asked.

"Leon had a bluetick hound. He loved the dog, but when he moved out, he left the animal with the kids because Peter loved the dog so much. The next time he came to pick up the kids, the dog was gone. The kids told him Coon got hit by a car and died. Leon thought Madison just got rid of it. And when you consider the unsavory characters she brought into the household on a regular basis . . ."

Shaking his head, Jorge fell silent. It was a moment before he spoke again. "Let me ask you a question, Sheriff Brady, and I fully understand if you're unable to answer, but do you think there's a chance that Madison Hogan played an active role in what happened to Leon—in the events that led up to his death?"

Suddenly Joanna found herself between a rock and a hard place. Jorge Moreno had been more than accommodating, but he was asking a direct question about what was now an ongoing investigation. She could refuse to answer entirely, or she could hedge. She opted for the latter.

"It's possible," she said.

"And would the motive by any chance have had anything to do with the death benefits she expected to receive from Leon's life insurance?"

"That might be a good bet," Joanna replied. "We know from questioning one of Leon's former co-workers that Madison spoke to the employer's HR department just yesterday inquiring about proceeding with a death claim."

"Already?" Jorge asked.

"The very next day after Leon's death."

That statement was followed by another silence, a longer one this time. Finally Jorge heaved a heartfelt sigh. "I'm so sorry, Lyn," the attorney said, addressing the Hogans listening in on the speakerphone rather than Joanna. "This is all my fault."

For a moment a puzzled Joanna looked back and forth between the desk phone and the attorney. "How could that be?" she asked.

"I'm the one who advised Leon to change his beneficiary designation. He asked if he should tell Madison about it. I told him no, that for the time being he should just let that sleeping dog lie. But it would appear I was wrong about that. If he'd told her, Madison would have known she'd have nothing to gain by killing him, and maybe Leon would still be alive."

Joanna could see that Jorge Moreno was hurting. She wanted to comfort him and to comfort Mr. and Mrs. Hogan as well.

"That might or might not be true, Mr. Moreno," she said quietly. "Unfortunately, crystal balls are currently in short supply."

Half an hour after leaving Jorge Moreno's office, Joanna was seated across the desk from DEA Agent in Charge Eugene Autry. He was a careworn fiftysomething who didn't seem overjoyed to have the sheriff of Cochise County visiting his office. Aware from other sources that the man had suffered a lifetime's worth of teasing as a result of his mother's enduring fan worship of the "Singing Cowboy," Joanna was kind enough not to pile on.

"What can I do for you, Sheriff Brady?" he asked.

"This is actually a courtesy call," she said. "One of my homicide investigations is about to intersect with one of your cases, and I wanted to be sure we're all on the same page."

"What case would that be?" he asked.

"Randy Williams," she answered.

She could just as well have set off an M-80 in the middle of his office. The man actually blinked. Eugene Autry would never have made it as a poker player. Too bad for him—Joanna had been playing serious poker for years.

"Obviously, I can't comment on ongoing cases," he said, which was in fact an outright admission that there *was* an ongoing case. "What homicide?" he added a moment later.

"You may have heard about our officer-involved shooting last week," Joanna said casually, "one in which a man named Leon Hogan was killed in a shoot-out with one of my deputies. The late Mr. Hogan and his estranged wife, Madison, were involved in a contentious divorce. I've just come from the divorce attorney's office. While investigating the wife's background, a private eye turned up the fact that she has an ongoing relationship with a Mr. Randall J. Williams. He also learned about your behind-the-scenes interest in Mr. Williams's . . . shall we say . . . activities?"

"Who's this private investigator?" Autry wanted to know.

Joanna forced herself to stifle a smile, but turnabout was fair play. "As you know," she repeated, "I can't comment on ongoing investigations."

"So why are you here, then?" Autry asked.

"If you want to keep your involvement with Williams under wraps, we need to work together. Your call. My investigation is moving forward regardless, and his connections to the drug trade will be out in public for all to see." With that, Joanna stood up and made as if to leave.

"Wait," Autry said. "Sit."

Joanna sat.

Autry took a deep breath. "I'm well aware that Randy Williams is the scum of the earth," he said, "but in this business occasionally we end up having to work with guys like that."

"You're using him as a confidential informant?" Joanna asked.

Autry nodded.

Joanna's Cochise County included eighty miles of U.S.-Mexico border. She understood that the DEA was trying to plug the holes that allowed illicit drugs to pour across that border. She also understood that having a CI inside the cartel-related drug scene could do a lot to interrupt the flow. But right now two innocent little kids were caught up in this drama as well.

"Okay," she said. "All cards on the table. I'm aware that Williams has the potential of turning into a valuable asset for you, but I'm here to serve notice. If he is somehow connected to our homicide, we're going after him full tilt. Do I make myself clear?"

There was a long pause. Finally Eugene nodded his assent. "Do what you have to do, Sheriff Brady," he said. "Let the chips fall where they may."

"Fair enough," Joanna replied, rising to her feet. "Thank you."

She left his office feeling considerably taller than five-four. She was a small-town sheriff who had just told the feds to back off, and wonder of wonders they had!

CHAPTER 25

WHEN JENNY finished with her final, she went back to Conover Hall and was relieved to see that Beth wasn't in the room. She had at least one final that day, maybe two. Jenny didn't remember how many exactly, but that's probably where she was. Outside, the weather was clear, yet warm enough that some of the accumulated snow was starting to melt.

With her last final still several days away, Jenny decided that spending some time outside was better than being locked up inside, so she put on riding clothes and headed off to see Maggie. The horse-boarding facility Jenny and several other rodeo-team members utilized for both boarding and training was on the Lazy 8 Ranch, located several miles out of town, partway between Flagstaff and Munds Park. There were barns and stables for boarding, along with both indoor and outdoor arenas for practice. The Lazy 8 was also home to Equine Helpers, a horse-therapy program for special-needs kids. In order to accommodate their activities, during the winter the ranch maintained a network of snowplowed trails that allowed less capable riders to enjoy wintertime riding adventures.

Jenny and Maggie spent the better part of two hours doing barrel-racing practice runs in the indoor arena. At the end of practice, though, sensing that Maggie

was restless after being cooped up for so long, Jenny
stripped off the saddle and the two of them ventured out
into the still-snowy landscape. Giving Maggie her head,
the two of them trotted along at a distance-eating gait
for close to half an hour.

Jenny loved being out in the snowy quiet with her
horse. It was exactly the break she needed from the
pressure of finals and the continuing drama with Beth.
When it was time to reverse directions, Maggie was
ready to go at a full gallop. Only toward the end did
Jenny pull the horse back to a cool-down walking pace.

Once in the barn, Jenny was delighted to run into
Nick Saunders, her best friend on the rodeo team. Nick
and his coal-black gelding, Dexter, were standing outside the horse's stall, where Nick was giving Dex a thorough grooming. Jenny slipped off Maggie and prepared
to brush her down as well.

"How're you doing, Saras," Jenny called over Dexter's
back.

"Sponda," Nick replied with a grin.

Nick, a junior at NAU, hailed from St. George, Utah,
originally. His mother, Lorene, was a widow in her
early sixties. His father, Marvin, a big-animal vet and
once a prizewinning bull rider in his own right, had
died of a heart ailment when Nick was a senior in high
school. When Nick was offered a rodeo scholarship to
NAU, the family jumped at the chance. And no matter
where the competitions occurred, you could count on
Lorene to be there in her camper with her two feisty
Pekingese along to keep her company.

Lorene was not just a fan, she was the team's volun-
teer den mother. The door to her RV was always open,

and she always had a pot of stew or soup available for hungry team members in need of sustenance. The first time Jenny met Lorene had been over a plateful of spaghetti covered with mouth-watering meat sauce at the table in the RV's tiny kitchen. In the course of the meal, Jenny and Lorene discovered a bit of common ground—they'd both been involved in Girl Scouts, Lorene as a troop leader and Jenny as a Scout.

By the time dinner ended, they were sitting at the table singing rousing versions of songs they'd learned at troop meetings and camp-outs—"Girl Scouts Together," "My Hat, It Has Three Corners," "White Coral Bells," "Kookaburra Sits in the Old Gum Tree." Much to their mutual surprise, they both loved the same round, which featured the lyric "Sarasponda, ret, set, set." By the time Jenny and Lorene finished belting it out together, Nick loved it, too.

Between Nick and Jenny, one of the nonsense words from the song became a traditional greeting between them. It was like a secret handshake, a code none of the other team members had so far been able to decipher.

"Cold enough for you?" Nick asked.

"Better than it was," Jenny said, slipping down to the ground. "I'm tired of being locked up inside, and so is Maggie."

"How are finals going?" Nick asked.

"Almost over. One to go—sociology—and that isn't until Friday."

"Want to grab a burger on the way home?"

"Sure," she said, "if you don't mind waiting until I finish grooming and feeding Maggie."

He didn't mind. There was a café in Munds Park that was popular with the rodeo set, and that's where they went for dinner. It was after dark by the time Jenny got back to Conover Hall. When she stepped into the room, she was surprised that the lights were off and no one was home. That was unlike Beth. She wasn't someone who hung out with friends. If she wasn't in class, she was usually in their room. Looking around, Jenny noticed that Beth's purse was there, so she must not have gone far. Maybe she was just down the hall doing laundry.

Jenny showered and pulled on the pair of sweats she usually wore as pajamas. She settled down on her bed and stared at her class notes for sociology. No matter how hard she tried, nothing seemed to penetrate, because by now a niggle of worry was starting to form in her head. Time slowed to a crawl. Her eyes kept going from her notes to the clock on her bedside table, which was now showing 7:46. Still no Beth. She wouldn't be doing laundry this long, so where was she? Since her purse was in the room, was it possible she was still in the dorm? Maybe she was really hanging out with friends, but did Beth Rankin have friends? Jenny didn't know of any.

Jenny's mind kept returning to how upset Beth had been over the weekend—upset but unwilling or else unable to talk about it. Was it a problem with the boyfriend, or was it part of the continuing problem with her mother? Jenny had no idea about that, either.

Picking up her phone, Jenny dialed Beth's number. It rang several times before going to voice mail. *"Beth here. I'm unable to take your call right now. Please leave a message."*

Jenny did so. "Hey, Beth, I'm back in the room. Where are you? Give me a call."

Hanging up, Jenny looked around the room again. There was nothing out of the ordinary and there was no sign of any disturbance. Beth's laptop sat on the desk where it belonged. Except for her down jacket and boots, her clothing all hung in the closet. Her makeup laid out on the counter in their shared bathroom was undisturbed.

Telling herself she was just being silly, Jenny finally gave up trying to study and turned on her small television set, more for the company than to actually watch anything. A cop show was just coming on. Jenny didn't watch enough TV these days to know where it was set, what the storyline was, or even who was starring in it, but as the credits rolled, she found herself thinking about her mother.

Years ago her mother had mentioned the abbreviation JDLR—cop shorthand for "just doesn't look right."

"Whenever that happens," Mom had told her daughter, "it's time to pay attention to your instincts, because if something inside you is telling you something is wrong, maybe it is."

And that's what this is, too, Jenny thought. *It just doesn't look right.* That's when she remembered her last conversation with her mother. Mom had said that if Jenny was worried about what was going on with Beth, maybe it was time to reach out to the boyfriend in order to get to the bottom of it.

Over the course of the evening, Jenny had tried Beth's number several times, always with the same result. Just after nine thirty, she tried again one last time while walking to Beth's desk. Again there was no answer, and by now Jenny's small tweak of worry had grown a lot more serious. Maybe something really was wrong.

Initially her plan was to log on to Beth's computer and locate Ron Cameron's name in the contacts list. But then Jenny remembered something else.

Earlier in the fall, shortly after Beth had purchased her new laptop, she'd been sitting outside one afternoon enjoying the crisp fall weather when her phone had slipped out of her jacket. When she finally noticed that the phone was missing, Jenny had shown her how to use her computer's Find My Phone app to do just that. A few minutes later, they'd located the missing phone, lying in the grass exactly where it had fallen. Dismissing the idea of talking to Ron, Jenny decided to go looking for the phone instead.

When Beth had first purchased both her phone and her computer all those months ago, she'd been completely inexperienced in their use and had turned to Jenny for help. Jenny had aided her roommate in setting up her devices, including creating accounts and establishing the necessary collection of passwords. Worried about possibly forgetting passwords, Beth—against Jenny's advice—had written all of them down on a single Post-it, which she kept in the top drawer of the desk.

That night Jenny was supremely grateful Beth had disregarded her password-protection advice. With the Post-it in hand, Jenny typed in the laptop's log-in code. On the start-up screen, Jenny noticed that Beth had eighty-seven new message notifications and thirty-five new e-mails. That seemed excessive, but intent on something else, Jenny ignored them. Instead she went straight to Finder, located the Find My Phone app, and turned it on.

Moments later the app had pinpointed the location

of the missing phone, marking a spot on a map with a pulsing green light. Jenny was able to expand the map until she could see that the phone had to be right there on campus, probably within a matter of blocks of Conover Hall. Had Beth tripped and fallen? Jenny wondered. Was she lying unnoticed in a snowbank somewhere nearby, unconscious and possibly freezing to death?

Desperate to find Beth before it was too late, Jenny pulled on her boots, grabbed her coat and the laptop, and raced from the room. Using her own phone as a Wi-Fi hotspot and carrying the open laptop in her arms, she headed out of the dorm and marched purposefully across campus, keeping an eye on the moving red dot on the computer screen as she went.

Eventually the red dot on the computer and the green dot came together as one. Looking around, Jenny saw nothing—no sign of Beth and no sign of her phone either.

Standing on a stretch of cleared sidewalk and hoping to be able to hear the phone ring, Jenny dialed Beth's number again. There was no sound, but when she looked around, she saw a small pink glow pulsing just under the topmost layer of icy snow.

Pawing through the pile, Jenny quickly located the phone and dug it out. When she looked at the glowing screen, she discovered there were now ninety-three new messages and fifty-four notifications. Was there a chance one of those might offer a clue as to Beth's whereabouts? Joanna had brought the password Post-it along. Digging it out of her pocket, she keyed the proper code into the phone. Once logged on, she went straight to Messages, where she opened the first one, from someone named Calvin. What she read there made no sense, so she opened the next one. That one came complete with photos, and as soon as she saw the first image, Jennifer Brady realized she had just stepped into a cyber nightmare.

CHAPTER 26

IT WAS almost ten o'clock at night. The kids were in bed, and the kitchen was clean as well. Over the course of the evening, Butch had made two batches of candy—fudge and divinity. "I can bake cookies in a crowd," he had told Joanna, "but making candy is a solo operation."

Now they were seated in the beautifully decorated warmth of their living room enjoying glasses of wine and a bit of adult conversation.

"So you took on the DEA and scored a win," Butch said. "Who'da thunk it?"

Joanna smiled back at him. "Indeed."

"So what's next?"

"We need to figure out if Williams had anything to do with Madison's showing up at Leon's house prepared to knock him off. We might not be able to get either one of them on an attempted-murder charge, but conspiracy to commit might do the trick. Now that we know scopolamine was involved, I think that increases the chances that Randy was in on it, too."

"That he was possibly the supplier?"

"Possibly," Joanna agreed. "The problem is proving it."

Joanna's phone rang. A call at this hour of the night usually meant a callout of some kind, so she gave her wineglass a wary look as she set it down and reached for her cell. When Jenny's face showed in caller ID, Joanna felt a wave of relief.

"Hey there, daughter of mine," she said cheerfully, switching the phone to speaker. "What's up?"

"Oh, Mom," Jenny blubbered into the phone. "It's awful. I don't know what to do."

Relief turned instantly to alarm. "What's the matter, Jen?" Joanna asked as her motherly mind sorted through a list of dreadful possibilities. "Dad and I are both here," she added. "You're on speaker. What's going on? Are you hurt? Did you have an accident?"

"It's Beth," Jenny sobbed.

Beth, Joanna thought. *Thank goodness it's not you.* Aloud, she said. "What's happened to her? Is she all right? Is she hurt?"

"I don't know if she's hurt or not. She's missing, Mom. I came home and she wasn't in the room. I've been calling all night long, and there's no answer. I finally used the Find My Phone app. I found her phone and not her, but what's on the phone is so terrible—" Jenny broke off and sobbed even more.

"What's on the phone?" Butch asked quietly. "Tell us."

There was a long pause before Jenny was able to gather herself enough to speak coherently. "She had close to two hundred messages—some texts and some e-mails—on the phone when I picked it up. There are more now, way more. They keep coming in all the time."

"What kind of messages?" Butch asked.

"A bunch of them show pictures of Beth," Jenny answered at last. "Naked pictures of her. Some of them show pictures of the men writing to her, and they're mostly naked, too. The messages are all addressed to 'Sweet Betsy from Pike,' and the things they're saying are so ugly, so gross—" Jenny broke off again. "I've heard people talk about sexting, but this is the first time I've seen it. I can't even say how awful it is."

"But if Beth is missing," Joanna said, slightly changing the subject, "when did you last see her?"

"This morning," Jenny answered, seeming to get a grip. "She was still asleep when I left for my final. She had two of them today. When I came home this afternoon, she wasn't there, but I didn't think anything about it. I went down to the Lazy 8 to ride for a while. Then I met up with Nick, and we had something to eat. When I came home tonight, Beth still wasn't in our room, but her purse was. I thought maybe she was doing laundry or hanging out with someone here at the dorm, but the longer I went without hearing from her and without her answering the phone, the more I started to worry. Finally I decided to go looking for her phone."

"Where did you find it?"

"Right here where I'm standing—in the middle of campus."

"Have you called the cops?"

"Not yet."

"You need to," Joanna said. "You need to notify the campus police right now before you go back to your room. You'll need to show them exactly where you found the phone because there might be other evidence there besides just that to tell them what happened. Call them first, and then call us back."

"You're sure the photos are of Beth?" Butch asked.

"I'm sure."

"How do you know?"

"Because of the tattoo," Jenny said. "At Thanksgiving her mother had a cow because Beth was using a cell phone. If she'd seen the tattoo she would have gone bananas."

"What kind of tattoo?" Joanna asked.

"I ♥ Ron with red ink in the heart," Jenny answered. "It's on her left breast. She showed it to me right after she got it. She was beyond proud."

"I'll just bet she was," Joanna said with a sigh. "Make that call now and then get back to us."

"Okay," Jenny said uncertainly.

"And don't worry," Butch added, attempting to reassure her. "I'm sure it's going to be all right."

"I don't think so," Jenny replied, "but I'm hanging up now."

For several moments after the call ended, Butch and Joanna sat in stunned silence. "I'm guessing it's the boyfriend," Butch said. "She shared nude pictures of herself with him. Then, when their romance hit a bump in the road, he shipped them off to a porn site."

"And not just the photos," Joanna replied. "He must have sent along her contact information as well."

"Contemptible!" Butch muttered.

"It's also against the law," Joanna said. "This is called sextortion. There was a panel on this at the last sheriff's conference I attended. Not only is this kind of extortion illegal, it's also dangerous. Most of the time, the victims are young and female, and many of them end up so ashamed that they commit suicide."

"So what do we do?" Butch asked.

"I happen to know that the FBI has a task force working on this. I'm calling Robin."

Robin was FBI Special Agent Robin Watkins. Several

years earlier she had gotten crosswise with one or more of the higher-ups in the D.C. office and had found herself banished to the hinterlands. From the hallowed halls of the J. Edgar Hoover building, Tucson might have looked like the back of the beyond and a suitable exile for someone regarded as an uppity female who needed to be brought down a peg. Unfortunately for them, Robin had taken to the Sonoran Desert like a duck to water. She and Joanna had worked together several times in the past, and Joanna had no compunction about calling at what many would have regarded as an inappropriate hour.

"What's up?" Robin asked cheerfully once she realized who was on the phone.

In as few words as possible, Joanna brought Robin up to speed. "All right, then," Robin said when Joanna finished laying out the situation. "If the boyfriend is in D.C. and the girl is in Flagstaff, thanks to the Internet this has already crossed state lines. I know some of the people working on these kinds of cases. I'll put them in touch with the campus cops at NAU. And give me Jenny's cell number, too. I'm sure they'll want to talk to her as well."

As Joanna finished giving Robin the number, Jenny called back, and once again Joanna put her on speaker. This time Jenny seemed to be more in control than she'd been earlier.

"I'm back in the room," she said. "When the cops showed up, they told me to come back here and wait for a detective to come interview me while they search the scene. But before they got there, I looked at the contacts list in Beth's phone, and it's really weird. There's no listing in her phone for a Ron or Ronald Cameron—

none at all. If he's Beth's boyfriend, why wouldn't he be in her contacts?"

"That is weird," Joanna agreed.

"While I was at it, I looked back through her call history. There are calls almost every night, right around midnight, lasting an hour or more, but they're always from a blocked number. And those are always incoming calls, not outgoing ones. It's as though Ron always calls her and she never calls him."

"That sounds pretty one-sided."

"Hey, Jen," Butch said from the background. "Do you still have that backup drive I gave you?"

"I have it," Jen replied, "but I haven't used it. Why?"

"The cops took Beth's phone, right?"

"Of course."

"Once the detective gets there, he's going to take her computer, too. But before he does, make a clone of her computer. Robin may be calling in the big guns from the FBI, but there might be a snippet on there, some detail that only someone who knows Beth well will be able to recognize. If that's the case, you might be able to help."

"Is that legal?" Jenny asked.

Joanna was the one who answered. "You had access to her computer and to her passwords, right?"

"Right."

"I doubt that would constitute an illegal search. Go ahead and make the copy."

"All right," Jenny said. "It'll take a few minutes, but I'm on it."

CHAPTER 27

JENNY DID her best, but before she was able to connect the external hard drive to Beth's computer, someone knocked on the door. When she opened it, a man and a woman—both clearly police officers—stood in the corridor displaying their badges. "Did you find her?" Jenny demanded.

The woman shook her head. "We have not," she said. "Are you Jennifer Brady?"

Jenny nodded.

"I'm Detective Ava Hunter and this is Detective Hank Weatherby with the Flagstaff Police Department. May we come in?"

Jenny stepped aside and allowed them to enter. "It's cold and it's dark out there," a worried Jenny said. "Where can she be?"

The woman helped herself to a seat while her partner loomed in the doorway. "We have people out searching," Detective Hunter said. "So far there's no sign of her. We're in the process of bringing in a K-9 unit. Would you happen to have a piece of Beth's clothing available?"

Rather than answer, Jenny retrieved Beth's pajamas from a hook just inside the closet door and handed them over. Detective Hunter passed them along to her partner, who took them and left the room without another word. Meanwhile Ava Hunter, preparing to take notes, retrieved an iPad from her purse and turned it on.

"We understand you're the one who located Beth's phone and reported her missing," Detective Hunter continued. "Is that true?"

Jenny nodded again. "I used an app on her computer to locate her phone."

"You have access to her computer?" Ava asked.

Jenny nodded. "I helped Beth set it up. She keeps all her passwords in her desk drawer." Still wearing her coat, Jenny pulled the crumpled Post-it out of her pocket and handed it over.

"So you and Beth are friends, then?" Detective Hunter asked.

"Roommates more than friends, I suppose," Jenny said. "Beth doesn't seem to have many friends. But I saw the pictures on her phone," Jenny added. "They were utterly vile, and they went out to all kinds of people, including names from her contacts list. I think Beth was too embarrassed to face anybody who might have seen them, and that's why she ran away."

"You think she ran away as opposed to being taken?"

"Wouldn't you?" Jenny asked. "I'm sure I would."

Detective Hunter made no reply to that. "You're sure the photos involved are of Beth Rankin?"

"I'm sure," Jenny said. "I recognize the tattoo."

"So who do you think took them?" Detective Hunter asked. "Her boyfriend, maybe?"

Jenny shook her head. "I think they're all selfies, and they were probably taken right here in our bathroom. Her boyfriend lives in D.C. I don't believe they've ever met face-to-face."

"The boyfriend's name?"

"Ronald Cameron. Beth calls him Ron."

"How long have they been . . . involved?" Detective Hunter asked.

"Since right after school started," Jenny replied. "They met online on one of those dating sites. I don't think Beth had ever had a boyfriend before."

"What does Ron do?"

"I'm not sure," Jenny answered. "I believe it's something to do with cybersecurity. I don't know if he works for a government agency or for someone else. He calls her almost every night, usually in the middle of the night when they can talk in private, but there's something weird about that. While I was waiting for the campus cops, I looked at her phone history. The incoming calls are there, but no outgoing ones, and there's no name or phone number associated with any of them. Also there's no number for Ron in Beth's contacts list. In fact, there's no listing for him at all."

"When was the last time you saw Beth?" Detective Hunter asked.

"This morning. She was still asleep when I left for a final. When I came home the first time, she wasn't here, and I didn't think anything about it because she had finals today, too. When I got back later this evening, her purse was here. . . ."

"It wasn't here earlier?"

"No, so I thought she might be somewhere in the dorm, maybe visiting someone or doing laundry, but then, as it got later and later, I started to worry."

"Why?"

"Because I was afraid she might have done something to hurt herself," Jenny answered. "She'd had a terrible weekend. I'm pretty sure she and Ron are in the process of breaking up, and she's taking it really hard. In fact, I was going to try calling Ron to ask him straight out about what was going on, but that's when I remembered the Find My Phone app, so I did that instead—I went looking for her phone."

Detective Weatherby returned looking decidedly unhappy and spoke briefly to his partner, whispering something in Detective Hunter's ear.

Scowling, she turned back to Jenny. "Your mother is Sheriff Brady from Cochise County?"

Jenny nodded.

"And you already spoke to her about this before you spoke to us?"

"She's my mother," Jenny said, pointing out the obvious. "Why wouldn't I talk to her?"

Detective Hunter turned off the iPad and stowed it in her purse. "Well," she sniffed, "it would appear that she's run the situation up the flagpole to someone at the FBI, and they're evidently taking over the cyber part of the investigation. We'll still be trying to locate Beth, but that's it. The feds will be doing the forensic analysis of Beth's devices, but we've been advised to take them into custody. So tell us, please, which of those two computers belongs to her?"

Jenny's and Beth's virtually identical computers sat side by side on Jenny's desk. Jenny retrieved the latter and handed it over. Clearly Detective Hunter was pissed about this turn of events. She took Beth's computer and stalked from the room without a word of thanks and without bothering to say good-bye either.

It was close to eleven when the detectives departed, leaving Jenny alone. She crawled into bed, not because

she expected to fall asleep but because she needed the
comforting warmth of her covers. She lay there in her
cocoon of blankets and thought about Beth Rankin outside and alone in the frigid cold and dark. It was enough
to leave Jennifer Brady feeling empty and broken.

CHAPTER 28

MOST OF Gerard Paine's neighbors in the town houses along West Placita Del Correcaminos in Tucson's Starr Pass neighborhood were retirees who spent their daytime hours playing golf or tennis or bingo or bridge. He did not. They walked or jogged or rode bikes. He did not. They did their shopping at grocery stores. He ordered most of his goods online, including some fresh items he had delivered from a local Safeway. They had pals and friendships. He was a loner.

They were all married or widowed or divorced. He was divorced, but if asked, he claimed to be a lifelong bachelor, because he didn't want to be cornered into mentioning the specific reasons behind his very rancorous divorce. Some of his neighbors were snowbirds who were half-time Arizona residents and half-time somewhere else. They all wore their home state's sports teams' colors and drove cars with out-of-state license plates. If asked, Gerard claimed he came from Tornado Alley—without specifying where—because he hated tornadoes. He didn't mention his years of teaching school in Oklahoma City because someone might have looked into the history of just why Gerard Paine had left the Sooner State with his tail between his legs.

So his fifty-five-plus neighbors lived their lives during daylight hours, while he inhabited the night shift. While

233

they did their Google searches with Safari or Duck-
DuckGo or Firefox, Gerard was a denizen of Tor and
the dark web. If his neighbors were good, Gerard was
evil.

His two-bedroom condo had once belonged to his
mother. Bernice Paine, a social butterfly and a killer
at bridge, had maintained an open-door policy with
round-the-clock guests and out-of-town visitors. Once
she passed away and Gerard moved in to take her place,
that open door slammed shut. Other than delivery
people, no one came or went from his door—absolutely
no one—and even the folks from UPS and FedEx never
ventured any farther than his front porch.

Gerard Paine was a recluse, and he liked it that way.
Obviously, he had enough money. Every two years he
leased a new Lexus that he barely drove, but as far as
anyone could tell, those biyearly new cars were his only
extravagance. He didn't travel. He was not a cruiser. He
was an odd duck, enough so that people were more than
happy to leave him alone.

Had anyone ventured inside his home, they would
have been astonished and probably more than a bit
puzzled by the sheer amount of computer equipment
scattered throughout. The kitchen and master bedroom
were relatively free of electronics, but every other
available space in the house was covered with either
computers, scanners, or printers. The walls were filled
with outsize monitors and screens. For Gerard the over-
whelming tech presence made perfect sense because,
as far as he was concerned, that's where he lived his
life—in those computers and on those screens.

There were plenty of people outside the immediate neighborhood who knew of his computer presence.

Some thought they knew him, or at least a version of him. For Beth Rankin in Flagstaff, he was Ronald Cameron of Washington, D.C. For Teresa Talbot in Fort Wayne, Indiana, he was Carl Draper, an IT guy from San Diego, California. For Samantha Toon of Billings, Montana, he was Leonard Cooper, a cybersecurity expert from Tampa, Florida. He was all of those and many more. What he really did for a living—his real life's work—was to run one of the most successful porn sites on the planet.

Once upon a time, he'd been an elementary-school music teacher, but then the world of coding had come along. His school district wanted to move with the times, and they'd paid for him to go back to school and study computer science. In the process they created a new computer-science instructor who, as it turned out, was also a computer-science monster.

Once news about his after-school dalliances with various students came to light, the school district let him go, doing so quietly in hopes of avoiding unwanted publicity, to say nothing of unwanted lawsuits. But then his wife found out about it. Once her accusations surfaced in public divorce proceedings, the jig had been up all around—and the lawsuits had returned with a vengeance.

Legal maneuvering had kept him out of jail but it was no wonder he was living quietly in Tucson and keeping himself out of the limelight in every way possible.

These days, at any one time, he had ten or more women on the hook to a greater or lesser degree. The younger they were and the more naïve, the easier they were to manipulate. He lied to them and cheated on them with impunity while at the same time demanding complete loyalty and absolute obedience on their part. And if they balked in any way—if they so much as hinted about stepping out of line—he dropped the hammer on them. By the time Gerard finished, most of them were too humiliated to even think about coming forward and speaking with the authorities. Had they attempted to do so, he was quite sure that his dark web–based identity was safely beyond reach.

When he first encountered Elizabeth Rankin the previous September, she was so incredibly unsophisticated that she could just as well have been gift-wrapped and dropped into his lap straight out of the fifties. In his opinion the name Elizabeth was a bit too highfalutin for a girl like that, and Beth went too far in the other direction. "Sweet Betsy from Pike" was a song he'd enjoyed teaching to his former elementary-school students. As far as Gerard was concerned, the name Betsy seemed to have just the right ring to it.

Until last night he'd had no idea that name was so offensive to his now-testy little victim, but it was, and when she'd suddenly turned on him in such a venomous fashion, that was it. Gerard Paine didn't nickel/dime around. He wasn't one of those people who would turn the other cheek or hang in long enough for a snake to strike at him twice. He didn't give Betsy a chance to come begging him to forgive her, not that he would have anyway. Instead, within a matter of hours, he dropped the bomb.

After all, he finally had the photos—ones it had taken months to wheedle out of her. And with the key-logger he'd installed on both her phone and her computer, he knew everything there was to know about Beth Rankin's online activities. He had access to her contacts list, and that was the first place he sent the album of nude photos—to everyone listed there. And then he sent the album to his own mailing list as well. His customer base of dues-paying members were happy to send him money as long as, from time to time, he sent them suitably explicit material to be enjoyed and savored in the privacy of their own homes.

The night before, he'd been a little surprised at the way Betsy had blown up at him, but it was time. She was supposedly very smart as far as things like chemistry and physics were concerned, but on a personal basis she was boring as hell, and he was happy to be rid of her.

Once Gerard finished with one of his many victims and turned his pack of pet jackals loose on them, he always savored the aftermath. Some of the girls reacted with helpless fury, while others vowed revenge. But the ones he enjoyed the very most were the ones who cried out their grief to friends and relations. He savored the ones who pleaded for him to take them back or who tried to gain direct access to him in hopes of forcing him to pull their damning images from the site. Not that he ever did. Once he had those photos in his possession, they belonged to him and to the world.

It had taken until five o'clock in the morning before he'd had everything in place to eviscerate Beth Rankin. Once he had done so, he went to bed and to sleep, expecting to spend this evening enjoying whatever radioactive fallout would be forthcoming. He fully imagined she would be one of the begging ones. Much to his astonishment, however, when evening came around, there was nothing from Beth—not a single word, not on her phone and not on her computer. If she was sharing her despair over what had happened, she wasn't doing it by text or e-mail, and her absolute silence on the subject was baffling. Never before, not once, had one of his victims gone completely quiet on him. He wanted a reaction—that was his reward. In this case he got nothing.

Gerard could see on his monitors that responses to the posted photos were still coming in on both her computer and to her phone. Between texts and e-mails, there were more than three hundred new notifications, but only one of those had actually been opened and read—a text from one of Beth's fellow students at NAU. After that she'd evidently lost interest and quit looking.

Gerard had other urgent pieces of business that required his attention, including several of those other members of what he liked to call his "Ladies of the Night." He had to maintain certain levels of cybersurveillance on each of them and supply the necessary doses of attention and input, but between times he kept switching back to Betsy. Hours passed, but whenever he checked, there was still nothing. Then, a little after nine, an alarm alerted him to the fact that Beth's computer had just flashed on. The problem is, it had come on with the Find My Phone app activated.

Gerard immediately switched to the computer's onboard camera. With that feed going to a separate monitor, he was able to use two screens to view whatever function the computer was currently performing as well as the face of the person operating the keyboard. Gerard fully expected to see Betsy's anguished face in one of them, but he didn't. Instead he saw what appeared to be a close-up of some kind of material—a jacket, perhaps. And rather than being stationary on a desk or a tabletop, the computer seemed to be moving—first down a corridor and then outside into the dark, where there were occasional flashes of light from streetlamps.

On the computer's screen side, there were two pulsing lights—a green one that didn't move and a red one that did, with the moving one gradually closing the distance between the two. No wonder Betsy had gone quiet. Obviously, she'd somehow lost her phone during the course of the day and was now using her computer to locate it.

Then, after close to half an hour of steady movement, it stopped, with the red dot almost on top of the green one. As the computer was placed on the ground, the face of the person carrying it appeared on the screen for only the briefest of moments. That one glimpse sent a shock wave through Gerard Paine's body as he realized that the person who'd been carrying and operating Betsy's computer wasn't her at all. It was someone else entirely—Betsy's roommate, Jennifer Brady.

For the next several minutes, Gerard waited and watched in stunned silence. Then another alarm sounded behind him as Betsy's phone came to life. Turning to that monitor, he saw droplets of water lingering on the face of the phone, as though the device had been left out in the rain—or maybe in the snow. And once again it was that other face, Jennifer Ann Brady's, peering back at him.

Gerard watched with some concern as Jennifer manipulated the phone. First she searched through the letter C in Betsy's contacts list. Gerard had no doubt that she was searching for the name Ron Cameron. When she came up crickets on that, she began scrolling though Betsy's phone history as well. And then, suddenly, the phone went dark—totally and completely dark—and it didn't come back on. Moments after that the computer switched off as well.

For the first time since he'd been doing this, Gerard Paine was concerned. He didn't know where Beth was, but Jennifer Ann Brady, the interfering daughter of a small-town sheriff from Hicksville, Arizona, was now nosing around in his business. Gerard was sure it was due to Jennifer's unwanted influence that Betsy from Pike had rebelled. He'd been close to done with Betsy, but he was sure she would have been good for at least a few more provocative photos. He had invested a lot of time and effort in bringing her along, and those missing photos would make for a dip in Gerard's bottom line. It was a loss that Jennifer Brady was destined to pay for, one way or the other.

But first he turned his attention to wreaking a bit of revenge on Betsy herself. Maybe she thought that by simply ignoring him she'd be immune, but that wasn't true. He knew all about her prudish parents. She'd spent hours on the phone bewailing her relationship with both of them, especially her mother. With a certain amount of glee, Gerard set about sending Kenneth and Madeline Rankin a care package. He'd been surprised to find no listing for Betsy's parents in her contacts list, and there was nothing in her e-mail or texting history to indicate they had any online presence. As a result there was no way to gift them with a digital copy of their daughter's nude photo album. That meant he would be forced to send them hard copies of the photos by snail mail.

He used latex gloves to put together an envelope containing glossy eight-by-ten copies of their daughter's degrading see-all poses as well as a printed note that said, "Please enjoy your daughter's first photo shoot. I think she has quite a career ahead of her." Next Gerard set to work locating a physical address for Kenneth and Madeline Rankin, and that took time. Once he'd done so and addressed the envelope, he applied self-adhering stamps, making sure they weren't enough to cover the cost of postage. That was his finishing touch. With no return address given, Betsy's parents would be forced to visit the post office and cough up cash to cover postage due. Not only was he sending the Rankin family an emotional time bomb, they would have to fork out extra money for the privilege of seeing it. That struck him as an appropriate way to add insult to the injury. Gerard had no doubt Madeline and Kenneth's world would be shattered. The only thing that bothered him was that there was no way he'd be able to witness it.

After dropping the letter in a drive-up collection box, Gerard returned home to do a deep dive into the life and times of Jennifer Ann Brady. He used information gleaned from Betsy's computer to locate some of the basics—like Jenny's home address on High Lonesome Road near Bisbee, for example. His clone of Betsy's computer gave him ready access to Jennifer's Facebook postings, which turned out to be a revelation. In addition to her mother, the cop, the girl had a stepfather named Butch Dixon. She had both a younger brother and a younger sister. She was a star member of NAU's rodeo team. Her prizewinning barrel-racing horse was named Maggie. Her best pal on the rodeo team was a guy named Nick Saunders. The two of them often volunteered their time with a horse-therapy program for special-needs kids at the Lazy 8, the ranch where they both boarded their horses and where they put in lots of practice time. Bingo! Knowing about Jenny's home away from home was just what the doctor ordered.

Gerard's use of the dark web allowed him to be in touch with a network of equally dark people—the kinds of folks who'd do almost anything for a price, including a murder-for-hire guy in Vegas who was willing to undertake the task of removing Jennifer Ann Brady from the planet. The death of the daughter of a small-town sheriff would likely cause quite a stir, but Gerard had absolute faith in technology and in the identity-shielding software and hardware he'd purchased at great expense. Jenny would get what she deserved, while at the same time Gerard would deal a death blow to Beth Rankin's very soul, and that was all to the good.

Gerard Paine had often heard the saying that "justice delayed is justice denied," and he felt the same should hold true for revenge. He wanted his to be swift and totally devoid of mercy.

CHAPTER 29

THE FIRST inkling Beth had that she was not alone was when the icy-wet nose of a panting dog hit her square on the face and jarred her awake. When she fled Conover Hall, she'd run off across campus with no sense of direction—of where she was going or why. Like a wounded animal, she had simply wanted to hide herself away, somewhere out of sight where no one could find her. When she'd seen a delivery truck backed up to a loading dock next to the North Heating and Cooling Plant with no one around and with a door gaping open behind it, she'd darted into that.

No people had been visible as she threaded her way past the mountains of rumbling machinery that struggled to supply steam heat to winterbound classrooms and office buildings. She made it as far as the back of the building. There, in an isolated corner, she found a worn cushion from a poolside chaise, probably stowed in that spot so someone working the long, lonely night-shift hours could grab an impromptu nap shielded from a supervisor's watchful eyes.

Not surprisingly, the heating plant was warm enough. Beth had stripped off her jacket and used that as a pillow while she lay there contemplating the wreckage of her young life. Ron had stripped everything from her, not only her clothing but everything else, too—her pride, her future, her education. There was no way she could go back to class and face her professors or her fellow students. She'd been shamed beyond redemption. And now, for the first time, she wondered if maybe her mother had been right after all when she'd insisted that access to cell phones was the source of all evil.

In the course of the late afternoon, Beth had heard people coming and going—talking, laughing, chatting, joking—in the unconcerned way workers do when they believe they have a job site all to themselves. She worried that someone might venture to the back of the enormous plant and find her, but no one did. At some point in the evening, the lights had mostly switched off.

Beth had no food or water with her, but she was neither hungry nor thirsty. In her despair she'd been wondering how long it would take to starve to death when she'd fallen asleep. She was fully awake now, and the powerful beam of a flashlight briefly blinded her.

"Back, Hooch," a male voice ordered, evidently speaking to the dog. And then, in a more concerned tone, he added, "Ma'am, ma'am. Are you all right? Are you hurt?"

I'm hurt, Beth thought, *but not in the way you think.*

"I'm okay," she mumbled aloud.

Nonetheless an EMT showed up and checked her vitals. While he did his examination, several uniformed officers milled in the background. They'd all come looking for her as part of an organized search party, but Beth couldn't help wondering how many of them had seen the photos. How many of them had seen her naked?

"How did you find me?" she asked.

"I believe your roommate is the one who called it in,"

someone replied. "She was worried about you and went looking for your phone."

Someone handed Beth a bottle of water and a granola bar. She still wasn't hungry, but the water tasted good. Eventually someone helped her to her feet and then walked along beside her, holding her arm as if she were ill. It turns out she wasn't ill so much as she was sick at heart. As they led her through the massive building, Beth's soul recoiled at the idea that there might be reporters waiting outside, to say nothing of television cameras. Once her image was posted on a news broadcast somewhere, how long would it take for someone to search the Internet and locate all those other images as well?

She hesitated, wanting to turn back, just as a woman wearing an FBI Windbreaker walked up to meet them. Introducing herself as Special Agent Adele Norris, she handed Beth a small blanket.

"You might want to put this over your head while we escort you out to my vehicle," she said.

"Reporters?" Beth asked.

Agent Norris nodded. "Lots of them," she said. "It turns out you're big news around here at the moment. But don't worry, Ms. Rankin, you're a victim, most likely a targeted victim. Your name has not been released to the media, and it won't be—at least not by law enforcement."

That was the first time Beth had even considered that she was the victim of anything. She had excoriated herself for being stupid, but she hadn't focused on the fact that Ron had specifically targeted her.

"Ron and I had a fight," she said.

"That would be Ronald Cameron?" Agent Norris asked.

Beth nodded.

"The FBI has already done a computerized search for Mr. Cameron. As far as we're able to determine, he doesn't exist."

Beth was offended. "You think I made him up?"

"No, Ms. Rankin," Agent Norris said. "We believe that the person or persons who did this to you made him up, and I'm hoping that by examining your electronic devices and by interviewing you we'll be able to find a trail that leads back to those responsible."

Beth spent the next three hours in a conference room at the Northern Arizona University Police Department, where Agent Norris, with the help of the department's female commander, LuAnn Maxfield, conducted an extensive interview. Beth, grateful that her interrogators were both women, answered their probing questions to the best of her ability. How had she and Ron first connected? What, if anything, had he told her about himself? To avoid their having to obtain search warrants, Beth offered them full access to the information available on both her laptop and her cell phone. An hour passed and then two. By hour three Beth's head was swimming. It seemed as though the questions were going around in circles and not getting anywhere.

"I'm done," she said at last. "I can't do this anymore."

"Where would you like to go?" Agent Norris asked. "We could put you in touch with your parents. . . ."

"No!" Beth said definitively. "Not my parents. I don't want them involved in this. Just take me back to the dorm."

They shut down the interview, and Agent Norris drove her home. It wasn't until they stopped in front of Conover Hall that Beth realized she had neither her purse nor her keys. She had left completely empty-handed, and the dorm's nighttime resident assistant wasn't thrilled to be summoned from her bed to let Beth in at such an ungodly hour of the morning. Once Beth reached the room, she had no choice but to knock on the door and wake Jenny in order to be let in.

The door was flung open instantly, as though Jenny had been standing on the other side waiting. "Oh, my God!" she exclaimed, pulling Beth into a warm embrace. "They called and told me they'd found you but . . . Are you okay? What can I do to help?"

In reply Beth simply allowed herself to lean into Jenny's protective arms, sobbing out the day's worth of tension and hurt.

"I'm sorry, sorry, sorry," Jenny murmured over and over, all the while patting Beth's shoulder.

Standing there together in the open doorway of their shared room, for the first time in her life, Elizabeth Rankin understood what it meant to have a real friend.

CHAPTER 30

AFTER THEIR wine Joanna and Butch went to bed but not to sleep. Joanna was a cop. She knew too much about the often tragic aftermaths of cyberbullying. Too many of the vulnerable kids who'd been targeted in school ended up committing suicide, and the ones who didn't die outright often suffered long-term effects, including debilitating cases of PTSD.

But Beth Rankin's current situation came with the very real possibility of dire consequences for Jenny's life as well. If there was a bad outcome for Beth, what were the chances of a similarly bad outcome for Jenny? Joanna recognized that her daughter was someone who cared about other people, sometimes too much. If Beth emerged from this ordeal with permanent emotional scars, would Jenny be similarly damaged? And because all those possible outcomes were completely beyond a mother's control, Joanna found herself utterly terrified.

When the phone rang at 1:00 A.M., she'd been in bed for the better part of two hours, tossing and turning and unable to sleep. Butch evidently wasn't asleep either, because as soon as she answered the phone, he turned on his bedside lamp and sat up. Jenny's photo was in caller ID.

"Did they find her?" Joanna asked.

"Yes," Jenny said. "They used a search-and-rescue bloodhound to track her down. She was hiding out in one of the heating and cooling plants right here on campus."

"And she's okay?"

"As far as I know. They told me they've taken her somewhere to be interviewed by the FBI and the campus cops. If they'd told me where she was, I'd be there right now."

Joanna let out a sigh. Beth was safe, and if the FBI was on the scene, that meant Robin had come through in a big way.

"I'm sure you would be," Joanna said. "But how are *you* doing?"

Jenny didn't answer right away. "I looked at the rest of those photos," she said finally.

The shock and revulsion in Jenny's voice made Joanna's heart hurt.

"They're awful, Mom," she continued. "Just seeing them made me sick to my stomach."

What Joanna wanted to say was, *Why on earth did you do that?*—but she held her tongue.

"I didn't mean to look," Jenny continued, "but I couldn't help it. I had glanced at them on Beth's phone, but when they showed up in my e-mail, I ended up clicking on them anyway. I think Ron must have sent them to everyone in Beth's contacts list."

Joanna was horrified. "Including her parents?" she asked.

"Probably not, because her parents aren't *in* her contacts list."

That seemed strange. "They're not?" Joanna asked.

"Why would they be? That's part of Beth's beef with them. They're terminally opposed to all kinds of electronic communication."

"In this case," Joanna said, "that's probably a blessing."

Butch joined the conversation. "Jen," he said, "would you like me to come up to Flag and serve as backstop? I'm sure Mom could hold down the fort here if you need me as moral support."

Jenny seemed to pause for a moment, thinking, before she answered. "You probably shouldn't come," she replied at last. "The way things are right now, I'm not sure how comfortable Beth would be with having a strange man hanging around."

"I'm strange, all right," Butch said.

"Dad," Jenny admonished. "You know what I meant—not strange as in odd but strange as in unknown. She's really broken right now—broken and fragile."

"Understood," Butch agreed at once. "You're the one who knows her, and you're in a good position to assess her current situation, but if you change your mind and decide my being there would be helpful, let us know. In the meantime be sure to take care of yourself, starting with deleting all those photos from your computer and your phone. They're bad for you, but they're poison to Beth."

"You're right," Jenny said. "I'll delete them as soon as I'm off the phone."

"And if I were you," he added, "I wouldn't mention to her that you've seen them. It would make Beth's sense of humiliation that much worse."

"Are you going to try to get some sleep?" Joanna asked.

"I don't think so," Jenny replied. "I don't have any exams tomorrow, so I should probably wait up for her."

"You're a good girl, Jennifer Ann Brady," Joanna told her, "a really good girl."

Moments later the call ended, and Joanna returned her phone to the charger.

"Crisis averted?" Butch asked as he switched off his lamp.

"Hopefully," Joanna replied.

Turning on her side, she tried to fall asleep, but it still didn't work. Her daughter was out in the real world dealing with some pretty ugly stuff, and there was nothing at all Joanna could do to protect her.

It was almost four before she finally drifted off. As a consequence it was a weary, bleary-eyed Sheriff Brady who showed up at the Justice Center just in time for roll call the next morning. Once that ended, she held a conference-room powwow with her Investigations Unit, where she brought her detectives up to date on everything she'd learned the day before, including recounting her conversation with Eugene Autry. Deb, who was due in court to testify in another case later that day, would be stuck in the office. Meanwhile Ernie and Jaime, the reunited Double C's, were tasked with going out to Sierra Vista to track down whatever they could find on Williams.

Back in her own office, Joanna stared at the phone, wanting to call Jenny while at the same time trying to resist temptation. She and Butch had discussed the matter earlier that morning before she left home. When she'd started to call, Butch advised against it.

"Look," he said. "Our daughter took a punch in the face from the cold, cruel world yesterday. If she needs us, she knows we're here and she can call on us, but Jenny's a sensible kid, Joey. We need to leave her alone and let her navigate this her own way."

Joanna could see that Butch's approach to handling the situation made sense on any number of levels. Even so, sitting at her desk and not picking up the phone to call wasn't easy. It also got in the way of her being able to concentrate on doing anything productive. Instead she stared at the ridge of limestone cliffs outside her window and thought about Beth Rankin and Leon Hogan. Both had been victimized. Beth's future was compromised, but Leon's had been outright canceled. Beth might recover, but there was no such possibility for Leon. In his case the best Joanna could hope for was to help his family pick up the pieces.

And then, in a moment of inspiration, Joanna realized that there was at least one piece that might indeed be recoverable. She reached for her phone after all, but instead of calling Jenny, she dialed Jeannine Phillips.

"Animal Control," Jeannine answered.

Animal Control was part of Joanna's department. There were several mobile Animal Control officers who patrolled the county and doubled as kennel workers when they weren't out on the road. As far as the office itself was concerned, however, it was a one-woman operation.

"Sheriff Brady here," Joanna said. "I need some help."

"What kind of help?"

"Do you remember that bluetick hound you took in a couple of months ago, the one you refused to put down?"

"Coon, you mean?" Jeannine replied at once. "Sure I remember him. He's a great dog. No way I was putting him down. Why?"

"The woman who brought him in, Madison Hogan, is involved in a homicide investigation," Joanna said.

"Right," Jeannine said. "I heard. She's married to the guy who died in the officer-involved shooting. How's Armando doing, by the way?"

It made sense that Jeannine remembered the dog's name but not the name of the woman who'd brought him in.

"Armando's doing better than anyone expected," Joanna replied. "He may end up being released from the hospital sometime early next week, but my concern right now is with the dog."

"How come?"

"I learned yesterday that Leon and Madison were estranged and headed for divorce. Coon was Leon's dog, but when he moved out of the house, he left Coon behind because his young son, Peter, was so attached to the dog. The next week, when Leon came by to pick up the kids, the dog was gone. The kids told Leon their mother said he'd been hit by a car and died."

"A lie," Jeannine said. "That dog was in perfectly good shape."

"But tell me about the guy who took the dog in, the one out in Double Adobe. If there was a chance Coon and that little boy could be reunited, do you think the new owner would be willing to give him up?"

"Are the kids still living with their mother?" Jeannine wanted to know.

"Yes."

"In that case I won't even ask," Jeannine said. "That Hogan woman already tried to get rid of Coon once. If he goes back home, chances are, she'll try it again, and this time she might make it work. I won't be a part of putting that poor animal in jeopardy."

Joanna couldn't help smiling into the phone. In Jeannine's world animals always came first.

"Maybe there's a way to have it both ways," Joanna suggested. "Leon's folks are here for the funeral. They drove down from Wyoming. I have no idea if they'd be interested in taking Coon home with them or not, but if they did, at least the kids would know the dog is still alive and maybe they could even see him every once in a while if they had a chance to go visit."

A long silence followed. "All right," Jeannine agreed, relenting at last. "That might work. The guy's name is Rusty Miller—Russell Miller really, but everybody calls him Rusty. Do you want me to check to see if the victim's parents are willing to take the dog?"

It turned out that Russell Miller, along with his wife, Kathy, were names Joanna remembered from her Christmas-card mailing list. Although she didn't know the Millers personally, they had evidently donated to her campaign. So maybe . . .

"No," Joanna said, "I'll look into it and let you know."

And that's what Joanna was sitting there thinking about when a call came in from Jenny.

"I'm so glad to hear your voice," Joanna said. "How are things?"

"Beth's sleeping now finally," Jenny said. "We talked until the wee hours, so I probably should be sleeping now, too, but I'm on my way to the food court to pick up something for breakfast. I know Beth won't want to go there herself. She doesn't want to show her face, because she's sure everyone she meets will know all about her."

"Even though they probably won't," Joanna put in.

"You know that and I know that," Jenny said. "Beth? Not so much. She thinks her whole life is ruined. I told her that the only way to make something good come out of this is for her and for us to do everything in our power to bring down the guy who invented Ronald Cameron. Beth seems to think she's the only person this has ever happened to, but that's not true. I've just spent an hour on the Internet coming up with at least a dozen similar cases. I doubt this particular jerk—her so-called Ron—is necessarily involved in any of those other cases, but they're all surprisingly similar. Perpetrators like this usually have multiple victims, and one of the things that keeps the bad guys from being brought to justice is that none of their victims want to come forward and blow the whistle."

"That's where the FBI task force comes in," Joanna suggested quietly.

"Exactly," Jenny agreed, "and that's what I tried to tell Beth, but I'm not sure she's hearing me. She's so unbelievably broken, Mom, and I don't know how to help her."

Joanna heard the pain and doubt in her daughter's troubled voice. "You're listening to her for starters and making sure she eats," Joanna said. "Both of those things count. What about her folks? Has she talked to them about any of this?"

"No," Jenny said. "I suggested that, but Beth's sure that if she tells them about what's happened, they'll say it was all her fault. In terms of having people in her corner, it looks like I'm it."

Shortly after Andy died, Jenny had found an injured rock dove out near the stock tank. Its broken wing was beyond repair, but Jenny had nursed it along for months, providing shelter for it as well as food and water. Eventually the poor creature had disappeared. It seemed likely that it had finally fallen victim to a predator of some kind—probably a coyote. And here she was doing it again, lifting up another broken bird, a human one this time around.

"Just keep doing what you're doing, Jen," Joanna advised. "You're being her friend, and right now that's what Beth Rankin needs more than anything else."

Once the phone call ended, Joanna sat for a while longer before arriving at an obvious conclusion and ending up laughing at herself in the process. *When it comes to fixing broken birds, like mother like daughter.*

Picking up her phone again, she checked her incoming-call list and dialed a number. "Mr. Hogan?" she asked when Lyndell answered.

"Yes."

"Sheriff Brady here," she told him. "If I stopped by the hotel, would you be available to visit for a few minutes?"

"Sure," Lyn said. "Our room isn't exactly spacious, so can we talk in the lobby?"

"The lobby would be fine," Joanna said. "See you in a few."

Ending the call, she left her desk and poked her head out the door. "I'm going uptown for a few minutes," she told Kristin.

"Any idea when you'll be back?"

"Nope," Joanna said. "I'm off on a mission of mercy. No telling when I'll be done."

Joanna parked at the bottom of Brewery Gulch and walked up the hill to the hotel entrance. The lobby was an old-fashioned, homey kind of place, with worn leather chairs scattered here and there on an aged hardwood floor. She found Lyndell Hogan seated on a couch tucked in behind the staircase.

"What's up?" he asked when she sat down next to him. "On the phone it sounded like something serious."

"It might actually be a bit of good news," she said.

"What's that?"

There was no point in beating around the bush. "For starters," she said, "it turns out Coon is alive."

"Really?" a disbelieving Lyn Hogan demanded. "Are you sure?"

Joanna nodded. "I'm sure." She then went on to tell him the story of how, shortly after Leon moved out, Madison had brought the dog to Animal Control, asking that Coon be put down.

"What a dreadful woman she is," Lyn muttered under his breath. "I'm the one who gave the dog to Leon in the first place when Coon was little more than a pup. Where is he, then? Where's Coon?"

"He was adopted by a fellow who lives out near Double Adobe."

"Where's that?"

"A few miles east of here," Joanna answered. "The guy's name is Rusty Miller. He lives on a ranch and apparently has a soft spot in his heart for bluetick hounds. I don't know him personally, but I know of him. As far as I can tell, he's a good guy, but here's the thing. If I showed up and told him how all of this came about, there's a possibility he might be willing to give Coon back."

"What good would that do?" Lyn asked. "He can't go back home to Sierra Vista, not with Madison in charge. She obviously hates him."

"That's all true," Joanna agreed, "but I wondered if you and Izzy would be willing to take Coon? That way he wouldn't be lost to Peter and Kendall completely. They might even be able to visit with him on occasion."

A long pause followed. Finally, without replying, Lyn Hogan got to his feet. "Hold on a minute," he said. "I'll be right back."

Joanna hoped he'd go up to the room and maybe check with his wife. Instead he walked over to the front desk and exchanged a few quiet words with the desk clerk.

"Okay," Lyn said when he returned. "The fellow over there tells me this here hotel is what they call pet-friendly. Do you want me to ride out to Double Adobe with you?"

Joanna shook her head. "That might make for too much pressure. After all, since Rusty was kind enough to take the dog in the first place, it's not fair to force his hand on giving him up. Let me go there first and test the water. If he's willing, we can make an appointment to effect the transfer."

Lyndell Hogan nodded. "Sounds like this Rusty fellow is a good enough sort. It wouldn't be fair to paint the poor guy into a corner. If he wants to keep Coon, he should."

CHAPTER 31

IT TOOK the better part of an hour for Jenny to cajole Beth into eating something and getting dressed, but when it came time to leave the room and head for the interview, Beth shut down.

"I can't go out in public," she said tearfully. "I can't face the people out there. I just can't."

"But you have to," Jenny insisted. "You can't stay in our room forever. I know it seems like everyone you meet will know what happened, but most of them won't. And if the few who do know about it try to hassle you, that will say more about them than it does about you. You were used, Beth, used and taken advantage of. You're the victim here, and doing this FBI interview is the only way to fight back."

"All right," Beth agreed at last, "but I'm not going unless you come with me."

Twenty minutes later they were in Jenny's dual-cab Ford F-150 and headed for the campus police department on Pine Knoll Drive. Once there, they met up with FBI Special Agents Adele Norris and Pete Flores. When Beth made it clear that she wanted Jenny's company in the interview room, Agent Flores shook his head, saying that wouldn't be possible.

"Then I'm not going in either," Beth told him, stopping just short of the door. "If it weren't for Jenny, I wouldn't be here in the first place. If she can't sit in on the interview, I won't do it."

Jenny was both surprised and gratified to see Beth sticking up for herself.

"It'll be all right, Pete," Agent Norris said. "What we're really looking for here is a comprehensive history, and maybe Jennifer will be able to add a bit of context from time to time."

Flores conceded grudgingly, and Jenny was allowed to enter. Once they were all seated, Jenny was relieved when Agent Norris seemed to take charge of the interview.

"Here's what we have so far," she told them. "As I told you last night, we're quite sure that the man you know as Ronald Cameron doesn't exist in the real world. So far the FBI has been able to find a number of Ronald Camerons, but none of those appear to be the one you have in mind. For the purposes of this interview, however, that's how we'll refer to him, as Mr. Cameron. Is that all right with you?"

"I guess," Beth said.

"So tell us again exactly how you and Mr. Cameron became acquainted."

"It was right after school started," Beth answered. "We met on a dating site. I posted a profile, and he responded."

"Which dating site?"

Beth told them. "It's one of the better sites," she said. "At least that's what I was told—that everyone who was on it was properly screened."

"Of course they were," Agent Norris said, but it was clear she didn't believe a word of it. "So how did you post the profile?" she continued. "Did you use your phone?"

Beth nodded.

"We've been examining that. So far we're unable to find any record of those early interactions," Agent Norris said.

"They're gone?" Beth asked.

Agent Norris nodded. "So what can you tell us about them?"

"We mostly just texted back and forth—getting-to-know-you kind of stuff," Beth replied. "Nothing important."

"Wait," Jenny said. "Don't you remember? To begin with you were using my phone because you didn't have one yet."

"Are any of those communications still there?" Agent Norris asked.

"Maybe," Jenny said. "Let me check."

There are plenty of people in the world who routinely delete their text conversations, but Jenny wasn't one of them. So while the questioning continued, she began scrolling back through months' worth of texting history before eventually finding what she wanted—a series of banal texts, one of which included Ron's photo from his profile. When Beth had shown the picture to Jenny, she'd been impressed by how good-looking he was and thought Beth lucky to have found him.

"Here's a photo of Ron," Jenny said, holding up her phone so Agent Norris could see the screen. "At least this is the one that was on his profile."

Agent Norris took the phone and studied it for a moment. "Do you mind if we borrow this?"

"Not at all," Jenny said.

Agent Norris handed the phone to her partner, who immediately left the room.

Now that Jenny was focused less on searching her phone and more on the interview itself, she found herself admiring the way Agent Norris went about it. Her questions were methodical, but not abrasive or threatening. One step at a time, she demonstrated how, by pretending to be interested in everything about Beth, Ron Cameron had gradually sussed out all the mundane details of her life, including several items that had provided him with the correct answers to various security questions on Beth's various media platforms.

"No doubt that's how Mr. Cameron managed to install the key-logging software on both your phone and your computer."

"A keylogger?" Beth asked. "What's that?"

Agent Norris explained. "It was a way for him to have access to everything you did on your computer—every word you typed, every Web site you visited, every text or e-mail you sent."

"You mean he's been spying on me?"

Agent Norris nodded. "And not just with the key-logger either," she added. "He had set the camera app on your computer so that if you happened to leave the lid open while it was on your desk, he could observe everything that happened in the room, even when the computer wasn't actively in use."

"So he was spying on both of us—on me and on Jenny?" Beth demanded.

"That would appear to be true."

That revelation left Jenny feeling shocked and violated. How many times had she undressed in front of that computer without having any idea that someone else—a stranger, really—was watching her and maybe recording her as well? Jenny wished she could simply sink into the floor. But when she looked in Beth's direction, she realized that something totally unexpected had happened.

All through the interview, as Agent Norris had laid bare Ron's whole grooming process, Beth's answers had been tentative and sometimes almost inaudible. As they came closer to the time of the photo shoot and the breakup that followed, Jenny feared that Beth would break down completely and bolt from the room.

But for Beth the revelation about Ron's Web-based spying was evidently the last straw. From that point on, she was finally angry enough to be willing to fight back. Her answers went from tentative to firm. When it came time to discuss the photos and the breakup, Beth related what had happened without a hint of hesitation.

"So on the night of the photos, everything was going well?" Agent Norris asked.

Beth nodded.

"But the very next day it all went bad. How did that happen?"

Instead of answering Agent Norris directly, Beth turned to look at Jenny. "It happened that night, as soon as you knocked on the door," she said. "I told Ron that I had to go because you needed to use the bathroom. When I hung up, I didn't think it was that big a deal. I still thought Ron and I were okay, but it turned out we weren't. The next time I talked to him, he was raving mad. He told me I had to stop being roommates with you and that I shouldn't go to Bisbee to spend Christmas with your family either."

"Then what happened?" Agent Norris asked.

"I got mad, too, and we ended up having a big fight," Beth said, "the first one ever. I told him that Jenny was my friend and I was keeping it that way. I told him he didn't get to boss me around like that."

"You see," Agent Norris explained, "that was the first chink in Ron's armor. For people like that, it's essential to maintain absolute control in any given relationship. Their whole game plan is to isolate their victims from friends and relations so they can dominate their lives completely. When you refused to abandon your friendship, Ron most likely felt disrespected because you'd chosen Jenny over him. As far as he was concerned, that was unforgivable, and from that moment on there was no going back."

"And that's why he sent out the pictures—to humiliate me because I stood up to him?"

Agent Norris nodded. "It's more than that, Beth. He doesn't just want to humiliate you. He wants to destroy you."

"But why?" Beth asked.

"Because you stopped playing by his rules," Agent Norris explained. "Once that happens, it turns into all-out warfare. That's why he distributed your contact information and why there are those hundreds of messages stacked up on your electronic devices—but take heart, Beth. There's a good chance one or more of those senders has left behind enough cyber bread crumbs to lead us back to Mr. Cameron and to his other victims as well."

"You think there are others?"

Agent Norris nodded. "I'm sure of it," she said. "In fact, you can take that to the bank. And once we finally do find him, I'm hoping you and some of the others will be willing to come forward and testify against him."

"In court?" Beth asked. "In public?"

Agent Norris nodded.

"Will the photos be there?" Beth asked. "Will they have to be entered into evidence?"

"It's more than likely they'll be an integral part of the prosecution's case."

There was a pause. "All right, then," Beth said finally. "If that's what it takes to destroy him, that's what I'll do. But you said earlier that this would turn into all-out warfare. What does that mean, and what am I supposed to do?"

"For one thing you go on with your life to the best of your ability," Agent Norris said. "If he reaches out to you in any way, don't respond. For the moment I'd advise you to avoid using electronic devices of any kind. That means no cell phone, no texting, no e-mails to anyone. You need to avoid posting anything online that might reveal where you are and what you're doing."

"Why?"

Agent Norris sighed. "Here's how this type of interaction usually proceeds. To begin with, there's the isolating relationship that devolves into sexting. When the inevitable breakup occurs, revenge porn rears its ugly head. We've already checked all those boxes. Unfortunately, things often don't stop there. If Ron is somehow able to gain access to your new account addresses or phone numbers, you're likely to be buried in masses of spam texts and calls. And after that . . ." Agent Norris paused.

"What?"

"Unfortunately," Agent Norris replied, "there are far too many cases where things have escalated into actual physical harm."

"You're thinking he might come after me?"

"I wish I could tell you that won't be the case, but I can't. People like Mr. Cameron have more than a couple of screws loose. Until we have him in custody, your safety is paramount. Don't wander around on campus alone. That goes for you and for Jenny here as well. If he's targeting you, he might also be targeting your friend. Follow a buddy system. If you're out and about, you both need to have someone with you at all times."

"But Ron lives on the other side of the country," Beth objected.

"That may be what he told you," Agent Norris corrected, "but that doesn't mean it's true."

As if on cue, there was a knock on the door, and Agent Flores stepped into the room. He was carrying a file folder in one hand and Jenny's phone in the other. He passed the phone to Jenny and the folder to Agent Norris.

"I ran it through our facial rec," he said. "This is what came back."

Agent Norris opened the folder and sifted through several documents inside before passing one of them along to Beth.

"Does this look familiar?" Agent Norris asked.

A surprised Beth glanced up from the photo and stared at Agent Norris. "That's the same photo that was on his profile," she said. "Does that mean you've found him?"

"Unfortunately, no," Agent Norris said. "The photo in your hand is lifted from the obituary of a young man named Michael Darrell Johnson, who died two years ago in a one-car rollover accident on Highway 79 south of Florence, Arizona."

Beth seemed mystified. "What does that mean?" she asked.

"It means that your stalker, aka Ron Cameron, used someone else's photo to create his dating profile. My guess is he probably has any number of aliases and any number of photos."

"So he can do this to other unsuspecting people?"

"Yes," Agent Norris agreed.

"Then we have to stop him, don't we?"

"Yes to that, too, but this photo raises another worrisome issue. Michael Johnson's death was big news in Tucson because it happened along almost the same stretch of highway where a movie star named Tom Mix died decades ago. So the story attracted a lot of attention here in Arizona, but I doubt it was big news anywhere else."

"Are you saying my stalker may have an Arizona connection—that he might even live here?"

"He might," Agent Norris said. "Remember what I said earlier about watching your back because the situation might escalate?"

Beth nodded.

"That goes double now," Agent Norris said, "and again, that means for both of you."

The interview ended a short time later, and Beth and Jenny headed back to the dorm. "Are you scared?" Jenny asked as she pulled into traffic.

"I'm too mad to be scared," Beth answered. "Mad at him for doing it and mad at myself for being so stupid."

In a way Jenny didn't quite understand, the interview that she'd expected to undermine and diminish Beth had instead invigorated her. Somehow Agent Norris's gentle questioning had put at least a few of Beth's broken pieces back together.

"What do you want to do this afternoon?" Jenny asked.

"I want to walk over to the food court and have lunch," Beth replied determinedly, "and I'm not going to wear a bag over my head either."

🌵 CHAPTER 32

KENDALL WAS asleep when the doorbell rang the next morning. She waited to hear if Mommy would go to the door. When she didn't, Kendall was torn. If the person at the door was a stranger, she wasn't supposed to open it, but what if it was Grandma Puckett? That was what she wanted more than anything—for Grandma to come back. Finally, unable to resist, Kendall slipped off the bed and went to answer.

When she opened the front door, no one was there. She was about to close it in disappointment when she saw a glass dish of some kind sitting on the front porch. Aluminum foil covered the top, and a small envelope was taped to the foil. Kendall tore open the envelope and found a note inside.

> *The class misses you. Hope you will be back soon.*
> *Mrs. Baird.*

The note made Kendall's eyes mist over with tears. When she lifted one corner of the aluminum foil, she found a miracle hiding inside. The whole thing was full to the brim with macaroni and cheese topped by a thick layer of crunchy bread crumbs and bacon bits. It smelled delicious, and when she picked the dish up, it was still warm.

Kendall turned to find Peter standing in the open doorway behind her, sleepily rubbing his eyes. "What is it?" he asked.

"Breakfast," she told him, "macaroni and cheese."

It was a feast. They both ate two whole helpings. When they were done, Kendall put what was left in the fridge and loaded the dishes in the dishwasher. Mommy didn't like to get up and find a mess in the kitchen. They watched cartoons for a while and colored, too, but the day seemed to drag.

"Why can't we go to school?" Peter asked.

"Because of Daddy," Kendall told him.

"Will we ever be able to go to school?"

"I hope so."

"When?"

"I don't know. Grandma Puckett told us that the funeral is on Friday, so maybe next week."

"I'm bored," Peter said.

"So am I."

At lunchtime they had another serving of macaroni and cheese. They were just finishing up when the front door opened and Mommy walked in. All morning long Kendall had assumed that their mom was just sleeping late in her room, but clearly she hadn't been home at all. Now she was, but she was also drunk and angry. Kendall recognized the symptoms.

Mommy staggered up to the table and pointed down at the partly empty glass dish. "What's that?" she wanted to know.

"Macaroni and cheese," Peter answered, although it was pretty obvious what it was.

"Where'd it come from?"

"Mrs. Baird brought it over."

Mommy was instantly irate. "You let someone into the house when I wasn't here?" she demanded.

We didn't know you weren't here, Kendall thought. She said, "I didn't let her in. She left it on the front porch."

"People should mind their own business," Mommy grumbled. "And clean all this crap up when you're finished."

With that she staggered off down the hall, slamming the bedroom door behind her.

"What's wrong with her?" Peter asked. "She was walking funny."

Kendall didn't want to tell him the truth. "She's probably just tired," Kendall said. "She'll be better after she has a nap."

They still had some of the DVDs that Daddy had left behind, so they watched *Frozen* and *Guardians of the Galaxy.* Kendall was in the bathroom when the doorbell rang again. She hurried to get there, but by the time she did, Peter had already opened the door.

"Is your mom home?" a woman's voice was asking.

"She's asleep," Peter said.

Kendall was getting ready to slam the door when she realized that the woman wasn't a stranger at all. She was Mrs. Walkup, their next-door neighbor, and she was holding a dish.

"I'm so sorry about your father," she said, "but I brought over a casserole. It occurred to me that you're probably having company visiting from out of town, and it's the least I can do."

Mrs. Walkup looked like she expected to be invited inside, but Kendall didn't think that was a good idea. "Thank you," she said, reaching out to take the dish. "I'll tell Mom you were here."

She closed the door and carried the dish straight to the kitchen, with Peter trailing along behind. "Is that what we'll have for dinner?" he asked. "What is it?"

Kendall lifted the lid and looked inside. She couldn't tell what it was, exactly. Some kind of meat-and-tomato dish with black olives scattered on top.

"Why are people bringing us food?" Peter asked.

"Because they feel sorry for us," Kendall explained, "because of Daddy."

"Is that what people do when someone dies?"

"I guess," Kendall said.

She was sorry about Daddy, too, but she was glad to have the food. Today, at least, they wouldn't go hungry.

CHAPTER 33

BY MIDAFTERNOON Joanna was back in her office at the Justice Center and feeling as though she'd accomplished at least one small good deed for the day. The meeting with Rusty Miller had gone as she'd anticipated it would. Once he knew the full story, he simply nodded.

"Sounds like these folks really want him back," Rusty said. "They've already lost their son. No reason they have to lose their son's dog, too."

After that he called Coon over, put him on a lead, and loaded him into the backseat of Joanna's Interceptor.

"He's a good dog," Rusty told her once the dog was in the SUV. "He's well behaved, housebroke, knows all about walking on a lead, and is great with kids. If the Hogans end up deciding they don't want him after all, I'd take him back in a heartbeat."

Joanna had driven the dog uptown, where a completely unruffled Coon walked into the lobby of the Copper Queen as if he owned the place. Joanna asked the desk clerk to call upstairs and let the Hogans know they had visitors. A few minutes later, when Lyn and Izzy Hogan stepped off the elevator, Coon went absolutely nuts. He broke free of Joanna's loose hold on the leash and raced over to give an ecstatic greeting to the new arrivals. Then, with his tail a-wag, he stood on his hind legs, put his front paws on Izzy's shoulders, and planted a wet tongue on her cheek.

"Why, Coonie!" Izzy exclaimed, laughing. "You funny old dog, you haven't forgotten me after all."

An embarrassed Joanna came racing to collect the lead, but Lyn beat her to it and waved her off. "It's okay," he said. "This guy was the runt of the litter. The breeder was going to get rid of him, but I talked him into giving him to me. Izzy brought him up, and then I trained him before we ever handed him over to Leon. I wasn't about to send an untrained dog to a family with a couple of little kids."

"That's the wonderful thing about dogs," Joanna said. "They don't forget the people who look out for them, and that's clearly the case with Coon."

While the Hogans set off on a shopping expedition to get a dog bed, food, and dishes for their newly retrieved animal, Joanna went back to the office. She was just settling in when Kristin called to say that Dick Voland was in the outer office.

Joanna's history with her former chief deputy was complicated. First there'd been their rivalry in that initial election, followed by her politically expedient move of appointing both her former rivals as co-seconds-in-command in her administration. Dick's tenure had ended abruptly when it became apparent that he had developed a crush on Joanna. Once she put the kibosh on that, Dick had left the department. His later entanglement and subsequent breakup with Marliss Shackleford hadn't helped matters. With all those complexities in the background, Joanna was grateful Kristin had given her a moment to put on her game face before ushering the man into the room.

She greeted him cordially. "Hey, Dick," she said. "How's it going?"

"I've got something I think you'll want to see," he said. Taking a seat in one of her visitor chairs, he pulled a small white vial out of his coat pocket and placed it on Joanna's desk. "In fact," he added, "you may want to ask Casey Ledford to run an analysis of the contents."

Joanna had seen a vial just like that once before—in an evidence bag of items collected from Leon Hogan's living room. With a nod she reached for her phone.

"Hey, Casey," she said. "Can you stop by for a minute?" Then she turned to Dick. "Assuming this is what we both think it is, where did it come from?"

"Let's just say I happen to know that Leon Hogan had been dosed with scopolamine and was completely out of his head when he was gunned down," he said. "How's Armando, by the way?"

Joanna didn't like hearing that the officer-involved shooting investigation had sprung a leak, but Dick had so many friends inside the department she let it go. It could have been anyone, and for right now she was better off not knowing who the leaker was.

"Armando's doing better than expected," she answered. "We're hoping he'll be released sometime next week, but when he comes back to work, it'll be desk duty only for the foreseeable future."

"Too bad," Dick muttered.

Joanna nodded. "Tell me about it, but if this turns out to be scopolamine, I need to know where it came from."

"And I need to protect my sources," Dick replied, "but here's a hint. You might want to take a long, hard look at Floyd Barco, the nighttime bartender at the Nite Owl. There's a lot that goes on in that joint that isn't exactly kosher. He sells these out of the glove box of his car as needed."

Joanna nodded. "I've heard about the Nite Owl," she said. "It sounds like a real hot spot, and not in a good way.

Just then Casey popped her head in the door. "Hey, hi, Dick," she said when she spotted him. "Good to see you." Then to Joanna she added, "You wanted to see me?"

Joanna picked up the vial and handed it to her. "How long will it take you to tell me if this is scopolamine?"

"Two shakes of a lamb's tail," Casey replied. "I'll let you know as soon as I get the results."

She departed at once, and Joanna turned back to Dick. "Have you mentioned any of this to Frank Montoya?"

"As a matter of fact, I just did," Dick said. "I told him there was a lot going on in his bailiwick that didn't meet the eye and maybe he should look into it."

"And?"

"He allowed as how he would."

"Did you tell him anything about a possible connection to the Hogan case?" Joanna asked.

"Not a word," Dick replied. "Didn't seem like a good idea to get caught in a crossfire between the two of you."

"Fair enough," Joanna said.

"As you know from Jorge Moreno, I was hired to work on Leon's behalf," Dick continued. "And that's how I ended up looking into the Nite Owl—because I learned Leon's wife and her boyfriend hang out there a lot. Randy can be a real jerk sometimes, and some of the other customers don't much care for him. The guy who gave me the tip this morning just happens to hate the guy's guts."

"A tip to what effect?"

"Randy's got a chance to buy into an important chunk of the local drug trade for an up-front cost of a hundred thousand dollars."

"The same amount of money as the expected proceeds from Leon's group insurance policy," Joanna murmured.

"You got it," Dick said. "So according to my source, Randy and Madison showed up at the bar last night and got into a hell of a fight. During the course of a very heated argument, Randy was overheard to say, 'If you ain't got the money, you worthless bitch, then we are done!'"

"That's probably the first he found out that the money he was counting on wasn't coming."

"And he wasn't happy about it either," Dick said.

"What happened then?"

"Randy left. Madison stayed on until closing time, kept right on drinking, and ended up leaving with somebody else."

Joanna's phone rang. "Contents test positive for scopolamine," Casey said when she came on the line

"Good," Joanna said. "Thanks."

"Anything else?" Casey asked.

"I'll let you know," Joanna said. She turned back to Dick Voland. "Sounds like I'd better touch bases with Frank," she said.

He stood up. "Sounds like," he agreed. "Again, the guy who's my source is a friend of mine. I'm not naming him. That way when questions start flying, he won't be singled out, but I'm pretty sure he'll talk, and so will others. As I said, Randy Williams isn't exactly Mr. Congeniality around there, and I don't think there'll be too many zipped lips."

"Thanks, Dick," she said. "I appreciate it."

"And for the record, Leon Hogan was a good guy who didn't deserve what he got."

Joanna nodded. "I'm pretty sure you're right about that, too."

Dick walked as far as the doorway and then turned around. "One more thing," he added as an afterthought. "When you talk to Frank, you might want to mention that Floyd Barco is a convicted felon, currently on parole. He drives a 1994 Chevrolet Suburban that is currently operating with a broken taillight, and he's known to keep an illegal handgun in his glove box, along with a ready supply of scopolamine. After the bar closes each night, he generally hangs around for a tipple or two after he finishes cleaning up, not that he does much of that."

"You took a pretty deep dive into the Nite Owl, didn't you?"

"We aim to please," Dick replied with a grin.

"Thanks for the background info," Joanna told him. "Appreciate it."

Once Dick was gone, she picked up her phone and dialed Frank Montoya's number. "I think we need to talk about the Nite Owl, Floyd Barco, and Leon Hogan," she said when he answered, "not necessarily in that order."

"You're right," he agreed. "It sounds like we need to do a lot more than just talk."

CHAPTER 34

WANTING PRIVACY, Jenny waited until Beth went into the bathroom to get ready for bed before calling her folks to report in.

"So how are things?" her mom wanted to know.

"Better," Jenny replied. "As we were heading for the interview with the FBI, Beth was still a basket case. I thought for sure she would fall to pieces, but she didn't. It was actually pretty amazing."

"What was amazing about it?" Joanna asked.

"The way Agent Norris handled her reminded me of when Jim Carter brought that wild mare to Clayton Rhodes and asked him to fix her. Remember that?"

Joanna did. For decades Clayton had been Cochise County's premier horse trainer. Because his land abutted the original High Lonesome Ranch, he'd also been Joanna's nearest neighbor. After Andy's death he had been a huge help in terms of pitching in with chores.

At some point Jim Carter, Jenny's 4-H leader, had bought a wild horse at auction that had been culled from one of the herds running loose on Bureau of Land Management pastureland. When Jim couldn't get anywhere with the animal, he brought it over to Clayton. The old man was in his eighties by then and unwilling to tackle actually breaking the horse, but Jenny had been old enough and interested enough to take a front-row seat at the patient way he'd gentled the terrified animal and brought her around.

"I mean," Jenny continued, "Agent Norris was asking about things that had to be really upsetting to Beth, and I expected the interview to turn into a disaster. Instead the process somehow made Beth better. It was fascinating."

"It's what cops do, Jen," Joanna said. "They're trained to establish a connection with the people they encounter, whether they happen to be suspects, victims, survivors, or family members. It takes rapport and trust to elicit information. So did it work?"

"I'm not sure how much useful information was added to the mix, but once we finished, Beth was ready to go to the food court for lunch. Before the interview I didn't think I'd be able to get her to leave our room. It was as if Agent Norris superglued Beth back together. We did learn one thing, though."

"What's that?"

"The photo Ron used to set up his dating profile was from the obituary for a guy from Tucson who died in a car wreck two years ago."

Jenny heard her mother's sharp intake of breath. "That suggests that whoever Ron is, he has some kind of Arizona connection. And if he decides to change from strictly cyberwarfare into something physical—"

"I know," Jenny interrupted. "Agent Norris already told us that Beth and I both need to be careful. One thing that came out in the interview was that Ron was really pissed about Beth and me being friends."

Beth emerged from the bathroom just then. Not wanting to say any more within her earshot, Jenny ended the call. "Okay, Mom," she said hurriedly. "Talk to you tomorrow. Good night."

"Your mom?" Beth asked as she settled onto her bed.
Jenny nodded. "I was telling her about the interview."
Jenny was starting to undress when an arriving text
dinged on her phone. The phone number wasn't one she
recognized, but the message made her heart sink.

Maggie is down in her stall. What do you want me
to do?

Maggie was sick? How could that be? The horse
had been perfectly fine the day before—with no sign of
lameness or fever, but if she was down, it was possible
that she'd suffered a career-ending injury.
"Oh, no," she said aloud.
"What's wrong?" Beth asked.
"It's Maggie," Jenny said as she texted a reply.

Okay. On my way.

She reversed course as far as getting ready for bed
was concerned. Instead of continuing to remove clothing,
she started putting it back on.
"Where are you going?" Beth asked.
"Where do you think? To the Lazy 8 to check on
Maggie."
"But it's the middle of the night," Beth objected.
"When a horse is down like that, waiting until morn-
ing to call a vet could be fatal," Jenny returned.
Beth made as if to climb out of bed. "Wait," she said.
"I'll come with you."
"You don't need to," Jenny said. "I'll be okay."
"What about the buddy system?" Beth asked.
Jenny was already pulling on her jacket. She was
tempted to ask exactly how much Beth knew about sick

horses, but she thought better of it. It seemed likely that if Ron were after anyone, it was Beth, but hadn't Agent Norris warned both of them to be careful? And if Jenny expected Beth to take her advice, shouldn't she do the same?

"I'll make a deal with you," Jenny said. "I'll call Nick and ask him to meet me at the ranch if you'll call the RA to come stay with you while I'm gone."

"Call the resident assistant?" Beth demanded. "I don't need a babysitter!"

"And neither do I," Jenny said, "but Nick's dad was a large-animal vet. He might be able to help me figure out what's going on with Maggie. I doubt you can."

Beth thought about it for a time before nodding in grudging agreement. While she dialed the resident assistant's number, Jenny called Nick, who answered after only one ring. When she told him what was up, his response was immediate.

"Sure thing," he said. "I'm on my way."

With her mind focused on whatever might have happened to Maggie, Jenny drove to the Lazy 8 faster than she should have. On the way she chatted with Nick on her cell phone's speaker, bringing him up to date with everything that had happened since they'd last seen each other.

Approaching the lighted entrance to the Lazy 8, she knew he was only half a mile or so behind her. As she slowed for the turn, she noticed that a vehicle of some sort—a small sedan—stopped on the shoulder of the road just ahead of her. It wasn't until she was almost even with the parked car that she realized someone was standing next to it. At that moment a lifesaving glimpse of the man's backlit silhouette revealed that he was holding a weapon in his hand, one pointed directly at her.

"Oh, my God!" she screamed into her phone as she jammed her foot on the gas pedal. The truck lurched forward as a bullet that had been intended for her pinged harmlessly off the bed of her truck.

"What's happened?" Nick yelled frantically into her ear. "What's going on?"

"There's a guy parked on the road!" she shouted back. "He just took a shot at me!"

"The hell he did!" Nick roared back. "Call 911!"

In her rearview mirror, Jenny saw the parked vehicle's headlights flash on. The driver seemed to be making a U-turn in order to follow her, but then another pair of headlights bore down on the turning vehicle and the scene turned into a dazzling whirl of headlights as Nick's truck plowed head-on into the much smaller sedan and sent it spinning.

"Nailed the bastard!" Nick crowed gleefully over the screech of rending sheet metal. "Now call the cops."

The uncontrollable trembling that assailed Jenny's fingers right then made it almost impossible for her to dial. Once she had summoned help, she made a U-turn and drove back the way she'd come. Nick's pickup, a powerful Dodge Ram, had been built to haul livestock and hay. Its air bags were deployed, but beyond minor damage to the front end it was barely dented, while all that remained of the sedan was a jumble of broken pieces. Nick had been wearing his seat belt. The shooter had not. Nick had hauled the guy out of the wreckage and dumped him in the dirty snow along the shoulder of the road, where he lay bleeding, writhing, and moaning. The weapon was nowhere in sight.

"The cops are on their way," Jenny gasped, falling gratefully into Nick's comforting arms.

The 911 operator, still on the line, speaking through Jenny's phone, was asking questions in the background. "He's hurt pretty bad," Nick said. "Tell her we need an ambulance as well as the cops."

Just then a dribble of blood ran down the side of Jenny's cheek. She looked up at Nick's damaged face and realized where it had come from.

"You're hurt," she said. "Your nose is bleeding."

Self-consciously Nick wiped his face with the sleeve of his jacket. "It's nothing," he said. "Air bag got me full-on, but I'm a helluva lot better off than he is. That asshole was trying to kill you, Jenny."

She nodded. "I know," she said.

"Unless I miss my guess," Nick added, "Maggie is perfectly fine."

And she was.

CHAPTER 35

BUTCH WAS in bed and Joanna was heading there, too, when Jenny called back. "A guy just tried to kill me," she said into the phone, almost choking on the words as she forced them out.

That jarring announcement left Joanna feeling as though her body had been plugged into an electrical outlet. With her legs no longer fully supporting her weight, she sank down onto the bed.

"Are you all right?" she asked weakly. "What on earth happened?"

"I got a message, supposedly from someone at the Lazy 8, saying that something was wrong with Maggie—that she was down in her stall and couldn't get up. I was getting ready to come check on her, and Beth wanted to ride along. When I told her no, we agreed that if she stayed home, I would call Nick. I was here and about to turn in to the ranch entrance when a guy standing on the side of the road took a potshot at me. Nick was a minute or so behind me. He rammed the guy's car and nailed him good. The shooter's not dead, but he's on his way to the hospital. The thing is, Nick wouldn't have been here at all if Beth hadn't insisted I have someone with me. She saved my life, Mom. She really did."

"What's going on?" Butch demanded from his side of

the bed. Belatedly, Joanna turned the phone on speaker and then repeated some of what Jenny had already said.

"Are you okay?" Joanna asked then. "Is Nick?"

"We're both fine. The cops are here now, and the EMTs are loading the shooter into the ambulance. I don't know how badly he's hurt. He was in his vehicle and starting to come after me when Nick slammed into him with his truck."

"I can't believe someone tried to shoot you," Butch said. "Are you sure?"

"I'm sure," Jenny declared. "We found a bullet hole in the bed of the pickup right behind the cab."

"But both you and Nick are okay?" Butch asked this time.

"We are."

"Then please give him a huge hug from us."

"I already did," Jenny said with a short laugh. "I hugged him for all I was worth. But the cops are wanting to talk to us now, so I have to go. I don't know how long that will take, but I'll let you know what's going on."

"Thanks, Jen," Joanna said. "And tell Nick from me that he's one good guy."

"So now Beth's cyberboyfriend is attacking Jenny, too?" Butch asked as Joanna pulled on her robe.

"I'd say so," she replied, "and it sounds like he's dangerous as hell."

"And do you think the guy who shot at her is the same guy who was messing around with Beth?" Butch asked.

"Not on your life," Joanna answered grimly, "not in person. Guys like that are cowards. They enjoy pulling the strings to mess with others without having the courage to show their own faces."

"What are you going to do about it?" Butch asked.

"What any right-thinking mother would do under the circumstances, and that means everything I can," she told him. "I'm guessing deputies from the Coconino County Sheriff's Office are the officers on the scene. First off I'm going to call Howie Fulton and let him know what's happened. Next I'm going to call the campus cops at NAU and ask them to keep an eye on Beth. Then I'm going to pull every possible string at my disposal and put the FBI on this case, too, because I'm pretty sure this guy is connected to Beth's Ron Cameron."

"Sounds like we're about to put in an all-nighter," Butch said, crawling out of bed. "I'll start a pot of coffee."

In the end it wasn't quite an all-nighter, but close. Sheriff Fulton was good enough to supply information as it became available, including the hit man's name— Aaron Morgan. He was in St. Jerome's Hospital in Flagstaff with what were deemed to be serious but non-life-threatening injuries that included numerous broken bones. He was also under arrest and would be interviewed by Phoenix-based agents from the FBI as soon as they could arrive on the scene.

It was almost one in the morning before Jenny finally called back. Two individual interviews had been conducted at the sheriff's department. Nick's had taken place in a single-person interview room. Jenny's had been done as a group-grope in a conference room where detectives from Coconino County, FBI Agents Norris and Flores from Phoenix, and Commander LuAnn Maxfield from NAU's police department had all joined in on the questioning process. Once the interviews were over, and with their vehicles currently impounded, sheriff's deputies gave Nick and Jenny separate lifts home.

"What's happening now?" Joanna asked.

"NAU is concerned that Beth's and my presence could put other students at the school in danger. Since a bad guy might be able to figure out when and where we'll be taking finals, we'll be having our last exams tomorrow during the day. We've both been told to show up at the president's office at ten o'clock in the morning. Someone there will administer our tests. In the meantime we've been instructed to speak to no one. That goes for Beth and me and for Nick, too."

"If you're done with finals a whole day early," Butch said, "does that mean you'll be home tomorrow evening?"

"I don't know how," Jenny said. "Beth doesn't have a car, and my truck is currently impounded as evidence."

"All right, then," Butch said, "since you're not old enough to rent a car on your own, I'll hop in one of ours and come get you."

"Would you?" Jenny asked. "You're sure you don't mind?"

"Are you kidding?" Butch returned. "If random bad guys are busy taking potshots at you, I'd rather have you here at home, safely behind our security shutters, than out driving around on your own."

"Thank you, Dad," she said gratefully. "I can't wait to be there."

It wasn't an easy night. As sheriff, Joanna was accustomed to being the one in charge and running the show. This time around she was on the outside looking in. About 3:00 A.M. a few more details slipped in under the official radar via a phone call from Special Agent Robin Watkins.

"Okay," she said, "here's what we know so far. Shooter's name is Aaron Morgan."

"I already knew that much," Joanna said. "Sheriff Fulton gave me the name, but not details."

"Turns out Aaron's an ex-con from Las Vegas who's about to go down on charges of attempted murder along with a weapons-possession charge. With an offer on the table of his pleading guilty to reduced charges, he's singing like a bird. According to him the real target tonight was Jenny."

A shudder of dread shot through Joanna while Robin continued.

"Morgan was hired to do this by someone who paid for his services via a Bitcoin transaction, half on signing and half on delivery. He's given the FBI access to his Bitcoin account. One of the FBI's blockchain agents in D.C. has suggested that we attempt to pull off a sting. We've asked the Coconino County authorities to report the incident as a fatality shooting with the identity of the victim being withheld pending notification. Meanwhile they'll have someone posing as Morgan report back that he's successfully completed the mission. When the final payment appears in the shooter's account, we may be able to use emerging technology to peel back the blockchains and establish a trace."

"Will the FBI do it?" Joanna asked.

"Looks like," Robin replied.

"And for now we're all supposed to pretend that the shooter succeeded and Jenny is dead?"

"That's the whole idea," Robin answered. "Fortunately, it was the middle of the night and there was no on-scene media coverage at the time. Everyone involved—Jenny, Nick, and Beth—is being asked to keep quiet about what really happened. As long as the bad guy thinks it worked, he's unlikely to try to make a second attempt, at least as far as Jenny is concerned. Just in case, however, LuAnn Maxfield has posted night-shift officers to keep all entrances to Conover Hall under surveillance."

That should have been some small comfort for Joanna, but it wasn't.

"How long is all this going to take?" she asked. "Until the bad guy is taken into custody, both Jenny and Beth remain in serious jeopardy."

"Agreed," Robin said, "and we're moving heaven and earth to make it happen sooner rather than later. In the meantime we've all got to pull together in order to make the unsub believe his hired gun succeeded. In other words, mum's the word."

"Understood," Joanna said, "I won't say a thing to anyone."

She and Butch finally crawled back into bed at four. "At least Jenny's safe," Butch murmured into Joanna's ear as she snuggled against him. "If it weren't for Beth and Nick, we'd be planning a funeral right now instead of planning Christmas."

"I know," Joanna said. "We were all very lucky."

And that was enough to let her fall asleep at last.

A bare three hours later, the smell of brewing coffee lured her into the kitchen, where Butch was up, dressed, and getting ready to head out.

"You're up early," she said.

He grinned at her. "I'm all for going and getting those girls. It's a five-hour drive, and I want to be there and ready to head back home when they finish up at noon. I sent a text to Carol letting her know what's up, and she's on her way over," he added as he poured coffee into two oversize thermal travel cups.

"Did you tell her why?"

"I told her Jenny was having car trouble."

"But doing two five-hour trips in one day is going to be tough on only three hours of sleep."

"Not to worry," he said cheerfully. "I'll drive up and have Jenny do the honors coming back home. I'm taking your car, by the way. There's more room in the Enclave than in my Subaru."

"Travel safe," she said, giving him a peck on the cheek as he headed for the door. She was tempted to go back to bed, but with Denny already stirring in his room, there was no point. She hit the shower instead.

CHAPTER 36

THE TEXT from Aaron Morgan came in on Gerard Paine's specially designated burner phone just after three in the morning. There was no explanation as to why it had taken so long for Aaron to get back to him after his mission, but the text consisted of a single word: DONE.

Gerard wasn't what you would call a trusting individual. All night long he'd been monitoring Flagstaff- and Phoenix-based news sites. On the ten-o'clock news broadcast in Flagstaff, there was a report of a shots-fired incident on Lazy 8 Road south of town, with details to come as they became available. That gave Gerard hope that his plan had worked. At 2:30 A.M. there was a breaking-news update on a Web site that reported an incident in which one person, an unidentified female student from NAU, had died from gunshot wounds.

In other words, Gerard was pretty sure Jenny Brady's death was a done deal well before Morgan sent the text. The GPS software Gerard had installed on Morgan's phone told him that the text had been sent from Kingman, Arizona. In other words, with his mission accomplished, Gerard's hired gun was on his way home to Vegas. Gerard was almost gleeful as he keyed in the codes for the Bitcoin transfer. Jennifer Ann Brady was dead. That meant that Beth Rankin would soon be carrying a lifetime's worth of guilt in that regard. To Gerard's way of thinking, it couldn't have happened to a nicer person.

As for the rest of it? Later today or maybe, at worst, tomorrow, his postage-due package would arrive on Madeline and Kenneth Rankin's doorstep. In that moment Gerard's plan of ultimate revenge would be complete.

Unfortunately for him, he was an individual who put far too much faith in technology. After sending the Bitcoin final payment, he went back to tending his flower garden and spent the next hour or so chatting up Samantha Toon in Billings. Had he checked the GPS on Aaron's phone, he would have seen something both surprising and chilling, because suddenly the phone was moving again, only this time it wasn't continuing north to Las Vegas. Nope, it was actually heading southbound—and not in a car either.

Shortly after leaving that gas station by car, the phone suddenly went airborne, having been moved from a Mohave County Sheriff's Office vehicle and loaded into a Phoenix-bound helicopter. Less than twelve hours later, his phone, along with Beth Rankin's phone and computer, would end up in the FBI laboratory in Washington, D.C., where a team of government IT experts would work frantically to tease out all of "Ronald Cameron's" many secrets.

The good guys were coming for Gerard Paine, and he had no idea.

CHAPTER 37

A SOMEWHAT bedraggled Joanna made it into the office in time for the end of roll call if not the beginning of it. She didn't like having to keep a tight rein on what was going on with Jenny in Flagstaff. The day before, she'd learned from Dick Voland that there was a serious leak somewhere inside her department, and she didn't want to take any chances that might further endanger Jenny and Beth or interfere with the FBI's efforts to take down Beth's tormentor.

Once roll call was over, Joanna ventured into the bullpen to huddle with her team of investigators. Seeing Ernie there conferring with Jaime and Deb made Joanna realize that she had not yet nailed down bringing on the next member of the team. With Ernie leaving in less than a month, she had to make that move soon.

"Hey, guys," she said. "What's up? And how did things go last night?"

In her late-afternoon phone call with Frank Montoya, the two of them had strategized over how best to deal with the Nite Owl issue. The bar was located close to the Sierra Vista city limits. When Floyd Barco closed up shop, there was a fifty-fifty chance that he'd head west into town or east into county territory. Joanna and Frank had agreed to plant patrol cars on both sides of the line with officers lying in wait.

"Turns out our guys won the toss," Ernie told Joanna. "Barco's in our lockup on a DUI charge along with drug possession. He blew a 0.15 on the Breathalyzer. Jaime and I have some paperwork to clear up here, but when we have our chat with him, care to sit in?"

"Yes, but I'll sit out rather than in," Joanna said, preferring to watch the proceedings from the far side of a two-way mirror rather than inside the room itself. "How do you plan to play this?"

"We know from several sources that there's a lot of drug dealing going on inside the Nite Owl and that Floyd Barco is part of it. We're going to lead him around to the scopolamine factor in Leon Hogan's death and see what breaks loose. If he thinks we're about to pin him on a conspiracy-to-commit charge, I'm guessing he'll talk."

"Have you discussed any of this with Arlee Jones?" Joanna asked.

Ernie nodded. "He says that if Barco plays ball and gives us the goods on Randy Williams and Madison Hogan, Arlee is willing to kick Barco's drug-dealing charge back to simple possession and drop the DUI charge altogether. He's going to have to get that taillight fixed, though," Ernie added with a grin.

"Okay," Joanna said. "Call me when he's in the box." She glanced around the room. "What else is happening?"

Deb raised her hand. "Later on today I'm planning on bringing Madison in for a little chat. With the Department of Public Safety off the case, she's probably thinking she's in the clear. I'll put her initial worries to rest by letting her know we're looking into drug activities at the Nite Owl. Later on I'll segue into what happened to Leon. Once we have her on tape, we can bring Randy in to see what he has to say."

Joanna nodded. "Okay," she said. "Compare and contrast sounds like a good strategy. Stay on it and keep me apprised."

On the way back to her office, Joanna stopped by Kristin's desk. "Is Garth Raymond on duty today?"

A few clicks on Kristin's computer brought up the duty roster. "He's off," she said a moment later.

"Thanks," Joanna said. She started for her desk, but Kristin held up her hand.

"Sunny Sloan just called and would like to have a word at your convenience."

"Tell her to come on in," Joanna said. "I'm available."

Sunny, the widow of Joanna's fallen officer, Deputy Dan Sloan, had worked in the department's front office for several years now. Joanna had offered Sunny a job as a way of helping a struggling single mom support her child but also as a way for Joanna to assuage some of her own guilt over Dan's death. When Sunny had first shown up, she'd been a diffident and almost painfully shy young woman. Now in her late twenties, she was gradually growing more confident and appeared to be coming into her own.

"You wanted to see me?" Joanna asked when Sunny showed up a few minutes later.

Sunny nodded. "I do. You know about my dad, right?"

"That you lost him a few months ago?" Joanna asked. "Yes, I'm aware of that, and I'm so sorry. How are you doing?"

"He'd been so sick for so long that it was a blessing for both Anne and me when he was gone. It takes time, but things are getting better."

Joanna knew that Anne Coyle was Sunny's stepmother. She also knew that when Sunny had first started working, Fred and Anne had both stepped up to provide child care for their granddaughter, Danielle, who was now a six-year-old first-grader.

"Did you know that after Daddy died, Grammy Anne invited Danielle and me to move in with her?" Sunny asked.

"I had no idea."

Sunny paused for a moment, as if reluctant to go on. Finally she found her voice. "I've loved my job," she continued. "When you first offered it to me, I didn't think I'd like it at all, but that's changed."

Uh-oh, Joanna thought, *she loves her job, but she's about to quit. Great! Just what I need, another job to fill!*

Sunny drew a deep breath. "But what I'd really like to do now," she said, "is become a deputy."

That pronouncement left Joanna utterly floored. "Really?"

Sunny nodded. "When Dan was here, I didn't really know any of the people he worked with, but I know them now. They're my friends the same way they were his friends. I've seen how everyone around here pulls together to help others, and I'd like to play a bigger role in that."

For a moment Joanna struggled to find a reasonable response, but the first words out of her mouth weren't her best. "You know that being a deputy can be a dangerous job," she cautioned.

"You think?" Sunny replied with a sad smile.

"It would mean your having to go through police-academy training," Joanna added after a pause. "You'd have to spend at least six weeks away from home in Phoenix."

Sunny nodded.

"And once you're a deputy, you'd be doing shift work."

Sunny nodded again. "I know that, too, and if it weren't for Grammy Anne, I wouldn't even be able to consider it, but she and Daddy started looking after Danielle while she was just a baby. Sometimes I think Grammy Anne is more of a mother to her than I am. But Anne knows this is what I want, and she's willing to do whatever it takes to make it happen. And as far as supporting my family, she and I both know that I'll make more money as a deputy than I do as a clerk. Besides," she added as an afterthought, "it would be my way of honoring Dan's memory."

Joanna knew there were plenty of biological mothers who had stepped into this kind of child-care role when necessary, but a stepmother? That seemed downright remarkable. Anne Coyle had to be someone special.

As for the wage disparity between office clerks and deputies? Unfortunately, Joanna knew that was all too true, and she found herself looking at Sunny with new eyes. She was young but dependable, trustworthy, and physically fit. In the last several years, she had earned an A.A. degree from Cochise College by taking classes both at night and online. She was smart, eager, and motivated, and it wasn't as though she was blind to the inherent risks of being a cop. In addition, she was a hometown girl. If the department paid her way through the academy, it wasn't as though Sunny would immediately take off for parts unknown.

"You really want to do this?" Joanna asked.

Sunny nodded. "I do," she said.

With Armando destined to be confined to desk duty for the immediate future and with another deputy—let's face it, with Deputy Raymond—moving into investigations, Sunny's offer was a godsend.

"Okay," Joanna said, standing up and reaching across her desk to shake Sunny's hand. "Deputy it is. I'll call the academy and see how soon they have an opening."

After Sunny left, Joanna didn't let any grass grow. She immediately called the Arizona Police Academy, where they just happened to have a class with an opening starting after the first of the year, on Tuesday, January 2. Joanna reserved a spot in Sunny's name and asked for enrollment forms to be forwarded directly to Sunny.

Once that was done, she sat for a moment or two, thinking. Now that she had inadvertently tricked herself into making up her mind on the upcoming detective vacancy, there was no reason to stall any longer. She picked up the phone and called Garth. He sounded surprised to hear from her.

"Are you enjoying your day off?"

"Yes, ma'am, I'm helping Gran put up the Christmas tree, but if you need me to come in . . ."

"Actually, I'd like you to do just that if you don't mind. I want to officially introduce you to your new colleagues."

"My new colleagues?" Garth echoed uncertainly.

"Yes, as of January first, when Ernie Carpenter retires, you'll be the newest member of my investigations unit."

"Really?"

"Yes, really."

. "I'll be there in an hour or so," Garth said, "maybe a little less."

When Joanna hung up the phone after that call, she realized that for the space of at least fifteen minutes she'd managed to keep from thinking and worrying about Jenny and Beth and about Butch driving north on far too little sleep. For right now not worrying was a good thing. With a sigh, she, like Jaime and Ernie, turned to do battle with that day's worth of paperwork.

CHAPTER 38

A CAMPUS cop arrived at Conover Hall at nine forty-five to drive Jenny and Beth to the admin building for their individual exams, which were overseen by a secretary in a conference room next door to the president's office. As expected, the sociology test was easy. Jenny breezed through it and finished up twenty minutes early. Beth worked on hers right up until time was called.

When they left the building together, another cop was on site, waiting to take them back to the dorm. Neither of them objected. The fact that someone had tried to murder Jenny the night before wasn't lost on either of them, and they both felt as though they were walking around with targets on their backs.

As they approached the dorm lobby entrance, Jenny felt a sense of relief, but then the door opened and she walked into a reality-based version of *Family Feud*. Beth stopped short just inside the door. "Mom? Dad?" she said uncertainly. "What are you doing here?"

"We came to get you," Madeline Rankin stated flatly. "I don't care what your grandmother wanted or what happens to her money. It can go straight down the drain and good riddance! We are pulling you out of this evil place and taking you home."

"You can't do that," Beth declared. "I'm not quitting school, and I'm not leaving."

"Yes you are," Madeline screeched back, waving a brown envelope in her daughter's face. "We've seen the pictures, Beth. This place is Sodom and Gomorrah, and it's turned you into a godless Jezebel. You are not staying here a moment longer. Not one moment!"

Jenny watched Beth's face turn white. Meanwhile the sound of raised voices was attracting a lot of undue attention around the lobby, including that of the dorm's on-duty resident assistant.

"Excuse me, ma'am," she interjected, coming around from behind the reception desk. "There are people here who are trying to study. Please keep it down."

"Keep it down my eye!" Madeline returned furiously. "What are they studying anyway, pornography? This place isn't a dormitory, it's a whorehouse."

"Ma'am, please," the RA insisted, "if you don't calm down, I'll be forced to summon a campus police officer."

"You do that," Madeline taunted her. "Go ahead. I can hardly wait to show him what people have been up to around here. They've defiled my daughter and turned her into a filthy piece of garbage."

With those words still hanging in the air, Beth fled into the elevator. Jenny remained in the lobby, realizing that everything her roommate had said about her awful mother was absolutely true. But Jenny's real focus was on the envelope in Madeline Rankin's hand.

"Those are pictures of Beth?" Jenny asked.

"Of course they're her pictures," Madeline snapped, "although they're probably only some of the pictures instead of all of them. God alone knows how many of these there are."

"How did you get them?"

"How do you think?" Madeline returned. "Someone

sent them to us in the mail. The envelope showed up at the post office this morning with more than a dollar's worth of postage due. Who are you?"

"My name is Jenny Brady. I'm Beth's roommate."

"Her former roommate, then," Madeline said. "You go on upstairs and tell her I said she should pack her things and get back down here. Kenneth and I are leaving, and so is she."

"I'll do no such thing," Jenny replied. "Beth has no intention of going with you, and she doesn't have to."

"Yes she does," Madeline said, "and if you won't go get her, I will. What room is she in?"

"I'm sorry," the RA put in, "I can't allow you to go upstairs. I believe your daughter has made her intentions clear. She has no interest in going anywhere with you. And since she doesn't want to speak to you either, I'll have to ask you to leave. As of now you're unwelcome guests trespassing on university property."

Beth's father attempted to intercede. "Come on, Madeline," he said. "We're not wanted here. We should go."

"I'm not going anywhere without my daughter," Madeline declared, "and don't you try to make me."

"Jenny," Butch said uncertainly, speaking from behind Jenny's back. "What's going on here?"

Jenny had been so focused on what was happening that she hadn't noticed the lobby door slide open and then close behind her. She spun around and found Butch standing there. "It's Beth's parents, Dad," she said. "They're upset."

"Upset?" Madeline echoed. "Are you kidding? I am not upset. I'm furious. These people have brainwashed my daughter into becoming something she's not, and I want her back."

By then the RA had returned to the reception desk and picked up the handset on the phone. No doubt she was dialing 911. Jenny knew that she and Beth had been given strict orders to stay under the radar and say nothing to anyone. Being caught up in an altercation that included an appearance by the campus cops didn't amount to keeping a low profile.

"I have to go, Dad," she said quickly. "I'll call you later." With that, Jenny, too, disappeared into the elevator. Even before she opened the door to her room, she could hear Beth's inconsolable sobs. She lay facedown on the bed, weeping into her pillow.

"He sent the pictures to my parents," Beth wailed when Jenny eased herself down onto the bed beside her. "How could Ron do something so awful?"

"Because he is awful," Jenny replied. "Because he's a scumbag who should be ground into the dirt like the cockroach he is."

"Yes, a cockroach," Beth hiccupped something that was almost a laugh. "That's exactly what he is," she added, taking a deep breath. "Are my parents still down in the lobby?"

"I doubt it," Jenny replied. "When I left to come up here, the RA was calling the cops. I believe they'll be encouraged to leave the campus, and I expect they'll have a police escort to make sure they do."

"I told you my mother was bad news," Beth said.

"Yes, you did," Jenny said, "but she's way worse than I ever imagined. So are you ready?"

"Ready?" Beth repeated.

"The other person who's down there now is my dad. We just had our last finals, and the two of us are on Christmas break, remember?"

Beth smiled weakly. "I almost forgot," she said.

"Get a move on," Jenny ordered.

Beth heaved herself into a sitting position. "I will," she said determinedly. "Because I'm going to Bisbee, and my mother and Ron Cameron can both go to hell."

"Right," Jenny said. "Let's do it."

They had both packed earlier in the morning, so now it was just a matter of gathering things together. When they were ready to head out the door, Jenny punched her dad's number into her phone.

"Is the coast clear? Are they gone?"

"It was either leave on their own or get hauled off to jail," he said. "Fortunately for all concerned, they chose the former."

"Good," Jenny said. "We'll be right down."

CHAPTER 39

AFTER GETTING off the phone with Garth, Joanna called Tom Hadlock to let him know her decision. He was pleased to hear it. Half an hour later, Jaime called. "Hey, boss," he said. "We're taking Barco into the interview room."

"Good enough," she said, "I'll be right there." On her way she stopped by Kristin's desk long enough to give her a credit card and ask her to go into town to pick up an assortment of pizzas.

"How come?" a puzzled Kristin wanted to know.

"It turns out we'll be having a departmentwide celebration early this afternoon."

As soon as Joanna caught sight of Floyd Barco, handcuffed to the table in the interview room, she recognized the type. He was a smarmy little man with a chip on his shoulder and plenty of attitude meant to make up for his diminutive stature.

"Look," he sneered, "you guys have me dead to rights—DUI, weapons charge, and more than my fair share of weed in the vehicle. So what's this all about? Just send me back to the pen and get it over with."

"It's not that simple," Ernie told him. "We're actually here to talk about a homicide."

Floyd's eyes bugged. "A homicide?" he repeated. "I've done lots of bad stuff, but I never had nothin' to do with something like that."

"We'll see," Ernie said. "Why don't you tell us about Randy Williams and Madison Hogan? I understand they're friends of yours, right?"

"They're not friends, they're customers at the Nite Owl. That's where I work, and they're regulars."

"So maybe they drop by for more than just good company and booze," Jaime suggested. "Maybe one or the other purchased another kind of goods from you fairly recently."

Floyd squirmed in his chair. "I don't know what you're talking about," he said.

"When you were taken into custody, the arresting officers noticed that you had several bottles of eyedrops in your glove box," Jaime mentioned.

"I've got allergies real bad," Barco said. "I have to use drops all the time, day and night."

"That's surprising," Ernie observed. "I didn't know scopolamine was good for allergies."

Floyd took a deep breath and said nothing.

"You might be interested in knowing that an empty eyedrop container just like the ones in your Suburban was found at the crime scene where Leon Hogan was shot to death," Ernie continued.

"So?" Floyd asked with a shrug, trying to regain some of his lost composure. "What does that have to do with me? Hogan was killed by some trigger-happy cop. Everybody knows that."

"What everybody maybe doesn't know is that Mr. Hogan was hopped up on scopolamine at the time he died," Ernie said. "Randy Williams's handgun was found at the scene. It would appear that someone dosed Mr. Hogan with scopolamine, possibly with the intention of killing the guy while he was out of commission and unable to defend himself. Not surprisingly, the most likely candidates on that score turn out to be Randy Williams and Madison Hogan. The only question now is whether you were in on it, too."

"Me?" Barco asked faintly.

"Yes, you, Mr. Barco," Ernie said. "As it happens, we've heard from more than one source that when it comes to scopolamine, you're the go-to guy in the neighborhood. We're also under the impression that Randy and Madison were looking to score a cool hundred G's in life-insurance proceeds by taking Leon Hogan out. So let me ask again, were you in on it or not? Did Randy and Madison pay you outright for the drugs they used, or were you in on the deal for a percentage of the take? Or is it possible you were going to be in on the cartel deal that Williams was cooking up?"

Floyd stayed quiet for a long moment. "I want a lawyer," he said finally.

"Absolutely," Ernie said. "And we'll see to it that you get one. At the moment, however, since we're holding you on other charges, we won't have to add conspiracy to commit homicide to the mix, at least not right now. But when your attorney shows up, you might let him know that possible charges on that score are pending, especially if either Randy or Madison drops the dime on you."

"But I . . ." Floyd began again, but then he seemed to think better of what he was about to say and fell silent once more.

"Fair enough," Ernie said. "Detective Carbajal here will be happy to escort you to your cell."

On Joanna's way back to her office, Butch sent a

text saying they were in the car and headed south with Jenny at the wheel. They were out of Flagstaff and coming home! Joanna's relief at the news was palpable. For the first time all day, it felt as though she could draw a full breath.

In Kristin's office she found Deputy Garth Raymond crouched down next to Mojo's bed, scratching the old dog's ears. He lurched to his feet the moment Joanna appeared.

"Good afternoon, Sheriff Brady," he said, wiping his petting hand on his pant leg. It was his day off. Rather than wear his uniform, he'd shown up in work clothes—a worn plaid flannel shirt, work boots, and jeans.

Joanna smiled back at him. "Don't worry about a few dog germs, Detective Raymond," she said. "I'm immune."

"Wait," Kristin demanded, leaping to her feet, "Did you just say Detective Raymond?"

"I did indeed," Joanna replied.

Kristin hurried around the desk to give Garth a congratulatory hug. "And that's why you had me pick up pizzas?"

"It is. Where are they, by the way?"

"In the conference room."

"Good," Joanna said. "Detective Raymond and I are going into the bullpen for a private introduction to the rest of the team, and then you can let everybody know that at one P.M. it'll be pizza time in the conference room. I'll make the official promotion announcement there."

In the bullpen Jaime, Ernie, and Deb welcomed Garth to the team. Later, during the conference-room party, Joanna made two announcements as opposed to one—Garth's promotion, of course, and also Sunny Sloan's recent decision about becoming a deputy.

By two o'clock everyone at the Justice Center—including the jail guards and the guys out in the motor pool—had tucked in on their share of pizza. Knowing that Carol would be making Jenny's favorite home-coming meal—green chili casserole—for dinner Joanna limited herself to a single slice of pepperoni pizza.

CHAPTER 40

IT WAS another forever day for Kendall and Peter. Mommy was sleeping late again, only this time she really was in her bedroom. Kendall had checked to be sure, and Mommy was snoring. She hadn't gone out the night before, and much to Kendall's relief, Randy hadn't come over. That meant Mommy had been home alone and drinking far too much. Kendall knew that, too, because she'd counted all the empty bottles in the recycling.

They had been outside playing and were about to go back inside for lunch when Mrs. Walkup's son pulled in to her driveway with a Christmas tree tied on the top of his car. Kendall and Peter watched while he cut the tree down and carried it inside.

"Are we going to have a Christmas tree, too?" Peter asked.

Daddy was the one who had always decorated the tree and helped them hang their stockings.

"I don't know," Kendall said with a shrug. "Ask Mommy."

It was after lunch and halfway through *Frozen* again when Mommy finally got up. Even though she was supposedly drinking coffee, she still smelled of beer, and her coffee didn't smell like plain coffee either.

"When are we going to put up our Christmas tree?" Peter asked.

"What Christmas tree?" Mommy snapped at him. "Who says we're going to have a friggin' Christmas tree?" Except she didn't say "friggin'." She said something else—a very bad word—and Peter fled the kitchen in tears while Kendall remained where she was, too shocked to say anything at all.

"Well?" Mommy snarled at her. "What are you hanging around for? I suppose you want a Christmas tree, too. Well, wanting one and having one are two different things."

Without another word Kendall followed Peter into the bedroom. She found him lying on his bunk sobbing. Eventually he cried himself to sleep. From out front Kendall heard the chatter and laughter of kids on the street as they made their way home from school. She couldn't help but wonder what they would be doing this afternoon. Maybe some of them would be at home putting up their own Christmas trees.

They probably wouldn't be hiding out in their bedrooms hoping their mommies would drink enough beer to fall back asleep.

CHAPTER 41

By 3:00 P.M. Joanna had almost finished wading through her daily mishmash of paperwork. Leon Hogan's funeral was scheduled for early afternoon the next day, and she planned on being there, but tomorrow morning she'd need to attend the board of supervisors meeting in order to discuss and defend her requested budget increases. That meant she needed to go home tonight with a clean desk and a clean slate. Otherwise, come Monday morning, she'd be buried.

"Hey, boss," Deb Howell said, popping her head inside Joanna's office. "Garth and I are on our way out to Sierra Vista to bring Madison Hogan in for questioning."

"I thought today was his day off," Joanna countered.

"It was," Deb replied, "but he wants to get his feet wet, and there's no time like the present. The more he can see or do before Ernie leaves, the better."

"Fair enough," Joanna said.

She put down the report she was reading and glanced out the window. Bright morning sun had given way to overcast skies. Without having caught a moment of TV news and weather, she was startled to see occasional wind-driven snowflakes whipping past her window.

It was winter, after all, and Bisbee was known to be a mile-high city. That meant snow wasn't completely out of the ordinary. Still, it surprised Joanna to see it. And suddenly, more than anything else, she wanted to be away from her desk and out of her office.

"Mind if I tag along?" she asked.

Deb frowned. "With Garth riding shotgun, someone will end up having to sit in back with Madison."

"Not to worry," Joanna said. "I'll drive myself. I never laid eyes on Madison at the crime scene. I'll be interested to see what she's like."

"Okay," Deb said. "See you there."

Butch called as Joanna emerged from the tunnel at the top of the Divide. "Hey," he said. "I just woke up from a long winter's nap. How's it going?"

"I'm on my way to Sierra Vista, following Detectives Raymond and Howell, who are about to bring Madison Hogan in for questioning."

"Did I hear you say Detective Raymond?"

"Yup, you certainly did. I gave him the news this morning and made it official at an impromptu pizza party at lunchtime. And that's not all. Sunny Sloan told me this morning that she wants to become a deputy. I was able to find her a training slot at the Arizona Police Academy starting right after the first of the year."

"Sounds like things are popping."

"They are. How are things with you?"

"I've been sleeping most of the way, and so has Beth," Butch told her.

"How is she?"

"Hard to tell. She hasn't said much. She's been through an emotional wringer and is pretty much worn out."

"How's the weather where you are?" Joanna asked. "We seem to be having a few snow flurries down here."

"Yeah," Butch said. "It's weird. The weather in Flagstaff was perfect—cold but clear. It started to sprinkle as we drove through Anthem, and it's a lot darker to the south."

"At least you have all-wheel drive," Joanna said. "Tell Jenny to be careful."

Butch laughed at that. "Not gonna bother," he said. "She goes to school in Flagstaff, remember? That means our daughter has way more experience driving on snow than you do."

Joanna could hear Jenny talking in the background.

"What did she say?" Joanna asked.

"Jen wants to know what's for dinner."

"Green chili casserole, of course," Joanna replied. "It's her down-home favorite. What did she think we'd be having?"

CHAPTER 42

WHEN THE doorbell rang a while later, Peter didn't stir, but Kendall did. She went as far as the bedroom door and peeked out through the crack in time to see Mommy, still in her pajamas and with a beer bottle in one hand and a lit cigarette in the other, stagger from the kitchen to the front entry. A ringing doorbell meant that the new arrival wasn't Randy, and Kendall hoped beyond hope that the person waiting outside on the porch would be Grandma Puckett.

Several verbal exchanges followed, with words that Kendall couldn't quite make out, but she heard Mommy's voice rising in anger. "What do you mean you want to take me in for questioning? What's to ask? The DPS said that cop did it. I don't see why you wanna talk to me."

Kendall slipped out of the bedroom and crept silently toward the front door until she was close enough to see that there were three people standing outside—two women and a man. One woman was wearing a blue pantsuit and the other a brown police uniform. The man was dressed in a plaid work shirt, jeans, and boots. The woman in the pantsuit, the one doing most of the talking, was tall and blond, while the shorter one in the uniform hovered in the background.

"Well, you can't take me in for questioning," Mommy

said. "I've got two little kids. I can't leave them here by themselves."

That surprised Kendall. As if Mommy didn't leave them there by themselves lots of the time! She was standing just behind Mommy and out of her line of vision, so when Kendall spoke, Mommy jumped like she'd been shot.

"You could always call Grandma Puckett," Kendall suggested quietly. "I'm sure she'd come stay with us."

"What the hell?" Mommy yelled. "What are you doing here? Get back in your room. Now!"

But to her mother's astonishment and to Kendall's own surprise, she didn't budge. She fully expected Mommy to slap her, but she didn't. She just took another angry draw on her cigarette.

"Your mother is in the area?" the woman on the porch was asking. "Perhaps you'd be kind enough to give her a call."

"I'll do no such thing," Mommy shot back.

"Then we may need to take your children into custody as well," the other woman said. "Once we get to the Justice Center, we can have someone from CPS come pick them up."

"Crap!" Mommy said. "Put them in foster care? Let me call and see what my mother says."

Kendall held her breath. First Mommy ground her cigarette stub out on the front porch, and then she fished her phone out of her pocket and struggled to make it work.

"Hey, Mom," Mommy said at last. "It's me. I need to go talk to some cops for a while. Can you come look after the kids?" There was a pause. "Okay, good.

Where are you, and how long will it take for you to get here? . . . Half an hour . . . that long? . . . Okay, I'll tell them.

"You heard, I guess," Mommy mumbled. "It'll take half an hour for her to get here."

That's when the woman in the background, the one wearing a uniform, spoke for the first time. "I'm Sheriff Brady," she said. "I'll be happy to stay here with the kids until your mother arrives."

"You sure?" Mommy asked.

"Positive," Sheriff Brady said. "It's no trouble at all."

"All right, then," Mommy said grudgingly, "I guess we can go."

"There's one other problem, Ms. Hogan," the first woman said. "You'll need to leave that beer bottle here. You can't take it with you—open containers and all."

"No problem," Mommy said, slamming the bottle down on a nearby table.

When she went to straighten back up, she tripped and almost fell, knocking over the bottle in the process. At last Mommy righted herself and stumbled out the door, while the man on the porch reached out and took one arm to steady her. Kendall was embarrassed that Mommy was still wearing her pajamas as he helped her into the car, but since no one else said anything about it, neither did Kendall.

She was about to turn and run to the kitchen to get something to clean up the spilled beer, but then she realized it must have been empty. The mess consisted of nothing more than a few drops. That was good news. Even better news? Grandma Puckett was coming to take care of them.

As the car with Mommy and the other two visitors

disappeared from sight, the woman in the uniform stepped across the threshold. She had short red hair and bright green eyes. There was a gold star pinned to her brown shirt. As she came inside, she held out her hand.

"My name is Sheriff Joanna Brady," she said. "What's yours?"

"Kendall," the little girl replied gravely, returning the handshake.

"And your brother?"

"His name is Peter."

"Where's he?"

"In our bedroom. He fell asleep a little while ago. I can wake him up if you want me to."

"That's not necessary," Sheriff Brady said. "If it's all right with you, we can just sit and talk until your grandmother gets here."

Sheriff Brady had a nice voice—a lot like Mrs. Baird's. Kendall Hogan liked her already.

CHAPTER 43

DURING HER years in law enforcement, there were several moments that remained seared into Joanna's memory. One of them was the gunfight off I-10 north of Benson, during which she'd taken cover and fired her weapon beneath the undercarriage of her minivan in order to rescue a little girl being held hostage by a fleeing gunman. Another was the middle-of-the-night journey she'd made, accompanied by Father Rowan, to inform a pregnant Sunny Sloan that her deputy husband was dead. But neither of those was as heartbreaking as walking into Madison Hogan's filthy house and meeting Kendall for the first time.

Joanna had remained in the background on a porch surrounded by a weed-choked front yard while Deb Howell and Garth Raymond had handled Madison Hogan—an argumentative train wreck of a woman. Only after the three of them left had she followed the little girl into the home.

"You can sit in here if you want," Kendall said shyly, ushering Joanna into the junk-strewn living room and sweeping a collection of toys and debris off a threadbare couch in order to clear a space for Joanna to sit.

"How old are you?" she asked.

"I'm seven."

As the child spoke, Joanna looked into her deep blue

eyes. They were eyes that were older than her age—eyes that had seen too much and known too much.

"I have a son who's seven," Joanna said. "His name is Denny, and he's lost a bunch of teeth. How many teeth have you lost so far?"

Kendall held up three fingers. A little boy appeared in the doorway across the room. "Who's that?" he asked, rubbing his eyes and pointing at Joanna.

"Her name's Sheriff Brady," Kendall answered. "Mommy had to go someplace. Sheriff Brady's going to watch us until Grandma Puckett gets here."

The little boy's face brightened. "Grandma's coming?" he said. "Is she going to take us to dinner?"

"I don't know," Kendall told the boy. Then, turning to Joanna, she added, "This is my little brother, Peter. He's five."

The kids didn't appear to be undernourished, but Joanna remembered that Kendall's teacher had told Detective Howell that the little girl had been spotted scavenging food from cafeteria trash cans.

"Do you like your Grandma Puckett?" Joanna asked.

Both children nodded enthusiastically. "She bought me chocolate-chip pancakes," Peter said.

"And a new dress for me," Kendall added. "She's nice."

"Where does she live?" Joanna asked. "Somewhere nearby?"

Kendall shook her head. "Somewhere far away," she answered, "in a place where only old people live. That's why we can't go stay with her. They don't let children live there."

"But you'd like to stay with her?"

Kendall dropped her eyes and said nothing. Finally she nodded reluctantly, but her apparent reticence didn't keep Peter from piping up on his own.

"Now that Daddy's gone, Mommy forgets to feed us sometimes."

Out of the mouths of babes! For a moment Joanna was too affected to say anything more.

"I'm sorry your daddy's gone," she said at last. "That's why my detectives and I came here today. We need to ask your mom about what happened."

Kendall's head came up. "They had a fight," she said at once.

"Who had a fight?"

"Mommy and Daddy," Kendall said, "that morning. I heard them, but when I tried to go see what was happening, the bedroom door was locked. I couldn't get out."

The hair on the back of Joanna's neck stood on end. "Where were you?" she asked.

"At Daddy's place."

"And when was that?" Joanna asked. "When did the fight happen?"

"That morning, just after the doorbell rang. I heard talking and then someone left. After the door closed Mommy started yelling at Daddy. Then there was a gunshot, and Mommy started screaming. There were a whole bunch more gunshots after that. When I climbed up on the dresser and looked out the window, I saw Daddy lying on the porch by the front door. I could tell he was dead."

Joanna was thunderstruck. Obviously Kendall could recall every chilling detail of what had happened that awful morning and do so in chronological order. That made this seven-year-old child the closest thing to an eyewitness there was to what had happened out in Whetstone. Now Joanna found herself wondering if Dave Newton had bothered to ask Kendall a single question. Had he even spoken to her? When Joanna glanced in Peter's direction, however, she found him gaping at his sister in openmouthed amazement.

"You saw Daddy dead?" he demanded.

Kendall nodded.

"Why didn't you tell me?"

"I couldn't."

"Why not?"

"Because you're just a little kid," Kendall said fiercely. "That's why."

And that was the moment that broke Sheriff Joanna Brady's heart.

CHAPTER 44

IT WASN'T exactly the kind of celebratory homecoming Joanna had hoped to have as the beginning of Christmas break. For one thing, everyone—Joanna included—was tired beyond bearing. Beth Rankin was a stranger to all of them. She was shy and withdrawn, and Denny's laserlike questioning didn't help matters. Who was she? Where did she live? Was she Jenny's best friend? What did she like to eat? How old was she? Did she have her own car? Did she know how to ride a horse?

It was a relief to all concerned when Butch banished Denny from the table to go take his bath. Minutes later Jenny grabbed Sage out of her high chair. "You guys visit, why don't you," she said. "I'll put Sage down, too."

"I'm really sorry to barge in on all of you like this," Beth said at last, speaking as if hoping to find a way to fill the conversational void.

"We're glad to have you," Joanna said. "They might have caught the shooter, but with that other guy still on the loose, there's no place I'd rather you and Jen to be than right here, locked inside our rolling shutters."

"I saw those when Jenny was closing them earlier," Beth offered. "They look pretty amazing."

"According to the company's sales brochure, even trained SWAT teams can't penetrate them."

"Good to know," Beth said.

An uneasy silence settled over the table. Finally, after glancing back and forth between Butch and Joanna, Beth said quietly, "I guess you know everything that happened, and you must think I'm really stupid."

"I don't think you're stupid at all," Butch said. "And believe me, you're definitely not alone. Have you ever watched a program called *Web of Lies*?"

Beth shook her head. "Never heard of it," she said. "As you might have noticed, my mother's a little weird. She doesn't approve of TV sets any more than she approves of computers or cell phones, and since that's how I grew up, I never got in the habit of watching."

"It's on a channel called Investigation Discovery," Butch explained. "Each show focuses on a victim of some kind of cybercrime—identity theft, cyberbullying, sextortion. That's what happened to you, by the way."

"Sextortion?" Beth asked, frowning. "That's what they call it?"

Joanna nodded. "That's what this so-called Ron guy did to you. It's when perpetrators blackmail their victims with threats of taking damaging photographs public. Only in your case he didn't bother with threatening. He just sent out the photos. But Butch is right, you might consider watching a few of those programs sometime. At least you'll see that you're by no means alone."

Beth nodded. Another short pause followed until she spoke again. "Before Jenny comes back, I have to say that I wouldn't have made it through all this without her. Even though I left Jenny out and didn't really tell her much about what was going on between Ron and me, when it started falling apart, she was right there for me. I've never had a real friend before—not ever. And to think she almost got killed because of me." Beth shivered. "If she had died, I never would have forgiven myself."

Reaching out, Joanna took Beth's hand. "But Jenny didn't die," she said reassuringly, "and neither did you. You're both here and safe, and no matter what, we're all going to have a wonderful Christmas."

Beth shot a glance in Butch's direction. "Did he tell you about my parents?"

"Not really, no," Joanna said.

The truth was, they had yet to have a moment of privacy when he could have.

"Ron sent my parents all those nude pictures," Beth said in a voice that was barely more than a whisper. "When my mother saw them, she went bananas. She thinks it's all my fault. She'll probably never speak to me again."

Joanna couldn't help but remember the often strained relations she and her mother had shared. "I wouldn't be so sure about that," she said. "Here's the weird thing about mothers. Yes, they get mad at their daughters from time to time, but eventually they come around. Maybe yours will, too."

Beth shook her head. "I doubt it. My grandmother would have forgiven me, but not my mother. I wish Grandma Lockhart were still here." Beth's voice broke, and she burst into tears. "Until I met Jenny, Grandma Lockhart was the only person who ever understood me. She's dead now, but she's the one who's making it possible for me to go to school."

"Your mother's mother?" Butch asked from his end of the table.

Wiping her tears on her napkin, Beth nodded.

"Why don't you tell us about your grandmother," he urged gently. "Grandma Lockhart sounds like a very interesting person."

CHAPTER 45

IT WAS much later. The dishes were done, and a weary Butch and Joanna were finally getting ready for bed.

"All I can say is, thank God for grandparents," Joanna told her husband as she stripped off her uniform. "When Deb and Garth took Madison Hogan in for questioning, her mother, Jackie Puckett, came riding to the rescue. If she hadn't been there to take charge of the kids, those poor little ones would have ended up spending tonight in foster care. And you should have seen them. As soon as Jackie showed up, Peter's face lit up like a Christmas tree. He was hoping she'd take them to dinner, and I'm sure she did."

"What about Madison?" Butch asked.

Joanna shook her head. "A pretty pathetic case, if you ask me. She was still in her pj's and drunk as a skunk in the middle of the afternoon when we got there. Had to be helped in and out of the patrol car. In the meantime here's poor seven-year-old Kendall stuck with looking after her little brother. If those kids had breakfast and lunch today, it was because she made it happen. Madison sure as hell didn't do it."

"Sounds like Kendall is more of a mother than Madison is," Butch muttered under his breath. "If you ask me, some people should never have kids to begin with."

"Funny," Joanna said, "that's the same thing Jackie

Puckett said to me earlier today—about her own daughter. She told me outright that with Leon Hogan dead, she's worried about the long-term welfare of the two kids, and so am I."

"Where are they tonight?"

"When I left, Jackie was getting them packed up to go stay overnight with her at the Windemere Hotel. She said she'd leave Madison a note letting her know they're with her and that she'll get them to the funeral on time tomorrow."

"So Madison is back home tonight?"

Joanna nodded. "Deb sent me a text saying that they had taken her back to Sierra Vista and cut her loose."

"The detectives let her go just like that?"

"Under the circumstances there's nothing else they could have done. We have no solid evidence that would allow us to charge Madison with anything. What we do have, however, is three hours' worth of video with her answering questions. The next step is to bring the boyfriend in to see if their stories match up."

"And if they don't, you try turning one against the other?" Butch asked.

Nodding, Joanna crawled into bed. "That's the way the game is played," she answered. "Divide and conquer."

That night there was no tossing and turning for Joanna Brady. She was asleep as soon as her head hit the pillow, because she was too damned tired to do anything else. She was still sound asleep and dreaming about riding a merry-go-round when the phone awakened her at 6:00 A.M.

"What does a guy have to do to get some sleep

around here?" Butch grumbled as Joanna reached for her phone.

When Joanna looked at the window for caller ID, Robin Watkins's face was the one showing. "Hey, Robin," Joanna said. "What's up?"

"An arrest warrant is being issued on a guy named Gerard Wayne Paine, aka Ronald Cameron. I have permission to offer you an engraved invitation to be on hand for the official takedown."

"A takedown?" Joanna echoed, sitting up in bed and switching the phone to speaker. "Does that mean you've found him?"

"It certainly does. He's in a fifty-five-plus community on Tucson's far west side near Starr Pass. Our bad boy is a seventy-three-year-old suspected-but-not-convicted pedophile living in supposedly respectable retirement on West Placita del Correcaminos. Correcaminos means 'roadrunner,' by the way. I looked it up. According to our tech guys, he's a regular night owl who generally does most of his work in the deep, dark hours of the night and then sleeps during the days. That's why we've scheduled the raid for nine A.M."

"This morning?" Joanna asked.

"Affirmative," Robin said. "It'll be morning for us, but for him it'll seem like the middle of the night, and he should be sound asleep."

"If the raid is at nine," Joanna said, scrambling out of bed, "what time do we rendezvous and where?"

"At Tucson PD headquarters at eight fifteen."

"All right," Joanna said, "but it's going to take me at least two hours to get there."

"Then you'd better hit the road pronto," Robin advised.

With a sigh and a glower over his shoulder, Butch

headed for the kitchen and the coffeepot while Joanna
dragged clothing into the bathroom to dress.

"I can't believe you caught him this fast," Joanna
said. Her phone sat on the bathroom counter on speaker
as she stripped off her nightgown and struggled to fas-
ten her bra. Showering was out of the question.

"We had a whole lot of luck on our side," Robin
replied. "The fact that we had access to Aaron Morgan's phone is what made it possible to locate Paine as
quickly as we did. And we're wasting no time now, because we want him in custody before he has a chance to
break down all his computer equipment and erase whatever's stored there. According to the utility people, he's
been using enough electricity to run a grow house. He
might've dodged prosecution back home in Oklahoma,
but we're dealing with federal charges here, and believe
me, this guy is going down."

"Good," Joanna said, "I couldn't agree more, and
you'd better believe I'll be there."

"By the way," Robin added. "How's the road situation
down your way? I heard it snowed pretty hard overnight."

"It snowed?" Joanna repeated. "In that case I'd really
better get moving."

She pulled on her uniform pants, hurried back to
the bedroom, and peered out through the burglarproof
window screens. The overhead sky was lit by a sliver of
waning moon, while the landscape all around the house
glowed an unearthly white.

"Crap," she muttered aloud. Her Interceptor was
equipped with all-wheel drive, but that offered scant
protection from the many nutcases who would be out
and about with less than zero understanding about how
to drive in inclement weather.

She arrived in the kitchen a few minutes later to find

a travel mug loaded with coffee sitting on the table. Next to it was a fried-egg sandwich.

"Eat that before it gets cold," Butch told her. "Can't have you riding off into battle on an empty stomach." He stood watching as she pulled on her jacket and retrieved her weapons from the laundry room's gun safe. "So they're going to get him?"

"Looks like it," she said, "and I've been invited to attend the party."

"By the way," Butch said, "I just got an e-mail from the school district. The roads are bad enough that school's been canceled for today. That means we'll be going into full-bore cookie-making mode."

Joanna kissed him good-bye. "I think an entire day of messing with cookie dough will be good for what ails Beth and Jenny both. It'll take their focus away from all the bad stuff and put it on some good."

Nodding, Butch hugged her close. "Stay safe," he murmured in her ear.

"I will."

A call to Dispatch as she left the ranch let her know that the worst part of the trip would be crossing the Divide north of Bisbee, where several cars had spun out onto the shoulder. Knowing that people would be wondering why she was driving past accident scenes without stopping to help, she turned on her flashing lights to give herself a visible and hopefully understandable excuse for ignoring them. Somewhere south of Tombstone, she remembered that morning's board of supervisors meeting.

"Siri," she said aloud, "call Tom Hadlock."

Joanna had copied him on her budget-request paperwork once it was finished, but she still had concerns about Tom's public-speaking capabilities. Under intense pressure would he be the best advocate for her department? Maybe or maybe not, but she hoped that today he'd measure up, because no matter what, Joanna was going to Tucson right now to participate in that FBI takedown. This was personal for her. Her choice had far more to do with her being a mother than it did with her being a sheriff. Gerard Paine had attempted to murder Jenny, and Joanna wasn't about to apologize that for this time at least she'd come down on the side of motherhood.

"What's up?" a groggy Tom muttered when he came on the phone. "And why are you calling so early?"

"It's time to wake up and smell the flowers," she told him. "And when you come to work, be sure to wear your dress uniform."

"How come?"

"This is your call to duty, Tom," she told him. "I hope you're up for an appearance before the board of supervisors, because you're pinch-hitting for me today."

"Are you kidding?"

"Not in the least. I'm on my way to Tucson to take part in an FBI raid to take down a guy who tried to have Jenny murdered and very nearly succeeded."

"Wait," Tom said, now fully awake. "Someone tried to kill Jenny? Where? When?"

"In Flagstaff," Joanna answered, "night before last."

"I never heard a word about this," Tom grumbled. Clearly he was offended that he'd been left out of the loop.

"The FBI asked us to keep the whole thing under wraps in hopes of catching him off guard, and it sounds like their ploy has succeeded."

"Who is he?"

"He's the ex-boyfriend of Jenny's roommate—a cyber ex-boyfriend at that, and a pedophile besides."

"Great," Tom said. "He sounds terrific, but if he's the roommate's ex-boyfriend, why would he target Jenny?"

"Because Jenny helped Beth stand up to him."

"I see," Tom said, but since he was a lifelong bachelor with no kids of his own, Joanna wasn't at all sure he did.

"Okay," he added after a pause, "dress uniform it is, and I'll do my best."

"I know you will," Joanna told him. "You always do."

By the time she reached St. David, the snow was gone completely, and she finally gave herself permission to eat Butch's now-cold sandwich. North of Benson she had just passed the exit ramp to Patagonia when her phone rang with Frank Montoya's photo in caller ID.

"Good morning, Frank," she said. "What's up?"

"I'm on the scene of a fatality fire," he said. "The Nite Owl burned to the ground early this morning. The fire was discovered around five A.M. By the time firefighters arrived on the scene, the building was fully engulfed. The remaining structure was so unstable that we weren't able to let investigators inside until just a little while ago. They reported finding two dead bodies in the debris and called for the M.E. Doc Baldwin says that the victims are a male and a female, both of them shot in the back of the head, execution style."

"Any IDs?" Joanna asked.

"Not at this time," Frank answered, "but Kendra says that when they went to transport the bodies, they discovered that the female was wearing pajamas."

"Pajamas?" Joanna echoed.

Because approximately half the human body is made up of water, Joanna knew that even during intense fires the area directly under a victim's body often remains relatively undamaged.

"My guess is the female is Madison Hogan and the male Randy Williams," she said.

"What makes you say that?"

"Because the last time I saw Madison Hogan, she was wearing pajamas. That was yesterday afternoon when we brought her in to the department for questioning. It was the middle of the afternoon, and she still wasn't dressed. She was also falling-down drunk. Her mother, Jackie Puckett, is currently staying at the Windemere Hotel, and Madison's two kids, Kendall and Peter, are there with her."

"What happened after the questioning?"

"Deb Howell and Garth Raymond cut her loose and took her back home to Sierra Vista. I have no idea what happened after that."

"All right," Frank said. "Based on all the connections between these two cases, I suggest we handle this as a joint operation."

"Agreed," Joanna said. "Tom Hadlock will be tied up in a board of supervisors meeting for most of the morning, but I'll let him know what's going on. And, Frank, whatever you need from us, just ask."

"Good," he said. "I'll send someone by the Hogan residence to see if Madison is or isn't there. My guess is that you're right and she's a goner. I'll also be in touch with Mrs. Puckett. Hopefully she'll be able to provide her daughter's dental information. Due to the fire, dental records are probably our only hope for getting a positive ID on either one of these individuals."

Frank signed off. Joanna tried calling Tom back.

When her call went to voice mail, she left a message letting him know about the situation in Sierra Vista and then drove on. Before the call from Frank, she'd been feeling upbeat and happy. The prospect of being able to be on hand as Gerard Paine was taken into custody had been almost too good to be true. Now Frank's disturbing news had burst her bubble. In less than a week, Kendall and Peter Hogan had lost not just one but both of their parents, and it seemed likely that seven-year-old Kendall was the closest thing to a mother Peter would ever have.

That was beyond unfair. It was downright tragic.

CHAPTER 46

JOANNA ARRIVED at Tucson PD in time for the coffee-and-doughnuts part of the joint operation briefing. FBI agents, including Robin, would make up the core arrest team, with part of them focused on taking Paine into custody while the rest were assigned the task of securing his electronic equipment. There was concern that he might have built some kind of self-destruct scenarios into his computers, and the tech guys would be on hand in order to keep that from happening if at all possible.

Paine lived on a street made up of three-unit town homes. His was an end unit in the last group on Correcaminos. The operation was being conducted inside a strict media blackout. Officers from Tucson PD were assigned to create a perimeter to keep gawkers away. They were also tasked with clearing neighboring units of residents prior to the arrest warrant's being served. Nearby streets would be closed to traffic in both directions. All officers and agents participating in the operation were expected to be armed. Considering the age of the target, a strategic decision had been made that the presence of a SWAT team wasn't required. Prior to the operation, the perimeter guys were doing their best to give Joanna the boot. Only Robin's timely intervention, arriving on the scene with her FBI shield in hand, kept Joanna from being sent packing.

She had left her Interceptor several parking lots away, but this was a neighborhood designed for older people, and there were shaded benches scattered here and there. Joanna settled on one of those across the street and two houses down from Paine's unit and waited to see what would happen. She watched while the residents from neighboring units were roused from their breakfast tables and, in more than one case, from their beds, to be ushered away from the buildings. Only then did the arrest team appear. They approached the unit's front door with one of them carrying a battering ram while the others held drawn weapons. Robin herself was the one who delivered the obligatory police knock.

"Open up!" she shouted. "Federal agents!"

No one waited around for Gerard Paine to answer or open the door. The guy with the battering ram delivered one fierce blow, and the door slammed open. After that there was a period of dead silence before Joanna heard Robin shout, "Gun!" The pause that followed couldn't have lasted longer than a second or two, but for Joanna, sitting outside and holding her breath, it seemed to go on forever. Finally there was another shout, a welcome one this time: "Get on your knees!" After another momentary silence, Joanna was relieved to be able to breathe again. Another period of dead silence followed, one that went on for a full five minutes. When agents at last led Gerard Paine out of the house, it was hard to imagine the wizened, handcuffed, and hunched-over bald guy tottering along on the sidewalk could be the source of so much evil.

As they ushered him toward a black Suburban, Joanna couldn't help thinking about the moment in *The Wizard of Oz* when Toto finally peels back the emerald-green curtain to reveal the wizard himself running the controls. Everything about Ronald Cameron had been just as fake as the wizard. The wizard was a frail little old guy, and so was Gerard Paine. When faced with the tall step needed to climb into the waiting Suburban, he had to be helped. Once the door closed behind him and the vehicle took off, Robin came looking for Joanna.

"That was efficient and effective," Joanna said.

Robin grinned. "We aim to please," she replied.

"I suppose you're on your way to the interview?" Joanna asked.

"What interview?" Robin returned. "He already asked for an attorney, so we won't be chatting him up, but we've got him, and better yet we've got all his computers. He must have fifty of them at least, each with a different password. It'll take time for us to access all of them, but we will, and there's no rush on that either—not with him cooling his heels in jail."

She paused for a moment and then asked, "How's Jenny?"

"She's okay," Joanna said. "Better than okay, actually. You really came through on this for all of us, but for Jenny and Beth especially. You should hear Jenny singing Agent Norris's praises. The interview she conducted with Beth was evidently something to behold."

Robin nodded. "There's a reason Adele Norris is on the task force. Victims in these kinds of cases are usually right at the breaking point and need to be handled with kid gloves, and that's something Adele knows how to do. She's a trained psychiatrist and was running a private practice when the Bureau recruited her."

"Believe me, Jenny was suitably impressed."

"What about you?" Robin asked. "How are you doing? I saw that your guy got cleared in that OIS."

"Yes, he did. Armando's still in the hospital at the moment and will probably need an extended time to recover. In fact, since I'm here in Tucson, I should probably stop by to see him for a moment before I head home. As for how I'm doing? A double homicide just turned up in Sierra Vista last night. Since it's related to my officer-involved case, I'm expecting we'll be doing some of the heavy lifting on that score, too. In addition, I've got a pair of little kids—a five-year-old and a seven-year-old—who've been orphaned this week. There's a good chance that their mother was partially involved in the homicide that killed their father. Unfortunately, as of early this morning on the day of their father's funeral, their mother is dead, too."

Robin frowned. "Will the children end up in foster care, then?"

Joanna nodded. "Chances are," she answered bleakly.

"Sorry," Robin said. "That's tough on everybody."

Someone appeared at the door of Gerard Paine's unit and waved for Robin to come back inside. "I'll let you know what we find," she said as she walked away. "And don't worry. You won't have to go through channels and across desks to get the information."

"Thank you," Joanna told her. "Thanks way more than you know."

The takedown had gone so smoothly and was over so fast that Joanna still had most of the morning ahead of her. She stopped by Banner Medical. Amy was back teaching school today, so Armando was there alone. Joanna spoke with him briefly, bringing him up to date on the status of the investigation, including the fact that Madison Hogan and her boyfriend were now likely deceased. Bare minutes into their conversation, however, a nurse showed up to take Armando to physical therapy, and that was the end of that. Joanna went downstairs, got into her car, and set her sights on Sierra Vista. That's where the action was at the moment, and that's where she needed to be.

CHAPTER 47

THEY COULD have eaten breakfast at the hotel, but Peter wanted to go back to IHOP, and Grandma Puckett let him have his way. Not that Kendall minded. She loved IHOP, too, but she didn't like chocolate-chip pancakes nearly as much as her brother did.

During the morning she'd noticed Grandma Puckett making several phone calls, or at least trying to make them. She dialed, but each time no one answered, and she ended each of the calls without speaking to anyone. Finally she looked something up and dialed a different number. This time someone must have answered.

"I'd like to speak to Sheriff Brady," Grandma said. "She's not? Then what about that lady detective? I believe Sheriff Brady said her name was Debbie something. Yes, Detective Howell. That's it, but she's not in either? All right, then, never mind. No, no message. I'll call back later."

Grandma frowned as she ended the call.

"What's wrong?" Kendall asked.

Grandma sighed. "I can't reach your mother," she said. "I spoke to her for a few minutes last night after dinner, but I can't reach her this morning. She's not answering the phone."

"Her battery's probably dead," Kendall said. "Sometimes she forgets to plug it in."

"I wouldn't be surprised," Grandma said at last. "She's always been such a scatterbrain." She turned to Peter. "Are you done?" she asked.

"Almost," he said. "Two more bites."

Kendall was afraid that if he ate any more, he was going to burst—or else have a stomachache—but she said nothing.

"All right, then," Grandma Puckett said, sounding a bit angry—and a little like Mommy. "Hurry and finish up. I'm not sure what time we're supposed to be at the funeral home. Your mom was supposed to let me know this morning. So we'd best go back to the room, change clothes, and get ready."

At the hotel, the moment they walked into the lobby, Kendall spotted someone she recognized. The tall blond police officer, the woman who'd come to take Mommy away the day before, was sitting on a sofa facing the entrance. As soon as she saw them, she rose and hurried to meet them.

"Mrs. Puckett?"

"Yes," Grandma said.

"I'm Detective Howell. Could I have a moment of your time?" Then, after glancing toward Kendall and Peter, she added, "In private, please."

Grandma looked slightly flustered, but then she opened her purse and pulled out a fistful of quarters. "Do you remember where the vending machines are?" she asked.

"I do!" Peter crowed. "They're down at the end of the hallway by the ice machine."

"Why don't you go get yourselves a treat while Detective Howell and I talk for a moment?"

Peter went skipping off without a care in the world. Kendall followed him, but she didn't like it—not one bit. When grown-ups had to speak "in private" like that, it almost always meant something bad for kids. She didn't know how bad, though, not right then. When Kendall and Peter returned from the vending machines a few minutes later with a bag of Doritos and a Snickers candy bar in hand, they found a pale and shaken Grandma sitting alone on the sofa. As soon as Kendall saw the expression on Grandma Puckett's face, she knew that something awful had happened.

"Are you all right?" she asked.

Grandma turned and looked at her—stared at her, really—but at the same time it felt weird, like she didn't know who Kendall was and didn't even recognize her face.

"It's about your mother," Grandma Puckett answered at last. "Two people were found dead this morning." She paused again as tears filled her eyes. "They believe one of them is your mother."

CHAPTER 48

AS SOON as Joanna hit the open road, she dialed Frank Montoya's number. "What's the news?" she asked.

"I sent my guys by to check on the Hogan place," he said. "A vehicle registered to Randall J. Williams, a Jeep Cherokee, was parked in the driveway of the residence, but no one was home. A search of the place showed evidence of a knock-down, drag-out fight— broken bottles, broken furniture, and blood—lots of that, enough to assume that someone got hurt real bad."

"Do you think Madison Hogan and Randy Williams are the two victims?"

"Yes," Frank replied, "pending a positive ID."

"And you believe they were kidnapped from her place and then taken to the Nite Owl, where they were finished off?"

"That's a pretty good bet, but we'll need to examine the physical evidence to know for sure. My CSIs are working the fire scene, so Casey Ledford is working the house."

"Any witnesses?" Joanna asked.

"No actual eyewitnesses so far," Frank answered. "In the course of the melee, a kitchen clock got knocked off a wall and broken. It stopped at 2:46, so that's the time frame we're guessing—just prior to three A.M. We've had people out canvassing the neighborhood.

"The lady next door, a Mrs. Walkup, told us that she's deaf as a post. Once she takes out her hearing aids at night, she doesn't hear a thing, but another neighbor, Lois Watson from up the street, has a security camera. We took a look at her overnight footage. It shows a vehicle with no headlights—an SUV of some kind— driving past her house in the direction of the Hogan place at two fifteen A.M. It departs the same way— again with no headlights—at three-oh-five, so the time frame fits. Naturally there's no license plate visible, and the resolution is crap, so you can't see any details other than the fact that the vehicle is an SUV."

"No make or model."

"Right," Frank said, "but we're on the lookout for security footage from other nearby locations that may tell us more."

"Has Madison's mother been notified?"

"Deb Howell handled that," Frank said. "She inquired about dental records. Mrs. Puckett said she knows that Madison had her wisdom teeth pulled a year or so ago. She's pretty sure it was a dentist here in town, but she doesn't know which one. We have people out looking. If and when we find the unknown dentist and her records, we'll get that information to Kendra immediately.

"Even without a positive ID, however, Mrs. Puckett said she would call Leon Hogan's parents and suggest that they either postpone the funeral or cancel it altogether, which seems like a good idea as far as I'm concerned. My heart aches for those kids, though—to lose one parent is bad enough, but both of them almost simultaneously?"

"Where are they?" Joanna asked. "The kids and Mrs. Puckett, I mean."

"At their hotel, as far as I know."

"I'm on my way back from Tucson right now. I'll drop by the Windemere and see them, unless you think there's a reason for me to come by the crime scene."

"No need," he said. "It's nothing but dirt and grit and ashes at this point. If you don't have to be there, don't go. But I didn't realize you were in Tucson. What were you doing there?"

"It's a long story," Joanna said. "I had a front-row seat at an FBI takedown. Maybe we can talk about it at Ernie's party."

"His what?" Frank asked, sounding surprised.

"Ernie's retirement party."

"He's retiring?"

"Yes, as of the first of the year," Joanna answered. "There's a party scheduled for the day after Christmas at the Rob Roy, and you're invited."

"What time?"

"I forget—five thirty, maybe? I'll need to check with them. Come to think of it, I need to invite Dick Voland, too. I'll have Kristin send out official invites, but pencil it in."

"I will," Frank said, "but be advised. I'm penciling in a recap on that FBI takedown at the same time."

Now that Joanna had determined she was going to the hotel to meet up with Jackie Puckett and the kids, she spent the remainder of the drive trying to put together what she would say to the children. No doubt by now someone else would have broken the terrible news to them, and she tried to see things through Kendall's and Peter's points of view. Yes, Madison Hogan had been a poor excuse for a mother, but she'd been *their* mother—the only one they'd ever known. Joanna's challenging situation with her own mother had been dicey at times, but once Eleanor Lathrop Winfield was gone for good . . . ? The grief Joanna felt afterward had been stunning.

Once in the Windemere's parking lot, Joanna stopped for a moment and drew a deep breath before heading for the hotel entrance. Inside, she swept the room with her eyes before approaching the front desk. Halfway there she caught sight of Peter Hogan, marching across the lobby toward the northwest corner of the building with an enormous dog, none other than Coon himself, walking sedately on a leash beside him.

She was both surprised and gratified to see Coon there. Beyond the boy and dog, in the far corner of the room, Joanna spotted the other members of the family—Izzy and Lyndell Hogan, Jackie Puckett, and Kendall. The little girl, decked out in a funeral-appropriate dark blue dress, was cuddled on a sofa next to Grandma Puckett.

The boy and dog walked over to the seating area. When Peter ordered Coon to lie down, the dog did so immediately, flopping onto the cool granite tile. Peter joined him, resting his head on the dog's rib cage. That was when Lyn caught sight of Joanna. He rose and came forward to meet her with Kendall on his heels.

"You heard?" he asked.

Joanna nodded. "I'm so very sorry about your mother," she said, addressing Kendall directly.

"She's dead," Kendall replied quietly, "just like Daddy. Grandma Puckett says she's in heaven."

"But she'll be back," Peter piped up confidently from his place on the floor. "Coon was dead, too, but now he's back."

And that was the second time one of the two Hogan kids broke Joanna Brady's heart.

She remained in the hotel lobby for the better part of an hour, a tough hour but also an inspirational one. She said very little about the double homicide. For one thing, it was an active investigation. For another, with the kids right there, any discussion of the gruesome way in which Madison Hogan and Randy Williams had perished was out of the question. There was only the merest mention of funeral arrangements. The service for Leon Hogan had indeed been postponed for the time being. As far as final arrangements for Madison? Those were too far down the road to even consider.

So rather than spending time on those tough topics, Joanna had the honor of being privy to an inspiring collaboration among three loving grandparents—one a blood relation and the other two not—trying to chart a path forward for two orphaned children, one that would keep them from being caught up in the state-run foster-care program.

Living with Jackie Puckett in her retirement community was out of the question, but months earlier one of Lyndell and Izzy's near neighbors had made a tentative offer to purchase their ranch. At the time they turned the proposal down cold, but as far as Lyn knew, it was still on the table. He allowed as how maybe it was time for them to sell out and retire to warmer climes.

"Compared to winter in Wyoming, Christmas in December in Arizona feels more like summer to us," he said. "And if we could buy or rent the right place, maybe the kids could stay on at the same school." He paused and looked at Kendall. "Would you like that?"

he asked. "Would you like living with Izzy and me and going to the same school?"

She nodded with no hesitation. "I like my teacher," she said. "Her name is Mrs. Baird. She brought us macaroni and cheese."

"If we live with you, can we have a Christmas tree?" Peter asked from the floor. It might not have looked as though he was listening, but clearly he was. "Mrs. Walkup has her tree up already, and I want ours up, too."

"I don't know about a Christmas tree," Izzy put in. "We'll have to see what we can do."

"But of course," Lyn said, looking at Joanna, "this is all dependent on whether or not the state will grant us custody. What do you think they'll do on that score?"

For an answer Joanna opened her phone, located a name in her contacts list, and then texted it to Lyndell's phone.

"I just sent you contact information for a guy named Burton Kimball," she said. "I know you have Jorge in your corner, but Burton is local, and he's been our family attorney for years. This might require formal adoption proceedings rather than simple custody arrangements, but if anybody can make that happen, he's the guy."

"I thought custody only happened when people got divorced," Kendall said quietly.

The comment took Joanna's breath away. Kendall, too, might have appeared to be simply observing from the sidelines, but in the course of her seven years this girl and her little brother had seen far too much.

"It means the court decides who's supposed to take care of minor children like you and Peter," Joanna explained.

"Like a judge or something?"

"Exactly," Joanna said.

"But why can't we just say what *we* want?" Kendall asked.

Why indeed? And as far as Hogan-based heartbreaks went, that counted as number three.

🌵 CHAPTER 49

WHEN JOANNA left the hotel, she went straight to see Frank at Sierra Vista PD so she could be updated on the progress of the investigation. An arson investigator from the ATF had discovered evidence of a flammable liquid—most likely gasoline—inside the charred ruins of the Nite Owl, along with a discarded plastic gas container that had been found in the desert behind the building's back parking lot.

It was still too early for results on the examination of the other physical evidence taken from either scene, and so far no additional footage of the mysterious SUV had surfaced. Where real progress had been made was in the area of electronic analysis.

While still working at Joanna's department, Frank Montoya had been her top guy when it came to obtaining cell-phone data, including call history and tracking information. He'd brought those valuable skills along with him to Sierra Vista PD and had passed along everything he knew. Now that transferred knowledge was paying off big time.

Two phones, one belonging to Randy Williams and the other to Madison Hogan, had been found in the wreckage of Madison's bedroom. Frank's tech guy—a kid who looked to be straight out of high school—was deep into tracking the devices' call histories and movements.

Frank led Joanna into the department's crime-lab facility where all that time-stamped information had been carefully mapped out and charted on a whiteboard, with Madison's phone represented in red and Randy's in blue.

The previous evening, starting shortly after Madison's return from the Justice Center, there'd been a series of phone calls back and forth between the two—with Madison's calls most likely emanating from her home in Sierra Vista and Randy's from his place on Hereford Road. Much later in the evening, over the course of half an hour or so, it was possible to follow Randy's phone's movements as it traveled from Hereford to Sierra Vista. Starting at 8:30 P.M., both phones began pinging off the same cell tower, one located three hundred yards from Madison's residence. That's where both phones remained until CSIs found them in the bloodied wreckage of Madison's bedroom.

"It looks like they buried the hatchet after their big blowup the night before," Joanna suggested.

"Evidently," Frank agreed.

Joanna stared at the board for some time before she spoke. "It looks like Randy came over, they had a drink or two, and then they went to bed, only to be awakened home-invasion style by person or persons unknown, who carted them off to the Nite Owl, where they were subsequently killed."

"Yep, that's our current set of assumptions, too," Frank said.

As they walked from the lab back toward Frank's office, an urgent text from Tom Hadlock appeared on the screen of Joanna's phone: Call me!

Most likely more bad news, Joanna thought. The board of supervisors meeting had probably blown up in his face.

"I need to go," she told Frank.

"Fine," Frank said, "but I'm not waiting around for the party to hear about what happened in Tucson this morning, and you're not leaving here until you tell me."

So she told him, giving him an abbreviated version of the story.

"All things considered," he said, "it sounds like a happy ending."

"Yes," Joanna agreed. "It was a close call with Jenny, and we're very lucky."

She wasn't feeling exceptionally lucky, however, once she got back into her vehicle and dialed Tom's number.

"I'm guessing our board of supervisors request went south," she said when he answered.

"Not at all," he said. "They were surprisingly receptive, and they're taking it all under advisement—even the bodycam request."

That was a far better result than Joanna had expected.

"Great job, Tom," she told him. "I'm so glad to hear it, but your text sounded urgent. What's up?"

"It's about Floyd Barco," he said. "The man was raising hell around here, bouncing off the walls—I mean literally banging his head on a brick wall—and yelling that he's got to talk to you. He says you're the boss, and he won't talk to anyone else. We tried sending him back to his cell, but he was so completely off the charts that I finally had to put him in solitary."

"What solitary?" Joanna asked. "Our jail doesn't do solitary."

"I put him on a suicide watch in one of the interview

rooms," Tom said. "He's handcuffed to a table with someone checking on him every half hour."

"When did all this happen?"

"He and some of the other inmates were in the rec room watching the noon news. Then, all of a sudden, all hell broke loose."

"He attacked someone else?" Joanna asked.

"Like I said. He attacked himself. If we hadn't been able to put him in the interview room, our next step would have had to be a straitjacket."

"And he only wants to talk to me?"

"That's what he said."

"Do you have any idea what story on the news triggered him?"

"The guards asked some of the other guys in the rec room. They said they were watching a story about two people being found dead after the fire at the Nite Owl in Sierra Vista early this morning. That's when he went berserk."

"All right, then," Joanna said. "I'm on my way. I'll be there as soon as I can."

On the drive into Bisbee, there was still snow on Juniper Flats at the top of the Mule Mountains, but the white stuff that had been on the road and along the shoulders earlier in the morning had melted away into nothingness.

Once Joanna arrived at the Justice Center, she entered through her own office and then headed for the interview rooms. A glance in through a two-way mirror showed Floyd Barco sitting alone in one of them. A paper cup with water and a straw in it was on the table and well within his reach, but the way he kept glancing uneasily around the room told Joanna that the smug attitude he'd exhibited the day before was long gone. The individual she saw sitting there now was scared to death.

He jumped when Joanna opened the door and let herself into the room. "You wanted to see me?" she asked.

Barco turned an anguished face in her direction. "There are cameras in here, right?"

She nodded.

"You gotta turn them off before I talk to you. If anyone finds out what I said, I'm a dead man, Sheriff. They'll kill me. Randy and me were friends and sort of partners, so I'm probably a dead man anyway."

"In the first place, the cameras aren't on," Joanna assured him as she sat down on the far side of the table, "so there's no need to turn them off. But who's going to kill you, Floyd, and what's this about Randy? Do you mean Randy Williams?"

It was Barco's turn to nod. "He's dead, ain't he? They said that two people were dead at the Nite Owl, and he's got to be one of 'em."

Joanna said nothing, neither confirming nor denying.

"And the other one's probably Madison," Barco went on. "That means they'll come looking for me next."

"Who'll come looking for you?"

"I can't say," he said, "and I won't, not until you get me into witness protection."

"Wait a minute, Mr. Barco," Joanna said. "I'm a county sheriff. Witness protection is a big deal, and it's way above my pay grade. I don't have any direct access to that."

"Then you need to get me to someone who does," he said, "because I can tell you all of it. The parts about Maddie and Randy wanting to knock off Leon, the parts about the goons who most likely took out the two of them, and the guy down in Agua Prieta who's running the whole show. He's an American citizen who lives in Mexico now, but he's the guy behind it all."

"You're claiming you can name names?"

"Big time," Barco replied, with just a hint of his old swagger.

"All right," Joanna agreed, "I'll call the U.S. attorney up in Tucson and see what he has to say. Maybe he'll want to talk to you, maybe he won't."

"What happens to me in the meantime?"

"You stay right where you are, here in the Cochise County Jail."

Barco's momentary swagger vanished. "But you don't understand," he whined. "He has people who can get to me even here."

"*Who* can get to you?"

"The guy I told you about, the one in Agua Prieta, but like I said, I'm not naming names. Not until I've got myself a deal."

Joanna rose from her chair. "All right, Mr. Barco," she said. "I'll see what I can do."

"Are you sending me back to my cell?"

She nodded.

"You can't. You got to put me somewhere by myself," he said. "Otherwise I'm done for."

"We'll see," Joanna said.

She left him there and headed back to her office, stopping by Tom's along the way.

"Well?" her chief deputy asked. "What's Barco want?"

"A private cell and witness protection," Joanna said. "He claims he can bring down a big-time drug-cartel boss from Agua Prieta. Barco's also worried that the guy will hire someone inside the jail to take him down just like they did Randy Williams and Madison Hogan."

"He knows they're dead?" Tom asked with a frown. Joanna nodded. "He does."

"Who gave him their names?" Tom asked. "You?"

"I didn't tell him, and I'm sure you didn't either," Joanna said. "As soon as he saw that piece on the news about the fire at the Nite Owl, he must have figured it out on his own and decided he was probably next up."

"What should we do now?"

"For the time being, let's lock him in one of the exam rooms in the infirmary. There's an emergency button he can press if he needs to use the john. Meanwhile I'll get on the phone to the U.S. attorney up in Tucson and see what he has to say."

Tom glanced at his watch. "Are you kidding?" he asked. "At four o'clock on a Friday afternoon?"

Joanna nodded.

"Good luck with that," he said.

And good luck was exactly what was needed. Joanna's initial attempt came to nothing. U.S. Attorney Matthew Mitchell was gone for the day, she was told. Would Sheriff Brady care to leave a message? She would not, but fortunately for Joanna she had a workaround. As of today, with the Gerard Paine takedown, FBI Special Agent Robin Watkins just happened to have a whole lot going for her as far as her agent in charge was concerned. Consequently, Joanna Brady had some points of her own with the man. She called Robin and gave her as much of an overview of the situation as she was able to provide and asked Robin to call her boss. Twelve minutes later a call on Joanna's direct line came in from a blocked number. Obviously the Tucson FBI agent in charge had access to Matthew Mitchell's cell-phone number.

"You wanted to speak to me, Sheriff Brady?" the U.S. attorney asked after introducing himself.

"I did."

"What about?"

Even though Joanna was reasonably sure Mitchell already knew what was going on, she told the story anyway, from beginning to end. Her recitation was followed by a long, thoughtful silence.

"And your informant, this Mr. Barco, said specifically that this concerns a U.S. citizen running a drug operation from Agua Prieta?" Mitchell asked finally.

"He did."

"And you have him sequestered in a safe place inside your jail at the moment?"

"We do. He's locked up in one of the exam rooms in our infirmary."

"Fair enough," Mitchell said. "I'll be dispatching a team of U.S. Marshals to pick him up later tonight. They'll be coming from Tucson, so I don't have a definite ETA. Thank you so much, Sheriff Brady. Your assistance in this matter is greatly appreciated, but we'll take it from here."

"What about those two homicides in Sierra Vista?" Joanna asked. "They're still under investigation."

"Frank Montoya's the police chief there, right?"

"Correct."

"Not to worry, then, Sheriff Brady. We'll coordinate with Chief Montoya from here on out."

It was a curt dismissal, but Joanna didn't even care.

She was done. She arrived home after eight, having left the house shortly after 6:00 A.M. and after putting in another twelve-hour day. She had stayed around the office long enough to turn a very relieved Floyd Barco over to the U.S. Marshals Service and send him on his way.

As Joanna drove back to the ranch, she should have been elated. After all, she and her people had helped break two major cases that day, but right at that moment they felt like a pair of hollow victories. For now the resolution of both cases was out of her hands. Gerard Paine was under arrest in Tucson, but whatever happened to him was up to the FBI and the department of justice. And the thug who might have played a pivotal role in the death of Leon Hogan was currently in the custody of the U.S. Marshals. Joanna had a sinking feeling that as far as Leon's death was concerned, true justice would never be served.

By the time she got home, heated up a bowl of leftover green chili casserole, and made it into the family room, Denny and Sage were both in bed and asleep, while everyone else—Beth, Jenny, Butch, and both dogs—were watching a screening of *It's a Wonderful Life*. They put the movie on pause long enough to hear what she had to say. She focused mostly on what had happened to Gerard Paine. What little she knew was way more than they'd seen on TV or in the media. Joanna was grateful to learn that at this point Jenny's name had not yet been mentioned as the intended victim in the Coconino County shooting. That would come soon enough, and when it did, all hell would break loose.

But for now Joanna was home. A two-homicide day that had started with a fried-egg sandwich eaten in a moving SUV ended with her snuggled on the couch next to Butch and nibbling on a freshly baked sugar cookie, one that had been colorfully if inexpertly decorated by Denny.

All in all, it qualified as a pretty good day.

CHAPTER 50

IT WAS Joanna's weekend to be on call, and nothing whatsoever happened, at least not on the crime front. Maybe all the crooks in Cochise County were too busy getting ready for Christmas to go looking for trouble. There were a couple of DUIs from overserved guests at holiday parties but little else, and nothing serious enough to require Joanna's presence out on the road. At home? That was another story.

The ten-o'clock newscasts on Friday night suddenly all got around to naming Sheriff Joanna Brady's daughter, Jennifer, as the target of Wednesday's attempted homicide south of Flagstaff. When Joanna opened the rolling shutters to let the dogs out early on Saturday morning, Marliss Shackleford's RAV4 was parked just beyond the fence. She exited the vehicle and started up the walkway.

"No comment," Joanna said before Marliss could open her mouth.

"My sources tell me that a Tucson resident named Gerard Paine is being investigated for multiple instances of identity theft and for being a major purveyor of pornography, and that he has an alleged history of sextortion, in which he has victimized any number of female victims. Was Jenny one of those?"

"No comment," Joanna repeated.

"Would it be possible for me to speak to Jenny herself?"

"Not on your life, Marliss. Now, get the hell out of here."

"You know that someone's going to have to interview her eventually. Wouldn't you rather it were a friend?"

"You're not Jenny's friend, and you're not mine either."

"What about what happened in Sierra Vista yesterday?"

"What about it?"

"Leon Hogan's widow and her boyfriend were both murdered."

"The incident at the Nite Owl occurred inside the Sierra Vista city limits. You'll need to talk to them about that."

By then Lady and Lucky had finished their business and were ready to go back inside. Joanna was, too, closing the rolling shutters behind her and leaving a frustrated Marliss stranded on the far side. It was a satisfying way to end that first attempted interview, but Joanna knew it was only the beginning of the media onslaught. Most of the calls that day went to the office, and people there fielded them as well as they could. A few of the more enterprising types somehow managed to access the landline phone at High Lonesome Ranch, and for hours it rang off the hook.

"Aren't you ever going to answer it?" Denny asked the third time Joanna let a call ring through to voice mail.

"Not this time," she said. "Whoever it is, I don't want to talk to them."

"Why not?"

"Sometimes Mommy just doesn't feel like talking."

"But what if it's not for you? What if it's for someone else?"

"Then they don't feel like talking either."

Nevertheless, there was a whole lot of talking going on that day, much of it between Beth and Joanna. Robin had called and warned Joanna that the FBI would need to speak to Beth at some length come Monday morning, and Joanna did her best to pave the way. The young woman found the prospect of another round of interviews daunting.

"Am I going to be stuck talking about this for the rest of my life?" she asked.

"Not the whole rest of your life, but until Gerard Paine is put away for good, you and Jenny both are going to be front and center. Believe me, I know it will be uncomfortable. But remember, the way the two of you conduct yourselves has the potential of making a big impact on many lives other than your own. By going public with this and taking Paine down, you'll be keeping similar outrages from happening to other unsuspecting young women. Unfortunately, there are countless jerks just like Paine out prowling the Internet and hunting for unsuspecting victims. By explaining how Paine targeted you, you'll be raising awareness and warning others to be on the lookout for those same kinds of behavior."

"I saw a picture of him on the news this morning," Beth said quietly. "Paine's an old man, like really old. The whole time I was talking to him, I was picturing that other guy—the dead one in the picture. It's creepy—like talking to a ghost."

"Yes, it is creepy," Joanna agreed. "By the way, have you ever seen the movie *The Wizard of Oz*?"

"Never, why?"

"You need to, because it turns out the wizard's pretty creepy, too," Joanna said. "Everybody thinks he's this powerful, all-knowing being, but in reality he's a cowardly little guy hiding behind a curtain, the same way Gerard Paine hid behind his computer screen. By the way, as of now we're putting *The Wizard of Oz* on our must-see movie list for this Christmas vacation. Come to think of it, I don't think Denny's ever seen it either."

Eventually the conversation turned to Beth's parents. "What should I do about my mom and dad?" she asked.

"After seeing them in action, Butch told me a little about your parents, and they sound . . . well . . . difficult," Joanna answered. "But here's the thing, Beth: You can't fix them. The only person you can fix is yourself. It might be wise for you to try to forgive them, because they probably did the best they could and were only trying to protect you. Unfortunately, that kind of protective isolation ended up leaving you totally unprepared for what was waiting for you out in the real world."

"I should forgive them?" Beth asked. "Really?"

Joanna nodded. "More for your own mental well-being than theirs, but to do that I think you're going to need professional help."

"You mean, like talking to a counselor?" Beth asked.

Joanna nodded. "Yes, but in person. I understand there's a Web-based support network for people like you, but I don't recommend your using it."

Beth shot Joanna a shadow of a smile. "Why?" she asked. "Because whoever's on the other side of the computer screen might not be the people they claim to be?"

For the first time, Joanna had a hint that Beth was getting it.

"Exactly," she said. "Now you're catching on."

CHAPTER 51

SUNDAY DAWNED clear but cold. Butch made waffles for breakfast. After that everyone, Beth included, went to church, where the junior choir—all ten of them, Denny included—stood at the front and sang "Away in a Manger."

During coffee hour Marliss Shackleford did her best to corner Jenny. "I understand you've had quite an adventure this week," she said. "Who's your friend?"

"She's my roommate," Jenny replied, "but I don't want to talk to you about any of this, Marliss. It isn't the time or the place."

"I'd be glad to set up an appointment."

"No thanks."

"But if someone was really trying to kill you, don't you want to be able to tell your side of the story?"

"No comment," Jenny said.

"Did your mother tell you to say that?"

"Actually," Jenny told her, "I was able to figure that out on my own."

As Jenny walked away, leaving Marliss fuming, she noticed that Beth was off having a quiet word with Reverend Maculyea. Butch had collected Sage from the nursery and was headed for the door, so Jenny collected Beth as well. Jenny wanted to have Beth safely out of the building before Marliss managed to target her.

"She's very nice," Beth said as they headed for the car.

"Who's nice?"

"Reverend Maculyea. A lot nicer than Reverend Ike ever was."

"Reverend Ike? Who's he?"

"He's the pastor at my mom's old church—the guy who says cell phones are evil."

"Marianne and my mom have been friends from junior high on."

Beth nodded. "She mentioned that. She also said that your mom had told her what happened to us. She said that if I needed to talk to someone during Christmas vacation, I was welcome to come see her."

"Will you?"

Beth thought about it for a moment. "Maybe," she said finally. "Did you know she doesn't get along well with her own mother?"

Jenny looked at Beth in amazement. "She told you that?"

Beth nodded.

"I had no idea," Jenny said. "None at all."

They went home from church and had a midday meal of roast pork, apple sauce, green peas, and mashed potatoes. By the time Sage went down for a nap, Jenny was feeling restless, so she pulled on her riding duds and headed for the corral.

As soon as Kiddo, Jenny's twentysomething sorrel gelding, heard her approaching footsteps, he pricked up his ears and trotted over to the fence in search of the apple treat he knew would be on offer. He was followed by Spot, the blind and once-starving Appaloosa mare her mother's Animal Control people had rescued from a foreclosed ranchette at Arizona Sun Sites.

Most of the time, Kiddo functioned as Spot's Seeing Eye horse. With both a deaf black Lab and a blind Appaloosa in residence, Butch liked to say High Lonesome Ranch had turned into a home for animals with disabilities.

Jenny had started her barrel-racing career on Kiddo. Once he'd outlived his barrel racing days, Maggie had been brought into the picture to serve as his replacement. Jenny knew that Butch rode Kiddo from time to time, but with her away at school, she was relatively sure the horse wasn't getting nearly enough exercise.

"How about if we go for a ride?" she asked him as he and Spot crunched their respective apples.

Kiddo didn't understand the words, of course, but the way he ducked his head up and down and pawed the ground made it look as though he did. Jenny grabbed a bridle from the barn and led him out of the corral before vaulting up onto him bareback. She loved feeling a horse's muscles moving under her without the intervening barrier of a leather saddle. As they headed out toward High Lonesome Road, Denny came charging onto the front porch.

"Hey!" he called after them. "Can I come, too?"

"Okay," she answered. "Go get Spot saddled up. We'll be back in a few minutes."

Jenny rode out to the end of the driveway and then bent down to unlatch and open the gate that allowed horse and rider to circumnavigate the cattle guard. Unsurprisingly, Lady and Lucky had come along for an afternoon romp. Horse, rider, and dogs trotted along together for a time, heading north on the reddish brown soil of High Lonesome Road.

After a mile Jenny turned Kiddo around and gave

him his head. He laid his ears flat and took off like a shot. They pounded back down the road at a gallop, churning up a trail of dust as they went. Jenny leaned forward into Kiddo's neck and let his golden mane whip against her face. Suddenly, for no reason at all, she found herself crying—because in spite of everything she was alive! She wasn't dead, because Aaron Morgan and Gerard Paine hadn't managed to kill her! That was what made it possible for her to be out here on this chilly afternoon with the sun on her skin, the wind in her face, and riding her beloved horse back toward the house!

In all her concern and worry about Beth Rankin, Jenny had somehow forgotten about herself. Now, in this exhilarating moment, she felt wonderfully alive and incredibly grateful.

When they returned to the yard, Denny and Spot were saddled up and ready to go, with Beth standing nearby observing the action. Jenny and Denny walked their horses out to the road and then traveled along at a gentle trot with Spot following close on Kiddo's tail and taking her cues from him. Glancing over her shoulder from time to time, Jenny was proud of the way Denny held his seat. He was already a good rider. Someday he would be an excellent one, all because Jenny had been able to teach him.

Once back from their ride, as Denny prepared to dismount, Beth patted Spot's muzzle and asked shyly, "Could I try, too?"

"Have you ever ridden a horse?" Jenny asked.

"I've never even touched one until now," Beth said.

Jenny slid off Kiddo's back and adjusted the length of the stirrups on Spot's saddle. "Let's see if this works," she said. "When you get on, you always do so from this side. Stick one foot in the stirrup, use the saddle horn to help boost yourself up, and then hold the reins loosely in your hands."

Beth managed to make it work on the second try. Jenny readjusted the length of the stirrups, and then she mounted up and off they went. This time there was no trotting. They walked along at a sedate trail-ride pace with Beth's leather saddle creaking beneath her.

"This feels really strange," Beth said. "How can you ride bareback like that?"

"Years of practice," Jenny told her with a smile.

They traveled the same route as before. It wasn't until they neared the gate on the way back that Jennifer Ann Brady had an epiphany. It was as though the world suddenly made sense to her in a way it never had before. Sometimes you need to gallop, sometimes trot, and sometimes even walk, but in order to really live, you need to be able to do all three.

CHAPTER 52

BY THE time Monday morning came around, Joanna was feeling relatively rested. She arrived at her desk after roll call to find a message from Amy Ruiz awaiting her. She went straight out to the front office and tracked down Karen Griffith, the older clerk who was a lifelong friend of Amy's mother.

"I just heard that Armando's being released today," Joanna said. "I've been so busy I haven't even asked. What's happening on their Christmas situation?"

Karen smiled. "Not to worry," she said. "It's all handled. Some friends and I went over yesterday and decorated the house inside and out, including putting up the tree. The presents are all wrapped and where they're supposed to be. When Armando comes home, Christmas will already be there."

Unable to help herself, Joanna gave Karen a quick hug. "Thank you," she whispered. "You're the best."

"I heard about Jenny," Karen said. "How is she, and how are you?"

Joanna felt a sudden flash of gratitude at the kindness of the people who worked with her. "She's fine, and so am I," Joanna said. "And thank you for asking."

By midmorning the FBI showed up in force to do interviews, bringing a flock of reporters with them. Joanna supplied the interview rooms and held off reporters as well. Two days of respite seemed to have benefited both Beth and Jenny. They appeared poised going into their individual interviews, and Joanna was relieved when more than two hours later they both emerged smiling.

"Are you heading home?" Joanna asked.

Jenny shook her head. "I'm going to drop Beth off uptown. She has an appointment to talk with Marianne. While she's doing that, I need to do some Christmas shopping."

Shortly after two o'clock, Burton Kimball and Lyndell Hogan showed up in Joanna's outer office.

"To what do I owe the honor?" she asked when Kristin ushered them inside.

"I wanted to thank you for putting us in touch with Mr. Kimball here," Lyn said. "We just now left the courtroom, and I wanted you to be among the first to know that Izzy and I have been granted temporary custody."

"Really?" Joanna asked, looking back and forth between them in nothing short of amazement. "It happened that fast?"

"That fast," Burton repeated with a smile. "I believe the judge decided that there were enough extenuating circumstances surrounding the case to make it necessary for him to award temporary custody on an emergency basis."

"What does temporary mean?" Joanna asked.

"It means that we can't take the kids out of state until the custody arrangement is made permanent," Lyn explained, "but that's not a huge problem. We'll just stay here for the time being. Izzy and I consulted a Realtor over the weekend. She showed us a house where the owner is being transferred and is desperate to sell. It's close enough that the kids won't even have to change schools. I told the seller that depending on how this morning's court hearing went, we could maybe finalize the deal this afternoon. I'm on my way to do just that as soon as we leave here.

"Tomorrow morning I'll fly home to Wyoming to tie up some loose ends there. I told the guy who wants to buy our place that he can have it. Izzy and Jackie will stay here and look after the kids together while I'm gone. I can tell you that after missing a whole week of school, they're both looking forward to going back tomorrow morning."

Joanna looked questioningly from Lyndell to Burton. In these kinds of situations, custody battles usually became pitched warfare, with relatives lined up on either side of a fence throwing stones. It was refreshing to realize that in this case all three grandparents were working together to present a united front. The other thought that occurred to Joanna just then had to do with the fact that if the elder Hogans could go out and purchase a new home at the drop of a hat, obviously Madison had made a serious miscalculation when she decided Leon was worth more dead than alive.

"It's still amazing that the judge allowed this to happen so fast," Joanna said finally.

"Izzy and I have a few resources at our disposal," Lyndell Hogan said modestly. "Once I showed the judge our current financial situation, he saw that we could offer the children a more stable environment than what would have been available to them in foster care."

"Sheriff Brady is right, of course," Burton put in. "Custody orders almost never happen with such speed.

In this case I believe character witnesses who phoned in their testimony from Wyoming as well as the in-person interviews conducted by Judge Atkins himself did the trick."

"What in-person interviews?" Joanna asked.

"Well," Burton said, "Jackie Puckett didn't exactly pull any punches in describing the kids' circumstances once they were left in the sole care of her daughter. Neither did Kendall. She delivered a number of telling details about the challenges of living with Madison Hogan. That little girl is something!"

"The judge spoke with Kendall directly?" Joanna asked.

Burton nodded. "He talked with both kids. All Peter seems to care about is getting his dog back and having Coon with him wherever he goes. Coon was the only item on his wish list—well, that and a Christmas tree."

Lyn got to his feet. "Our son may be gone, but I wanted you to know that at this point I don't even mind that we missed having a funeral for Leon. He loved those two kids with all his heart, and getting to have them with us feels like getting a piece of our boy back. So thank you, Sheriff Brady," he added, coming around the desk to give her a heartfelt hug. "Thank you so much for everything you did—for us, for the kids, and for Coon, too."

"You're more than welcome, Mr. Hogan," she said, "but I was only doing my job."

CHAPTER 53

THE DAYS leading up to Christmas sped past. In the legal world, things seemed to have accelerated into warp drive. In Flagstaff, Aaron Morgan was allowed to plead guilty to conspiracy to commit murder on the condition that he testify against Gerard Paine. Meanwhile the mastermind himself remained in federal custody as the number of felony charges against him continued to mount.

On the Floyd Barco front, there was total radio silence. If there were plans in the works about bringing in the guy from Agua Prieta and charging him for the brutal murders of Madison Hogan and Randy Williams, no word of it leaked out to either Joanna or Frank Montoya. Whatever the feds were doing on that score was occurring behind a strict cloak of secrecy.

Real-estate dealings, too, seemed to be moving at lightning speed. Since Izzy and Lyndell were paying cash for their new house, the closing was accomplished in a matter of days. Then, after waving her Amex card and spending a day in Tucson with an interior designer, a personal shopper, and a U-Haul truck at her disposal, Isabella Hogan had the place furnished, wall to wall and soup to nuts. Her purchases included furniture, beds, bedding, pots, pans, dishes, glassware, and silverware. For the first time in their young lives,

Kendall and Peter had their own rooms, and their rickety old bunk bed went to the junk heap where it belonged.

Joanna stopped by one day to say hello just in time to see movers unloading the truck. Inside, the arranging process was being directed by a woman who was, according to the Hogans' Realtor, Sierra Vista's primo professional house stager. In this case she staged the house for someone who would be living in it rather than selling it.

"But what about your things back home in Wyoming?" Joanna asked. "What happens to them?"

"Oh, those," Izzy said with a dismissive wave. "Most of the stuff up there is as old as the hills. Some of it came from Lyndell's mother and some from his grandmother. This is the first chance I've ever had to get my own brand-new stuff, and I'm taking full advantage. By the way, we're going to have an afternoon open house on the Saturday before Christmas. A few people have hinted around that given everything that's happened, it's too soon for the kids and for us to have any kind of celebration. I say screw 'em. These kids have had enough sadness to last a lifetime. It's time for them to have some fun."

"I couldn't agree more," Joanna said.

"Speaking of kids," Izzy said, "Kendall tells me you have a little boy about her age."

Joanna nodded. "His name is Denny. He's in second grade, too."

"Well, feel free to bring him along," Izzy said. "I've invited some of the families from the kids' school, but I don't know how many will show up."

"The Saturday before Christmas," Joanna said, consulting the calendar in her phone. "What time?"

"Two to four or so," Izzy said.

"We'll be there," Joanna said. "My husband, my son, and my two-year-old, Sage. I have an older daughter who's home from college, but I'm pretty sure she and her roommate will be otherwise engaged."

With Denny in school for the remainder of the week, Joanna was pleased to learn from Butch that Jenny and Beth were going riding together almost every day, coming home with their cheeks flushed and smiles on their faces. Without the crutch of a cell phone in her hand, Beth was learning to saddle, bridle, and curry horses. She even allowed at dinner one night that once she and Jenny returned to Flagstaff, she hoped to be able to spend some time volunteering with the Lazy 8's horse-therapy program.

Beth had spent several long sessions with Marianne Maculyea and seemed to have emerged with the understanding that if Marianne could get through life minus a close relationship with her mother, Beth Rankin might well be able to do the same.

At the Hogans' open house, Joanna had to admit that the stager had done an amazing job. The results were spectacular, including a ten-foot-tall lushly decorated Christmas tree.

During the party Joanna saw a sparkle in Kendall's blue eyes that hadn't been there before. She spent much of the party glued to Jackie Puckett's side. Izzy and Lyndell Hogan might have offered the children a permanent safe haven, but it was Grandma Puckett who had first come to their rescue. That obviously counted for something.

When Kendall wasn't plastered to Grandma Puckett,

she was in her bedroom playing Uno and Chutes and Ladders with Denny. The two of them hit it off like longtime pals. Meanwhile loner Peter was content to be out in the backyard throwing either tennis balls or Frisbees, all of which Coon obligingly returned every single time.

On Christmas Eve, Joanna received a surprise gift in the form of a phone call from Claire Newmark, her closest ally on the board of supervisors. "I think we've finally got the votes," Claire said. "Your budget request, bodycams included, should sail through with no problem."

"Thank you so much for letting me know," Joanna said gratefully.

"And how's Deputy Ruiz?" Claire asked.

"He's home and recovering well, as far as anyone can tell."

"Thank God for small favors," Claire said. "I'm so glad to hear it."

Christmas Day itself was an absolute circus. Since Beth had never before experienced a full-on family Christmas celebration, she seemed taken aback by the chaos that left the entire living room awash in discarded wrapping paper. The next-to-last gift wasn't under the tree because it was *on* it. It consisted of a tiny box with Joanna's name on it. Inside were a pair of eye-popping emerald pierced earrings.

"To match your eyes," Butch told her when she delivered a thank-you kiss.

Finally only one unwrapped gift remained—Beth's. On Christmas Eve, Butch had made a quick trip to Tucson to bring it home. Jenny, knowing what was up, was the one who delivered it into Beth's hands.

"What's this?" Beth asked.

"Open it," Jenny urged. "You'll see."

Beth did. When it became apparent what it was, she looked at Jenny in dismay. "An iPhone?" she asked. "But I thought I wasn't supposed to have one of these."

"Mom talked to Agent Norris. With Gerard Paine under lock and key and with his network shut down, she says there's no reason you can't go back online, as long as you have a new number, new address, and all new passwords."

That afternoon the entire household, including Carol Sunderson and her two boys, gathered in the family room to eat popcorn and watch a DVD of *The Wizard of Oz*.

"The wizard really was creepy," Beth murmured as the credits rolled. "I see now why you wanted me to watch it, and I'm glad Dorothy and Toto took him down."

CHAPTER 54

THE EVENING of Ernie's retirement party, the kids all stayed home and had pizza while Butch and Joanna, dressed to the nines and with Joanna sporting her emerald earrings, headed for the Rob Roy. Joanna had made it known that uniforms were banished for the evening. Everyone had been directed to show up in their best bibs and tuckers while off-duty officers from Pima and Graham counties were handling patrol duties throughout Cochise in order for Joanna's people to be able to attend the festivities.

The Carpenters had outdone themselves. Ernie showed up looking amazing in a tuxedo with a beaming, evening gown–clad Rose on his arm. Joanna knew they had to be dealing with a tumult of conflicting emotions right then, but none of that showed. They'd made up their minds about how they would deal with the situation, and they carried it off without a hitch.

As promised, the food was great, and considering who-all was in attendance, Myron Thomas made sure no one was overserved in the drinks department. The end-of-the-evening roasts were hilarious and delivered with the kind of laughter, jabs, and barbs that can only be shared among people who've known and cared for each other for years.

Joanna was the next-to-last person to speak. She

didn't even try to do a roast. "When I came here nine years ago, I was a babe in the woods. I knew nothing about law enforcement, but yet all of a sudden I was the sheriff. If it hadn't been for people like Frank Montoya and Dick Voland," she said, nodding to each in turn, "I wouldn't have made it. They, along with Ernie here, taught me everything I know.

"Yet it turns out those other guys were both short-timers. Frank and Dick didn't hang around for the long haul, but you did, Ernie, and I thank you from the bottom of my heart. Go if you must. Have fun. I'm just not too sure I believe all that stuff about your going fishing."

She sat down to a round of applause, and Ernie himself stood up. "I've worked for the Cochise County Sheriff's Department most of my adult life," he said. "When this little red-haired dynamo first turned up on the scene, I figured we were close to bottoming out. But you know what? I was dead wrong about that. So I'd like to propose a toast to Sheriff Joanna Brady, the best boss I've ever had."

EPILOGUE

NEW YEAR'S Day was supposed to be a holiday, but since Tom Hadlock had covered Christmas Day, it was Joanna's turn to handle this one. She was in the office that Monday afternoon, but things were blessedly quiet. Kristin was off, and only a skeleton crew was at work out in the front office. Sunny Sloan was on her way to Peoria, where she was due to start classes at the Arizona Police Academy the following day.

Butch was planning on leaving early the next morning to drive Jenny and Beth back to Flagstaff. Having the girls there for Christmas had been fun, but after dealing with company for the better part of two weeks, Joanna was looking forward to having their household shrink back down to normal.

She was surprised when shortly after noon there was a tap on her doorjamb and Jenny stepped inside.

"Why, hello," Joanna said. "Where's everybody else?"

"It's just me," Jenny said. "We need to talk."

Uh-oh, Joanna thought, *isn't this where I came in?*

"What's up?" she asked as Jenny slipped onto a chair.

"When you first got elected, I hated the fact that you were sheriff," Jenny admitted. "For one thing, I was afraid you were going to die, just like Daddy did. I hated that you worked such long hours. It was all about catching the people who do bad things. I knew it was important, but it made me mad when you couldn't be at school events the way other kids' mothers were. I guess I was just jealous."

"I'm sorry—" Joanna began, but Jenny held up a hand to stop her.

"Don't apologize, Mom," she said. "I'm not here asking for an apology. The last couple of weeks have been real eye-openers for me. Your job is about way more than just catching bad people; it's about helping good people, too, and about putting broken lives back together. And I want to tell you I'm proud of you."

Not knowing what else to say, all Joanna could manage was a murmured, "Thank you."

"That evil man almost destroyed Beth, and he might have gotten away with it if you and Robin Watkins and Adele Norris and LuAnn Maxfield and Marianne Maculyea hadn't all worked together to help her. I want to say thank you for that, too."

"You're welcome," Joanna said, but somewhere out there, just out of earshot, she was waiting for that other shoe to drop. Eventually it did as Jenny continued.

"I realized the other day that sometimes you have to walk and sometimes you have to gallop, so I'm galloping now, Mom. I haven't told Dad this yet. I'm telling you first. You know that all my life I've wanted to become a vet, but I've changed my mind about that. When I get back to Flagstaff, I'm planning on changing my major over to criminal justice. Someday I hope to join the FBI and become an agent just like Adele Norris."

Jenny finally ran out of steam and fell silent. For a long moment, neither of them spoke, Jenny because she'd said what she had to say and Joanna because she was torn between two diametrically opposed emotions—incredible pride and absolute dread!

"Well," Jenny prodded finally, "aren't you at least going to say something?"

Without a word Joanna rose from behind her desk, walked around the side of it, and then hugged her daughter for all she was worth.

"From what I've seen, you'll make a great one," Joanna said, "and I couldn't be prouder."

Next up for J. A. Jance fans . . .

Read on for a sneak peek at J. P. Beaumont's latest riveting investigation, in which he is approached by a visitor from the past and finds himself drawn into a missing person's case where danger is lurking and family secrets are exposed.

YEARS AGO, when J. P. Beaumont was a homicide detective with the Seattle PD, his partner, Sue Danielson, was murdered. Volatile and angry, Danielson's ex-husband came after her and, with nowhere else to turn, Jared, Sue's teenage son, begged Beau for help. As Beau rushed to the scene, he urged Jared to grab his younger brother and flee the house. In the end, Beaumont's plea and Jared's quick action saved the two boys from their father's violent rage.

Now, almost twenty years later, Jared reappears in Beau's life, seeking his help once again—this time, he needs assistance in finding Chris, his missing younger brother. Still haunted by the events of that tragic night, Beau is unable to refuse. Taking on the case, Beau follows the lead into the wilds of wintertime Alaska and encounters a tangled web of family secrets in which a killer with nothing to lose is waiting to kill again.

NOTHING TO LOSE

**Coming soon in hardcover
From William Morrow**

PROLOGUE

"HEY, BABE," Mel called to me from the bathroom doorway, "the shower isn't draining and neither is the toilet."

At 6:30 on a cold, dark winter morning, those were ominous words indeed, and for more than one reason. In some relationships, being addressed as "babe" might be a term of endearment. Coming from Mel Soames, however, the word landed with the same impact as when, without ever raising her voice, my mother used to address me as Jonas Piedmont Beaumont. In those instances, and in this one as well, it was time for me to wake up and smell the coffee.

I also didn't make the strategic mistake of getting out of bed to go see for myself or of asking, "Are you sure?" If Mel said that was the situation, that *was* the situation. Nor did I caution her to avoid flushing again. Mel happens to be a smart woman, and my offering her unneeded advice is never a good idea.

Her words were worrisome for another reason, and that's this: I am not now nor have I ever been a handyman. Yes, I've seen all those *America's Funniest Video* clips where the kids yell, "Hey, Dad, there's water coming out of the bathroom." The panicked father races to the scene only to discover that his rug-rats have set out a long line of plastic water bottles marching in single

file from an open bathroom door and out into a hallway.
The hapless father is left muttering a series of bleeped-
out words while the happy pranksters double over with
laughter. That joke might be funny on TV but not in my
own bedroom and certainly not at that ungodly hour of
the morning.

With Mel still occupying the bathroom, I crawled
out of bed and headed for the kitchen. When Mel and
I had purchased and remodeled our sixty-five-year-old
mid-century modern home, I had no idea that the house
came with radiant heat throughout. As I padded from
the bedroom to the kitchen, I was grateful for the comforting warmth of the heated flooring on my bare feet.
A check of the kitchen sink showed no sign of a backup
there, and so, with a grateful heart, I turned on the coffee machine.

While our DeLonghi Magnifica put itself through its
morning warm-up exercises, I turned around expecting
to find Sarah, our recently adopted Irish Wolfhound,
at my side and ready to go do her morning necessar-
ies. She was nowhere in sight. When I went looking, I
found her still in the bedroom, curled up in a ball and
snoozing away in her toasty-warm nest next to my side
of the bed.

Before I go any further, a word about dogs. I'm not
a lifetime dog lover. The dog that had dragged me into
this new and relatively unfamiliar territory was another
Irish Wolfhound named Lucy. Mel serves as the chief
of police in Bellingham, Washington, north of Seattle.
She's still gainfully employed while I am not-so-happily
retired. Lucy came into our lives in the aftermath of a
domestic violence incident in Mel's jurisdiction. When
a battered wife took her children and fled to a shelter

situation, they were unable to take Lucy with them, so Mel ended up bringing her home.

After years of chasing bad guys first for Seattle PD and later for the attorney general's Special Homicide Investigation Team, aka SHIT, I had inevitably become the person tasked with keeping hearth and home in order. As a consequence, Lucy became my responsibility, a job I grudgingly accepted but only with a good deal of griping and a singular lack of good grace. All that changed, of course, when the abusive husband from the domestic violence incident got let out on bail and came gunning for Mel—knifing for her actually rather than gunning. When the chips were down, Lucy had come racing to Mel's defense. If that isn't enough to turn a guy into a dog lover, I don't know what is.

I would have been happy to keep Lucy permanently, but that wasn't in the cards. Mel and I may have fallen for her, but once Lucy met our granddaughter, Athena, Lucy voted with her paws and made her preferences clear. We may have loved Lucy, but Lucy loved Athena, and that's where she is now, living with Athena and her other grandfather in Texas. But by the time we gave up Lucy, Mel and I both knew that there would be another dog in our lives sooner or later. The answer to that turned out to be sooner, and unsurprisingly we took pains to locate another Irish wolfhound.

Sarah is a former mommy-dog rescued from a now-shuttered puppy mill outside Palm Springs. We had adopted her in early October, but since she had spent most of her life living in a metal shed giving birth to one litter of puppies after another, she had no social skills and almost no muscle control in her hindquarters, leaving her rear end so weak that she could barely stand.

392 J. A. Jance

After arriving in Washington, Sarah had spent six weeks at the Academy for Canine Behavior in Woodinville, regaining her physical strength and learning how to be a family dog with some basic command training thrown in on the side. She had finally come home to live with us only a couple of weeks earlier on the Friday after Thanksgiving.

As with Lucy, since I'm Sarah's primary caregiver, she's now clearly *my* dog as opposed to *our* dog—and her side of the bed is also my side of the bed—and that's exactly where she was when I went looking for her. Lucy always bounded up and out the moment my feet hit the floor. Sarah is your basic slugabed and has to be coaxed to rise and shine, especially on a cold winter's morning.

"Out," I ordered, pointing at the door. Sarah delivered a series of sleepy-eyed blinks before slowly unfurling her very long legs. Once she was upright, she gave me a flappy-eared shake of her head as if to voice a personal objection to being awakened before sauntering reluctantly out of the bedroom. Due to her southern California roots, Sarah does not like the cold, so I followed along to make sure she didn't take an unexpected detour somewhere along the way. After all, at that very minute, it was cold indeed in Bellingham, Washington, even for people who are relatively acclimated to inclement weather.

Two days earlier what meteorologists refer to as a Polar Vortex had plunged a long knife of frigid weather down through British Columbia and into the US, with Bellingham right on the westernmost edge of it. At the same time, what our weather gal calls a "Pineapple Express" was rolling in off the Pacific, bringing with it drenching rains all up and down the West Coast. The two opposing weather patterns had merged somewhere north of Seattle resulting in blizzard conditions that had brought Bellingham to a complete standstill.

Mel's and my house on Bayside Road in the city's Fairhaven neighborhood sits on a bluff overlooking Bellingham Bay. Because we're so close to the water, we're usually in a banana belt situation as far as snow is concerned—usually, but not this time around. If it hadn't been for the all-wheel drive on Mel's Interceptor, she wouldn't have been able to make it up and down our driveway. My S-class Mercedes is an older model 4-Matic, but when it comes to driving on snow and ice, I'm not especially proficient, and I try to avoid driving and walking in that kind of weather as much as possible.

The previous morning, before the snowstorm hit, it had already been icy cold outside. When I had sent Sarah out into our frigid back yard to do her thing, I had made the mistake of thinking she had completed the job. That was an error on my part. Sarah evidently likes walking on icy cold ground as much as I do. Much later in the day, I learned she had avoided freezing her huge but dainty paws by leaving an Irish-wolfhound sized package gift for me under the roofline of the front porch. Rather than walking around the house to the proper receptacle, I had resorted to the lazy-man's shortcut of flushing the by-then frozen pile of doodoo down the guest room toilet. Standing in the kitchen the next morning and waiting for the coffee to brew, I should have been smart enough to put two and two together and figure out what had happened with the plumbing, but as I mentioned earlier, I'm no handyman.

After filling Mel's and my thermal mugs with coffee,

I made a pit stop of my own in the powder room without attempting to flush. Then I picked up my iPad and found the number for Roto-Rooter in the home vendors section of my contacts list. That's another side issue of owning a home that dates from the middle of a previous century. It's a good idea to have a talented plumbing guy and an electrician or two on speed dial.

By the time I'd managed to get an ETA on the plumber, Mel was dressed and having her typical on-the-go breakfast, which generally consists of a piece of buttered toast accompanied by a couple slices of pepper-jack cheese.

"What's on your agenda for the day?" I asked, joining her on an adjoining stool at the kitchen island.

"A working lunch with the mayor at noon," she replied, "and a city council meeting this evening, unless they call it off due to weather. The trucks are out plowing the snow and spreading sand, but the streets are impassable again almost as soon as the trucks and plows are gone. You probably didn't hear them," she added, "but they already plowed our street and driveway."

"Rank hath its privileges," I muttered.

She gave me a beaming smile. "It certainly does," she agreed.

"When's the cold-streak supposed to end?" I asked.

"Tomorrow," she answered, "but don't hold your breath. It's going to warm up tomorrow or the next day, but before that happens, they're predicting another record snowstorm."

"Great," I grumbled. "Alternating layers of snow and ice. Looks like I'll be settling in for another long winter's nap."

Mel gathered her coat, purse, and coffee, and then stopped by where I was sitting on her way out.

"As long as you're stuck at home," she suggested, giving me a wifely good-bye peck on my cheek, "why don't you think about putting up the decorations?"

She said it with a smile and a kiss. It was more of a hint than an order, but once again, just like the water problem in the bathroom, I knew I needed to pay attention.

CHAPTER 1

LARS JENSSEN, who started out as my AA sponsor and ended up becoming my step-grandfather after marrying my widowed grandmother, used to tell me, "We get too soon old and too late smart." I like to think I wised up before it was too late. And that's why, once I finished my morning coffee and my daily crossword puzzle, I got my rear in gear and set about dealing with the Christmas decorations, starting by hauling a dozen or so boxes in from the garage.

Supposedly, we have a three-car garage. That's what the Realtor told us. The reality is somewhat different. Once we came to Bellingham and Mel had the use of a company car, she had unloaded the Porsche I had given her years earlier. So now, one of the three bays holds my S-class Mercedes and one holds Mel's Police Interceptor, while the third bay is devoted solely to Christmas— Mel's doing rather than mine.

The space devoted to Christmas in our garage is a direct result of Mel's lifelong conflict with her father. She grew up as an army brat, and she's always had a problematic relationship with her dad, who retired as a full-bird colonel. He's gone now, and I'm more than happy to take her word for it that he wasn't a nice guy. For him Christmas was nothing but an annoying afterthought. Naturally, Mel begs to differ.

When she divorced her first husband and moved to Seattle to go to work for SHIT, she drove cross country hauling a U-Haul trailer loaded with . . . you guessed it—her vast collection of Christmas decorations which for years were stowed in a rented storage unit. After we married, whenever it came time to decorate our condo for Christmas, Mel would go to the storage facility and come traipsing home with a collection of boxes that turned our unit into a winter wonderland that the grand-kids absolutely adored. The whole family loved it, yours truly included, but I couldn't help but wonder how she did it, because each year the end result seemed to be totally different from the year before. The reality of the situation didn't come into focus for me until after our move to Bellingham. That's when she shut down the storage unit and transferred her amazing collection into the garage.

Mel is nothing if not organized. The boxes are loaded onto four heavy duty rolling shelving units. The three boxes containing the pre-lit tree are pretty much self explanatory: top, middle, and bottom, with the tree skirt neatly folded in the one labeled "bottom." All the other moving boxes are labeled on every visible side: red balls; silver balls; white balls; blue balls; poinsettias, one red one white; holly sprigs; ribbons; bows; angels; Santas; nutcrackers; and wreaths. As I surveyed the assortment of boxes, I realized this was like one of those gigantic Lego sets my grandson, Kyle, loves so much. Everything I needed was there—some assembly required.

Since I didn't remember seeing blue ornaments on any previous tree display, and since blue is my favorite color, I chose the box labeled "Blue Balls." It seemed to me that white poinsettias would be a good bet with blue balls, so I took along a box of those as well as ones labeled "Angels," "Santas," and "Nutcrackers." I also set aside boxes marked "Christmas Linens" and "Ribbons." After hauling all of those inside, I went to work.

Before Karen and I divorced, I remember Christmas decorating mostly as an ordeal of organized chaos. I wasn't exactly encouraged to participate, and for good reason. Because I'm over six feet and Karen was only five-five, it was usually my job to install the angel at the top of the tree, a task that was always accomplished *after* the tree was decorated. One year, after having a bit too much holiday spirit (I believe I already mentioned I've been in AA for years now), the ladder and I came to grief and so did the tree, right along with a large number of decorations. Karen started speaking to me again sometime after New Year's, and from then on my help with the angel was no longer required.

This year, doing the job on my own and determined not to repeat that disaster, I decided to put the angel on the top of the tree *before* I put the tree together. I unloaded the angels from their box, lined them up on the kitchen island, and picked out one with a blue skirt. Then, using a pair of zip ties, I fastened that angel to the top in a fashion that I doubt even an earthquake could dislodge. Only then did I finish putting the tree together. Fortunately, all those little multi-colored LED lights lit right up without the slightest hesitation.

I was somewhat disappointed when I opened up the box labeled "Blue Balls." What I'd had in mind was something truly blue—royal blue, I suppose you'd call it. These were more turquoise than deep blue—some shiny and some frosted. I didn't use all of the balls in the box, but I think I hung most of them. Then I filled in the blanks on the tree with dozens of white poinsettia blossoms and punctuated those with a flock of silver bows and ribbons.

I was standing there asking Sarah what she thought of my decorating job (yes, I do talk to my dog when no one else is around), when the doorbell rang. Sarah beat me to the door, but due to our security system's monitor in the entryway hall, I knew without cracking the door that the guy ringing the bell was Ken, our regular Roto-Rooter guy, come to present the bill.

After putting Sarah on a sit and stay, I opened the door. "All done?" I asked.

"Yup," Ken said.

"What was it," I asked, "a tree root of some kind?"

Ken glanced at me and then sent a reproachful glare in Sarah's direction. "By the time I was able to scope it, it looked to me as though someone tried to flush a gigantic dog turd down a toilet. The damned thing got hung up on an ice dam in the main sewer pipe and stopped everything cold. Fortunately, I finally managed to break it up. That'll be three-fifty—card, cash, or check?"

I used my Amex and paid the $350 with a happy heart, grateful as all hell that Mel hadn't been home to hear the cause and effect which, as it turns out, were both entirely my fault. Then I went back to decorating. I lined up the angels, Santas, and nutcrackers on the island in preparation to actually deploy them. Then I opened the linens box. The top layer of that was a stack of white and red guest towels. I knew from past experience that those needed to be rolled up and put in the basket on the counter in the powder room. Then I sorted through the holiday tablecloths, runners, and doilies. Once I had those distributed on various flat surfaces throughout the house, I arranged the angels, nutcrackers, and Santas in sad little groupings of three, like so many trios of lonesome carolers.

It wasn't exactly the elegant effect that Mel usually produces. My results were more ham-fisted than beautiful, but I figured Mel could do some gussying up once she got home. In the meantime, giving myself a pat on the back, I settled into my favorite chair by the gas-log fireplace with a newly made cup of coffee to enjoy my handiwork.

The whole process had become more or less a meditation on Christmases past, first remembering that Christmas tree screwup with Karen and the kids and then going all the way back to Christmases when I was a kid. My mother was a World War II–era unwed mother. She was engaged to my father and pregnant with me when he died in a motorcycle accident. Rather than giving me up for adoption, she had—against her father's wishes—chosen to keep me and raise me on her own. We lived in a small two-bedroom apartment over a bakery in Seattle's Ballard neighborhood. She supported us by working as a seamstress, making clothing on a Singer sewing machine that sat on a worktable that took up a good third of her bedroom.

Naturally, she was always busiest in November and December as clients wanted new duds for holiday events. Usually on those cold winter nights she was still up working long after I went to bed, but at some point she'd be done, and the next morning something magic would have happened. I'd come out of my bedroom and find that the living room and dining room had been transformed overnight into a Christmas wonderland. We always went to church on Christmas Eve and then hung our stockings on the mantel of our non-working fireplace. Christmas morning, both of our stockings would be filled, but it wasn't until after I was old enough to get a job as an usher at the Baghdad Theater that she finally opened her stocking on Christmas morning to find something she herself hadn't put there.

I was sitting there, half drifting and half dozing, thinking about what an unsung hero my mother had been, when the doorbell rang again. Since I wasn't expecting any visitors, I thought maybe Ken had come back to give me a revised bill of some kind, but the security screen in the hallway revealed the presence of a stranger wearing a long woolen coat—unusual in the Pacific Northwest—and carrying what appeared to be an old-fashioned satchel. He was a handsome looking guy in his late twenties or early thirties. The distinctive white collar around his neck told me he was also most likely a priest. That made me wonder. Was the local Catholic parish sending priests out passing collection plates door-to-door these days?

I sent Sarah back to her rug in the living room before opening the door. Thanks to her academy training, she did exactly as she was told.

"May I help you?" I asked the stranger out front.

"Detective Beaumont?" he said.

People who know me now don't call me that, so obviously this was a voice out of my past.

"Yes," I replied uncertainly.

"You probably don't remember me? I'm Jared," he said, "Jared Danielson—Father Danielson now. I hope you'll forgive me for stopping by this way."

The words "Jared Danielson" took my breath away

and opened a window on one of the darkest days of my life. It took me a moment to gather myself after that. It had been close to twenty years since I had seen him.

"Why of course, Jared, you're more than welcome," I said at last, extending my hand and ushering him into the house. "So good to see you. How are you and what are you doing these days?"

He stepped inside and stood there on the entryway rug, stomping off the ice and snow that had clung to his boots. "I'm here because I need your help, Detective Beaumont," he said.

The last time I had seen Jared Danielson was years earlier when he'd been a lanky kid of thirteen who had just lost his mother. Now he was a well-built grown man, but a shadow of that long ago tragedy still lingered in his eyes.

"Call me Beau," I told him. "I stopped being Detective Beaumont a long time ago. Come have a seat and a cup of coffee while you tell me what you've been up to since I saw you last. Black or cream and sugar?"

"Black is fine," he said.

As I walked Jared Danielson into the house, it seemed as though all of that recently installed holiday cheer had instantly vanished. Suddenly I was traveling through time and space into a very dark place in my life, headed somewhere I definitely didn't want to go—a hell I had visited in nightmares countless times through the intervening years.

First there is an explosion of gunfire from somewhere out of sight. When nothing more happens, I realize the bad guy is dead and turn back to check on my partner. Shot in the gut, a bloodied Sue Danielson sits leaning against a living room wall. She is holding my backup Glock in one hand, with the weapon resting on her upper thigh. As I watch in horror, her fingers slowly go limp and the gun slips soundlessly to the floor.

In real life, that's when I knew for sure that Sue was gone. Her ex, Richard Danielson, had shot her dead.

NEW YORK TIMES BESTSELLING AUTHOR

J.A. JANCE

The Brady Novels of Suspense

JUDGMENT CALL
978-0-06-173280-5

REMAINS OF INNOCENCE
978-0-06-213471-4

DOWNFALL
978-0-06-229772-3

FIELD OF BONES
978-0-06-265758-9

Discover great authors, exclusive offers,
and more at hc.com.

JB2 1021

MASTERWORKS OF SUSPENSE BY
NEW YORK TIMES BESTSELLING AUTHOR

J.A. JANCE

Featuring Detective J.P. Beaumont

UNTIL PROVEN GUILTY
978-0-06-195851-9

INJUSTICE FOR ALL
978-0-06-195852-6

TRIAL BY FURY
978-0-06-195853-3

TAKING THE FIFTH
978-0-06-195854-0

IMPROBABLE CAUSE
978-0-06-199928-4

A MORE PERFECT UNION
978-0-06-199929-1

DISMISSED WITH PREJUDICE
978-0-06-199930-7

MINOR IN POSSESSION
978-0-06-199931-4

PAYMENT IN KIND
978-0-06-208636-5

WITHOUT DUE PROCESS
978-0-06-208638-9

FAILURE TO APPEAR
978-0-06-208639-6

LYING IN WAIT
978-0-06-208640-2

JUSTICE DENIED
978-0-06-054093-7

PROOF OF LIFE
978-0-06-265755-8

SINS OF THE FATHERS
978-0-06-285344-8

Discover great authors, exclusive offers,
and more at hc.com.

JAN1 1021